Soldier of Rome:
The Legionary

SOLDIER OF ROME:
THE LEGIONARY

A novel of the Twentieth Legion during the
campaigns of Germanicus Caesar

James Mace

iUniverse, Inc.
New York Lincoln Shanghai

Soldier of Rome: The Legionary
A novel of the Twentieth Legion during the campaigns of Germanicus Caesar

Copyright © 2006 by James M. Mace

iUniverse books may be ordered through booksellers or by contacting:

iUniverse
2021 Pine Lake Road, Suite 100
Lincoln, NE 68512
www.iuniverse.com
1-800-Authors (1-800-288-4677)

This is a work of fiction. All of the characters, names, incidents, organizations and dialogue in this novel are either the products of the author's imagination or are used fictitiously.

ISBN-13: 978-0-595-41737-7 (pbk)
ISBN-13: 978-0-595-86077-7 (ebk)
ISBN-10: 0-595-41737-X (pbk)
ISBN-10: 0-595-86077-X (ebk)

Printed in the United States of America

"Thrice happy is the nation that has a glorious history. Far better it is to dare mighty things, to win glorious triumphs, even though checkered by failure, than to take rank with those poor spirits who neither enjoy much nor suffer much, because they live in the gray twilight that knows neither victory nor defeat."

—Theodore Roosevelt, *The Strenuous Life*

Dedicated to the men of Company C, 2nd Battalion, 116th Cavalry

"Cobra Strike!"

Acknowledgements

All of us have a story to tell. And yet, even with the most diligent and talented of writers, it becomes obvious that our stories cannot be heard through our efforts alone. Behind every author is a group of friends and family who were there with advice, inspiration, editorial assistance, and above all belief in the author and the story. The following are those who believed in me, and in "Soldier of Rome," without whom this story would have been left filed away in the recesses of my mind, never to be heard.

Foremost I thank God for giving me what many have referred to as "the gift." My ability to write and to tell this and other stories is indeed a gift from the Divine.

To Mum, Dad, and my sister, Angela. For your love and support that was both inspirational and practical. Thanks for sending me all of those Roman history books so I could conduct my research while I was in Iraq!

Don LaMott, for helping me to fund this project, and without whose laptop this story would never have been written. Justin Cole (the real Vitruvius) for your visual and artistic input. Christopher Harvey, for introducing me to the publishers and giving me the guidance necessary to get this project off the ground.

Mike Lower, for being my biggest editorial critic, as well as one of my strongest supporters. Thanks for motivating to write like an actual professional. Clint Hanson, Jake Smith, and Gary Brock for taking the time in the middle of a combat zone to read the initial drafts of this book. You guys made me believe that I could succeed as a writer. Nic Fischer, Ryan Small, David Gehrig, and Chris Irizarry, for refusing to allow me to doubt myself and for pushing me to see this through.

And finally, to my other brothers-in-arms that I served with in the Iraq war. You are the Legionaries of this age!

CHAPTER 1

▼

TEUTOBURGER WALD

Teutoburger Wald, Germania
August A.D. 9

The mass of trees grew thicker, the sky darker, and what had started off as a mild summer shower had turned into a torrential downpour. The small contingent of Roman horsemen were already soaked and shivering, their Germanic guides laughing at their plight. Soon after entering the mass of trees they came upon a bog. The mud was thick and slimy, the water smelled rank with stagnation. The group halted as the Germans gazed around. Their leader's face broke into a sly grin as he saw the path he was looking for. They were getting close.

"How much further?" one of the troopers asked, the rain continuing to douse them, in spite of the tree canopy.

"Not far," the lead guide answered, "I promise, it will all be over soon."

"The gods curse this weather," another Roman muttered.

"Which gods?" still another one grunted.

As the cold rain slowly trickled down the back of his neck, the barbarian guide laughed to himself. *The weather will soon be the least of your worries,* he thought. Just then a Centurion rode up to him.

"What in Hades is the holdup?" he asked, irritated. "You were supposed to find the most expedient route for our column, and instead we're at a virtual standstill!" He was soaked and freezing, though he did not notice, so hot was his anger. Centurion Calvinus hated and deeply mistrusted the Germans. He could not for the life of him figure out how Varus had ever grown to trust them. The barbarian calmly turned his mount around to face him.

"It was your Commanding General who entrusted us with the leading of your men through the Wald. I am sorry that a little summer shower has soured your mood; however, I take it that you are not questioning his judgment." There was a sneer of defiance on the German's face, something that only further enflamed Calvinus. He brought his horse along side the German's and leaned forward so that their faces were just inches away.

"Don't think that just because you connived your way into Varus' inner circle that you can take on airs with me, *Arminius*. If you don't find us a way through this bloody mess right now, I will gut you myself!" The threat was very real, though Arminius' face remained calm.

"I already have," he replied mildly, "there past that fallen oak and the cluster of rocks, the path that will lead you straight through Teutoburger Wald." Calvinus gazed over to where the barbarian was pointing. Sure enough, there was a path that lead through the bog. However it was very narrow, only wide enough for maybe three to four Soldiers to walk abreast in places. Steep rock formations rose up on the left side further down.

"You want us to march along *that?*" His anger was boiling over. With the rocks on one side, and an impassible bog on the other, the path was the perfect lane for setting up an ambush. "One would have to be either insane or a complete half-wit to attempt that!"

"Your own auxiliaries are already up on the slope, protecting your flank, but if you think you can find a better way, feel free," Arminius replied with a board sigh. "In the meantime I suppose I should go and tell Quintilius Varus, Senator and Governor-General of Germania, that one of his Centurions does not trust his judgment and indeed thinks him to be half-witted." As Arminius started to turn his horse back around, Calvinus grabbed him gruffly by the tunic.

"I smell treachery on you, barbarian! If you in any way prove me right, I will follow you straight into the pits of hell and destroy you, be you Quintilius Varus' friend or no."

"Shouldn't you be getting back to your Cohort, *Centurion?*" Arminius asked as he jerked away from Calvinus' grip. As he rode away, he thought to himself that it didn't matter if this Roman trusted him or not. In fact, it did not matter if the entire army mistrusted him! All that mattered was what Varus thought, and he had Varus in the palm of his hand.

Arminius was a Germanic warrior of great distinction, war chief of the Cherusci, and had previously served as an auxiliary commander of Germanic cavalry for the Romans. This had greatly appealed to the impressionable Varus, so much so that he had even taken Arminius to be one of his closest confidants.

What a fool you are, Quintilius Varus, Arminius thought. *Your head and your bloody Eagles will soon be mine!* He took a glance over his shoulder to see if the rather troublesome Centurion was still behind him, but Calvinus had gone.

"That Roman's become too suspicious," one of other scouts remarked as he rode up along side his War Chief.

"It matters not," Arminius replied, "his bones will soon be trampled into the mud, along with the rest of the Army of the Rhine!"

As Calvinus made his way back to the column, his Cohort Commander rode out to meet him. The man had his cloak wrapped around him, though it was soaked completely through. He was shivering and miserable, as were the rest of their men.

"What's the delay up there?" the senior Centurion asked impatiently.

"The barbarians claim to have found a way through, but I must tell you that I sense a trap!" The Cohort Commander lowered and shook his head. *Here we go again,* he thought.

"Calvinus, for the last time…"

"Gods damn it, why won't any of you listen to me?" Calvinus barked in a complete breach of protocol. He was at his wits end and tired of being ignored. For weeks he had been warning his fellow officers about his suspicions, and he was desperate not to allow the Army to take the path that he knew in his heart led to certain death. His Commander's eyes grew wide in anger at the sudden outburst from his subordinate, but Calvinus was not about to back down.

"I keep telling you about all the signs that say 'this is an ambush,' yet no one will listen! I smelled a rat as soon as this expedition was announced. A few zealous tribesmen murder a Roman tax collector and his staff and we send *three* Legions after them? Then Arminius assures Varus that there would be no resistance, that the tribes were mostly docile. Since when have Germanic tribes *ever* been docile? And was it not Arminius who convinced Varus to allow the Soldiers to take their families and camp followers with them? That is the biggest breach of Army doctrine I have ever heard of in my career!" The Cohort Commander listened impatiently to the same rant he had heard nearly a dozen times in the last week alone. "And how about that older German, Arminius' father-in-law Segestes? *He* even warned Varus that Arminius plans to betray us! I'm telling you…"

"No I'm telling *you*, Centurion!" The Cohort Commander barked. "If you do not cease and desist immediately, I am going to drag you before the Commanding General myself! Do not forget that Varus wanted to strip you of your rank and position the last time you were rude to one of his native guests, and that it was my intervention which prevented it! And now you dare to get insubordinate with *me?* I will deal with you later, Calvinus; though I must tell you that you will be lucky if you leave Teutoburger Wald with your rank intact, if I have anything to say about it! Now return to your Century!" As Calvinus rode away, he turned back to his Commander.

"Sir, we'll be lucky if any of us leave Teutoburger Wald with our *lives* intact." He turned away and rode back to his men, rightly suspecting that he would never see his Cohort Commander again.

"We'll ride ahead and make sure the way is clear," Arminius told the bedraggled Roman contingent that still accompanied his scouts. They hardly even acknowledged him, each man off in his own world as he fought the rain and the cold. Arminius and his Germanic companions galloped off, leaving the Romans well behind. As they rode along the path, he heard the sound of crow cawing. They brought their mounts to a halt as one of his scouts answered the call. Arminius looked to his left, along the top of the rock outcroppings. He saw an older warrior step out from behind a thicket of bushes. He was bare-chested and carrying a broadsword. It was his uncle, Ingiomerus. Arminius waived in salute and dismounted his horse. His scouts did the same and followed him up the steep slope to where the rest of their fellow warriors lay waiting.

What a fool you are, Quintilius Varus!

Metellus Artorius Maximus looked around in disgust. He was thoroughly miserable as the Legions passed deeper into Teutoburger Wald, a thick and nearly impenetrable forest. Arminius had assured the Romans that this was a safe and more expedient route.

Yeah right! Metellus thought. He was cold, soaked and had absolutely no idea where they were going.

At nineteen years of age, Metellus had been in the army for a little over two years. He was a strong, intelligent, good looking Soldier with a promising career ahead of him. He wrote often to his family about how proud he was to be serving in the Seventeenth Legion. His younger brother, Artorius, had so wanted to come with him, to live the life of the Legions. Metellus laughed briefly at the memory.

"If only you knew what you'd be getting yourself into, little brother!" he said to himself as he tried to wipe the rain from his eyes. Leaves and branches slapped his face constantly as he struggled to move through the quagmire. He looked around to see where the rest of his Century was. His friend Clodius was close by, head hung low as he plodded along. The rest of the Century was starting to scatter. This was not boding well in Metellus' mind. Intervals and formations were becoming nonexistent in the confusion and the rain. As he looked behind him, he stepped right into a swampy mess, sinking halfway up his calf.

"By the gods, I'm going to kill the bastard who convinced Varus to take this route!" he swore in a low tone. Clodius stifled a laugh as he reached down to help his friend out.

"What a damn mess," he observed as he pulled Metellus out of the mire and then surveyed the area. There was nothing but trees and swampy marsh to be seen. "I thought that barbarian, Arminius was supposed to be showing our reconnaissance cavalry the quickest way to go. I can't believe this is the route they picked!"

"And just how in Hades do they expect the baggage trains to get through this?" Metellus asked. "Not exactly the best job of prior planning." The rain was coming down harder and his irritation was increasing. It wasn't supposed to rain like this during the summer!

"And what idiot put out that we wouldn't be needing our leather rain covers for our shields?" With no cover on his shield, it had become waterlogged and felt like it weighed a ton. His leather pack felt as if it was overflowing with water as well. He sighed and started walking again. They moved out quickly, trying to catch up to the rest of their Century. Metellus was also concerned because it seemed that no one was paying attention to anything going on around them. Normally, Centurion Calvinus would have already been in his face, beating him with the vine stick for having fallen out of formation. Where was he, anyway?

Soon they came upon a narrow path, the only place that did not seem to be overflowing with water and muck. Soldiers were already moving in a narrow file along the lane, oblivious to everything around them except the torrential rain and the ground at their feet.

"No way the baggage carts will be able to use this," Clodius observed. Metellus only shrugged.

"At this point, it's not really our concern," he replied. Clodius raised an eyebrow at that.

"It will be if we end up sleeping on the ground tonight."

Arminius watched the bedraggled Soldiers pass before him. It was time. The moment for him to strike at the very soul of Rome and shatter her sense of invincibility had arrived.

Now! War horns sounded, battle cries deafened anyone within earshot, spears and arrows flew, and what seemed like the every Germanic tribe charged in a mass of men and spears. The sheer force of their charge shattered the Roman lines like a demonic beast. So caught off guard were they, that only a few were able to disgorge their javelins before they were overwhelmed. Formations were completely forgotten, and Soldiers soon found themselves isolated and having to fight individually. Like a tide coming over the sands, they soon disappeared in the wake of their doom. The Romans who survived the initial shock were now in a fight for their lives against insurmountable odds. The outcome was never in doubt. The sheer force of the wave of barbarian warriors knocked many Romans into the swamps, their heavy armor and weapons dragging them to a murky and watery grave in the blackness below.

Metellus was surprised and appalled when he heard the sound of the war horns. He looked to his left and saw a massive hoard of barbarians pouring down from the hillside.

"Where are those damned auxiliaries?" he shouted to himself, referring to the native fighters enlisted to fight along side the Legions. They had been tasked with providing some semblance of flank security, and should have given ample warning of any potential threat. He soon had his answer. For no sooner had he spoken those words then he saw a large number of auxiliaries amongst the charging barbarians. They were still dressed in mail armor, wearing Legionary style helmets. So much for loyalty!

"Treacherous bastards!" he said through clenched teeth. He watched in horror as his Century disappeared amongst the mass of men and metal. This couldn't be happening! Metellus had been reared on the concept of Roman invincibility from the date of his birth. Fighting together as a cohesive unit, his Century had always been unstoppable. Nothing could stand up to them! But by the gods where were they now? In the mass of barbarians, he could not see anyone from his unit. He then realized that he and Clodius were alone. His friend was seething in rage.

"Traitors from Hell!" he screamed as he threw a javelin at one of the turncoat auxiliaries. The weapon slammed into the side of the man's neck with such force, that the shaft whipped around and tore his esophagus away. The auxiliary fell to his knees and then to the ground, his head practically severed from his spine. Clodius then drew his gladius and charged headlong into the fray. Metellus

watched horrified as a massive barbarian bear hugged his friend and pinned him against the side of the rocks. Clodius spun his gladius around and stabbed the man in the small of his back. He then disappeared from view.

As soon as he lost sight of his friend, panic welled up inside Metellus and he did the unthinkable for a Roman Soldier; he turned and started to run. So great was his overwhelming fear, that he was not even aware of what he was doing.

He ran for what felt like hours. His legs ached and his lungs burned as he tried in vain to suck in enough air. He found he could no longer hold on to his shield or his pack. Without even slowing down, he dropped everything he was carrying, including his javelins, which had become tangled in the thick underbrush. He didn't even know where he was running to. All he knew was that he had to get away from that swarm of death and destruction. As he passed through a mass of branches, he tripped over a tree root and fell face first into a marsh, completely submerging himself. Again, he panicked, thinking that he was drowning. He literally leaped to the surface, gasping for air. He looked around and saw that all was black around him. It must have been getting late in the day. Combine that with the thick canopy of trees over him and the black clouds that dominated the sky, and he found that all was dark and he could scarcely see his hand in front of his face.

As he stood trembling in the water, his breathing started to slow down. The rain had stopped, and a cool gentle breeze seemed to rip into his very soul. Suddenly he was filled with something stronger than fear. He was filled with utter shame. He had committed the ultimate sin; he had run away from a battle. He had left his comrades to their doom. He placed his head in his hands as he fought back tears of despair.

He looked around and saw that he was alone. He could not see the battle, though in the remote distance he could still hear the clash of arms and the hellish screams that accompanied it. Nothing like this had ever happened. He had never been on his own in a battle. His unit had always fought together, working as one had made them invincible. To fight on ones own was unthinkable! Now he *was* alone.

Suddenly he found his resolve. There was only one thing he could do to find redemption. He had to find his companions. Surely, somebody from his Century was still alive! Metellus found it impossible to comprehend that all had been wiped out. He started wading through the swamp, slowly making his way towards the sounds of the battle. It was so dark that he tripped and fell face first against a gnarled tree. His face caught the nub of a branch, gouging his cheek. He bit the inside of his cheek and swore quietly as he tasted the blood that was seep-ing from the wound. He reached up and ripped off a piece of skin that was hanging from his face. This in turn caused him to swear even more as he continued to struggle to find his way out of the swamp.

Once he reached a bank, he lay on his stomach and found some stray branches with which to pull himself out. He found that the mud and slime had plastered itself to his sandals and legs, weighing him down. He reached for handholds and found some stray branches with which to pull himself out.

At this rate, the battle will be over before I even get back to it, he thought.

Once he was out, he pulled himself upright and sat back against a tree, catching his breath. He leaned over as he heard the sounds of many running feet heading towards him. Not knowing whether they were friend or foe, he laid flat along side the tree. In the gloom of the thick forest, he could not see a soul, but soon he heard voices, voices that were not speaking in Latin. Their tone was excited and their unholy chanting caused him to shiver.

He closed his eyes and tensed up as he heard the excited voices of numerous Germanic warriors running by. Slowly he unsheathed his gladius and braced himself against the ground, ready to spring. Soon the sounds moved past him and he started to breathe easier. Then he heard a loud crash and splash as someone fell into the swamp he had just crawled out of. He heard the sounds of cursing unlike anything he had ever heard before. He listened intently as the irate individual slogged through the water, heading directly towards where he lay. Metellus held his breath as he caught the form of a man pulling himself out of the water. He could just make out the long club the barbarian carried, and he could also see the unkempt mop of hair on his head.

It would have been easy to just lie there and wait for the man to pass him by, but something burned inside Metellus. He felt that he had to do something to atone for his earlier cowardice. As the German struggled to pull himself up, Metellus lunged forward, smashing his helmeted head into the barbarian's, knocking the man senseless. He then fell on top of the German, and with one hand over his victim's mouth, he rammed his gladius into the side of his neck. The barbarian thrashed about in his death throes, blood spurting from his jugular, all over Metellus' hand. He worked his gladius in a rough sawing motion, trying to expedite his enemy's death. So violent were the barbarian's convulsions that Metellus was almost thrown off. Once death had finally claimed the man, he slowly staggered to his feet and starting moving in the direction the barbarians had gone. For where they went, surely his friends would be.

Had it been hours that had passed, or days? Metellus was not sure. Though the rain had long since stopped, the sky was still black. He heard the sound of crying, as if from a young child. He instinctively ran towards the sound. He saw that it was in fact an infant toddler, standing next to the bodies of his murdered father and mother. A burley German was laughing over the corpses and was preparing to stab the child with his spear. Metellus rushed forward, however he was not fast enough. The warrior ran his spear clean through the wailing toddler. He then hefted his spear with the child hanging off it, laughing as if he had skewered a wild boar. In a blinding rage, Metellus grabbed the barbarian, spun him around and drove his gladius into the his pelvis. The German howled in surprise and pain as Metellus stabbed him repeatedly in the abdomen. As the man fell dead, Metellus bent down to console the child, whose cries had subsided. It was still alive, but coughing up blood and convulsing violently. Metellus' heart was filled with anger and sorrow at the same time. It was not the child's fault. Damn his parents! Damn all who had condemned their children this way! How could anyone have thought that a campaign was the appropriate place to bring one's family, especially young children? He looked up to see a group of Germans pointing at him through the trees. They turned and started running in his direction. He realized that he could not hope to save the child. In spite of the guilt that burned inside him, he turned and ran.

"Please forgive me," he said as much to himself as to the child that he knew was to soon be murdered. As he ran, he turned back and watched, unable to avert his gaze as one of the barbarians hacked the child's head off with an axe, laughing all the while. Metellus wretched, sobbed quietly and turned away. As he crashed through a thicket, he came to a small clearing where he saw a sight that gave him cause for relief. There stood Centurion Calvinus, Commander of the Fourth Century. His relief was short-lived, when he realized his Centurion was fighting for his life against several barbarians. Metellus had hoped to see the rest of the Century fighting along side Calvinus; however, there were only two legionaries with him.

This can't be right, Metellus thought. *Where in the name of Jupiter and Mars is everyone else?* As he ran into the clearing, Metellus saw that there were in fact only the two Legionaries with Calvinus, and that all three were engaged in mortal combat with five Germanic warriors. Three of these were attacking Calvinus. Seeing his distinctive armor and the crest on his helm, they had recognized him as an officer, a Centurion no less. Killing a Roman Centurion would bring much prestige and glory to the warrior responsible.

Metellus gave a loud cry and rushed forward to save his Centurion and his friends. He lunged forward, plunging his gladius into the nearest barbarian's chest. The man tried to scream as his lungs quickly filled with blood. As he collapsed to the ground, Metellus' gladius became stuck in the ribcage of his stricken foe and was ripped from his hand. Ignoring this, Metellus attacked another German with his bare hands. He quickly got inside the warrior's shield and spear. An elbow to the wrist knocked the spear away; one to the face dazed his adversary long enough for Metellus to grapple him to the ground where he hammered his fist into the man's face and head. He tried to choke the barbarian, but the German was incredibly strong, and not so easily dispatched. He bucked violently, nearly throwing Metellus off. His left hand came loose and banged against the dagger on his belt. His dagger...of course! With a flick of the wrist, Metellus drew his dagger and plunged it as hard as he could into the man's eye. It buried itself four inches before stopping. Warm blood spurted all over Metellus' hand and wrist. He leapt off the German, who was thrashing on the ground as his body convulsed uncontrollably. Metellus then walked over to the body of the other barbarian he had slain, and with a violent jerk pulled his gladius free of the man's chest. Blood dripped from the blade. He then looked up to see Calvinus thrust his gladius under his remaining assailant's jaw. The two legionaries had dispatched their attackers as well and were looking to their Centurion for answers to their dilemma.

"What the fuck do we do now, Calvinus?" one of them asked. His voice was near panic. He was clutching his arm, which had been punctured by a German spear, and was in obvious pain.

"We find whoever else is still alive and we cut our way out of here," Calvinus answered, panting slightly, but still surprisingly calm.

"Where's the rest of the Century?" Metellus asked.

"They're dead! Everyone's dead!" the other Legionary answered. His hands were on his knees, his head hung low.

"Sir?" Metellus asked, looking to his Centurion.

Calvinus lowered his head, nodding. "I'm afraid so. And as far as I can tell, the four of us are all that remains of the Cohort, maybe even the whole damn Legion! Cassius Chaerea of the Nineteenth seems to be the only senior officer in the entire army that hasn't lost his head. He's established a rally point not too far from here, and hopefully hasn't been overrun. We'll link up with him and then fight our way out from there."

"If we can even find him in this gods' forsaken nightmare," one Legionary muttered. Calvinus ignored the man's remark. The sounds of Germanic war cries and men crashing through the woods alerted their senses. "Alright, let's move out."

Calvinus was more than a Centurion and commanding officer to his men. To them he was like a second father, hard as iron, yet compassionate to the needs of his men. A tough, battle-hardened veteran with nearly fifteen years in the Army, he was the one who always had the right answers and knew the solution to any situation, no matter how desperate. He would get them out of this!

Getting to Cassius' formation required crossing a large portion of the battle-field. As they ran through the dense woods, they found the bodies of most of their Century and Cohort. They were a ways from the narrow lane on the bog, and Metellus realized that they must have been conducting a fighting retreat, for there were many barbarian corpses amongst the slain Legionaries. Had it all been in vain? Had the barbarians' numbers been too great? Were there no other survivors? Metellus tripped over a corpse and fell face first into the dirt. He rolled over to see that it was the body of Clodius. His face was split down the middle with an axe embedded in it, his mouth agape in horror. "Clodius," Metellus whispered, a tear coming to his eye. "No." The sheer despair of the disaster was becoming insurmountable.

A jerk from one of the Legionaries pulled him to his feet and back to his senses. "Come on! There's nothing you can do for him!" The sound of their Germanic pursuers was getting closer. As they moved through the thickets and undergrowth, they came upon even more carnage. Here many of the camp followers had been slain. The bodies of Soldiers were mixed in amongst the dead, cut down as they tried to protect their families and loved ones. Metellus saw one dead Soldier with his throat cut, lying on top of the bodies of a woman and young girl, the wife and daughter he had tried in vain to save. He thought briefly of the child he had failed to save. It was obvious from the positioning of the bodies, as well as the blood oozing from their private areas, that both women had be viciously raped and then mutilated. The young girl had even been decapitated as a final insult. Metellus shuddered at the sight, realizing that the Soldier had probably still been alive and had been forced to watch the horrifying spectacle before his own life was brutally ended. Metellus thanked the gods again and again that he had declined the opportunity to bring his beloved Rowana on the expedition with him. At least she would be safe!

Metellus suddenly felt that he would never see her again. This in turn caused him to seethe with rage and despair. It wasn't going to end this way! He thought back to the day he had said goodbye to her.

"Promise me you'll be careful," she had said as she clung to him. "I need a live husband, not a dead hero."

"Do not worry yourself, Love. It's simply an expedition to route a few rebellious barbarians. Besides, I am with the best armed and best trained army in the world. Nothing can stop the Seventeenth! I *will* see you again." With that, he had given her a lingering kiss before he had turned and walked away. Not once did he allow himself to look back. Metellus started to feel a sense of desperate determination at the memory. He could not allow that to be the last time he would ever see her. He *had* to keep his promise!

Metellus shook his head, forcing such thoughts from his mind. He had a battle to fight, and his survival depended on staying focused. Suddenly he saw his salvation. Cassius' rally point was in sight, a mere three hundred meters away. So close, yet seemingly impossible to reach. There were maybe one hundred and twenty Legionaries lined up in a box formation, the last bastion of Roman might and practically all that remained of the Army of the Rhine. Their shields were linked together, swords at the ready. Most of the barbarians ignored them, looking for easier prey. Occasionally a zealous group would crash into the formation, only to be beaten back.

"There it is!" Calvinus pointed the position out to his men. With renewed energy, they rushed towards sanctuary. A call came out from the rally point. Some of the Legionaries started to move towards Calvinus, but were quickly pulled in by their officers. Maintaining formation was the only hope any of them had, so Calvinus and his men would have to make the final dash to safety on their own. The Legionaries in the formation cheered them on, frustrated that they could not rush out to help. They started shouting and pointing off to the left of Calvinus' small band where another mass of barbarians was running out of the woods towards them.

"*Stand ready!*" Calvinus shouted as he set into his fighting stance. The Legionaries quickly followed suit. The Soldiers in Cassius' formation couldn't bring themselves to look away as Calvinus and his men disappeared from view. They readied themselves to charge forward and help, only to have an even larger band of warriors crash into their lines once more.

In spite of lacking a shield, Calvinus still used his left hand to punch one of his assailants before ramming his gladius hard into the man's groin. The Centurion then grabbed him by the hair and threw the barbarian, who was howling in immeasurable pain, into his companions. Metellus and the other Legionaries fought with equal tenacity, each man holding his own against the onslaught.

One barbarian carried a massive cudgel, which he swung as hard as he could at Metellus. The blow caught him flush on the side of the head, knocking him to the ground and tearing off his helmet. Blood streamed from behind his ear where the helmet had torn a nasty gash that nearly severed his ear. The blow caused blinding vertigo, and Metellus retched violently. Dazed and confused, he struggled to his feet, his head throbbing. Through his blurred vision, he saw the two Legionaries tackle his assailant and stab him repeatedly. He also saw Calvinus cut down two more Germans in rapid succession. Their fellows suddenly halted their attack, their uncertainty apparent. Calvinus gave an unholy howl of rage and lunged at their nearest adversary. He slashed hard with his gladius, something Romans practically never did. Yet so ferocious was his blow that it cleaved the man's head from his shoulders.

Dizziness overcame Metellus again and he fell to the ground. He pushed himself up to his feet and saw his companions sprinting away. He ran as hard as he could, yet he found himself unable to clear the cobwebs from his head as he stumbled and fell further behind. The men in Cassius' formation had beaten off the latest attack by the barbarians; however they were in a desperate state and could not hold out for much longer.

"*Calvinus!*" he heard Cassius shout, "*we have to get our of here now!*" Just then, Metellus felt a crushing blow to the small of his back and he was knocked to the ground. As he impacted the damp earth, he somehow managed to maintain control of his gladius. Suddenly he was awake, alert, every fiber of his being fighting for survival. He rolled over to see a massive barbarian bearing down on him with a cleaver. He could smell the man's rank breath and foul body odor. He quickly raised his gladius to block the attacker's blow. Unfortunately, he managed to only partially deflect the strike. The cleaver slid down his gladius and impacted hard on his right thigh, opening a massive gash. Metellus howled in pain, and in desperation swung his gladius up in a backhand slash. The blade connected with the German's throat, slicing it open. The warrior fell to his back, clutching at his throat, his screams muffled by the gurgling sound of blood gushing from his jugular.

Metellus slowly pulled himself to his feet, clutching at the wound on his leg where dark crimson blood flowed freely. He did not even bother trying to stifle his cries of agony. He knew that there was no chance of stopping the bleeding; the wound was arterial. Metellus was in great pain, and his leg refused to function properly. Calvinus was immediately at his side, his own helmet now gone and he was bleeding from a long gash that ran from his left eyebrow down to his cheekbone. That entire side of his face was purple and swollen, his eye forced shut. Calvinus grabbed Metellus by the shoulder, examined his wound, and then looked away downcast. Turning back, he looked Metellus in the eye. Both men knew that the wound was mortal.

"Go," Metellus gasped to his Centurion, looking at the two Legionaries. "You have to get these men out of here, Sir. Just…please…tell Rowana…" his words were cut off as he choked up and found himself unable to continue.

"I will," Calvinus answered as he clutched Metellus by the shoulder. He nodded in acknowledgement and ran back to his remaining Soldiers. The war cries and din of battle behind them was growing ever louder. Before resuming their flight to Cassius' detachment, all three Soldiers turned back briefly and saluted Metellus with their swords. Metellus returned their salute and then turned to meet his fate. His vision was starting to blur, the loss of blood quickly taking its toll. He saw an entire band of Germanic warriors coming his way. He struggled into a fighting stance, his weapon at the ready, rage in his eyes. They would not take him so easily! He just hoped he could cut down a few before he succumbed to his wounds.

At the head of the charging hoard was a young, slender barbarian, body painted blue, wearing nothing but a torque around his neck. The man looked like he was demon possessed, and he was clearly much quicker than his fellows were. Metellus readied himself to fight the man, but was surprised when the fleet-footed German ran right past him. He was ignoring Metellus, eyes obviously on the bigger prize ahead, the Centurion with his back turned! Metellus realized that his companions were oblivious to the barbarian pursuing them, and that they had no chance of outrunning him. With the last of his strength, he turned and flung his gladius, falling to his hands and knees as he did so. His vision was now almost completely blurred, yet he still managed to see his sword tumble end over end, embedding itself deep into the base of the madman's spine. Metellus smiled to himself. He knew then that his friends would be alright. His breath was coming in deep gasps now as he lay on his stomach. He could no longer see or hear the battle around him. The forest, his friends, the German hordes, Cassius' formation had all but disappeared in the darkness that was overtaking him.

Calvinus and his men rushed through the ranks of the formation. The Legionaries gave a cheer, taking solace in that at least someone else had survived. Cassius ran over to Calvinus, the Tribune placing his hand on the Centurion's shoulder. Calvinus was bent over, hands on his knees, gasping for breath.

"You guys alright?" Cassius asked.

"We're alive, if that counts for anything," Calvinus replied, looking up at the Tribune. He noticed right away that Cassius too had lost his helmet. His face was cut in numerous places, his gladius and armor were soaked with blood. Cassius bit his lip hard and nodded in acknowledgement. He then patted Calvinus on shoulder before turning back to his own men.

"Alright, listen up!" he shouted. "We're going to cut our way back, heading due west until we reach the river. We will then head south to our bridges, and pray they have not been overrun. Keep it tight, lads! If we stick together, we *will* survive! *Move out!*" He then turned his attention back to Calvinus as the formation started its slow march.

"Come, old friend," he said, "let's leave the hell of this accursed place forever."

"You may be leaving this accursed place," Calvinus replied under his breath as Cassius walked away, "but I will return!"

For Metellus, he knew he was breathing his last. He wished for the end to come, though he sorrowed at the thought of what affect his death would have on his Mother, his Father, little Artorius…Rowana. Then, out of the shadows, he saw Rowana walking across the glade. He closed his eyes tightly and opened them again, but this was no dream, for there she was. She may not have been there in the horror of Teutoburger Wald, yet somehow, across time and great distance, the merciful Fates were allowing him to see her one last time. She turned towards him and stood in the middle of a beacon of light that shown through the darkness. She wore a white gown, her auburn hair flowing freely around her shoulders. Her arms were wrapped around herself, her eyes filled with infinite sadness.

She knows, Metellus thought to himself.

"My Love, I'm so sorry," he whispered, reaching for her with his right hand. Suddenly a German spear was slammed through the back of his skull. His world went black and he knew no more.

CHAPTER 2

▼

AFTERMATH OF DISASTER

What a fool you were, Quintilius Varus! Arminius surveyed the carnage that spread as far as he could see. The ground was littered with corpses both Roman and German.

Here was the greatest feat of arms in our time, he thought to himself. Three entire Legions had been destroyed. The Army of the Rhine had virtually ceased to exist. Now was the time to strike into the heart of Roman territory. With the Army of the Rhine destroyed, the provinces in Gaul were left practically undefended. A rapid invasion could annex all that land for the Cherusci and their allies. However, when it came to dealing with the Germanic tribes, nothing ever came rapidly. It had taken Arminius years just to unite the tribes to strike as they did against Rome. Now, when the opportunity to achieve so much more was within their grasp, it was quickly slipping away before the bodies of the slain had even cooled.

The warriors would plunder the Roman dead. That would take time. The tribal chiefs would then bicker and squabble over their share of the wealth. Thankfully, there were no slaves to be had, as that would take even more time and resources to deal with. All who had survived the battle would be sacrificed in reverence to their deities, in thanks for giving them this victory. Once the bickering over plunder ended, there would be further quarrels regarding what to do next. Arminius and his closest allies would push for immediate invasion of Gaul while their army was still intact. Others would wish to ravage and plunder the entire province around the Rhine bridges. Still other tribes would simply go home, basking in the glory, yet shunning responsibility when time came for retribution. To go home and do nothing else was the worst course of action that Arminius could imagine, and yet it was the one that they would most likely take. Unless he could keep all of the tribes united, he would not have the forces necessary to invade Gaul.

Then there would be Tiberius to deal with. Arminius shuddered at the thought. He knew that after such a disaster as this, the Emperor Augustus would not hesitate to send his best General to deal with the situation. Varus had been a coward and a fool. Tiberius Claudius Nero was another matter completely. In fact, had Tiberius been in command of the Army of the Rhine, Arminius highly doubted that he would have even contemplated such a bold move that had just brought him victory. Surely, the outcome would have been different with Tiberius in command. Arminius' father and uncles had all faced Tiberius and his brother Drusus in battle and felt the full affect of their wrath. Two uncles had been slain, one by Tiberius' own hand. Mercifully, Drusus had died in a horse riding accident years ago, but his brother had lost none of his skill or venom. Arminius' one surviving uncle, Ingiomerus, still walked with a slight limp from a javelin wound in the thigh, gotten in battle with Tiberius' army.

Lesser known was Tiberius' nephew, Germanicus, so named in honor of his father Drusus' military achievements in Germania. Arminius scoffed at the very notion. Germanicus was the protégé of Tiberius, having served directly under him in Pannonia. There was little doubt that he would accompany the General, possibly even in a position of high command. Still, while Germanicus was virtually an unknown factor, Arminius knew that he had been trained by his uncle, who surely had passed on some of his cunning, tactical savvy and sheer ruthlessness on the battlefield.

If I face Tiberius on the battlefield, I will have sealed the fate of the entire Germanic nation, Arminius thought to himself. While he was brave, knowledgeable in the tactics and techniques of the Roman Army, and had won one of the greatest feats of arms in memory, he was no fool. He knew his limitations, and he was not too proud to admit when he was outmatched. Tiberius was skillful, his troops so well drilled, that most battles were virtually over before the first blow was even struck. No, against Tiberius there could be no victory, even if he were able to keep the numerical advantage. At that moment, he made his decision; he would pull his army back across the Rhine. They would continue to conduct raids and skirmishes to harass the Romans, of course. But above all, they would pray to their gods that Tiberius would not venture across the Rhine.

*   *   *   *

News of the disaster came hard to Rome. Families wept, mourning the loss of loved ones, and a general panic ensued. Many citizens were convinced that with no army to speak of on the frontier, it was only a matter of time before the barbarians reached the gates of Rome itself. Such thoughts were nonsense to the sensible person, however so had been the destruction of the Army of the Rhine. How could this have happened? How could an entire army have been annihilated? Stories ran rampant about how Germania was a land of seven-foot tall giants, who could crush Legionaries with their bare hands. And there were thousands of them! Tens of thousands in fact…no, hundreds of thousands! They spawned in those dark forests, watching, waiting for the moment to strike. And now they had come for the head of Rome itself!

None took the news harder than Augustus Caesar, Emperor of Rome. Three of his Legions, the Seventeenth, Eighteenth, and Nineteenth were gone. The barbarians had taken his beloved Eagles, the sacred symbols of each legion. Such a disgrace was unbearable. Equally appalling was the sheer loss of life. Twenty-thousand Roman citizens had perished in the holocaust. Now the Emperor had to make some rapid decisions before the barbarians invaded the provinces in Gaul. Retribution was a given; the barbarians *must* be made to pay for this atrocity. However, the first thing that needed to be done was securing of the Rhine bridges, and eliminating any chance of invasion. And by the gods, somebody had to quell the masses that were panicking and spreading stories borne more out of fantasy and fear than fact! For these things, he looked to Tiberius and Germanicus. They would save Rome, or else nobody would. The Emperor was so consumed with grief and despair that he could do little to help in preparations for war. In the midst of council, he would suddenly cry out, "Quintilius Varus, give me back my legions!" The seventy-two-year-old Emperor would be of little help when it came to planning the actual campaign. Late one night, Tiberius and Germanicus were pouring over a map of the Rhine frontier, when Germanicus brought this point up to his uncle.

"Let Augustus mourn," Tiberius said without looking up from the map. "And let the public see that he mourns with them. Retribution, securing of the frontiers, and salvaging the public's sanity is now our responsibility."

Germanicus nodded in assent. "We have two legions, Second Augusta and Twentieth Valeria that we can send to the frontier almost immediately. Auxiliaries can be picked up at garrison stations along the way. I suggest we expedite the move by leaving the artillery wagons, at least temporarily, and stripping all baggage trains to the bare essentials."

"Leave the auxiliaries as well," Tiberius said. "They take too long to get organized; when what we need right now is speed. They can be picked up later with the follow-on forces. Right now, all that matters is getting to the bridges as quickly as possible. I'll take both Legions and start immediately. I've already sent dispatches to the Legates of each. Once we reach the frontier, we'll secure and reinforce whatever forts remain. Supply won't be an issue while on the march. It may be another matter once we reach the Rhine. I don't know what's been plundered from the frontier forts, nor do we know if the countryside has been scavenged or not."

"I've already taken care of that," Germanicus replied. "I've sent word to the auxiliary commanders to send out as many foraging parties as they can. They'll have extra stockpiles of rations available for pickup. We can use them to escort the baggage trains and artillery wagons as well once they come up, thereby freeing up more legionary forces. I'll bring them as soon as I can rally at least another Legion."

"You're not coming," Tiberius said, "at least not right away. There has been much panic since word of the disaster broke out. Augustus feels that you'd be best suited staying back to calm the masses for the time being."

"My place is with you, uncle," Germanicus protested. "My place is with my men!"

"Your place is where the Emperor tells you it is!" Tiberius snapped. Germanicus looked crestfallen. Tiberius was a hard, practical man, but he was not entirely unsympathetic. He remembered what it was like to be left behind on an important campaign. In his case, it had been the campaign where his beloved brother had died. Oh yes, he understood how his nephew felt. He suddenly felt the need to console the young man who had served him so well in the past.

"Germanicus, I know your quality as a Soldier and as a leader of men. You have learned your lessons well, both in study and on the battlefield. I dare say you rival your father as a tactician." Germanicus smiled at the compliment.

"I also know," Tiberius continued, "that you have a way with the people of the city. They look to you for inspiration and guidance. The Emperor, while dearly loved, is an old man. He is tired. He looks to the young to breathe life and hope back into the city. You alone can do that. You have the gift. It is the gift that many lack, to include myself."

Tiberius, while a capable administrator with strong ethics and principles, lacked the ability to convey these to the public. He was seen as a bitter, spiteful individual, preferring solitude over companionship. This of course was an exaggeration brought on by the gossips. His closest companions were philosophers and scholars. And that damn astrologer of his! At forty-nine, he was still in amazing health, though his face bore the scars of acne and his body the scars of war. Drusus, his late brother and the father of Germanicus, had been a good looking and charming young man, with the same gift for words that his son now possessed. The sheer force of his aura and personality could inspire even the bleakest of souls to do great things. He had been adored by the public and loved like a father by his men. And he had been one of the few people Tiberius himself had ever truly loved. While he did possess a certain fondness for his own son, also named Drusus, for some reason the feelings just didn't run as deep as they should have between a father and son.

Besides his brother, only two other people in his life had Tiberius loved. The first was his father, divorced by his mother while she was pregnant with his brother. He had died when Tiberius was still a boy. The other was his now ex-wife, Vipsania, whom Augustus had forced him to divorce years ago. Tiberius had then been forced into a loveless marriage with Augustus' daughter, Julia. That had been among the prices he had had to pay in order to ensure his succession, and it was something he would always regret. For in reality, Tiberius had no desire to be Emperor. He was especially bitter that he was selected to be Emperor by default, every potential successor having died a very premature death. Yet in spite of everything, he still loved Rome. The city and the empire were in his soul. And though he had no desire to rule the known world, he truly felt that he was the one most capable of it, and therefore obligated to take the reigns of power. He knew he would serve Rome until his dying day.

In his heart, he wished that years ago he had had the courage to tell Augustus what he could do with that whore of a daughter of his. The result would have been forced retirement from public service; no longer would he have been able to serve Rome. And of course, there was the possibility of banishment. That he could have handled, for at least he would have still been with Vipsania, and perhaps he could have been a more active father in their son's life. It was the one time he had truly felt like he had been a coward. But sadly he could not undue the past. Vipsania had remarried; Julia had been banished to a desolate island when her father discovered the truth concerning her adulterous ways; Drusus the younger grew up practically alone. All that was left was a lonely man destined to rule the world some day.

Germanicus, like his father, was attractive, extremely athletic, fair-haired, and almost Apollo-like in appearance. He was scholarly when it came to military study, and at the same time aggressive and adaptable when it came to practical application. Like his father, he was loved by the public and seen as a father by his troops, in spite of the fact that he was younger than many of them. His wife, Agrippina, was the younger sister of Vipsania. He was very much in love with his wife, and his children were the source of his pride and joy. He was also very protective of his younger brother, Claudius, who walked with a limp and had a serious speech impediment. But above all, he was a statesman and a Soldier. He would do his duty, wherever that may be. He left to go and face the hysterical mob that had formed outside the palace.

*   *   *   *

It was a warm sunny day. A young boy ran through the glades, waiving his toy sword about. He pretended he was with his brother, off in the Legions, fighting for the glory and honor of the Empire. It was getting late in the afternoon, and he would soon have to come in for his lessons. He did not particularly enjoy these, especially on days such as this. However, it was something that he knew was necessary if he were to live up to the promise he had made to his brother before he left two years before. He thought about his brother as he walked towards his home. What was life in the Legions really like? His brother had sent him letters telling him about his home on the Rhine, of his brothers-in-arms, even of the beautiful young woman he had fallen in love with. Though Roman law did not recognize the marriages of Soldiers below the rank of Centurion, it did not stop these men from settling down and starting families. He wondered if Metellus intended to start a family with this woman. It was something eleven year-old Artorius thought to be silly. After all, he was not yet at the age when girls became interesting.

As he ran down the hill towards his home, he saw a pair of riders on the road. They were heading towards his home as well. He couldn't be sure, but it looked like they wore the uniforms of Legionaries. He was immediately filled with excitement. Could it be Metellus, come home for a while? Did that mean that the stories he had overheard about a disaster on the Rhine were not true? He immediately started sprinting towards home. His elation was cut short when he saw the riders dismount and hand a parchment over to his father. His mother was standing with her hands covering her face. What could be wrong? Did these men bear news concerning his brother? If so, what could it be? He slowed to a walk as he approached the house. The two Soldiers looked less than pleased with the task they had of delivering their message, and seemed anxious to leave. One stood with his head downcast, clutching at the bridle of his horse. The other shifted nervously from one foot to the next, unsure of what they were supposed to do next. Artorius walked over to the man who was standing with his horse.

"Are you a friend of my brother's?" he asked, looking up at the man. The Soldier just closed his eyes and turned away. He was obviously shaken.

"Artorius," his father said with his arms now around his wife. "Go inside, lad." Instead, the young boy turned and walked away towards the river nearby. Incomprehensible thoughts crossed his mind and he started to run. His father did not try to stop him.

*   *   *   *

Several weeks later Tiberius stood at the gate of the Rhine fortress that now housed the Twentieth Legion, Valeria. A small band of refugees was being escorted in. Rumor had it that these were more survivors from the Teutoburger disaster. A reconnaissance party had spotted the ragtag bunch and had almost attacked them, when one of them starting spouting off in perfect Latin that he was a member of the Eighteenth Legion and had survived the massacre. There had only been a couple other groups of survivors found so far. The largest had been lead out by Cassius Chaerea, a Tribune with the Nineteenth. One hundred and twenty had been with that group. Another group of about fifteen who had escaped being captured turned up a week later. This latest group looked like it had been hit the hardest. There were only six of them, and they were a frightful sight.

Tiberius was stone faced as he watched the men pass through the gate, yet his heart broke for them. Two were borne on litters hastily constructed by the reconnaissance party. The others stood, heads hung low in shame, and their clothes tattered, bodies covered in lacerations and bruises.

"What are we going to do with them, Tiberius?" a Centurion asked. "I mean after we feed them and treat their wounds of course."

Tiberius' expression remained unchanged. "We welcome them back. We tell them that the fault of the disaster is not theirs. The blame rests with one man alone, who now burns in hell. These men will take their proper places back amongst the ranks."

"But sir, what of the Emperor's standing order about not accepting back Soldiers who have been publicly disgraced? I pity them, yes, but I do not know if it would be proper, in the Emperor's eyes at least, to accept them back as if nothing happened."

Tiberius turned to face the Centurion. "Centurion, you as a professional Soldier and a practical man should realize that with the sheer loss of life we have suffered, we need every man we can get. The shame and disgrace lies *not* with these men."

"Yes Sir." The Centurion smiled and nodded. He felt the same way, but had to be sure of his Commander's feelings and intentions.

Without further delay, Tiberius walked up to each Soldier in turn. He placed his hands on each man's shoulders and kissed them all on the forehead. He next grasped each of the litter-bound Soldiers by the hand in a sign of friendship. He then took a step back and with a sweeping gesture of his arm towards the camp said, "Welcome home, my friends."

The Soldiers stood dumbfounded. After all, they had just returned from the biggest disgrace an army had suffered since any could remember. No one could remember a time when a single Eagle had been taken, let alone three! Yet here was the Commanding General of the Army of the Rhine, a man all of them knew was destined to be the next Emperor of Rome, welcoming them back. They slowly started to walk towards the interior of the camp, where a mass of Legionaries stood ready with fresh clothes, bandages and medicine for their wounds, hot food for their empty stomachs, wine and companionship to salve their shattered souls. Theirs was a bond only Soldiers could understand. Yet one Soldier stood fast where he was. Tiberius walked over to him. The man was young, in his early to mid twenties. He had little to no facial hair, in spite of his lack of a shave. His eyes did not look as lost as his companions did. Rather they were filled with stark awareness of horror and sorrow.

"Why do you not join your companions?" Tiberius asked the young Soldier.

"What right do I have to join them?" the Soldier asked; his voice breaking as he looked at the ranks of the Twentieth Legion. "We failed you, Sir. We failed the Emperor, we failed Rome. Worst of all, we failed each other. I'll never forget the savage horrors we witnessed. I can still hear the screams of the tortured as they begged for death. Some had their tongues cut out. The barbarians, in their twisted logic thought that by eating the tongue of a Roman, they might learn to speak Latin. Some were crucified and eviscerated. Others yet they put in wicker cages and burned alive. My friends, my brothers, and yet I was helpless to do anything for them." He closed his eyes hard as tears streamed down his face. He was beyond being shamed by them. "I swear their ghosts haunt me. I don't know how I can ever forget the horror, the pain, the sheer suffering. How do I live again, Sir? How do I find redemption?" He was now looking Tiberius straight in the eye. Tiberius placed a hand on the man's shoulder.

"What is your name, Soldier?"

"Macro, Sir. Platorius Macro. Formerly of the Nineteenth Legion, Third Cohort, First Century."

"Platorius Macro, you can live again by doing them justice, by ensuring that your survival was not in vain. Rejoin your comrades in the ranks, and in time I promise, you will find redemption." Macro nodded and without another word went to rejoin the other survivors. As he walked off Tiberius said to himself, "And you shall have revenge!"

Germanicus would join his uncle on the Rhine two years later. After capturing and repairing the Rhine bridges, Tiberius led many sorties into the frontier. These were limited at first, as he did not have the resources available for a massed campaign. As the months went by, fresh troops, mostly recruits, started to rebuild the Army of the Rhine. Varus was publicly damned and the numbers XVII, XVIII, and XIX were never again used to number a Legion. Units were transferred from all over the Empire, increasing the army's strength to eight Legions. Soon they would be ready to launch an offensive unlike anything Arminius had ever witnessed.

Late in the year of A.D. 13, in the forty-second year of the reign of Augustus, Tiberius was recalled to Rome.

＊   ＊   ＊   ＊

As his chariot approached the gates of Rome, Tiberius looked upon the Eternal City with nervousness and dread. On the frontier, he had never felt more alive. That had been his true calling, to be on the front lines of Rome's battles. He knew full well why he had been recalled. The aged Emperor was nearing the last of his days. The succession and transition of power would have to come swiftly and smoothly in order to prevent chaos and unrest.

Many in the Senate pined for the days of the Republic, when they alone ruled the Roman Empire. In truth, very few could even remember what that time had actually been like. The political infighting, the corruption, and the unchecked abuses of power were conveniently forgotten. Augustus had ruled for so long that a large proportion of the masses knew of no other system of government and were very much reluctant to even think about returning to the days of the Republic, where in its death throes there had been numerous civil wars and internal strife.

Rome had expanded its borders so far as to make a true Republican system virtually ineffective. Someone had to keep the Senate and regional administrations in check, to ensure that all worked together for the greater good, which now expanded far beyond the borders of Italy. From Gaul to Egypt, all known civilizations and peoples fell under the domain of the Empire. To effectively rule an Empire required an Emperor. The Emperor was dying and his successor felt the full weight of the world coming down on his shoulders.

Tiberius stopped his chariot in front of the Imperial Palace. He knew right away where to go. Though he had been away from Rome and the Imperial estates for nearly five years, he knew the area like the back of his hand. Servants came and took the reigns of the chariot from him as he ascended the steps into the palace proper. He saw his mother, Livia pacing slowly back and forth in front of the door leading to the gardens.

"It is good you have returned," she said without even looking his way.

"How did you know I was back in Rome?" Tiberius asked. "I've only just arrived." Livia smiled a half smile.

"I have my sources. They keep me well informed," his mother replied. She had a determined, yet sad air about her. Though it was plain that her one intent had been to get her son elevated to the highest position of power, the final step of that transition would be very painful for her. After all, she had been married to Augustus for more than fifty years. The man she had shared the vast majority of her life with was slowly slipping away.

"So how is he?" Tiberius asked. His real concern was how long he had until he had to take on the task he had been preparing for, and yet dreading his entire life.

"He's in the garden," Livia replied. "He asked to see you once you returned. He spends most of his waking moments in his garden, off in his own little world. He knows his time is growing short, and so he takes the most pleasure in the simplest things in life. He'll want you to assume the majority of power immediately. You will become Emperor in everything but name, ruling jointly with him until he breathes his last. Go to him." She motioned with her head towards the door leading outside. Tiberius took a deep breath and walked through the door. He was still dressed in full military garb, his helmet held under his arm.

As he walked through the gardens, he came upon the aged Emperor. Augustus was seated on the edge of a fountain, a small pot with a sapling in his hands. He had just finished planting it and was marveling over something that only he could see.

"You sent for me, Caesar?" Tiberius asked, standing at attention. He had never felt comfortable in the presence of the Emperor, preferring their relationship to be confined to correspondence from the opposite end of the Empire.

"It's a marvelous thing that something so small and frail as this will one day grow to be big and strong," the Emperor stated, still gazing at the potted sapling he held. "It will grow slowly, over the course of the ages, like our Empire. And if well maintained, it will live for hundreds of years, maybe even thousands. It will watch everything, its gaze immortal in the eyes of men. It will see the passing of our Empire, and what will come beyond her. Yet it will linger and flourish long after we are gone." He smiled sadly and placed the pot down on a tray where there were several other plants that he had been toying with. He then turned towards his stepson.

"Sit with me," he said, motioning towards a nearby bench. Tiberius hesitantly took the seat, his helmet in a virtual death grip beneath his arm. Augustus still held the same smile.

"You know, Tiberius, I have been less than fair with you over the years," the Emperor began. Tiberius looked away and cringed. He knew that Augustus would bring up certain topics that he wished would otherwise remain buried in the past. There was nothing for it, after all. He had paid a heavy price to be where he was, on the brink of sole ruler ship of the known world. And yet he did not want it.

"The fairest thing would have been to leave me in retirement on the Isle of Rhodes, or else on the frontiers with the army," he replied. Augustus nodded, though never relaxing his contented smile. He leaned forward, closing the distance between himself and Tiberius.

"When one is destined for greatness, one cannot escape it," he replied. "You are destined to serve in a far greater capacity than you ever imagined, or even wanted. It seemed like everything and everyone, including yourself, fought against your becoming my successor. I myself never even toyed with the idea of you succeeding me until the hour had grown late." He sighed and shrugged, so many memories of the last forty-two years flooding back into his conscience. Tiberius remained silent.

"I underestimated you, I really did," Augustus continued. "I had always based my selection of a successor on emotional attachment, rather than on practicality and qualifications. Your mother kept reminding me of your true worth, but I did not listen. I think now of all those whom I had groomed for this position, and how much better my efforts could have been spent had I given you your just due. My old friend, Marcus Agrippa was my first choice, though I knew that it would be unlikely for him to succeed me for any length of time. After all, I was only a few months older than him."

Tiberius closed his eyes at the name of his former father-in-law, the father of his still beloved Vipsania. Agrippa had died long before. Tiberius of course was then forced into that loveless debacle of a marriage with Agrippa's widow and Augustus' own daughter, Julia. Tiberius found it to be rather twisted that he was to divorce his wife in order to marry her own father's widow. Augustus loved Agrippa and Agrippa's sons, perhaps because they were his own grandchildren. When it came to Agrippa's daughters, it seemed like his feelings ran cold. Perhaps it just wasn't convenient politically at the time. Never mind that Tiberius and Vipsania had truly loved each other, and were not married for political reasons.

"The other candidate during that time had been my then son-in-law, Marcellus. Sadly he died of a summer chill. Years later, when Agrippa died, that left me with his children, my grandsons. Oh how I looked to them to breathe life into the Empire once I had gone!"

He's not making this any easier, Tiberius thought to himself. He noticed how Augustus never once mentioned his own daughter, and he knew better than to bring her up.

"Sadly neither Gaius nor Lucius survived," the Emperor was looking past Tiberius, into the remote past. It was as if he were having a conversation with himself rather than with his stepson and heir. Tiberius noted that Augustus failed to mention his surviving grandson, Posthumous Agrippa, who had been banished following a series of bad conduct and brutish behavior. "It was after their deaths that I turned to you, my old war horse. You and your brother, the gods rest him, were the ones who really kept the Empire running." Augustus was looking at Tiberius once more, as if drawn back to the present.

"I admit we have not always seen eye-to-eye, but once your mother forced me to look upon your real talents, I could ignore you no longer. It was as if the gods themselves were forcing my hand. I swear your position as my successor has been *divinely* chosen. You have been my champion, albeit a reluctant one. Any crisis this Empire has faced, I have sent you to meet it head on, yet I always took you for granted.

"And now we will set about making things ready for the next generation! There are many things you must become accustomed to if you are to succeed as Emperor. While I have no doubts as to your administrative talents, your political machinations could use some work."

"I have always left politics to the politicians," Tiberius replied.

"Well now you *are* a politician, or rather the supreme politician," Augustus replied. "You're not on the Rhine frontier anymore, Tiberius. You must learn what it is to rule Rome from Rome. As for the Empire's safety, I have no doubts.

You were always the finest military commander I had ever met. Though it pained me to admit it, I even told the Senate on more than one occasion that you would have been more than a match for my uncle, the Divine Julius Caesar himself! No, I will leave this world content in the reassurance as to her safety.

"Your dealings with the Senate and the Senators themselves are what concern me. Therefore, tomorrow I shall grant you joint Consulship with me, and you shall be appointed head of the Senate. You shall also be known as my peer, sharing the reigns of power with me. I dare say, your mother probably told you of this already. I swear that woman knows of my intentions usually before I do!" Augustus laughed at that. Tiberius sighed. He knew full well why it was that Livia seemed to know Augustus' thoughts and intentions before he did. It was because many of his thoughts and intentions were of her design, craftily worded to make the Emperor actually believe that he thought of them. It was her way of ruling through him. In this way, Livia was going to be terribly disappointed when her son assumed power.

CHAPTER 3

▼

THE RECRUIT

Town of Ostia, Italy
January A.D. 15
Six years after Teutoburger Wald

The day had finally come for young Titus Artorius Justus. It was his seventeenth birthday, a day that had been six years coming. Six years since that god's awful day. Artorius remembered that day clearly. It was the day that changed his life forever. He had been playing in the hills outside his family's home when the riders approached. They wore the uniforms of the Legions. The site of the riders had excited Artorius. Was it Metellus, home for a visit from Germania?

He had heard stories, terrible stories, stories that could not possibly be true. Every time someone mentioned the Rhine, the Legions, or Metellus, Artorius was quickly ushered away, never privy to such conversations, yet he knew. It had confused him at first. His parents, Primus and Persephone had always freely expressed their pride in their eldest son, and his achievements in the army. Artorius loved reading the letters his brother sent to him from the Rhine. They were his motivation for doing well in his studies. Metellus had promised that he would write to him, provided he studied hard and learned to read.

"Strengthen your mind as well as your body," Metellus had told him once, "for with a strong mind and a sound body you can accomplish anything." They were words that Artorius never forgot. He saved the letters his brother had sent him, cherished them as one would cherish gold. Metellus never wrote or spoke to

Artorius like one would to a young boy. He wrote to him in the same language and manor that he would use towards a peer or a friend, something Artorius always remembered him fondly for. Then the letters stopped coming. As much as he tried to suppress his feelings, his gut told him that something bad had happened. The hushed conversations in his presence when his brother's name was mentioned further added to his anxiety. He was not so young that he wasn't aware of the change in his parents.

Then came the official dispatches from the Rhine. Along with news of the disaster came lists of the survivors who had fought their way back to friendly territory. There were not many, and Metellus' name was not among them. It was soon after this that the riders came. Metellus was now officially listed as dead, and with no body to bury or burn, his burial fund was being paid to his family. Artorius remembered running down from the hill, stopping some distance away as he saw his mother collapse into his father's arms. She made not a sound, but her body shook uncontrollably as she quietly sobbed. The two Soldiers looked obviously shaken, cursing that they had to perform such a bitter task. His father's face was as hard as stone, but even he could not control his tears. Artorius had turned and walked away.

As he walked he tried to comprehend what all of this meant. He then came to understand that his brother would not be coming home, not then, not ever. He was gone. Artorius started to run. He ran as hard as he could until he reached a small stream, branches of the trees growing along it trailing in the slow current. He sat next to the water and cried, trying in his young mind to fathom the loss. As the reality sunk in, he thought hard about who had caused this, who had murdered his beloved brother. He thought of the Germans, those unclean, uncivilized barbarians to the North. These people had murdered his brother! Artorius was suddenly filled with rage. His fury was compounded by the fact that he was too young to do anything to avenge his brother. But he would not stay young forever. He swore then and there that as soon as he was old enough, he would join the ranks, he would become a Legionary, and he would avenge his brother.

Persephone was still trying to recover from a summer chill when news of her son's death came. Her condition grew worse, turning quickly to pneumonia. She refused to eat, refused to see the doctors, and slowly wasted away. As she lay dying, she clutched her husband's hand.

"I go now to be with our son," she whispered. These would be her last words. Primus was ready to follow his wife and son into the afterlife. One thing kept him from taking that final journey. He still had another son, and to abandon him was unthinkable. So Primus lived only for his son, for all else had become black and meaningless in his life.

Artorius thought back to those dark days and it only hardened his resolve. He knew that it would be difficult convincing his father to write the necessary letter of introduction that would verify his citizenship and allow him to enlist in the Legions. For only Roman citizens could become Legionaries. Non-citizens could still serve, but they would serve as auxiliaries, less trained, less well equipped, and consequently with a much higher mortality rate than their brothers in the Legions. Artorius *would* become a Legionary. He just had to face the daunting task of asking for his father's blessing. Breaching the question was what troubled him. He would ask Juliana. She always knew how to talk to his father. Anytime he ever needed to discuss something with the elder Artorius, he always went to her first. He started to walk down the path leading to her house.

Artorius was a strong youth, both in mind and body. He was of average height, but powerfully built. He had heard legends regarding the impressive strength of the Germanic warriors, and he figured he had better be of equal or greater strength. He spent hours in his self-made gym, adding massive size and power to his frame. His feats of strength were impressive. Equally as impressive was the strength of his intellect. One minute he would be pressing great stones over his head or wrestling with bulls, the next he would be reciting Aristotle from memory or giving a dissertation on mathematics. Such fetes were quick to impress the young ladies in and around Ostia. In particular was young Camilla, whom Artorius had had a crush on since he was old enough to take an interest in the opposite sex.

On mathematics Artorius was always bested by his friend and sometimes mentor, Pontius Pilate. Pilate, a few years older than Artorius had already gone off to join the Twentieth Legion, Valeria. A member of the patrician class, Pilate had been given an appointment as a Military Tribune, a rank that Artorius knew he would never see. Word also had it that his skill in mathematics and the principles of trajectory had earned him a place as the Legion's chief of artillery.

Aside from having to deal with asking for his father's endorsement, he also had to break the news to Camilla. She and Artorius had grown very fond of each other as of late, and he knew that his leaving to go to war on the Rhine would break her heart. He gave a sad, audible sigh as he thought about that.

Artorius arrived at Juliana's small cottage. She and her family had been neighbors of Primus and Persephone since Artorius could remember. Her husband had died of a mysterious disease, and her daughter had died giving birth to her grand-son around the same time as Persephone's death. Sadly the infant had perished as well. Juliana's son-in-law thought the family to be cursed and abandoned her. She had been left alone in the world. Primus and Artorius took pity on her and strengthened their friendship with her. Though she never tried to replace Perse-phone, in some ways she became the mother figure that Artorius lacked.

Juliana was working outside in her small garden when Artorius arrived. She was still a very striking woman, maybe a couple years older than his father. Pri-mus spent many days at Juliana's and Artorius was growing impatient with his father for not taking his relationship with her further. She looked up from her gardening when she heard him approaching and smiled at him. "Hello, Arto-rius."

"Beautiful morning," he replied.

"Your father's just left," she told him.

"I know. But I did not come looking for him, at least not yet," he replied.

"I see," she sighed, still smiling, "you've got another dilemma that you have to discuss with your father, and you don't know how to do it." He hung his head sheepishly. She set down her gardening tools and motioned towards a bench.

"Well let's not waste the day. Come sit down and let's discuss what ails you. Wine?" she asked him.

"Yes please," he answered. When she had served him, she sat on a bench across from him, her chin on her hand, that smile never leaving her face. How had his father not fallen in love with that smile? He took a long draught of wine before starting.

"You know today is my seventeenth birthday. I am now of age and eligible to join the army. I need Father to write me a letter of introduction that I can take to the recruiting station. Without proof of citizenship, I cannot hope to join. I am not certain how to tell him of my intentions."

"He already knows," Juliana said her expression unchanging.

Artorius was dumbfounded, "what do you mean he knows?"

Juliana stifled a laugh, "my dear Artorius. Do you really think you could hide such a thing from him? He is your father after all. He's known of your intentions for six years. He could read it in your face. He could see it in your eyes. He could see it in how you continued to study the campaigns of Scipio, Marius, and Caesar into the late hours of the night." She was no longer smiling. "You know he came to me last night to discuss this very thing. He didn't leave until just a little while ago."

"I knew he hadn't come home last night," Artorius said, "I just figured that maybe you two were..." he stopped and looked away, realizing what he had almost said. Juliana burst out laughing.

"Gods have mercy! You really thought we were..."

"Well he was gone all night!" Artorius' face was completely flushed. "I've wanted to tell him for years that you are the best thing to come into his life in so long. And that he was a fool if he didn't, you know, make something more of it."

Juliana looked at him with much affection in her eyes. "You know that I do love your father dearly. He was there when everyone else had abandoned me. He gave me life." She paused for a moment, "but I never tried to take it any further. I may have been alone, but he still had you. I could not bring myself to try and replace your mother." She looked away.

Artorius took her hand in his. "You've been as much of a mother and a friend as anyone could hope for. Your love and understanding have always been without question."

She reached up, touched the side of his face, and then kissed him on the cheek. There was a tear in her eye. She took a deep breath and wiped her tear away. "Now we need to deal with the dilemma with your father. You know that he already knows of your intentions, so just go and ask him. He's very protective of you, Artorius, but he knows what is in your heart and that you will not be dissuaded. So just *ask* him."

Artorius smiled, kissed her hand, and turned to leave. "Thank you," he said, "you always have the simplest, and yet the best answers." With that he left.

Juliana smiled and turned back towards her garden, "and so young Artorius, you begin your new life as a man."

Artorius decided to make one final stop on his way home. He found Camilla pacing back and forth amongst the trees outside her family's home. She was just a year younger than Artorius, and he had been infatuated with her since they were small children. Camilla was petite in stature, a good half-foot shorter than Artorius, though very athletically inclined. As the youngest of four daughters and three sons, thoughts of her potential marriage were almost an afterthought to her parents. This left the way open for her and Artorius, though he knew that if he left to join the Legions, any chance of a union between them would have to be placed on hold for a very long time. Would she wait for him?

"I knew this day would come," Camilla said as he approached. Her back was to him, her arms folded across her chest. "You'll be leaving to join the Legions, to share the same fate as your brother." Her cold words struck Artorius hard. Of course she had always known of his intentions; however up until this point she had always spoken well of it. She had said how brave and noble it was for him to do.

"How can you say such a thing?" he asked as he walked up and put his hands on her shoulders. She turned to face him, arms still folded, yet tears were in her eyes. "I will return, you must know this."

"All I know," Camilla answered as her voice broke, "is that your hatred and desire for vengeance is stronger than any love you may bear for me." She broke down and wept, her head on his chest, hands clinging to the back of his tunic tightly. "I'm so afraid for you. Those aren't even men that you will face on the frontier; they are animals, savage, brutal, disgusting animals."

"Yes they are," he replied as he wrapped his arms around her tightly. "They murdered my brother, and drove my mother to her death. Don't you see? If I don't do something, then I will never be at peace. I cannot let such abominations go unpunished." Camilla leaned back and placed both of her hands on the sides of his head.

"Just promise me that you'll write, and that you *will* come back to me alive," she managed to say through her tears. "I cannot imagine losing you. Since we were children, I have always felt that my place was with you." With that she kissed him very tenderly, turned and walked away. Though his heart ached, deep inside he felt as if his saying goodbye to Camilla was little more than a formality. He would keep his promise and write to her, of course. Yet in the back of his mind he sensed that she would not wait for him. He hoped he was wrong.

*   *   *   *

Tiberius was Emperor at last. After having spent his entire adult life in service to Rome, he now possessed ultimate power over her. Though publicly he considered himself to be little more than the senior member and representative of the Senate of Rome, in reality he was sole ruler of the known world. When Augustus died the year before, he had taken the reigns of power with great reluctance. Now he had no choice but to leave the war on the Rhine in the hands of Germanicus. While the campaigns against Arminius were by far the most important issues to be dealt with, they certainly were not the only ones. The task of effectively administering an empire was astronomical. Tiberius wondered how Augustus had done it for more than forty years. The deceased, and now deified Augustus had lingered for almost a year after Tiberius' recall to Rome. Only when he felt secure in the knowledge that Rome was left in capable hands did he finally allow himself to pass into eternity.

Shortly following the death of Augustus, Tiberius' chief rival, Posthumous Agrippa, met his end. Even in exile he was still viewed as a potential threat, being as he was the sole surviving natural grandson of Augustus. Though he had not given the order, and was in fact as surprised as any when he was informed of the young man's execution, Tiberius could not help but feel a sense of relief. Posthumous himself could have personally done little from his remote island prison, however there were plenty who would gladly usurp the current Emperor in favor of someone of Augustus' own bloodline.

The Emperor sat behind a desk, pouring over documents and protocols requiring his attention. He looked down at his hands and forearms. There was still a lot of strength left in them. Some senior Centurions managed to stay in the army well past his age. Suddenly he envied them. They at least were where the action was, out on the line. Were it up to him, Tiberius would still have been there with them. He sighed. Such was not the case. As much as he had loved the life of the Legions, he had to admit when it was time to pass the reigns off to the next generation.

The door opened and Livia walked in. Tiberius sighed again, without having looked up from his work. His mother was the only person who would dare enter without so much as knocking. Even his son Drusus only entered with his expressed permission.

"What is it, Mother?" he asked, pretending to be deep in concentration. "I'm rather busy today."

"Oh and is it my *son* who greets me so warmly today?" Livia asked, sarcastically. The widow of Augustus and mother to the present Emperor was a Roman matron of all the old virtues. In spite of the fact that she was a woman, Livia considered herself to be a servant of Rome as well. Many claimed that while Augustus ruled the world, she had ruled him. Such was not the case with her son. "Perhaps you've forgotten who it was who helped you to become Emperor in the first place." Tiberius slammed his stylus down onto the table.

"Yes, and thank you so much for reminding me of the hateful predicament you put me in!" He hated admitting it, yet it was true. Had it not been for Livia's profound influence over Augustus, one of a dozen other potentials would have become Emperor instead of him. There were many days when he wished one of them had. "Augustus told me that my succession was decreed by the gods. In reality it was decreed by Livia!" His mother ignored the remark.

"Your nephew sends word from the Rhine. He asks that you send him some-one to help him in the administrative details concerning the enormous army he now finds himself in charge of." Never one to waste words, Livia immediately set about discussing business. Tiberius threw his hands up in the air.

"By the gods, how is it you manage to know what's happening on the frontiers before I've even read the dispatches?" Livia only smiled wryly at the comment. Her network of gathering information amazed even herself sometimes.

"I have my sources. Besides, I know that while very much capable, Germani-cus cannot run the campaigns on the Rhine alone. No doubt you heard about the mutiny he had to squash the moment you left."

"Yes, of course," Tiberius answered, picking up his stylus and continuing to work.

"It would seem like you left him a handful to deal with. And I'm not just talk-ing about the Germanic hordes he still needs to suppress." Livia was always overly critical of her son's administrative decisions. The only thing that had been harder than living up to the expectations of Augustus had been living up to the expecta-tions of his own mother.

"I've already taken care of it, *Mother*," Tiberius answered curtly. "Caecina Severus should be here soon. I'm sending him to aid Germanicus." Livia smirked at the name.

"Sending the man who bailed you and your brother out so many times? Well at least you've made one sound decision."

"I thought my brother did no wrong in your eyes," Tiberius retorted.

"Aside from his infatuation with the archaic system known as the Republic, you mean?" Livia rose and made her way to the door.

"You know many think that given your staunch support for this hereditary monarchy we now find ourselves in, that you did not even mourn his loss. Some think that you saw him as a threat to the system." These words struck Livia hard, though she did her best not to show it. Tiberius knew that it was not true of course. Though publicly she had never shown any outward sign of emotion, Livia had been inconsolable when word of Drusus' wounding and subsequent death reached her. She had lain at night in Augustus' arms, sobbing uncontrollably. No matter what differences she may have had with her sons, Livia still felt the same devastating loss that all parents felt who had the unfortunate task of burying a child. Tiberius immediately regretted his choice of words.

"You know I never believe what is said about you," he said. Livia did not reply until she had reached the door. She opened it to find Severus waiting just outside.

"When he was dying, Augustus called you the last hope for Rome," she said, turning back to her son. "He may have never told you, but he always loved you, as I do." She immediately left the room. Tiberius lowered his head. His mother never ceased to amaze him. In fifty-five years, not once had she ever expressed any form of affection towards her eldest son. He looked up and waived Severus in.

Aulus Caecina Severus was a couple years older than the Emperor, though he hid his age remarkably well. He was a tall, handsome man, and like all traditional Romans he was clean-shaven, keeping his hair short and well groomed. He wore the muscled cuirass typically worn by a Legionary Legate. It was old, well worn, and bore marks from the blows of countless adversaries.

How does he do it? Tiberius thought to himself. *He's older than I am, has seen more campaigns, and yet he looks almost young enough to be my son!*

Severus stood rigid, eyes straight ahead, and saluted Tiberius. The Emperor was a bit shocked by this, especially since he considered Severus to be a close personal friend. Out of respect he rose to his feet and returned the Legate's salute.

"You sent for me Caesar?" Severus asked, still standing rigid.

"Oh come off it man," Tiberius laughed, waiving Severus to a chair. He was a bit unnerved to see that Severus remained rigid, almost standoffish. Tiberius sat down and leaned back in his chair, his fingers intertwined.

"Yes, I sent for you," he said at last. "Rome has need of your services..." Severus breathed out hard through his nose and finally looked the Emperor in the face.

"Rome has had need of my services for more than forty years," he replied bitterly.

"And she calls on you again, one last time," Tiberius continued, keeping his patience. Severus shook his head and looked down.

"Caesar you know as well as I that there will never be a 'one last time.' There will always be conflict, always a crisis. It will never end; not for you and apparently now not for me." The Emperor's face hardened at the remark.

"You're right; it will never end for me. That is the price I pay for being where I am. It is also the price you must be willing to pay. You are a Senator and magistrate of Rome. You have known this your whole life. I remember when you taught me what duty, honor, and courage meant. My reputation as a Soldier stems from what *you* taught me! It was from you that I learned how to be a decisive strategist, and still lead from the front; that my life was not worth more than the men I led. All those times I placed myself at the head of a charge, being the first to crash into masses of men and spears, were because of the utter selfless example that you set. Why the change?" Severus looked downcast. He was obviously feeling shamed by his conduct.

"I know my duty, Caesar. It's just that I've been doing this for so *long*. I've spent more years on campaign than most of the other Senatorial Legates combined. My grown children scarcely know me! And yet, I admit that in battle I never felt more alive; but now I'm tired. Tell me Tiberius, do you know of anyone else in the whole of the Empire with more actual combat experience than me?" Tiberius shook his head. He knew there were none, not even him.

"It is precisely for that reason why I have recalled you," he answered. "You mentored and served myself and my brother well. I freely admit that many of my early victories were won precisely because of your leadership. We now face a crisis unlike any seen by Rome for a generation. You know this. I take it that's why you kept your armor in such good repair." He pointed to Severus' uniform to emphasize the point.

"I *need* you, Severus," the Emperor continued. "Germanicus is a good Commander, and he will do well. However, he cannot do this alone. He has eight Legions to command. The mutiny on the Rhine gutted some of these of experienced, albeit corrupt, officers. The Legion I am placing you in charge of lost forty-percent of its Centurions in the shake-up. The men who replaced them are in many cases a lot younger and less experienced then I would like to see going into this campaign. They need not only leadership, they need inspiration. I can only trust the conducting of this campaign, not to mention the eight Legions involved, to my two best men."

"What about Drusus?" Severus asked. Tiberius took a deep breath and dropped his head slightly. His son, whom he had named in honor of his late brother, had been somewhat of a disappointment to him. Drusus tried hard to please his father, and Tiberius knew that with the right kind of mentoring he could potentially make a fine officer. However, in many ways he still acted like a young schoolboy; his vices, namely gambling and whoring with his Judean friend Herod Agrippa, gravely affected his focus and duty performance. It simply would not do for the men to see their commander still half-drunk and reeking of prostitutes on a regular basis. Tiberius cringed at what it would take if his son were to ever have a chance of succeeding him as Emperor of Rome. Granted, Germanicus was his actual successor, however if Tiberius had learned anything from Augustus' mistakes, it was not to place all his hopes on one potential candidate for the Imperial Throne. He knew his son had potential, he just wasn't ready yet.

"Drusus will come into his own some day, but not now. This is not the time for me to train him. Right now I need men who can get results on their own, without my having to personally watch over every move they make. No, I'm sending Drusus to suppress an insurrection in Pannonia." Severus smiled and nodded. "Besides," Tiberius said with a wave, "I know you would like nothing more than to personally get your hands on the traitor Arminius." Severus clenched his fists at the name. Arminius had served under him as an auxiliary commander, and he regarded his treachery as a personal insult. As tired as he was, he knew in his heart that nothing would please him more than having his final campaign be one of retribution against one who had betrayed him so grievously. Such concepts gave him strength that he thought had faded a long time ago.

"Alright," he said. "Tell me what you need me to do." Tiberius returned the smile and nod. He pulled out a large map of the Gaul and Germanic provinces. Strategic positions, along with the placement of all eight Legions were marked. He also produced a parchment with unit names and the names of their senior officers.

"Here are the units you will be working with, along with their commanding Legates." Severus noticed that space for the name of the Legate of the Twentieth Legion was left blank. Tiberius was quick to explain. "Technically you will be the Legate for the Twentieth. However, your primary duty will be to act as second-in-command of the entire army. In the event you two decide to separate your forces and act independently, you will take overall command of one of those elements."

"That will mean leaving command of the Twentieth in the hands of the Chief Tribune," Severus observed. "It will take one hell of an officer. Who is it, by the way?" He knew that in accordance with Roman law and tradition, the Chief Tribune was usually a young Senator with little to no actual experience. Tiberius produced a document with the roster for the Twentieth Legion.

"Gaius Strabo is his name," he answered.

"Strabo," Severus said, "why does that name sound familiar to me?"

"His uncle, Seius Strabo, is Commander of the Praetorian Guard. I hand picked him myself. He's a good young man, intelligent and level-headed, like his uncle. He seems to listen well and is anxious to learn. You've got a good Master Centurion to work with as well."

"Who might that be?" Severus asked, glancing through the roster.

"Flavius Quietus," Tiberius answered. Severus laughed at the name. He had known Flavius back when he was a young Legionary, thirty years before. Even if Strabo proved not to be the competent officer Tiberius thought he was Flavius would keep him in line. He also glanced at the names of all the Legion Commanders. Most of the names he recognized. He nodded his consent.

"I can work with this," he said after reviewing everything. "One thing though. When this is over, I retire…for good this time!"

*   *   *   *

Primus was walking through the vineyards as he often did on days such as this. It was here that Artorius would find him. It was amongst these vineyards that Primus and his sons had had many of their talks. He remembered back when Metellus had come to him, asking for the same letter of introduction that his other son would soon request. He would sign the letter, just as he had for Metellus. And they would make the same trip to the recruit depot. From there his task as a father was done. He wondered if he would really be doing the right thing, sending his last son off to join the army, given his brother's fate. He also thought back to his own experiences in the army and how painfully that had ended at the end of a Pannonian spear. He still walked with a slight limp and nowadays was rarely seen without his walking stick. He had thought hard about what had happened to him and to Metellus, as well as his beloved Persephone. He also realized that in the end it really was not his choice to make. Artorius had made his decision, and it was after all his life to live. As he contemplated these things the younger Artorius came running up the path towards him. Primus watched his son as he slowed to a walk.

He is strong; he thought to himself, *he is intelligent. I just worry about the rage and the hatred in his heart. I do hope he can find peace and satisfy his rage before it completely consumes him.*

Artorius approached his father. His voice was shaking with nervousness as he spoke. "Father, I know you know of my intentions." As Primus did not reply right away, Artorius continued, "I wish to join the Legions, to serve Rome as my father…and my brother before me."

"Walk with me," Primus replied. They walked amongst the vineyards for some time before Primus spoke again. "You say you wish to join the Legions to serve as your brother and I did. Tell me this, my son, would you wish to share the same fate as us; To end up half-crippled, or worse, dead? I only served in the Legions for four years before my injuries forced me out. Your brother was in for two years before his death. And let us not forget that your maternal grandfather was killed at Actium. You of course understand my concern for you, being as you are my only remaining son," he paused before continuing, "but in truth what concerns me the most is your real motives for joining the army. I saw the hatred in you grow from the moment we heard word of Metellus' death. I too had the same rage burning inside of me. Believe me; I wanted nothing more than to avenge my son, and my wife. In time I learned to quell my desire for revenge, to calm the raging spirit inside of me. You, my son have not done this. Your lust for vengeance has only grown over time."

"It is not just vengeance, Father. It is *justice* that I seek. We both know that the Emperor is planning to launch a massive invasion of Germania soon. Tell me, what kind of man would I be if I allowed this one chance to pass me by? It is like I can feel Metellus' soul crying out for justice."

"And suppose you do go to Germania and you do exact justice without getting yourself killed, what then?"

"Then I will continue to serve Rome. The army is the one truly honorable profession left in the civilized world, besides being a teacher." Primus smiled at the compliment, though it was a sad smile.

"Very well," he said, "I shall write your letter, just as I did for your dear brother. And I shall pray nightly to the gods that you do not suffer his fate. Only remember this; to seek justice is a good and noble thing, to seek revenge out of sheer hatred is something that will devour your very soul. You are a strong, intelligent young man, Titus. Do not let hatred rule your fate." Very little was said after that. They continued to walk the vineyards, discussing other things, anything but the army and the impending war.

The next day they left without ceremony for the recruit depot located by the docks in Ostia. There Primus delivered both his son and the letter of introduction that would allow him to join the ranks of the Legions. There was sadness in the elder Artorius' face, but there was also pride. He had sent a letter the night before to Pontius Pilate, asking that he check in on Artorius periodically.

"I'll be alright, Father," Artorius said with what he hoped was an air of confidence. Primus forced a smile before embracing his son.

"Remember what I told you," he replied. "Let *justice* be your guide. The army is only as noble and honorable as the men who serve in it."

"And I hope to one day find myself worthy of such honor," Artorius replied. As he walked towards the gate where a number of potential recruits stood waiting, he turned back and faced his father.

"When I do return, Father, I hope that you will have done the right and honorable thing by Juliana. She is the best thing to have come into your life, and you would be a fool to think otherwise." Without another word, Artorius turned away. Primus could only smile and marvel at what his son had said.

As soon as Artorius had disappeared within the confines of the recruit depot, Primus started his lonely journey home. He had work to do in the vineyards that day and lessons to prepare…no he would stop and see Juliana first.

*   *   *   *

There were about twenty young men waiting inside the recruit depot for their physical screenings and interviews. They had come from all over the region. Some were the sons of shepherds and farmers who wanted to rid themselves of the monotony of their fathers' professions. Others were of the poor and destitute who had nowhere else to go. Still others came from the city's middle classes, who were educated and wished to make an honorable profession out of the military.

Artorius took a seat on a bench outside the medical screening room. The other recruits sat in silence, nobody saying a word. Most were young, no older than he was. In spite of his eagerness, he was still a bit apprehensive. He had never been away from home before, and now he was on the verge of leaving forever. Artorius saw similar looks in the faces of the other recruits. All were nervous, yet excited. These men were no conscripts; Rome had ceased using conscription generations before. No, every last man who served in the Legions was a volunteer. These men *wanted* to be there. After what seemed like a long time, the door opened.

"Next," an orderly said, waiving Artorius in. The examination room was long, with a table and stool at one end.

"Let me see your hands," the orderly directed. Artorius did as directed. "You've done work with these," the man observed. "No noticeable scars or deformities," he continued as he wrote on a small pad. Next he held up a small stick.

"Follow this with your eyes," he ordered as he moved the stick around Artorius' head. He then made some more notes on his pad. He then required Artorius to squat down and walk with his hands on his hips. A few more brief calisthenics and he waived Artorius out.

"Alright, it looks like you are fit for duty," he said without looking up as Artorius left.

As he sat back onto the bench, Artorius thought to himself that the medical screening was too brief, almost rushed. What with the need for additional Soldiers on the frontier, it seemed that if you possessed all of your fingers and toes and did not have any mysterious diseases evident, then you were accepted. The pre-selection interview was equally rushed. Artorius couldn't even remember what they had asked him. They were then taken over to the money changers where they would draw an advance on their pay. This excited most of the recruits. Finally they were ushered into a holding area where they would await transport to the Legions on the frontier.

Artorius decided to make conversation with one of the other recruits. He walked over to a powerfully built lad, who looked like he was halfway intelligent. The mop of blonde hair on his head betrayed less than purely Latin roots, though this was becoming more and more common. At least he didn't smell like sheep excrement!

"So now we hurry up and wait," Artorius said, trying to break the ice.

The young man snorted at the remark, "yeah, they rush us through the physical screening and interview so that we can get to the frontier faster, only with our luck there's probably no transportation available for the next three days!" His sarcasm was thick.

Artorius laughed. "Well at least they were good enough to pay us for our time. I'm Artorius," he said, extending his hand.

"Magnus," the other recruit replied.

"So what brought you into the service of the Emperor's Legions?" Artorius asked.

Magnus pondered his response. "Well, my oldest brother took all the profitable shares of Dad's business; he sells textiles by the way. My next oldest brother is now an oarsman in the navy, which pays really well, however it's utterly monotonous. Plus I get seasick. And since I didn't feel like finding a real job within the city, I thought I would join the army. What about you?"

"Revenge," Artorius replied without pause.

"Oh," Magnus raised an eyebrow, and then shrugged it off.

Their banter was interrupted when the door opened and as two fully armored Legionaries walked in. One had his left arm was in a sling and in his right hand he held some documents. With them came the Centurion who had conducted their interviews.

"Lads," the Centurion said, "this is Sergeant Statorius and Legionary Decimus of the Twentieth Legion. They'll escort you to your post. Any questions concerning your assignment you can direct towards them." With that the Centurion left.

"When I call out your name, sound off, and fall out outside," Statorius said, *"Antoninus!"*

"Yeah," the young man replied. The Sergeant lowered the scroll and walked over to the young recruit, a deep scowl scoring his face. Antoninus started to realize his error as the Sergeant stood with his face just inches from his ear.

"Is that how you address a superior?" Statorius shouted. *"When I call your names, you will sound off with 'here Sergeant!' Is that clear?"*

"Yes, Sergeant!" all the recruits sounded off together. The Legionary named Decimus held his fist over his mouth, trying to stifle a laugh.

"Now, let's try this again. *Antoninus!*" Statorius shouted.

"Here, Sergeant!"

"That's better. *Artorius!*"

"Here, Sergeant!"

"Gavius!"

"Here, Sergeant!"

"Magnus!"

"Here, Sergeant!"

As soon as their names were called, they rushed outside to see twenty horses saddled and waiting for them.

"This is how we are getting to the Rhine?" the recruit whose name was Gavius asked nervously.

"What's the matter, can't ride?" Decimus asked as he came walking out.

"It's just that I've never ridden a horse before."

"Well you've got two weeks to learn," the Legionary said, smiling.

"Two weeks?" Artorius asked.

"What, you didn't think we were just going to fly to the Rhine, did you?" Decimus did not wait for an answer. Just then, Sergeant Statorius came walking out. He walked briskly over to his mount, and with some effort, having only one good arm, managed to get mounted.

"Alright, stow whatever personal belongings you have into the saddle bags," he directed. "You've got two minutes to be mounted and ready to ride!"

Good horsemanship was not something many Romans possessed, so it was rather amazing that all of them were in fact ready to ride when the Sergeant gave the order to move out. Gavius struggled with his mount for most of the first day. Very little was said for the first few hours of their trip. All of them wanted to garner whatever information they could from the Sergeant, but none seemed willing to try and talk with him. Artorius, bored with the silence, decided to make conversation with Statorius.

"Excuse me, Sergeant?" he said.

"Yes?"

"Did they send you all the way down from the Rhine just to come pick us up?"

"I was wounded in action several weeks ago and I was convalescing in Ostia until just yesterday. I was on my way back when I got tasked with taking you all with me."

"May I ask how you got wounded?"

"Sure," Statorius replied. There was a silence that followed. Artorius realized that the Sergeant was waiting for him to ask.

"So how did you get wounded?"

"I messed up."

After another long silence, Artorius realized that this particular conversation was going nowhere. Decimus rode over and nudged him.

"Don't worry about the Sergeant. He's a little irritated right now. Besides, he doesn't talk much anyway." Artorius looked over at Statorius, who seemed to be brooding about something. He turned his attention back to the Legionary.

"Could you please tell us about where we are going?" he asked.

"Yes," Magnus piped in, "tell us about the legendary Twentieth Legion, Valeria."

"Valeria?" Gavius asked, still struggling with his horse.

"It means valiant," answered Artorius.

"That is correct," replied Decimus, "a lot of times a Legion will be given an honorary name to add to its title. The Second Legion is known as 'Augusta' since it was formed by the former Emperor. Some monikers aren't so flattering, though. The Twenty-First Legion is known as 'Rapax,' which technically means 'The Predator,' however it has been taken to mean 'greedy.' As for Valeria, it is indeed a Legion full of valiant men. The place we are headed to is called Cologne. It's a good sized place. What with two Legions stationed there, many feel it will soon boom into a full-blown city. We share a double-size fortress with the First Legion, Germanica. They're a pretty good lot. Gaius Caetronius is their Commander.

"Most, in fact I think all of you are being assigned to the Third Cohort. Four of you, Artorius, Magnus, Antoninus, and Gavius are coming to the Second Century, where I happen to be assigned."

"Century," Antoninus said, "so that means there are a hundred men assigned to it?"

"Actually that's a misnomer," Decimus answered, "A Century is made up of ten tent groups, or sections, of eight men each. The senior Legionary in each section acts as its Sergeant. So in actuality there are eighty men in a Century, eighty-four if you count the senior officers, when we are at full strength, which is practically never. Sergeant Statorius and I come from the same section.

"The Centurion is the man in charge of the Century. All are highly experienced Soldiers who've come up through the ranks. Most have between fifteen and twenty years in the army by the time they see promotion. Our Centurion, Platorius Macro is one of the younger ones. In fact, he was just promoted within the last year. Come to think of it, there are a number of young Centurions in the Twentieth. There was a big shake-up amongst the ranks after the entire army damned near mutinied."

"The army mutinied?" Magnus asked.

"Didn't hear about that back home, did you?" Decimus stated more than asked. "That doesn't surprise me. Anyway, that's a story for another time. Like I was saying, you've got the Centurion who runs the Century. Directly beneath him is the Optio. The Optio is second in command of the Century and he takes care of a lot of the day to day business. Our Optio's name is Valgus.

"The other predominant figures within the Century are the Signifier and the Tesserarius. The Tesserarius takes care of all the duty rosters, the watch words of the day and the training schedules. He's somebody you definitely want to make friends with, especially if you want to avoid certain details like digging out the sewage pipes every time they get backlogged with shit." The recruits all wrinkled their noses at the thought. Decimus laughed and continued, "The Signifier is in charge of all the Century's pay and allowances, and is also third in command of the Century. You'll learn to love him on pay days. He is also the one who carries the Century's standard into battle, which he uses for relaying visual signals and orders to other units. Flaccus and Camillus are our Tesserarius and Signifier. There are also some various special duty positions like the Chief Weapons Instructor. Sergeant Vitruvius holds that position. You'll get to know him *very* well over the next few weeks." Statorius started laughing, as if at some inside joke that only he and Decimus were privy to. Decimus continued his dissertation on the makeup of the Roman Legion.

"So now you know the basic structure of the Century. The *Cohort* is made up of six Centuries, and it is commanded by the ranking Centurion, known as the *Centurion Pilus Prior*. The Pilus Prior is always assigned to the First Century. Valerius Proculus is the Pilus Prior for the Third Cohort. Ten Cohorts make up the bulk of the Legion. Cohorts Two through Ten are structured exactly the same. The First Cohort is a bit different. It only has five Centuries instead of six, but each of these is at double-strength of one hundred and sixty men. All Soldiers in the First Cohort are hand picked veterans and are considered to be the elite of any Legion. Their Centurions are each given the title of *Centurion Primus Ordo*. They are the most experienced, and the senior ranking Centurions within the Legion. They outrank even the Cohort Commanders. They in turn are lead by the *Centurion Primus Pilus*, sometimes known as the *Chief* or *Master* Centurion. He is the senior ranking Centurion within the Legion, and third overall in the chain-of-command. It is the highest rank an enlisted Soldier can ever hope to achieve, though most will never see it. Remember, there is only one per Legion, and there are currently twenty-five Legions in the Empire. You can do the math on that one. Flavius Quietus holds that position in the Twentieth. He's a hard ass old school Soldier. Has a soft spot for the lads, though.

"The Equestrian Class of society provides the Legion with its military Tribunes. There are six in each Legion. They serve as staff officers, mostly for only six-month tours. We pay little attention to them as very few take a serious stab at being career army officers. Pontius Pilate, our Chief of Artillery is one of those few." Artorius' ears perked up at the sound of his old friend's name.

Decimus continued, "The senior Tribune in the Legion comes from the Senatorial Class, just like the Commanding General, or *Legate* as is his official title. Caecina Severus is the Legate of the Twentieth. Gaius Strabo is the Chief Tribune, and second in Command."

The new recruits tried to absorb as much of this information as they could during the two weeks that it took them to reach their home on the Rhine. They stayed at various road stations along the away, sleeping in the stalls next to their horses, or wherever they could find a place to lay down. The further north they went, the colder it became. Snow covered the landscape as they closed in on their destination. Artorius had never dealt well with the cold, and he clutched his cloak as tightly around him as possible. One afternoon they finally saw the town of Cologne and the fortress coming into site.

CHAPTER 4

▼

FROM CIVILIAN TO SOLDIER

"There it is lads," Statorius said, "home of the Twentieth Legion, Valeria." The recruits grew excited as they rode closer. The fortress was an impressive site indeed. What made it impressive was the permanence of the structure, and its sheer menacing appearance. There were several ditches surrounding the walls that were filled with jagged spikes and tangle foot obstacles, though with the snow on the ground, the recruits could not see the contents of the ditches. The walls themselves were of stone and masonry, as were the guard towers. The gate was reinforced with metal strips. It was open, and there were several guards on duty just inside. Statorius showed them some papers and they ushered him in.

The fortress resembled a small city more than anything, only it appeared to be cleaner and more organized. There were long rows of barracks, stables, black smith shops, bakeries, bath houses, just about anything one could need. It looked as if one could get easily lost.

"How does one find their way around here?" Magnus asked.

"It's not hard, once you understand the layout," Decimus said, "plus once you've been inside one fortress, you can find your way around any, since all are identical in their layout. Here we are." They stopped at a stable where some grooms came to take their horses. The grooms were Germans, though they had better hygiene and grooming standards than one would expect from "barbarians."

"From here we walk," Statorius said. They walked over to what looked like a headquarters building. From there most of the recruits were escorted off by waiting Legionaries. Only four, Artorius, Antoninus, Gavius and Magnus remained with Sergeant Statorius. He walked them over to another building. This one was L-shaped. It was really long on one side, where Artorius assumed all of the billets were for the men of the Century. The shorter end housed the Centurion's quarters as well as the offices. They walked into the outer office, where a Soldier was sitting behind a desk, filling out paperwork. The Soldier looked up and smiled when he saw Statorius.

"Look who's decided to come back to the land of the living," he said.

"Good to see you too, Camillus," Statorius replied, grasping his hand.

"So, what have we got here?" Camillus asked.

"Fresh ones, straight out of the turnip patch. Do you have any idea where we're putting them?"

"As a matter of fact," Camillus said, shuffling through some papers, "this one, Antoninus is getting assigned to Ostorius' section. The rest..." he paused, "are going with you."

Statorius looked surprised. "I didn't think I had three vacancies."

"Yeah well, that one new kid you had, what was his name, Falerius, I think. Anyway, he took a bad fall during a night march in some bad country. It busted his leg up pretty good. The doctors said that the leg probably would never fully heal, and that while he may walk again, marching and fighting were definitely out of the question. So yes, you had three vacancies. Now you and Ostorius are about the only sections that are at full strength."

"Well we will be, once these kids make it through training. When do they start?"

"Tomorrow," another Soldier said as he walked in from the outside. He was also dressed in full armor, and he carried a long staff with a knob on the end of it, a symbol of his rank. "Statorius welcome back," he said, shaking the Sergeant's hand.

"Valgus," Statorius said, "good to see you. Lads, this is Valgus, the Optio for the Second Century."

Valgus nodded in acknowledgment. "Let me get out of my gear and I'll take them over to supply to draw their basic issue. In the mean time why don't you go bathe and relax for a while? You look like hell," he said to Statorius.

"Yes, I definitely need to hit the bath house."

"I'm already there!" Decimus shouted from the doorway as he left.

"When do we get to use the bath house?" Artorius asked, realizing that his own smell was more than a little ripe. Valgus walked over and placed the end of his staff underneath his chin.

"Who in the hell gave you permission to speak, *recruit? If* your scrawny ass makes it through training, and *if* we actually decide to let you become a Legionary, then you can speak! Until then you will shut the fuck up unless spoken to!" The Optio gave his staff a slight nudge to emphasize his point. Artorius was taken aback that he had called him 'scrawny,' given that he had about twice the amount of muscle mass as the Optio. Without missing a beat, Valgus withdrew his staff and continued calmly, "In answer to your question; later, after you get all your equipment and settled into your quarters."

As soon as Valgus had changed he took them over to the armory. An older Legionary stood behind the counter along with a couple of Gallic assistants. There were shelves and bins of gear and weapons behind him.

"Line up single file, and start trying on your equipment," he said, curtly. The first thing they drew was one pair of Legionary sandals with cold weather leggings. Next they were sized for their red tunics, of which they were issued four. Artorius required the largest size of tunic available to fit around his massive frame. Next, they were each issued a belt with groin protection in the front, a dagger with scabbard, a Gallic-style helmet with cheek guards, and body armor, known as the lorica segmentata. Again, Artorius required the largest size of armor available. The armor was a bit of a puzzle to figure out. It consisted of a horizontal metal bands that wrapped around the torso. It also had extra bands for the shoulders and neck. In addition to all of this, they were issued a basket, pick, saw, some linen for their bunks, and a long Y-shaped pole with a leather sack with which to put everything in.

"No other weapons?" Magnus asked, holding his dagger.

"Until we show you how to use them properly, all you dumb-asses will do is hurt yourselves!" Valgus yelled from the door.

"You'll get those at the end of training, after you've sworn the oath of allegiance," the veteran Legionary answered.

With great difficulty they managed to haul all of their gear over to their quarters in the Century's main hall. They were shown to a room where there were eight bunks. Five of these showed signs of occupancy. Two Legionaries were dozing on their racks. There was a small table and some chairs in one corner and a small cooking stove in the other. There was also a doorway leading to another room directly behind it. In here there were a number of shelves and bins. The shelves were set up for the Soldiers to stow their body armor, helmet and weapons. Five shields were standing up against the wall, and a bin in the corner held a number of javelins. Eight other bins were set up to hold all of the Soldiers' entrenching gear. Another was filled with palisade stakes. A door on the far wall of this room opened directly to the outside. Each recruit claimed a bin and a shelf and stored their gear as best they could. About this time, Statorius, Decimus and one other Legionary came in through the outside door. They wore fresh tunics and their hair was still damp from the bathhouse. Statorius' arm was still in a sling, though he seemed to be refreshed and in a much fairer temper.

"Ah, I see you've found where we live and where all of your equipment goes," he said.

"So what happens now?" Artorius asked, nervously.

"Dinner," replied Statorius. He then called to one of the Legionaries asleep on his bunk, "hey Carbo! Get off your fat ass and get started on supper! It's your turn today!" Carbo, the Legionary in question, groaned as if in pain and reluctantly rolled off his bunk. He then started the fire underneath the cooking stove.

"What's with him?" Magnus asked.

"Little too much wine and spirits last night," the Legionary who came in with Statorius and Decimus said.

"And a little too much of that trashy tavern wench, Lolia" Decimus added, smiling fiendishly.

"I told you!" Carbo bellowed from the other room, "it was that tavern bitch and her sister!"

"Like hell it was," the Soldier piped in, "you were so wiped out last night that you were probably seeing double!"

Carbo grunted under his breath and started to place some wheat cakes and bacon onto the skillet, all the while grunting about wenches and their sisters.

"Anyway lads," Statorius started, "these are our newest recruits. Artorius, Magnus and Gavius; meet Praxus. Of course, you have already met Decimus and you've now been introduced to Carbo, sort of. The other poor sod passed out over there is Valens. I think he may have had a little too much of Lolia and her 'sister' last night as well." He paused and then in a low voice asked Praxus, "Lolia doesn't actually have a sister, does she?"

"I don't think so," Praxus answered.

"Hmm, well anyway, once these new fellows get through the next eight weeks of training and officially become Legionaries, we'll actually have a full crew for once!"

"The training is eight weeks?" Gavius asked.

"Don't worry, it goes by pretty fast," Praxus said.

"Yeah, you're too tired and wiped out every night to have any concept of time," Decimus added with a smile.

"You'll be alright," Statorius said, "besides, the real beatings don't begin until weapons drill in a couple of weeks." Given their 'warm' reception at the hands of the Sergeant, as well as Optio Valgus, the recruits did not like the sound of that.

"And they never end either. Especially with Vitruvius as our Chief Weapons Instructor," Decimus said, showing the bruises on the back of his hand and forearm.

"Anyway, let's eat," Statorius said as he walked over and elbowed Valens in the ribs.

*   *   *   *

Training started early the next day. Statorius had woken them all up well before sunrise, and had instructed them to don their tunic, helmet, belt and dagger and fall out outside in front of the barracks. Optio Valgus stood there waiting for them. He was dressed in full armor and he carried his staff with him. Antoninus came out from another section of the barracks to join them.

"Recruits," Valgus said his voice hard, "today you will begin the transformation from civilians into Soldiers. The first thing a Legionary needs to be is strong in the mind and the body. During the first couple of weeks, we will condition both. To start the day off we will go for a little run." Valgus led them on a jog around the inside of the fortress wall. The pace felt good at first to Artorius. In addition to being immensely strong, he was well conditioned, or so he thought. The pace quickened as they made each turn along the wall. On the final stretch, they were nearly at a sprint. Artorius was gasping for breath by the end of the run. He looked over to see that his fellow recruits faired little better. Though Valgus was laughing out loud, he did not look pleased.

"By the gods, how is it that you sorry lot can be winded after a mild jog? You are *pathetic!* Now get on your feet and start acting like Legionaries, instead of like a bunch of whipped Greek schoolgirls!"

Without giving them time to rest, he had them run over to the parade grounds. There were several heavy balls made out of hide, lying off to one side, each weighing about thirty pounds. He paired them up and had them throw the balls back and forth to each other as hard as they could. Artorius found this to his liking. He paired up with Magnus, and he found it amusing that he almost knocked Magnus down several times with the force of his throws. Of course, he soon began to tire and several times dropped the ball. This in turn brought a sharp rap across the back from Valgus' staff. He never said anything, he would simply smack a recruit sharply each time one of them dropped their ball. Finally, when it seemed like none of them could even hold their arms up anymore, he gave the order for them to stop and rest. Artorius' arms felt weak and his legs wobbly. He was strong, but he did not possess the conditioning that he thought he had.

Valgus had them form up, and marched them back over to the barracks. He ushered them into the main office. Each of them had just sat down when Camillus, the Signifier walked in.

"Good morning, recruits," he said, "today you will learn a bit about the history of the Twentieth Legion, our rank structure and where your place will be within her.

"The Twentieth was first mustered more than forty-six years ago by the Divine Augustus. It was first stationed in Hispania and took part in the campaigns against the Cantabrians. Later it served under Tiberius in the Pannonia insurrection. During this campaign, the Legion found itself cut off and surrounded. In spite of insurmountable odds, they managed to route the enemy and make their way back to friendly lines." He continued to lecture them for a couple hours, at the end of which in walked a man they knew immediately to be their Centurion.

"On your feet!" Camillus called out, as he immediately stood up.

"At ease," the Centurion said. On Camillus' cue, they all took their seats.

The Centurion was not very old, perhaps thirty. There was something about his demeanor though that just commanded respect. He was not overly large in the frame, but one could tell just by his very aura that he possessed incredible strength. His face bore several scars, as did his hands and forearms. Artorius thought, *he probably has many scars, though I doubt if any are on his back.* He also carried a short vine stick in his hand. Like the pole that Valgus carried, it was one of the symbols of his rank.

"Men, my name is Centurion Platorius Macro. I am the Commanding Officer of the Second Century. Currently there are seventy Soldiers assigned to this Century. Once you get through your training that number will raise to seventy-four. You may or may not have heard about the upcoming spring campaign, and right now, we need every Soldier we can muster. Therefore, your training will be accelerated in order that you may be able to accompany us. However, do not think this means that your training will be any easier, or that you will be given less than the full measure of what you are expected to learn.

"I expect my Legionaries to be fit, both physically as well as mentally. I need Soldiers who can make tough decisions instantaneously on the battlefield, and be physically able to carry them out repeatedly. I accept only the highest standards of discipline and conduct while you are on duty. In addition, know that I will hold you accountable for all of your actions, be they right or wrong." He smacked the vine stick across the palm of his hand to emphasize the point. "Optio Valgus, they're all yours," he said as he left the room.

"Alright recruits, head back to your billets. Supper should be waiting for you. I also highly recommend that you each hit the bath house tonight; I don't want you stinking up my parade field in the morning!"

Artorius looked outside and saw that the sun was setting. He did not realize how late in the day it was. He also realized that they had not eaten all day and that he was very hungry. When they arrived back at their billets, he saw that Statorius and the others had already made their dinner.

"Hey, here's our babes back from their first day of training," Praxus said as he motioned them towards where their food was cooking. There was the usual staple of wheat cakes, but there were also strips of meat, fresh fruit, vegetables, and wine. Artorius grabbed his mess tin and immediately started to pile on the food. He looked down and saw that his hand was trembling; he was so tired and hungry. Just being able to eat was a joy and a relief.

"That's one nice thing about the Roman army, you never go hungry," said Valens, who was looking a lot more lively than the night before.

"Could have fooled us!" retorted Magnus, "this is the first we've eaten all day!"

"Well I don't think that was intentional," replied Statorius, "but with your training having to be accelerated, they have to cram a lot more into each day to make the most of it. I guess today they just forgot about breakfast."

"You mean they don't intentionally starve us to make us stronger?" Gavius asked.

"What an asinine concept," Praxus retorted.

"Come off it, man, this isn't Sparta!" Carbo piped in. He also was looking better than he did the night before. He was a bit pudgier than the other Legionaries were, and was red in the face as if out of breath. He definitely did not look the part of a Legionary.

"I thought the Spartans were the toughest race in the ancient world," Gavius said.

"They were overrated," Statorius said through a mouth full of food.

"You're not kidding," Carbo continued, "I mean think about it. They starved their soldiers because they thought it would make them tougher. They even forced them to go on long marches without so much as shoes. Their only means of motivation was through fear. You screw up once and they cut your throat! Talk about an army with morale problems! Sure, the scare tactics may have worked for a while, but where is Sparta now?"

"Nothing but a sad memory of a failed race," Decimus said.

"That's right," Carbo replied, "now look at us. Yes, there is the discipline that is required if we are going to succeed in battle. Believe me; I have felt the Centurion's vine stick more than once. However, there are also many benefits of being a Soldier. Our pay, even at the lowest ranks, is certainly no meager wage. Moreover, it is consistent. And they feed us pretty damn well."

"Some of us more than others," Praxus said as he poked Carbo in the stomach.

"Yeah, feed on my ass, you scrawny little sewage rat!" Carbo retorted as everyone laughed. Just then, there was a knock at the door and Flaccus, the Tesserarius walked in.

"Hey Statorius, just wanted to let you know that your section has rampart repair tomorrow," he said.

"Where at?" Statorius asked.

"Over by the North wall, there's a section of wall on the rampart that's falling apart. Vitruvius' guys took care of all the stone cutting today."

"No problem. We'll get it done."

As soon as Flaccus had left, Artorius asked, "Do we get to help you with this detail tomorrow?"

"No," Statorius replied, "You guys get to do more physical conditioning and training with Optio Valgus tomorrow. No need to worry, you will get plenty of time to build walls and roads and dig ditches soon enough. Alright lads, it looks like we all have an early day tomorrow, so we'd better hit the rack."

Soon the lamps were out and everyone was sound asleep. Artorius lay on his bunk thinking of all that had transpired over the last few days. He had made it to the Legion; however, he was not officially a Soldier yet. He hoped that his training would go fast. The sooner the training was over, the sooner they would be on campaign; and the sooner he could have his revenge.

The next morning they stood tall outside the barracks as Optio Valgus walked up and inspected each one in turn. When he got to Magnus he came unglued.

"Recruit, why in the hell have you shown up for formation with a dirty tunic?" he shouted into Magnus' ear. Magnus had elected to wear the same tunic that he had the day before, and it was covered in sweat and dirt. *"Did I not tell you not to come stinking up my parade field?"*

"I thought that since we were going to be getting dirty this morning anyway, no sense in…" his reply was cut short by a hard smack across the back from the Optio's staff.

"I don't care if you plan on crawling through pig shit, you will come to my forma-tions washed and with a clean tunic! Do you understand me, Recruit?" He gave Mag-nus another blow across the back to emphasize the point. Magnus stifled a yelp of pain.

"Yes Sir!" he answered awkwardly. As he stood there, shaken, Valgus stuck his face next to his ear.

"So what are you waiting for?" he whispered. "Get out of here and into a fresh tunic. *Move!"*

Artorius was shocked to see how quickly Magnus was able to run back into the barracks and change into one of his clean tunics. It didn't seem like even a minute had passed before his friend was standing tall before the Optio again, albeit looking a little sheepish. Valgus acted as if the whole incident had never happened.

The first week consisted of physical training, as well as classes on the principles of Roman warfare. Classroom study was one thing; it would be a different matter to have to execute it first hand. For that, they needed to learn individual weapons drill.

*   *   *   *

Sergeant Vitruvius was an imposing figure to say the least. He was slightly taller than average, and was completely bald. His muscles were even bigger than Artorius', and they looked carved out of stone. Unlike most veterans, his body was conspicuously devoid of any noticeable scars, and he had a voice that could carry over long distances without having to yell. He was a complete professional, taking his assigned duty as Chief Weapons Instructor very seriously. Rome taught her Soldiers to fight in lines of battle as a team. It was Vitruvius' job to make cer-tain that every Soldier on that line was an unstoppable killing machine. He pos-sessed a reputation for being immensely strong, incredibly fast with the gladius, and he never missed with the javelin. Every stroke with his weapon was deliberate and precise. In short, he was the perfect killing machine and none was better suited to teach other men how to kill each other.

"Everyone needs to grab a training shield and gladius from the cart and follow me," he said to the recruits, pointing out the equipment cart to them. It was early in the morning, and the sun was just beginning to warm the cold earth.

Artorius picked up the wicker shield and wooden sword and was somewhat surprised. Even with his superior strength, they still felt unusually heavy. He shrugged and followed the instructor to where numerous six-foot poles were sticking out of the ground. They had lines painted horizontally on them at the neck and hip level, and all looked beaten and worn.

"First thing you need to do is assume a good fighting stance," Vitruvius started. "It must allow for maximum mobility, balance, and power, while at the same time it must be comfortable. Take your shield in your left hand and your gladius in your right. Place your feet about shoulder width apart, with your right leg slightly back." He demonstrated and everyone followed his lead.

"Now on a service shield there is a metal boss right in the center. Can anyone tell me what that is for?"

"Is it to protect the hand?" Antoninus asked.

"That's part of it," Vitruvius answered, "but can anyone tell me its primary use?"

"To smash the enemy in the face," Artorius said.

"Absolutely right," Vitruvius replied. "When you make contact with your opponent, the first thing you want to do is throw him off balance. In order to do that, you smack him with the boss on your shield. Now remember, when you punch somebody you do not want to just use your arm. No matter how strong you are, you're not going to get maximum effect." He punched the pole hard to demonstrate. It hardly budged.

"The real source of power," he continued, "lies in the hips. When you punch, turn your hips into it, and draw your power from there. Like this," with that he slammed his shield into the pole. It rocked violently back and forth, and the recruits thought he might uproot it. "Now you try it."

The recruits all smacked their shields into the poles. Some found it awkward at first. Vitruvius would check each recruit in turn and make corrections as necessary. For Artorius it seemed to come naturally. He felt the pole move underneath the force of his blows. He tried to think it was a Germanic warrior; perhaps even the one who killed his brother. He became incensed as he slammed it repeatedly. He did not even notice Vitruvius was standing next to him until the Sergeant grabbed his shield and almost pulled him down.

"Good power, good intensity. Need to be quicker on the retraction," Vitruvius told him. He then addressed the group, "Make sure that when you strike, either with the shield or the gladius that you pull back quickly. Your first shot may not throw your opponent off balance right away. If he has an axe or some kind of hooked weapon, he can snag your shield and yank it out of your hand. Or worse, he can pull you off the line completely." They continued to practice slamming their shields into their wooden opponents until Vitruvius was satisfied. All the recruits were panting, out of breath. Artorius was breathing heavy, but the exertion felt good. After a few strikes, he let his shield bottom rest on the ground as he caught his breath. He had no sooner set his shield down when he felt a sharp pain as he was struck across the back.

"What the hell do you think you are doing?" Centurion Macro screamed into his ear, his vine stick held high for another blow.

"Sorry, I just got tired and thought…" Artorius began. Before he could continue, the Centurion smacked him across the back of the legs. Pain shot through them, and he almost fell to his knees.

"You thought *what?* That it would be all right if you decide to take a break while a barbarian skewers you like a wild boar? Get your shield back up and strike your target!" Artorius immediately brought his shield back up and started punching at the stake again. His arm ached and he was dripping with sweat, yet he dared not set his shield down, lest he incur the Centurion's wrath again. He heard a hard slap and a yelp as he caught another recruit committing the same crime. Their instructor seemed to take the Centurion's beating of recruits as a matter of course.

"Alright, now that you've knocked your opponent off balance with a blow from the shield, the next step is to move in and kill the bastard as quickly as possible," Vitruvius explained. "If you look, you'll see that the gladius has a sharp point to it and a short blade. That is because it is designed for close combat, and it is primarily used for stabbing. Most barbarian swordsmen use great swords that are the same height as the wielder. They like to heft them in an elaborate overhead slash. Such fighting styles, while flamboyant, are practically useless. Anyone know why?"

"Because it shows your intent and gives the enemy time to defend against it," Magnus answered.

"It is slow and less likely to hit," Gavius responded.

"It leaves their body wide open, thereby they are more easily killed with a rapid stab," Artorius said.

"All correct," Vitruvius said, obviously pleased. "Recruit Antoninus, step up here." Antoninus came forward and faced the others. "Now raise your sword arm like you were going to slash." Antoninus did so.

"If you look," Vitruvius said, "you'll notice that with his arm up, his torso is stretched out and his body is wide open for attack. Plus, it puts him off balance."

With that, he shoved Antoninus to the ground with little effort. He then extended his hand and helped the recruit get back to his feet.

"As I said, the primary use of the gladius is as a stabbing weapon. You rattle your opponent with a blow from your shield; you finish him with a quick stab to his vitals. The ideal spot is just below the ribcage. If you can strike him underneath the ribs and up at an angle, your blade will go right to his heart or lungs. You want to avoid stabbing directly into the chest, as there is the probability of your blade ending up stuck in the ribs. The abdomen and bladder region also work. Usually these areas are not immediately fatal, however your opponent will be out of action, and he will die soon enough. For a quick kill, you can also aim for the throat or just beneath the jaw. If you cannot get a shot in at the vitals, aim for the legs. A quick stab to the thigh will put him on the ground quickly. Now you try it. Remember, just as with a shield punch, draw you power from the hips. Alright, go ahead and do it."

Vitruvius and Macro watched as the recruits went to work stabbing away at the wooden poles. Artorius again visualized a hulking German in front of him. He imagined the sheer agony he would put the man in when he stabbed him in the abdomen, or the throat, or underneath the ribs and into the lungs. Once he was satisfied that things were progressing well, the Centurion left.

"Hold your weapon firmly, but do not keep a death grip on it," Vitruvius told the recruits as they practiced. "Your weapons should become an extension of your arms. They should become a part of you." After a while, he had the recruits cease in their exercises.

"Alright, you've started to grasp the most rudimentary basics of individual combat. Are there any questions before I release you for your afternoon meal?" Vitruvius asked.

"Yes Sergeant," Magnus said. "I understand that battles can sometimes last for hours. I also understand the need for us to be in extremely good physical shape; however these weapons seem to be excessively heavy."

Vitruvius smiled, "is there anyone else who thinks that their training weapons are excessively heavy?" There was a pause before he continued. Obviously, the recruits did not want to appear weak in front of the Sergeant. "Understand that yes, the training weapons are heavier than service weapons, twice as heavy in fact. You are right, Recruit Magnus. Conditioning is extremely important for a Legionary. If you can sustain the fight using these training weapons, then using your actual service weapons will come easy. That is it for weapons drill today. Next will be your afternoon meal, followed by classes on Century battle drill and then more physical training with Optio Valgus."

That afternoon they went over the basics of maneuvering a Century as part of a larger element, the Cohort. Centurion Macro taught these classes himself, since he was the one who would direct such maneuvers on the battlefield. The recruits returned to the practice field, where the Centurion had a large parchment stretched out on an easel. There were numerous diagrams drawn on it.

"While individual fighting prowess is important, it will do you no good if you cannot work together and fight as a team," the Centurion began. "The lowest element of any Legion is the Section, which consists of eight Soldiers. Ten sections make up a Century. When deployed for battle, the Century will usually form up on line, facing the enemy. The Centurion always takes the position at the right of the line and in the front rank if the Century is in column formation. The Optio takes the position at the extreme left or at the rear of the formation if the Century is in a column. Their job is to make certain that the Century holds the line, stays in formation, and executes properly. The signifier will position himself next to the Centurion. He is the one who will relay all signals and orders.

"The Cohort consists of six Centuries. Normally it is the smallest unit that will ever operate independently. Standard battle formation for the Cohort is Centuries on line, one behind the next. Soldiers in each rank will be staggered with those to their front. This will ensure proper overlapping coverage, and make it easier when the Cohort conducts a passage-of-lines."

"Excuse me Sir, but what is a passage-of-lines?" Magnus asked. The Centurion didn't miss a beat in explaining.

"You may recall that the old Greek phalanx consisted of many ranks, often sixteen or more, that were stacked one behind the next. Each phalanx would crash into the other and they would maul each other with massive spears until one broke. If you were in the first few ranks, chances were you were going to end up dead. No matter how decisive a victory was for one side, both would always suffer appalling, and unnecessary losses. The passage-of-lines is one of the Roman innovations that help us to avoid this. Once Soldiers in the front rank become fatigued, the Centurion will give the command 'set for passage-of-lines.' At this time, the Soldiers in the front rank will set in place and quit advancing forward. The Centurion in the next rank will then give the command 'execute passage-of-lines.' The Soldiers in the second rank, moving together as one, will rush past the Soldiers in the front rank, and smash into the enemy lines. This must be executed with precision, and all Soldiers must remain together on line for it to inflict maximum shock on the enemy. The Soldiers who were previously in the front rank will then police up any dead or wounded, and make their way back through the remaining ranks to the rear of the formation. Are there any questions concerning this?" There were none.

Afternoon physical training consisted of a going for a run around the inside of the fortress, only this time with a log pressed over their heads. As much as this added to the degree of difficulty, Artorius found that he was not as winded as he was after his first run. That night there was the usual friendly banter around supper with the rest of their group. Their companions were more than friendly, though there was definitely that degree of separation that would continue to exist until they completed training. Afterwards, it was a brief trip to the bathhouse before going to bed. Artorius was finding sleep easier to come by at night. He knew his conditioning was improving, he was learning the ways of the Legion, and he was slowly transforming into a Soldier. He longed for the day when he would be a civilian no longer.

The next day offered more of the same. Problem was Artorius' arms and back still ached from the day before. It was not long before they started to wither under the strain of having to wield the practice gladius and shield for so long. He began to seriously regret not having included more endurance exercises in his old workout regime. He was immensely strong; he just did not possess the muscular stamina necessary to go for long periods of time.

Sweat seemed to gush from every one of his pours. His arms felt ready to fall off as he continued to strike his wooden adversary that only the day before he had attacked with such zeal and fervor. Just when he felt like he couldn't go any further he heard a loud yelp as one of the other recruits felt the wrath of the Centurion's vine stick.

Where had he come from? He glanced over to see Magnus leaning on his shield while Centurion Macro alternately screamed in his ear and smacked him across the back with his vine stick.

"You worthless bag of pig excrement!" the Centurion bellowed. *"You say your body hurts? I'll teach you the meaning of hurt!"*

The young recruit gritted his teeth and kept his eyes front as the Centurion continued to chastise him both physically and verbally. Finally with a yell of rage and determination he lunged forward and attacked the wooden stake with renewed energy.

"Better," he heard Macro say aloud. "Keep it going, Recruit." Artorius immediately renewed his own assault, lest he too fall victim to the Centurion's wrath.

That evening he sat in the heated pool in the bathhouse for some time, allowing the hot water to do its magic on his tight and aching muscles. He watched as Magnus slowly limped into the pool. He had several marks across his back, though none looked to have caused any kind of long-term injury. Still, Magnus winced as he lowered himself into the water.

"Certainly knows how to motivate, doesn't he?" Artorius asked sarcastically.

"Artorius," Magnus muttered with his head lying back against the side of the pool, "would you take offense if I told you to go screw yourself?" Artorius laughed at his friend's plight.

"Seriously though," Magnus said, looking his way, "I suppose I should be grateful to Centurion Macro for helping me to strengthen my body and my mind." Artorius wasn't sure if he was serious of if he was being sarcastic.

"And to think we actually volunteered for this," Artorius mused to himself, his eyes shut.

"Ha!" Magnus snorted. "I swear the Centurion's not even human. Nor is that Sergeant who's out there teaching us weapon's drill. That man is some type of unholy machine. Either that or he's a god of some sorts."

"Oh relax," they heard Praxus say as he lowered himself into the pool. "I assure you, Vitruvius is quite human." Magnus looked down into the steaming water.

"I have got to watch what I say until I know who may be listening," he muttered.

"It's no big deal," Praxus replied. He seemed vibrant and full of life. Obviously he had not just had his backside beaten by an enraged Centurion with a vine stick. "Trust me; I've been there myself on more than one occasion, to include after I got out of recruit training."

"When was the last time you ever got the vine stick?" Artorius asked, suddenly curious.

"About a year and a half ago," Praxus answered, looking down. "I was on sentry duty. I had spent the night before letting loose and cavorting, knowing full well I was to be on duty the next day. Well about halfway through my shift I decided to use my shield as a prop and catch a quick nap. Lo and behold if Centurion Macro doesn't wake me up with a blow to the back of my helmet. He caught me so hard, my helmet actually came off! He then walked away, without saying another word. As soon as I got off shift, I received one of the worst beatings I have ever taken in my life.

"What made it harder was there was a set of orders sitting on Macro's desk, promoting me to Sergeant and giving me command of my own section. Needless to say, those got burned; I lost my immune status as well. It was only within the last few months that I got that back. And to be honest, I'll be lucky now if I *ever* see Sergeant." He paused for a few seconds, while contemplating things. "But then again, I did get off pretty easy. Falling asleep on sentry duty can be considered a capital offense. Macro could just as easily have had me crucified or hanged." As Praxus finished his story, Valens and Decimus joined them.

"Valens, you haven't been out with one of your concubines have you?" Praxus asked, pretending to be annoyed.

"Just came from there!" Valens announced, grabbing at his crotch.

"Well I hope you washed that thing before you get in here!" Praxus retorted. "Gods know what you'd get in the water!"

"Actually our Valens here has stepped up in the world," Decimus announced. "I saw this one. She actually had all of her teeth!" Praxus frowned and nodded.

"I have to say Valens, I'm impressed," he replied. Artorius laughed and climbed out of the hot water as the others continued in their tasteless banter.

"Get your packs ready and fall out outside!" Statorius bellowed to the recruits the next morning. Immediately they all grabbed their packs and started to don their body armor.

"Leave the armor. Helmet and cloak only," the Sergeant called out.

As Artorius and the others fell out outside, they saw the rest of the Cohort's recruits were heading to their position as well. Flanking them was a Century's worth of Legionaries in full body armor and kit. Valgus was dressed the same, as was a Centurion whom the recruits had never seen before.

"Recruits, this is Centurion Dominus, Commander of the Fourth Century. Today the Fourth is going on a little road march to stretch their legs. In order to get your weak asses in shape, you will be joining them. Fall in on the center of the formation!" With that, Optio Valgus stood in the front rank, at the head of the Cohort's recruits. The Centurion stood at the front of the column, along with the Fourth Century's Signifier.

"*Century!*" he bellowed. "*Forward...march!*" With much awkwardness, the recruits stepped off with the regular Legionaries. It wasn't until they reached the gates of the fortress that they finally got in step with the other Soldiers.

Artorius was surprised at the quickness of the pace that the Fourth Century set. Regardless of individual height, their strides were long and rapid. It stretched his legs well; however he wondered how long he could keep up at such a pace. It was no wonder that the Legions were able to cover long distances on an average day's march. He noticed how the regular Soldiers' eyes and heads all swiveled slightly, scanning their surroundings, as well as the horizon. Since there was little threat on their side of the Rhine, he figured it all came instinctively to them.

The air was cold, and he could see his breath. However the pace kept the blood flowing and prevented the cold from penetrating. Snow crunched underneath their feet as they marched in step. Artorius listened as the belts and equipment from the Legionaries bounced in rhythm off their armor, creating its own cadence to match their step. Though he started to feel winded after the first few miles, he found that by focusing on the sounds of the march, he was able to push the fatigue from his mind. The steady cadence became almost hypnotic, and he found himself lost in a dreamless trance.

"Century...halt!" The Legionaries took one extra step and then stopped together. The recruits, lost as they were in their own reminiscing, stumbled and crashed into each other. One poor fellow had the misfortune of bumping hard into Optio Valgus, who in turn spun around and smashed him on top of the helm with his staff.

"You clumsy oaf!" he yelled into the hapless recruits face. "Pay attention to what is going on around you! I swear I will castrate the next one of you who falls out of step!" With that he smacked the recruit across the back of the helm, causing it to spin a quarter turn until the left cheek guard was over his face.

"And for gods' sake tighten up your damn helmet straps!" he yelled as he hit the recruit yet again across the helmet. Centurion Dominus seemed to be laughing, though when he caught the recruits looking this way, his face immediately turned to a scowl.

"What the fuck are you jackals looking at?" he hollered at them. Immediately they turned their eyes to the front and the Centurion resumed his chuckling.

It was nearly dark by the time they returned to the fortress. The Legionaries were mildly tired and worn, though nothing compared to the sheer exhaustion felt by the inexperienced recruits. In spite of their exhaustion, not one fell out of step or missed a command from the Centurion. Once Dominus had dismissed his Century, Valgus turned and faced the recruits.

"Alright, nice leisurely stroll today, twenty miles, without body armor, shield or javelins. The average march is twenty-five miles, in full body armor. And let's not forget that at the end of a march comes setting up camp, digging ditches, building palisades, and of course the rotating sentry watch. When you can conduct the full twenty-five miles in full kit without passing out like a bunch of eunuch-looking faggots, you might be ready to become Legionaries. *Dismissed!"*

CHAPTER 5

▼

PREPARATIONS FOR WAR

Germanicus looked across the table at the assembled host. The Legates, Chief Tribunes, and Senior Centurions from eight Legions were present. Along with them were the senior auxiliary infantry and cavalry commanders. An enormous map showing all the known routes past the Rhine bridges as well as the general location of all the major tribes lay on the table.

Next to Germanicus sat Caecina Severus, Legate of the Twentieth Legion, and appointed by Tiberius to be the Deputy Commanding General of the Army of the Rhine. Severus was fast approaching sixty; however, he barely looked a day over forty. He was a Soldier of immense tactical experience and skill. He had served with both Tiberius and Drusus, and he knew Arminius personally. Arminius had commanded one of Severus' auxiliary regiments, and his betrayal burned Severus deeply.

"Friends, brothers in arms," Germanicus began, "today we plan the first major campaign in what will ultimately lead to retribution for what has become the greatest act of betrayal in our time." He paused to let his words sink in. "Our war is not just against Arminius and the Cherusci. He formed a coalition of what amounts to almost every major tribe within Germania for his attack in Teutoburger Wald. That coalition is fragile at best, many of the tribes having gone home, and wishing nothing more to do with Arminius. Nevertheless, all are guilty of this heinous crime, and all will pay for it. Every tribe will bleed until the rivers and marshes run red. Afterwards, those who do not repent and come back into the fold of Roman allies will face extermination." He turned his attention to the map.

"The Bructeri and the Marsi will be our first major targets. The Marsi are a smaller tribe and under the protection of the Cherusci. Most of their land is actually open farmland. Therefore it will be easier to cordon off. The Bructeri are much larger. Their land to the east is mainly thick forests and swampland. Trapping them will be more difficult."

"One question, Sir," a voice asked. It was Flavius Quietus, Master Centurion of the Twentieth Legion. "If we move east against the Bructeri, then our rear will be exposed to attack from the Cherusci in the west. Even if they don't engage us directly, they can still cut off our access to the Rhine bridges."

"We've already planned for that," Severus answered. "We will split our forces in half upon crossing the frontier. Four Legions, plus auxiliaries under Germanicus will try to cordon off and smash the Bructeri. The rest of the army, under me will demonstrate against the Cherusci and prevent them from flanking us or cutting off our access to the bridges. We will also take care of the smaller Marsi tribes."

"Very good, Sir," Flavius answered.

"I do not expect you to run from a major battle if it is offered by the enemy," Germanicus said. "However I doubt that this will be his intention. At the same time, I do not wish for you to go out of your way to try to force a major engagement. There are several Marsi settlements that will be in your sector. Your destruction of those will alert the Cherusci. Destruction of the Marsi will have two major effects. One, they will pay the price for their part in the Teutoburger massacre. Two, it will show that Cherusci protection is worthless and that any tribes under their protection need to rethink their allegiance. Now gentlemen, we need to hammer out the specifics of how we are going to do this."

Soon every piece was set on the map board. All the major players knew their roles in the upcoming campaign. The Twentieth Legion would head west with Severus to demonstrate against the Cherusci and smash the Marsi. Severus relished the thought of a major battle against his old comrade and now nemesis. However, he agreed with Germanicus, that it was highly doubtful that Arminius would force such an encounter. Though they would not take part in the larger campaign against the Bructeri, there would still be plenty of work for his Legionaries to do.

*　　　*　　　*　　　*

Weapons training had upgraded past the wooden stakes. The recruits would now face human instead of wooden opponents. Other Legionaries from the Century came out to provide sparring partners. Artorius did fairly well on his first endeavor. Usually most individual fights only lasted a matter of seconds, however Artorius lasted several minutes against his first two opponents before being cut down, and he actually beat his third opponent. He found that his lack of patience was his biggest challenge. He would sometimes get frustrated if he could not get the quick 'kill.' This would lead to his making a mistake, which usually ended with a rather painful jab to the face, neck, or stomach. He was then glad that these were not real weapons.

At the end of their training session, he walked over to where Sergeant Vitruvius was pulling a canvas tarp over the cart full of training weapons.

"Excuse me, Sergeant," he said.

"What is it, Recruit?" Vitruvius asked.

"I know that you've shown us the basics of individual weapons drill, yet I feel that there is a lot more that we can learn from you."

"Here, give me a hand with this," Vitruvius said as he tied down one corner of the tarp to the cart. Artorius helped him tie down the other three corners before continuing.

"Everyone I know of says you're the best there is at hand-to-hand fighting," he said. "I've noticed that you do not have the visible scars that most of the veterans have."

"That's because I don't like pain," Vitruvius replied.

"What I'm getting at is I want to know what you know. I want to become the best there is in this Legion," Artorius said.

"Pretty high aspirations for someone who is still a recruit in training," Vitruvius said. He took a second to think about it and then said, "Alright. I know that your training will be over soon. Once you have become a Legionary, then you come see me. The first Thursday after you swear the oath we will meet out here. Then I will start you on your lessons."

"Thank you, Sergeant," Artorius said as he turned to leave.

Vitruvius smiled. "You may not be thanking me later."

A few days later, the recruits came to the practice field where instead of practice swords, there were long javelins placed in the cart. They were seven feet long, the last three of which was a long metal shaft with a point on the end.

"The javelin, otherwise known as the pillum, is among the best shock inducing weapons in our arsenal," Sergeant Vitruvius said, presenting the weapon to the recruits. "A service weapon's metal shaft and point is made of a pliable metal that will bend upon impact. The purpose of this is to make it so that the weapon cannot be thrown back. If the enemy blocks your throw with his shield, the bending of the metal makes it almost impossible to extract, thereby renders the shield useless. These practice javelins are of the same weight as service weapons, however the metal ends do not bend. This allows us to retrieve and reuse them quickly."

"Sergeant, why are these weapons not double the weight like our practice swords?" Antoninus asked.

"Because if you were to practice with a weapon that was double the weight, you would not learn to balance and throw a service weapon accurately. You would end up over compensating for the weight and most likely end up overthrowing your target.

"Now, when you prepare to throw, you will notice that the handgrip just past the metal shaft has a weighted ball at the end. Place your throwing hand there; heft it up to your shoulder." He demonstrated as he talked through it. "It should feel balanced. When you throw, you take a few steps forward, cocking your arm back. Your last step should be with your throwing side leg. As you step, throw your javelin, keeping eyes on your target as you do so. This will help with your aim, ensuring greater accuracy." He then took a few steps forward, and with a low grunt cast his javelin at one of the wooden stakes. The practice spear stuck directly beneath the line marked at head level.

"Alright, javelins ready!" the Sergeant called out. The recruits hefted their javelins up to their shoulders. Artorius picked out a target stake about twenty-five feet to his front. "Ready...throw!"

With a bit of awkwardness, they threw their javelins at their wooden opponents. Gavius struck his right at the base. Artorius' javelin skipped off the top of the stake and stuck in the one behind it. Antoninus and Magnus missed entirely.

"Antoninus, Magnus, you owe me two laps around the drill field...*move!*" Vitruvius shouted. Immediately, the two young recruits took off at a dead sprint around the field.

"Gavius, you hit your target, however you did not score a fatal hit. Therefore you owe me one lap around the field." Gavius did not even wait for the order to move before he took off running.

"Artorius, I would say that that was a good throw, were I to believe that you meant to strike the target directly behind the one to your front. You owe me one lap as well."

The drill field was quite large, and it took the recruits some time to complete each lap. Once all had finished, Sergeant Vitruvius immediately made them pick up and throw another volley of javelins. This time they faired a little better. Gavius managed to hit his target at knee level before his javelin fell out and landed on the ground. Antoninus and Magnus each hit theirs in the groin, with Antoninus' javelin falling out as well. Artorius struck his target directly in the head. Vitruvius continued to make corrections and assess penalties for each inaccurate throw. Artorius even had to run another lap because the Sergeant could not believe that he actually meant to hit his target in the head. On the next volley, he struck his target in the head again, as did Gavius. This time Vitruvius was convinced that it was in fact intentional.

*   *   *   *

Ingiomerus sat upon his horse, gazing at the river. Scouts were fording the river below, in spite of the extreme cold. It was a risk they had to take, since the bridges were now guarded by the Romans. He had a fire going, and ushered the scouts over to it as soon as they had crossed the Rhine. He had barrels of ale waiting for them as well.

"So what did you find?" the old war chief asked as soon as the scouts had gotten some ale and had started to warm themselves by the fire.

"There are eight Legions encamped on the other side of the Rhine," the lead scout answered, shivering as he tried to warm up. "They also have a full compliment of auxiliaries. This will not be a series of raids or skirmishes. This will be a full scale invasion." Ingiomerus smiled.

"At last!" he shouted. "Finally we will get a chance to finish the Romans once and for all."

"That is if Arminius can be convinced to face them in open battle," one scout remarked as he downed a full bladder of ale.

"Let me handle my nephew," the old warrior stated.

*   *   *   *

Training continued for a couple more weeks. Road marches became more frequent. Like all phases of their conditioning, the degree of difficulty was gradually increased. Before he knew it, Artorius found that he could complete the full twenty-five miles in full kit without feeling exhausted. He also realized that he was becoming more and more proficient at weapons drill. He would use his sheer strength to knock his opponents off balance, and he was becoming faster with the gladius with each passing day. His accuracy with the javelin improved as well. Eventually he was able to call a spot where he was aiming and score a precise hit every time. Only Gavius seemed to rival him in precision with the javelin.

One afternoon, Valgus took them to a different part of the training field. There was a small ballistae set up on a stand. Out in front of it were bales of hay staggered at different ranges. Each bail had human silhouettes painted on them. Standing next to the ballistae was a Centurion from the First Cohort and a Tribune that Artorius recognized right away. It was Pontius Pilate, his old mate from school. Pilate smiled and nodded at Artorius in acknowledgement. The recruits formed up directly behind the ballistae.

"Recruits," the Centurion began, placing his hand on the weapon, "this is the Scorpion. With me is Tribune Pontius Pilate, the Legion's Chief of Artillery. I am Centurion Dionysus, the Centurion of Artillery. Today we are going to show you men how to operate, maintain, and fire the Scorpion. There are sixty of these in the Legion. During a campaign, each Century assigns two Soldiers to operate a Scorpion. These Soldiers then come over and work with our catapult crews and us. The Scorpion crew consists of a Loader and a Gunner."

With that, he stood next to the Scorpion where there was a basket full of bolts. The bolts were a couple of inches in diameter, and about a foot in length. They had a sharp metal point on one end with four thin wooden guides on the back. There was a hand crank on each side of the Scorpion. Dionysus and Pilate each grabbed one and started to turn them rapidly. This caused the drawstring to pull back. When the cord was at maximum tension, the Centurion placed a bolt into the feed tray. Pilate assumed the Gunner's position behind the weapon. At the end of the weapon was a pair of raised stakes. In between the stakes were two sticks laid horizontally. This acted as a sight that Pilate was looking through.

"When firing," he said, "you need to make a quick assessment of the range to your target. The Scorpion is accurate out to about two hundred meters. For close range targets, place the target in the center of your sight. Then," with that, he hit the release that fired the weapon. The bolt flew straight at the nearest bale, hitting precisely in the center of the man silhouette. The recruits were obviously impressed. Dionysus and Pilate quickly cranked the drawstring back again and Dionysus placed another bolt into the feed tray.

"For targets further out, you'll have to adjust the elevation," Pilate said. "At maximum range, you should just barely be able to see the top of your target's head in the sight." He then looked down the sight and fired again. The recruits watched as the bolt flew in an arc and impacted right in the center of the farthest target.

"Are there any questions?" Pilate asked. The recruits had none. "Very well. Antoninus, Gavius, you're up first." Loading the scorpion was easy enough, but each recruit in turn struggled with hitting even the closest target.

"Don't worry too much about it. It takes practice to get good at this," Dionysus said upon seeing the frustration in Gavius' face. "Pay attention to where the bolts strike and adjust the elevation accordingly."

Artorius and Magnus had the same difficulties at first. Getting the left to right azimuth was easy enough, but inducing just the right amount of elevation was becoming a nightmare. *Pilate must have spent hours practicing on this,* Artorius mused to himself. Finally, after much frustration and more than a few profane remarks, the recruits were able to hit most of the targets with decent accuracy. Only the farthest target continued to elude them.

"Something to keep in mind," Pilate told them once he felt they were comfortable with shooting bales of hay, "most of the time your targets will not be stationary. When engaging a moving target, you must remember to induce lead, depending on how fast they are moving. You will also need to induce lead if there is a strong crosswind. Unfortunately we have no real way of practicing this here, so that is something that will just have to be learned first hand."

After they had finished practicing and as the other recruits were leaving, Pilate walked over to Artorius, who snapped to attention and saluted. Pilate smiled, returning the salute.

"I see you finally made it over here," he said.

"I couldn't let you go off to war alone," Artorius replied. "I admit it was a bit nerve wracking having to ask Father to bless off on my joining."

"And how is my old tutor?" Pilate asked.

"He's doing well," Artorius answered. "I think he finally may be getting around to seeing Juliana as more than just a friend."

"Ah, dear Juliana," Pilate mused. "She's a good woman. Your father could scarcely do better."

"Sadly I have not heard from Camilla for some time," Artorius continued. "I used to get a letter from her at least once or twice a week. It's been three weeks now since I last heard from her. I guess there is only so much we can really say to each other when we are hundreds of miles apart."

"I hate to be the one to tell you this, old friend, but you'd be best to give up any hopes of a future with her. She's attractive and very nice young girl; but that's just it, Artorius, she a still a *girl*. You may only be a year older, but your experiences here will age and mature you far beyond your years. The distance between you will be measured in more than just the physical miles. My advice to you is stay focused on the task at hand, complete your training, and then find yourself a little harlot to take your mind off things." He paused for a few seconds. "Do well in your training, Artorius. Listen to the officers and Legionaries who have been at this for a while. These are good men. They will look after you. Take care, old friend." They exchanged salutes before going their separate ways.

"You know that lad?" Dionysus asked Pilate after the recruits had left.

"An old school friend," Pilate replied. "His father was one of my teachers. I see a lot of potential in him. He is strong, incredibly intelligent; there is just the issue with his constant burning rage that worries me." The Centurion looked at him, puzzled.

"His brother was killed in Teutoburger Wald," Pilate responded to the unasked question.

"So he's here seeking revenge," Dionysus stated. "He'll get his chance soon enough."

CHAPTER 6

▼

THE LEGIONARY

It was morning and the sun shone through the window of the barracks. Artorius woke up; it was the first time since arriving that he had not been woke up before dawn. He looked over to see the other recruits were still in their bunks, but that the other Legionaries were gone. Just then, Sergeant Statorius walked in. He was wearing all of his armor and it looked as if he had taken the time to shine up his armor and helmet.

"Alright ladies, wake up!" He said, kicking at their bunks. "You've got ten minutes to be dressed, body armor, everything."

As the recruits wandered into the back room where there equipment was, they saw that to their kit a gladius and scabbard had been added.

"The gladius goes on the right side of your belt," Statorius said. "Get dressed and follow me outside."

As soon as they were dressed, they walked outside to see the entire Century had formed up in a column six ranks deep. Valgus was standing in the center behind the formation. Camillus stood in front of the formation, holding the Century's standard. He also wore the traditional wolf's skin over his helmet and shoulders. Centurion Macro stood next to him. He was carrying a rolled parchment in his hand.

"Recruits Antoninus, Artorius, Gavius and Magnus, post," he said. All four stood between Macro and the rest of the Century, facing the Centurion. "Draw your swords," he told them. "Swear the oath!"

The oath of allegiance was something the recruits had memorized long before this day. Artorius was so full of excitement that he hoped he would not forget any of the words. The recruits held their swords high in a salute and recited the words they had been longing to speak:

"In the name of the Senate and the People of Rome, and in the name of the Emperor, the Divine Tiberius, I do swear my allegiance. My loyalty to the Twentieth Legion, to my fellow Soldiers, and my integrity to them shall be above reproach. The orders of my superior officers I will obey without question. I am a Soldier of Rome, protector of the Empire, and the right hand of the Emperor Tiberius."

At the completion of the oath, they each replaced their swords into their scabbards. Macro unfurled the parchment and turned it so the letters faced them.

"From this day forth you are now entered onto the rolls of the Legion," he said, "You men are no longer civilians, you are no longer recruits. You are now Legionaries, Soldiers of Rome." He rolled the parchment up. In a low voice that only they could here he said, "welcome to Century, men. Now join your brothers in the ranks."

As they turned around, a loud cheer erupted from the men of the Second Century. The new Legionaries found their place with Sergeant Statorius and the rest of their section. Centurion Macro dismissed the formation, and the men headed back to their barracks. On the way back in, Legionaries from the Century kept coming up to Artorius and the others, clasping their hands and welcoming them. It was the greatest feeling Artorius had ever felt. *Finally*, he was a Soldier of Rome! Optio Valgus stood at the door leading into the barracks. He was practically beaming with pride as he took each man by the hand.

"Welcome to the Century, Soldier," he said to each as they shook his hand and made their way into the barracks. Seeing the pride his Optio felt towards him added to Artorius' sense of accomplishment.

As he put his armor and helmet back onto his shelf, he saw that there were three more shields lined up against the wall. They were the full-length rectangular curved shields, with a metal boss in the center and brass strips lining the outer edges. Each shield was painted red, with golden wings coming out of the boss. Artorius found his and smiled at the inscription that was on the inside towards the top. It read:

T. Artorius Justus, Legionary
Legio XX, Cohort III, Century II

It was late afternoon and the small town outside the fortress was crammed with Soldiers. With the upcoming campaign, the Legion's senior officers felt that it was in the men's best interest to relax and unwind a bit before the campaign commenced. It was the first time that Artorius had been in town. The Legionaries were allowed to leave their armor and helmets in their rooms, but they were required to each carry their gladius and dagger. Auxiliaries guarded the entrances and exits to the town, so the Legionaries felt somewhat secure, though one could never completely let their guard down. They were after all, on the border of the frontier and very close to hostile territory.

Artorius and his companions sat around a table in the tavern. After numerous weeks of training, it felt good to unwind. A serving wench brought them a picture of wine. She winked at Carbo as she set it down. She looked to be in her late thirties, though in reality she was probably much younger. Hard life on the rural frontier did not help the locals to age well. She had probably been pretty at one time, though now she looked weathered and tired.

"That must be Lolia," Artorius said.

"That's her alright," Praxus said. "The love of Carbo's life!" He grabbed his friend by the back of the neck.

"Kiss my ass," Carbo said as he took a long draught of wine, "I told you I was incredibly drunk at the time."

"And well on your way to becoming incredibly drunk once again," Decimus piped in.

"And whom may I ask is that?" Magnus asked, pointing towards a fetching young Gallic woman.

"That? Oh that's Varinia," Praxus said. "Five sesterci and she's yours."

"Say again?" Magnus asked. Then in realization, "Oh, so she's one of *those!*"

"And a damn good one too," Decimus said, reaching down and grabbing at his groin. "And, she has a sister!"

"Really? So can I get both of them for say ten sesterci?" Magnus asked.

"I don't know, probably," Decimus answered.

"Right, I'll see you guys later," with that Magnus promptly left.

"Ah, the lecherous young whelp. Just can't wait to empty his loins, can he?" Gavius remarked.

"Humph," Praxus snorted, "If you want to see lecherous, you should hang around with Valens more often. I swear if it were not for the mandatory savings program instituted by the army he would go broke on wine and prostitutes, well on prostitutes anyway. He actually doesn't drink a whole lot. Speaking of which, where is he?"

"I saw him go wandering off with that broad from the butcher's shop a little while ago," Carbo answered.

"The one with all the missing teeth?" Praxus seemed shocked. "Just how drunk was he?"

"I'm not sure. He didn't look drunk, at least. Besides I think they took off towards her house just minutes after we got here."

"Where's this house at?"

"Two blocks north, right hand side."

"Oh this I've got to see!" With that, Praxus left with Carbo right on his heels.

Artorius watched them leave before starting a fresh conversation with Decimus. "Decimus, there's a few things I've been curious about."

"What's on your mind?" Decimus asked before taking another pull off his wine.

"When we were on our way up here, I asked Statorius how he got wounded. All he would say is that he messed up. I'm just curious as to what happened."

"Well it was like this," Decimus said, "we were on a sortie against some band of renegades that had crossed the Rhine and were causing trouble. Things were going pretty well once we closed up on them. We threw our javelins and they panicked before we even charged. We drove them back to the river. Well, the problem was that with nowhere to run to, they turned and started fighting like wild animals. Statorius then broke one of the basic rules of close combat. He lunged too far forward to attack one of the barbarians. He stabbed the man in the chest and his gladius became stuck. It was then that one of them hooked his shield with an axe and yanked it away. With no shield and his sword stuck, he was in an awkward position. And remember, all of this took a matter of seconds to unfold. Anyway, one of the barbarians lunges in and catches him in the upper arm with his spear, just as Statorius got his gladius unstuck. Thankfully, we had just initiated a passage-of-lines and the second rank blitzed right past where he was and took care of the barbarians. We helped him back to the rear, and he spent the next six weeks convalescing in Ostia. He learned his lesson, though. Especially since Vitruvius never lets him live it down. Make no mistake though, Statorius is an excellent Sergeant and he looks after us pretty good. He just made a mistake is all." He emptied his wine goblet and poured some more.

"So what about this mutiny that nobody heard about back home? You had made mention of it during our travels from Ostia," Artorius asked. Gavius leaned forward, fascinated.

"Oh boy, that's a story that's going to require some more wine. *Hey Lolia! Bring us some more wine, you saucy little tart!*" Once more wine had been brought to them, Decimus started to tell the story, at least as he saw it, of the mutiny on the Rhine.

"I had just joined the Legion shortly before Teutoburger Wald. Once we got word of the disaster, we rushed here to secure the bridges against invasion. Things were going ok, except that there was a lot of corruption amongst the junior and even the senior officers. Another issue was the numerous Soldiers who had served out their tenure. They were looking to retire. Instead, they ended up stuck here on the Rhine for gods know how long.

"Once Tiberius was recalled to Rome, things went to hell in a hurry. It seemed like every Centurion in the entire army was corrupt. They extorted money from the junior enlisted, as you would not believe. I mean, come on. Centurions make five times what we do, and yet they still felt the need to pinch their Soldiers for every sesterci they had. If a Soldier was due for leave or furlough, it cost him. If a Soldier wanted to quit showing up on the latrine duty roster, it cost him. This made the Tesserarius' job infuriatingly difficult, as it was his responsibility to ensure that all details were evenly distributed. When we complained to the Tribunes, they did nothing. In fact, some of them thought that extortion was an easy way to make money, so they started doing it themselves!

"It became worse when the Centurions started demanding payments for no reason whatsoever. Soldiers who could not pay or who were just unwilling to felt the wrath of the vine stick. It seemed as if we were fighting a two-front war, one against the barbarians, and the other against our own officers. Tiberius had kept us in check. It is not just that he was a tough disciplinarian. In truth, we did not want to disappoint him. Whatever his reputation back home, he was very much adored by the Legions, and we could not let him down. Once he left for Rome to assume the reigns of ultimate power, it seemed like all hell broke loose. All discipline evaporated and we became a frenzied mob. The Centurions and Tribunes responsible for our misery were rounded up and beaten.

"So, Germanicus shows up to try and restore order. In a mass meeting with the mob, some lads even tried to make him Emperor instead of Tiberius! Of course, most of us knew deep down inside where our true loyalties lay. Germanicus knew this as well. He even offered to fall on his sword if we did not return to our posts and show our loyalty to the Emperor. This was a theatrical gesture to say the least, especially when one fellow actually tried to hand Germanicus his own blade because he said it had a sharper edge. Of course, this was all despicable behavior. All of us knew better, and all of us were in fact loyal to both the Emperor as well as our Commander. The constant corruption and abuse had just driven us over the edge.

"Unbelievably, it actually took a woman to quell the whole damn thing. Fearing for his family, Germanicus sent his wife and children away from the camp. Many of the lads saw this. Roman Soldiers may be some hardhearted bastards, but most are sentimental inside, especially when it comes to our women and children. Agrippina came back, and the site of her carrying their newest babe, Gaius, all dressed up in a miniature Legionary costume, well the lads just lost all anger. They even dubbed the little boy 'Caligula' because he even wore little Caligae boots like ours.

"Once order was restored, Germanicus and Severus had to get the army back on its feet, and in a hurry. The ringleaders of the riot were summarily tried and executed. This was mainly because the front line of a war is not the place to commit mutiny, especially when there are thousands of bloodthirsty barbarians just waiting to catch us with our guard down. Caetronius, Commander of the First Legion, was given the dubious task of overseeing the trials. Representatives from every Century within the army stood in front of the tribunal, swords drawn. I was one of those who actually volunteered for the task. Each accused man was on a raised platform and was pointed out by a Tribune. If the Soldiers shouted out that he was guilty, he was thrown headlong and cut to pieces. We even gloated over the bloodshed as though it gave us absolution. Nor did Germanicus check us, seeing that without any order from him; the same men were responsible for all the cruelty and all the odium of the deed." [1] Decimus took a pull off his wine and shuddered at the memory.

"How many of the accused were executed?" Gavius asked.

"I don't recall," Decimus answered, shaking his head. "What I do remember is seeing a couple of my friends, friends who I had known since recruit training, being found guilty and cut to pieces by the ravenous mob. And yet I felt nothing; no, I felt loathing and rage. Rage that in reality was directed towards myself for having been involved in the whole affair, yet I directed it towards those who I was at the time convinced had been the cause of our plight. In reality, all of us were guilty."

"What of the corrupt officers?" Artorius asked.

"Those bastards were also put on trial. Since technically they had not committed a capital crime, Germanicus could not execute them. Too bad; I can only imagine the venom and wrath their bodies would have received from us.

"However, he did dismiss and throw out of the army all the officers who were convicted of abuse. In order to accomplish this, the General revised the list of Centurions. Each, at his summons, stated his name, his rank, his birthplace, the number of his campaigns, what brave deeds he had done in battle, his military rewards, if any. If the Tribunes and the Legate commended his energy and good behavior, he retained his rank; where they unanimously charged him with rapacity or cruelty, he was dismissed from service. [2] Many of these Centurions had more than enough years to retire, and yet now they had nothing! Served the bastards right. Of the fifty-nine Centurions in the Twentieth, twenty-seven were convicted and dismissed. This included four of the Cohort Commanders. That shook things up amongst the ranks, and led to promotion opportunities for many of the Optios. Hence why there are now a number of younger Centurions in the Legion. That is how Macro was promoted. He was our Optio and had fought for a long time against the practice of extorting money from Soldiers.

"Anyway, we soon took to the field on a punitive expedition against some of the local tribes that had assisted Arminius. Several battles later, our spirits were revived and the scourge of mutiny was laid to rest. No one talks of it. It is something that we are not proud of, and we'd be glad if it were never mentioned back home."

"That was an interesting story," Gavius said. "More wine? You looked parched."

"Yes, thank you," Decimus said.

Just then they heard a loud voice shouting, *"come back here, you rat-bastard!"* They turned just in time to seeing Praxus, laughing uncontrollably, come rushing into the tavern. He was being chased by a thoroughly enraged, and equally naked, Valens who was swinging his gladius wildly. No one took much heed of the weapon, as it was still in its scabbard. As Praxus rushed past the table where his friends were, Valens threw the sword at him. Decimus very calmly grabbed the wine picture and his goblet off the table as the gladius crashed into Artorius' and Gavius' drinks, sending goblet shards and wine everywhere. Praxus was still laughing to himself as he sat down. Decimus handed him the wine picture, which he immediately started to drink out of. Once he realized that several dozen sets of eyes were fixed on him, Valens gave a nonchalant shrug.

"What?" he asked as he turned around and casually started strutting towards the door, all the while making no attempt to cover his exposed nether regions. "Praxus, be a good fellow, and bring my gladius back to the barracks, will you?" he called over his shoulder. Praxus gave him the thumbs up while attempting to finish off the pitcher of wine in one pull.

They spent the rest of the night drinking and chasing the tavern wenches. Somehow, everyone actually managed to find their way back through the main gate and to their barracks. Artorius had not drunk quite as excessively as the rest, though he still felt the aftereffects and slept late.

The next morning Artorius walked gaily around the inside perimeter of the fortress. He was feeling vigorous and full of life, in spite of his excesses of the night before. As he walked back towards the barracks, he saw a lone Soldier sitting on the ground, near a secluded section of the wall. He thought nothing of it until he saw that it was Gavius from his section. He was sitting with his back against the wall, his knees curled up into his chest and his arms wrapped around his legs. The young Legionary seemed to be disturbed about something.

"Hey Gavius!" Artorius called, waiving to him. Gavius just nodded his way and continued to stare off into space. This puzzled Artorius, so he walked over to the man who only the days before had been a recruit like him.

"Something the matter?" he asked. Gavius just ignored him. "Oh come on, don't tell me you didn't have enough coinage on you last night to score you a little strumpet!" He elbowed his friend good naturedly. He composed himself when he realized there was something more serious at work in Gavius' mind. Artorius sat down next to him.

"Are you going to tell me what is on your mind, or do I have to drag Magnus over here and have him beat it out of you?"

"I'm afraid, Artorius," Gavius finally replied. Artorius looked at him, puzzled.

"Afraid, of what?" he asked.

"Failure," Gavius replied. "I try to come across as strong, both in body and spirit. Truth is I'm scared out of my mind. I have no family. I was orphaned when I was only a child. I lived poor and in the streets. Only my name allowed me to join the army. I have a better chance at life here than I have ever had. To fail here will mean that I failed in life."

"I fail to see how you could see yourself as a potential failure," Artorius conjectured. "We all struggled through recruit training, but we made it. You're one of the best javelin throwers I've seen. You fight well enough when we spar, so what is it?"

"I guess I've never had anyone expect anything of me before. I feel so overwhelmed at the possibility of letting these men down, especially the veterans who work with us. They've become the big brothers that I never had. I know we've only been in the army a short while and have barely made it through training. I just feel that in that short time I've become a part of something. That something is much larger that I can ever be. To be successful at it is a heavy burden."

"Yet it is a burden we all accepted willingly," Artorius answered. "And truth is, to be a Soldier of Rome takes more than any man can give in and of himself. There is only one way that any of us can succeed in this life, and that is by working together. A man in the ranks is not best judged by how he performs as an individual. What best judges him is how well he uses his talents in conjunction with those of his brothers. Our combined skills, yours and mine, are worth more than those of ten men who cannot work together. That is how the Roman Army has won so many of its battles when greatly outnumbered. Together we hold the very fabric of the Empire together." He clutched his hand in a fist to emphasize the point.

"And if we fail to hold that together?" Gavius asked. Artorius smiled and shrugged.

"We don't, because it is not an option. Accept the fact that you are a valuable part of this Century, Gavius. If you weren't you wouldn't be here. None of us will fail, because we don't let each other fail." Gavius smiled and nodded at that. Artorius rose to his feet, smacked his friend on the shoulder and started to walk away.

"Looking forward to your first sparring session with Vitruvius tomorrow?" Gavius asked.

"No," Artorius answered, without looking back. "I'm starting to think I may have lost all control of my senses on that one!"

Praxus and Sergeant Statorius passed by the drill and practice field. They turned to watch as two Legionaries sparred with each other. Both were big men, ripped with muscle, though one was slightly taller and even larger than the other. Within seconds, the larger man had beaten his opponent down and was standing over him with his training gladius pointed at his opponent's throat. Praxus and Statorius just smiled and shook their heads.

"Seems like our Artorius is getting the first of his personal lessons from Vitruvius," Statorius remarked.

"I wonder how long he'll last," Praxus said as they watched Vitruvius help the young Legionary get to his feet before they squared off again. Within seconds, Artorius was on the ground again, this time he was doubled up, clutching at his stomach. Praxus dropped his head while stifling a laugh.

"I'll be surprised if he comes back after today," he said. In the background, Artorius got to his feet, still breathing heavily and set into his fighting stance once more.

"I don't know," Statorius replied. "There's something about him. He's eager, yes. But there is something more to it than that. I think these sparring sessions could work wonders for him." They watched as Vitruvius beat Artorius into submission yet again. This time he did not get up so fast.

"Provided Vitruvius doesn't kill him first," Praxus laughed as they turned and walked away.

"Gods have mercy, but that hurt!" Artorius gasped as he lay on his back.

"You're talking, so you can still breathe well enough," Vitruvius remarked as he leaned against his training shield and removed his helmet. "You've got good aggression, Soldier. However, you are far too reckless. You're too anxious to end your fights quickly. You need to learn a bit of patience. There's nothing that says the fight has to end with the first blow struck."

Artorius rolled to his side and winced. He still couldn't figure out how a big man like Vitruvius could thrash him not only with sheer power and intensity, but also with the speed and finesse of a cat.

"You end your fights quickly enough," he remarked as he sat up. Vitruvius snorted.

"That's only because my opponents usually make it all too easy for me," he said with his eyebrows raised. He reached down and helped Artorius to his feet. "That's enough for today. Remember what I told you. Practice on the training stakes, and we'll see next week what you've learned."

"Yes, Sergeant."

After he put away his training weapons and stowed his helmet, Artorius headed over to the bath house. Though he himself was covered in dirt and sweat, it seemed like the Sergeant had not exerted himself at all. As he walked towards the bath house, Magnus came running over to join him. He couldn't help but smile when he saw his friend's sorry state.

"So how was your first sparring session with Vitruvius?" he asked, knowing full well the answer. Artorius said nothing. He just grimaced as he walked along with a slight limp.

"That good, huh?" Magnus persisted.

"I swear that man's not human," Artorius muttered. "I mean, how can a man with so much size and brute power be that quick? He's even bigger than I am, so one would think that I would have the edge in speed and agility. Ha! It's not even close!"

"Think you'll get anything out of working with him?" Magnus asked.

"Besides frustration and a lot of pain?" Artorius retorted.

"Hey, you're the one who volunteered for this!" Magnus remarked. Artorius laughed in spite of himself. He still wasn't sure why exactly he had asked Vitruvius to tutor him one-on-one. He didn't just want to be the best there was, he was actually curious to see for himself if the Sergeant really was invulnerable.

"I wonder how he learned to be this good," Artorius said as they walked into the front of the bath house.

"A lot of trial and error I suppose," Magnus replied.

"I doubt there was much error," Artorius remarked. "I don't think anyone has ever even scratched him!"

Artorius' body ached the next day as he along with approximately twenty Soldiers from the Century headed out on road repair detail. It was his first time doing such a task, since they had just barely come out of training. They had been allowed to leave their helmets and armor behind, though every Soldier carried his sword belt with him. They marched smartly out the gate, with several oxen carts bearing pre-made paving stones in the center of their formation. Just ahead of them, two Centuries were marching out the gate, fully armored.

"Where are those guys off to?" Artorius asked aloud.

"They're from the Eighth Cohort," Valens replied. "They're conducting patrols of the area, checking to see if any enemy raiding parties have crossed the river."

"Is that a common thing for us to be doing?" Magnus asked.

"Not usually," Valens replied, "especially at this time of year, and since we hold all of the Rhine bridges. However one can never be too cautious." Artorius and Magnus watched with interest as the two Centuries maneuvered into a line formation and starting sweeping through a grove of trees towards the river.

It was several miles to the point where the repairs would be taking place. Artorius still walked with a slight limp, however he felt the walk was doing his body some good. After the first couple miles, he felt loosened up and he no longer ached as much. He knew immediately when they came upon their designated work site. The pave stones had crumbled and washed away, leaving a ragged mess.

"Well here we are, lads," Flaccus said. As the Tesserarius, it was his responsibility to supervise the work detail. "Alright, all sections fall in online, parallel to the road. Each Soldier will take a five-block section. Once the area has been cleared and leveled, we will begin replacing the stones. Any questions?"

As Artorius and the others in his section fell in on their piece, he looked at what would need to be done to fix the road. He had never done this kind of work before, and it wasn't what he'd expected to be doing as a Legionary. He pointed this out to Valens, who happened to be working next to him.

"What, you think all the roads that hold the Empire together just magically appeared?" Valens retorted sarcastically.

"Well no, I just thought that perhaps we used slave labor," Artorius replied as he started scraping and clearing away loose rubble. Valens scoffed at that.

"Slaves cost money," he said. "They are expensive to feed and house. And besides, their craftsmanship leaves a lot to be desired!"

"That's no joke," Carbo piped in. "You let slaves do any kind of construction like this, and you end up redoing it yourself anyway."

"I know what you mean," Magnus said. "My dad tried using slaves in his textile mill for a while. Thought he would save money on labor. Instead he almost went completely bankrupt!"

"What happened to the slaves?" Artorius asked.

"Most he sold to some gladiator trainer," Magnus answered, "though a few of the women he kept, saying that we needed extra maidservants. In fact, they weren't much good at housekeeping either. Come to think of it, the only place I ever did see them go was his bedroom." Magnus furrowed his brow in thought as some of the Legionaries that were listening burst into laughter.

"You'd be surprised at the number of skills required of a Legionary that have nothing to do with fighting," Valens continued. "Leatherworking, metal smith, stone working, surveying, cooking, these are all skills that make the army flourish."

"And if you excel at any given skill that the army is looking for, there can be incentive pay and special duty in it for you," Carbo said. "Notice how Praxus and Decimus are conspicuously missing from this detail?"

"Not to mention every other less than desirable detail!" Valens added.

"Yeah, I had noticed that," Artorius replied.

"That's because they are on what is called *immune* status," Valens said. "Praxus is an expert at curing and working with leather, so while we get to do details such as this, he gets to work in the leather shop, working on packs, saddles, straps for armor and sandals, that kind of stuff."

"They get out of all the less desirable duties, plus they get paid more than the rest of us," Carbo remarked, somewhat annoyed.

Artorius just laughed as they went back to working on the road. By the end of the day their section of the road was repaved and ready for usage. As soon as they arrived back at the barracks, Artorius decided to check the duty rosters before heading to the bath house. Duties for each individual Soldier were posted a month out. He looked down the list, interested in what duties everyone else had drawn. Gavius had been tasked to work in the bakery for the next week, while he and Magnus were tasked with road repair for the next two days, and then rampart repair along with the rest of the section, minus Gavius and those on immune status. Praxus would be in the leather shop, while Decimus would spend three days assigned as the Centurion's aide before spending the rest of the week in the armory. He was surprised to see that all duties ended that next week, on the last day of February. After that all Soldiers were listed as *in Century* on the roster. It could mean only one thing.

CHAPTER 7

▼

THE FIRST CAMPAIGN

On the East Side of the Rhine Bridges, Germania
March A.D. 15

It had been a long day, and Artorius was glad to be able to lay his head down and get some sleep. He thanked the gods that he did not have watch duty that night either. The days before had been spent packing all of their equipment into their carrying sacks, loading the baggage carts with tents, food, and provision, as well as all of the artillery wagons. They had linked up with the rest of the army early that morning and had just managed to reach the east side of the Rhine before setting up camp for the night. Eight Legions were camped there, along with a huge number of auxiliaries and cavalry. Their camp was enormous. One could not hope to make it from one end to the other without a horse. In the morning, the army would split into two groups. Four Legions, plus the bulk of the auxiliaries would head east with Germanicus to destroy the Bructeri. The remaining four Legions, to include the Twentieth, would head west to demonstrate against the Cherusci. However, that was tomorrow. Right now sleep was all that concerned Artorius.

In another part of the camp, the lamps were still lit in a large headquarters tent. Inside Germanicus, Severus and the Legates of each Legion were planning the specifics of their missions the next day. The next day would mainly involve long road marches deep into enemy territory. Contingency plans had to be made in case Arminius had gotten word of their intentions and mustered a large force against them. This was highly unlikely; however, they still had to plan for it. It was more likely that the Germans would set up linear ambushes along the routes, using hit-and-run tactics against the Romans. Of course it was also just as likely that the Cherusci and Marsi did not know of their presence, and that they would be able to conduct the first phase of their operations unopposed. Only time would tell.

＊　　　＊　　　＊　　　＊

Artorius awoke to the sound of the Cornicens' horns. Though the day before had been long and hard, he was surprisingly refreshed. The weeks of training, right before going on campaign had done him good. He and his tent mates got up, dressed, and proceeded to pack their tent and all of their gear. Gavius and Valens were cooking breakfast for the crew when Flaccus came walking down the line, talking to all the groups in turn.

"Hey Statorius, just so you guys know we're moving out in about an hour," he said, "Apparently the cavalry screen found some scattered villages about half a day's march from here."

"Are they Marsi or Cherusci?" Statorius asked.

"They couldn't tell," Flaccus answered. "We definitely know they aren't friendly, though. There are no friendly tribes on this side of the river. We know that some of the Marsi were settled to the west, we just didn't think they had migrated this close to the Rhine."

"They're getting bold," Vitruvius said as he walked up.

"They won't be once we get done with them," Statorius said.

Vitruvius smiled a sinister smile. "Yes, it has been a while since my sword tasted fresh meat," he said, his right hand rubbing the pommel of his gladius.

"A few scattered villages? You'll be lucky if you get to kill a cow, Vitruvius!" Flaccus said.

"Well, it's still fresh meat, isn't it?" Vitruvius laughed.

Artorius listened to the conversation in silence as he helped his friends load their tent onto a waiting cart.

"So what will this mean for us?" he asked Praxus.

"Could mean a couple of different things, none of them very exciting though," Praxus answered. "When we're dealing with villages on a punitive expedition the first thing we do is cordon off the entire area. Nobody gets in and nobody comes out. We then send an assault element through that clears the entire area of anything living. Once done, they set fire to the place and we move on."

"So we just kill everything in the village?" Magnus asked.

"Pretty much," Valens answered. "Of course sitting on the cordon is boring as hell most of the time, though assaulting a village usually gets messy. Moreover, there is not a lot of glory and prestige to be had in killing a few farmers and some livestock, mind you. Occasionally you'll get lucky and find something worth pilfering."

Artorius thought about Valens' words. Would this be how he got his revenge? By killing a handful of farmers and burning their crops? He still held out hope that the Cherusci would come and face them on the battlefield and that they would be able to exact their revenge properly. It was not that he had any issue with the killing of Germanic farmers, far from it. All were guilty, and all would be punished. He just figured that a major battle would resolve the issue that much quicker.

Just outside where the headquarters tent was being dismantled, Master Centurion Flavius Quietus was reviewing the plans for their part of the operation with the Cohort Commanders. Normally this task would fall upon the Commanding General, but since Severus now had four Legions plus auxiliaries to command, the task fell to his subordinates. As Chief Tribune, Strabo was technically the one left in charge of the Legion; however, he was wise enough to allow those with the proper experience plan the attack. Flavius took a staff and drew a rough overlay of their sector on the dirt. He drew up prominent terrain features, as well as the placement of all the known settlements.

"Gentlemen," he started, "this is our sector for this operation. It is not very large, and to be honest, using an entire Legion for this is overkill. However, we are in enemy territory, and there is no way of knowing for sure what we will be up against.

"We will leave here Cohorts in a column. First Cohort will provide the vanguard; the Sixth will provide rear security for the baggage trains. Auxiliary infantry will provide security on our flanks and the cavalry will screen our front.

"Behind this ridge, the cavalry will hold fast and await our arrival. They will then take the long way around the settlements, utilizing the woods for cover, finally pushing out past the villages and continue to screen our front. The auxiliary infantry will push out on the flanks, for at least a good mile, and prevent anyone from entering the area. This gully on the northeast side leads away from the village. This is their most likely route of escape, should they become alerted to our presence. The First Cohort will secure the gully and make certain no one uses it to escape. The Second, Third, and Seventh Cohorts will conduct the actual sweep of the area. The Third will take the right, the Second the center and the Seventh will take the left. The rest of the Legion, minus the Sixth Cohort, will provide the close cordon of the area and ensure that nothing escapes. The Sixth will set up security around the baggage trains, one terrain feature behind the eastern section of the cordon. Once the sweep is complete, the assault elements will form back up in a column, the rest of the Legion collapsing on them. Once the auxiliary infantry have linked back up with us, we will push forward to where the cavalry should have our campsite staked out. It is about half a days march from here to the ridgeline, so we'd best start moving." He then took a few moments to answer any questions the Cohort Commanders had. Soon the Legion was on the march.

Artorius watched the countryside slowly roll by. The area had a lot of open ground, though it was still infested with the massive forests that seemed to permeate the entire country. He half expected that they would come under attack at any moment, that there would be hoards of barbarians storming their flanks. Of course, Severus was better prepared than Varus had been. Auxiliary infantry had pushed out on the flanks and cavalry screened their front. If any force did come at them, the auxiliaries would more than likely be able to repel it. And even if they weren't they would at least provide ample warning to the Legionaries. His mind at ease in terms of the danger they faced, his thoughts wandered to their task ahead. "Think we'll see any real action today?" he asked Magnus, who was marching next to him in formation.

"From what the vets have said, I kind of doubt it," Magnus answered. "Sounds like these operations are almost boring in nature. Kill a few farmers, torch their crops, and then move on."

"That's what I was figuring," Artorius replied.

Magnus gave him a searching look. "Anxious to exact your revenge, are you?" he asked.

"If only you knew," Artorius answered. He was suddenly angry.

"Artorius, I'm your friend. And if I'm going to be able to help you exact your revenge in any way, you might as well tell me. What is it that burns inside of you? Everybody sees it. Praxus, Decimus, Carbo, heck even Sergeant Vitruvius mentioned something to Statorius the other day. He said that in your little sparring sessions every week, which by the way makes me think that you are either mad or have a high threshold for pain and a masochistic streak, that you fly into a blinding rage each time you two come to blows. He said you mutter curses against the Germans, almost acting as if he is one of them." Artorius looked almost embarrassed.

"Don't get me wrong," Magnus continued, "Vitruvius thinks it's productive. He just worries because you become so incensed that you lose focus. That's why he thrashes you all the time. I've heard him say that you have more raw talent than any Legionary he has seen in a long time. You just have trouble controlling your rage."

"Alright," Artorius said, "If you really want to know what fire burns inside of me," he then told Magnus about how Metellus had been killed in Teutoburger Wald, the subsequent death of his mother, and how he promised himself that he would avenge their loss.

Magnus was fascinated, though by no means surprised. "I understand," he said.

"Make no mistake," Artorius continued, "I think the army is the most honorable profession a Roman can choose. When this campaign is over, I intend to make a career out of this. Right now, the hardest battle I am fighting is not so much conquering my hate, but rather using it to my advantage."

"If it makes you feel any better, you're not the only one," Magnus said. Artorius gave him a puzzled look. "I don't mean me," Magnus said when he saw the look of confusion, "what I mean is; didn't you ever think that maybe there are some Soldiers in the Legion who were actually there and survived Teutoburger Wald? Think about it. Tiberius welcomed the survivors back after the disaster. Chances are most of them are still around."

"I wonder who they are," Artorius pondered.

"That I don't know," Magnus answered.

They walked on in silence for the next few hours. Around midday they came to the base of a ridgeline. They watched as several cavalry scouts rode towards the marching column from the ridge. They linked up with the First Cohort, and after a short halt, started leading most of the cohorts around the ridge to their places on the cordon. The Third Cohort stood fast, along with the Second and the Seventh. Macro had briefed them all on their mission before they moved out that morning. Now Macro and the other Centurions had ridden forward to work out the final details of the attack with the Cohort Commander. A couple of scouts were there as well, giving the finer details of the Cohort's sector. Artorius and the other Legionaries could not hear what was being said. From the Centurions' gestures it didn't look as if they were overly worried about how the operation was going to go. Soon the Centurions rode back to their Centuries. There they dismounted and had grooms take their horses back to the baggage trains, where the Sixth Cohort was stationed in reserve.

"Cohort on line, skirmishing formation!" Proculus, the Pilus Prior called out. All six Centuries formed up in a long line. The Second on the extreme right, with the First, Fourth, Third, Sixth and Fifth falling in on their left. Skirmishing formation meant that everyone spread out further than the usual interval, though they could form up tight if a serious threat suddenly materialized. Artorius looked to his right and saw that Centurion Macro was the last Soldier on the line. The Second Century would be the extreme right of the entire assault. Just behind Macro was Camillus, dressed in the traditional wolf's skin that adorned his helmet and shoulder guards. He carried the Century's Standard, which he would use to relay visual signals, and to act as a rally point in emergencies. As simple as this operation seemed, nothing was being left to chance. Standing next to Macro was Sergeant Vitruvius and his section. Next to them was Sergeant Statorius' section. Artorius and Magnus found themselves right next to their Sergeant. Decimus was on the left of Artorius, followed by the rest of the section, and subsequently the rest of the Century.

"Post javelins and ground your gear," Macro told his men. All did as they were told. "Every fourth man will carry one torch," Macro added as Flaccus walked down the line handing out torches. Decimus was the last Soldier to draw a torch. As soon as this was done, Camillus gave the signal that they were ready. Once all Centuries had done the same, the Signifier of the First Century signaled the other Cohorts that they were ready. Once Strabo saw this, he sent the signal back, giving the order to advance. Soon three Cohorts were advancing towards the ridgeline and the woods at the top.

Artorius watched as the wood line grew closer. Not a word was said by anyone. Most of the time he stayed focused on maintaining formation. This proved to be difficult on the rough terrain going uphill. His heart was pounding as they moved through the wood line. Towards the end, the order was given to halt. About three hundred meters beyond the woods was a broad expanse of small villages surrounded by farm fields. The crops had barely been sown. People milled about working their fields or tending to livestock. There were silos containing what remained of the last season's harvest.

"Doesn't look much like a people bent on the destruction of Rome," Magnus mused.

Artorius looked at him, eyes filling with hate. "How in Hades can you say that? These people are among those responsible for the Teutoburger disaster. They are responsible for my brother's murder. For all we know, one of those damn farmers could have been the one who killed him!" His breathing increased as adrenaline flowed through his veins. He did not care anymore that this was not a major battle they were facing. He only cared about vengeance. All were guilty! Germanicus had even said so. He was grasping the handle of his gladius roughly, waiting for the order. He did not have to wait long.

"Gladius...Draw!!" Simultaneously the entire Cohort drew their swords. Artorius seethed. People in the fields stopped and looked about for the source of the disturbance.

"Advance!" As one, the Cohort moved down the hill at a slow jog. The people in the fields looked horrified. There was no central organization, no way to sound an alarm and set up an organized defense. Many ran towards their homes, either in hopes of evacuating their families, or to find weapons with which to fight the Romans. Others stood fast, either frozen in disbelief, or else determined to make their final stand where they were.

Artorius saw Germans on his left being cut down rapidly as the Legionaries advanced. Farm tools were definitely not suited for combat. He watched as Carbo smashed his shield into one young barbarian. The lad was knocked to the ground and Carbo quickly finished him with a stab to the throat. Carbo was just two positions over from Artorius, but he knew better than to break formation to get in on the killing. Soon barbarians emerged from some of their huts bearing swords or spears. Even the women came out to fight alongside their men. The resistance was in no way organized, and each was quickly slain as they fought in vain to defend their homes.

Two men and one woman came out of their huts and rushed at Artorius and his section. The men each carried a spear, the woman bearing a pitchfork. The two men attacked Decimus and Artorius, the woman rushed Magnus. Decimus calmly settled into a fighting stance and engaged his attacker.

Artorius saw that his opponent's eyes were wide with terror. He knew he was going to die, and he was afraid. This only inflamed Artorius. He gave a cry of rage and lunged at his attacker. With his shield he quickly knocked the man's spear to the side and smashed him in the face with the boss. With a rapid stab to the thigh, the German was on the ground. Artorius looked at the barbarian, his hatred only intensifying and he smashed his shield into his face. He then looked over to see Decimus pin his opponent against the wall of a hut and stab him underneath the ribcage. He also watched Magnus plunge his gladius into the woman's belly. There was nothing else for them to fight as they made their way through the village. The farmers had few items of any value, which negated any hopes of plunder.

Once it was confirmed that all the villagers had either fled or been otherwise eliminated, the Century lit its torches and walked back through, setting fire to anything that would burn. Soon they came back to the hut where they had been attacked. The man that Artorius had wounded still lay on the ground. He was breathing rapidly and he was in obvious pain, blood oozing from the wound to his leg and his face a bloody pulp. An evil thought then came to Artorius' mind. He sheathed his gladius and snatched Decimus' torch from him.

"Hey, what the hell?" the startled Legionary shouted.

Artorius then walked over to where the German was lying on his back, clutching his injured leg. His face was a bloody mess from the blows of Artorius' shield. Artorius smiled wickedly and then slammed the torch into the man's face. The German screamed in horror and pain as the flames started to slowly burn his face and hair. Artorius started to grind the torch against his face, screaming at the stricken barbarian.

"*Burn, you son of a bitch, burn!* It is time *you* became a sacrifice to your foul gods!"

The man's head was soon completely consumed in flames. He was thrashing and screaming, clawing at his face, tearing hunks of burning flesh off. Artorius drew his gladius and with several hard slashes, cleaved the barbarians head from his shoulders. He looked up to see Decimus and Magnus staring at him.

"You know, usually we use the torches on the buildings," Decimus said calmly as he retrieved his torch and set fire to the hut. Artorius gave a growl and kicked the burning head towards the hut. He was immediately calm again, not giving a second thought to what he had just done. He heard the screams of those who had tried to flee the destruction, only to be cut down by the Soldiers on the cordon. It was over as quickly as it had begun.

As the huts burned, the Cohorts continued to advance through the farms, destroying everything as they went. Livestock were slaughtered, silos burned, and the dead inhabitants left where they fell. Once they reached the end of the settlements, they formed back into a column. Horns sounded and the rest of the Legion moved in towards their position, Cohorts taking their respective places in the column. The Legion then moved out, leaving behind a valley of burned settlements and scores of barbarian dead. No casualties had been suffered by the assault elements, and only a few minor injuries were sustained by Soldiers as they navigated the difficult terrain on the ridgelines.

It was nearly nightfall by the time they reached the site selected by the cavalry scouts for their camp. Soldiers immediately set up security, pitched tents, and threw up defenses. Artorius and Magnus were among those tasked with digging the standard ditch and palisade. They worked in silence for a while, both men absorbing what had happened that day. Finally Artorius broke the silence.

"I'm not crazy, you know," he said.

"I know," Magnus answered. "You just had some pent up rage you had to satisfy. And believe me; compared to what these barbarians have done to our people, what you did was mild."

"I thought about Metellus, and could he have been one of the ones those bastards burned alive. I've heard stories about what these people do to their enemies. The thought of doing what I did never even crossed my mind until I saw the torch that Decimus carried. I couldn't control my anger at that point." He was obviously disturbed by everything.

"Well you'd better learn how too soon," Magnus said. "It's one thing to lose control when burning out some farmers. Once we engage their armies en mass, it will be a different matter." He paused for a minute. "You know I'm actually a bit troubled by the woman I killed today. Did you notice she was pregnant?"

"No, I didn't," Artorius answered.

"Well she was. Probably just a few months along is all. Still, it felt kind of weird."

"Look at it this way," Artorius replied, "you may have prevented another Arminius from ever being born."

"I guess so. Still it kind of messes with you, though. I mean, here we are on a campaign to avenge twenty-thousand Roman murdered, and the only thing I've done is stab a pregnant woman in the belly."

"Perhaps our little demonstration will draw the Cherusci out in force," Artorius said, not really confident in his assessment.

"Come on, Artorius. You don't believe that any more than I do. By the time the barbarians rally enough forces to cause us any major problems, the campaign season will be damn near over and we'll be on our way home."

They finished up their section and headed back to where their companions had set up their tent and had supper cooking. Decimus and Carbo were cleaning their weapons; Praxus was repairing a broken strap on his body armor; Valens and Gavius were finishing up cooking supper, and Sergeant Statorius was engaged in conversation with Vitruvius, Ostorius and some of the other Sergeants from the Century.

"Grab your mess tins, it's just about ready," Valens told them as they set down their entrenching equipment. Artorius and Magnus were subdued as everyone engaged in their usual conversations regarding wine, women, home, gambling, their favorite gladiators or chariot racers, and more women. Decimus and Carbo were the only other members of their section to kill anyone that day. Gavius had only succeeded in killing a chicken and setting fire to a silo. Statorius seemed to know what was bothering his newest Legionaries.

"Not like you thought it would be, was it?" He asked, "Killing your first human being, I mean." They were both silent.

"Artorius went absolutely berserk on that one fellow," Decimus said.

"I saw that," Statorius replied, "Did it make you feel any better?"

"No," Artorius said finally. "I can't really describe how I felt. Consciously I know that all of these tribes are allied with the Cherusci and they are all involved in the wars against Rome. There's just that pang of what I guess is guilt. Is it always like this?"

"It's natural human emotions. I would start to worry if you ever *stop* feeling it," Statorius said. "It's different on the battlefield, though."

"Yeah," Decimus added. "Out there, there's no doubt whatsoever as to whom the enemy is, and that they deserve to die. Besides, if you thought today gave you an adrenaline rush, wait till we face a horde outnumbered five to one!" With that he stood up, patted each of them on the back and walked off.

"So am I the only one in the section who hasn't killed anyone?" Gavius asked.

"Don't worry, you'll get your chance soon enough," Praxus replied. "Besides, like I'm sure Magnus and Artorius now understand, be careful what you wish for. It's not all that you think it is."

"I agree with Decimus, it *is* a bigger rush on a battlefield," Carbo mused. "Then again, I suppose that is at least in part because you are fighting for your life out there, and you know it."

"So what happens tomorrow?" Artorius asked, anxious for a change of subject.

"My guess is we'll stay here for a while," Praxus answered.

Carbo added, "Chances are Arminius knows by now about Germanicus and his strike against the Bructeri. I'm sure he also knows that we are here, so I doubt that he'll try anything serious."

"Yeah, we'll probably send patrols out from here, seeing if Arminius will take the bait or not," Decimus said. "There aren't a whole lot of settlements around here that we haven't destroyed already. Remember, there are three other Legions out here besides us and I'm sure they were busy today."

*   *   *   *

The other Legions had been busy. At the headquarters of the Twentieth Legion, Severus met with all of the Legates, Chief Tribunes, and Master Centurions from the Legions to assess the day's events. Though they were not part of the main effort against the Bructeri, they had been busy enough. All settlements within their immediate area of operations had been destroyed. A few survivors had been allowed to escape towards Cherusci territory.

"Well done," Severus said after he had read the last report and checked everything against his map. "We've drawn first blood on this campaign. Now we'll see if Arminius takes the bait. All Legions will hold in place. Fortify your camps, and send out sorties. Sorties need to consist of no less than three cohorts. Messengers will send status reports to here every three hours."

"Sir, if our sorties do become seriously engaged, do you want us to press the fight?" one of the Legates asked.

"Have riders sent with every sortie to act as messengers. If you do become heavily engaged, then yes you will force the issue. If you have any doubts about your ability to crush the threat, swallow some of your pride and send word to the other Legions. There is no room for vanity in this, gentlemen. We will mutually support each other, not seek our own vain glory. I trust you will use your best judgment on this. Is there anything else?" When there were no other questions, the meeting broke and all the senior officers returned to their units. Strabo and Flavius stayed back.

"You performed very well today," Severus told Strabo.

"I had more than a little help," Strabo said, nodding towards the Master Centurion.

Flavius smiled. "I helped you come up with the plan, Sir. You executed it," he said to the young Tribune.

"Well I don't care how you did it, what matters is you destroyed one of the largest settlements in this sector, and you did it without sustaining any casualties," Severus piped in. "You both are to be commended."

CHAPTER 8

▼

AMBUSH AND PHILOSOPHY

Decimus had been right. The next day, three cohorts that had not taken part in the previous day's assault were sent out. As predicted, they went on a sortie to try and lure any wandering barbarian war bands into a fight. None took the bait. The rest of the Legion passed the day standing watch, improving their defenses, or catching up on sleep. Artorius was at first grateful for the break, but soon became restless. He wanted to be able to avenge his brother properly, and killing some farmers was not the way to go about it. He hoped that the barbarians would be lured into a real battle. It would not happen that day. He was standing watch when he saw the cohorts coming in from their sortie.

"Looks like no one took the bait today," Praxus observed. Artorius realized that he seemed to draw sentry duty with a different person just about every single time. Magnus was the only one whom he had done multiple shifts with.

"Doesn't look like they're going to take it at all," Artorius muttered, leaning on his javelin.

"Oh I don't know, sooner or later they'll get tired of us being here and they'll try and send us a message of sorts." Artorius looked over at the older Legionary. He never really speculated on how old the other men were in his section. Most were young, though their experiences made them seem older.

"Can I ask you something, Praxus?" Artorius asked.

"Sure, what's on your mind?"

"Why are you here? In the army, I mean. What drives you as a Soldier?" Artorius was genuinely interested in knowing more about the man whom all the other recruits had started looking to as a mentor.

"It's hard to say really. I mean what drives any of us?" Praxus answered. "My father was a Soldier. Retired after twenty-five years, got himself a nice plot of land to call his own, and a place in the Noble Order of Knights."

"So he retired as a Centurion then?" Artorius asked, realizing that the only way a commoner could attain the status of an equestrian was to retire from the army at a minimum as a Centurion.

"Yep, retired after having commanded his own Century for seven years. Seemed like a good life to me. Of course I was just a boy when he retired, plus I never did see him much when he was still in. My older brother was able to get appointed as a Tribune. I on the other hand had to settle for enlisting as a grunt Legionary."

"My father was wounded and forced out of the army after only four years," Artorius replied.

"I heard that. I also heard about your brother." Artorius face hardened at the last remark. Praxus immediately picked up on it. "I'm sorry. I know it's a difficult thing to have to live with, especially coming back here."

"Coming here was the only way I could think of dealing with it," Artorius replied. Praxus nodded at the thought.

"Makes sense to me," he said after a minute. "As for me, I see it this way; I put my life on the line for Rome. Rome in turn grants me a nice pension when I'm done with it. In the meantime I try and make the most of the adventure along the way. Personally, I find that the best things in life are good wine, good friends, and good women."

"So you don't go looking for women in the same places as Valens then?" Artorius remarked as both men laughed.

"No. And you shouldn't either," Praxus replied.

"Don't worry, I prefer women who have all of their teeth, and who bathe regularly."

"You know, Valens swears that there is some merit to finding a woman with missing teeth. Quite frankly I think the lad is just embarrassed after every one of his escapades and he looks to find any positives that he can. I honestly think he suffers from some sort of addiction." Artorius shuddered at the thought. He then laughed to himself. He had always heard back home about the glory that is Rome, and the prestige of her Legions. Legates and Senators always spoke of it, yet nobody seemed to ask the Soldiers themselves what they thought about such things. Then again, he doubted that posterity would want to read that the heart of Rome lay in men who just wanted to drink wine, gamble, play sports, and chase women.

A few days later Artorius was sitting outside his section's tent, writing a letter to his father, when the Cornicen's started sounding the call to arms. He put his paper and stylus away and immediately donned his armor. Soldiers were coming from all directions, falling in on their gear.

"What's going on?" he asked Praxus as the later laced up the ties on his armor.

"Sounds like the sorties out in sector just came into contact," Praxus answered.

Within a matter of minutes the cohorts not on camp guard were formed up and ready to move. Artorius saw Severus and the Legion's cavalry riding out the gate well ahead of the infantry.

"Battle formation! Six ranks!" came the order as soon as all troops were outside the gate. Within each Cohort, each Century formed up on line, with one Century falling behind the other. Soldiers marched in tight formation, with no more than three feet between them, javelins at the carry. All five Cohorts were on line with each other, with about thirty feet in between each. Cohort Commanders rode up and down the lines, shouting words of encouragement and making certain that all units stayed in formation.

"At the double-time, march!" As one, all cohorts quickened their pace to a slow jog. The Second Century was in the second rank of the Third Cohort, and Artorius struggled to see past the Legionaries in front of him. However, soon he was able to see the forms of friendly Soldiers in the wood lines. There the ground rose steeply, ending at a small ridge. This was occupied by Soldiers providing security for the sortie. There was a lot of activity going on at the base of the high ground.

Soon the relief force slowed to a walk and halted as Master Centurion Flavius of the First Cohort rode out to meet the other Cohort Commanders. As the Soldiers stood and caught their breath, Artorius saw that the commotion was coming from what appeared to be a casualty collection point. There were about a dozen Soldiers being attended to, with several more being borne in on litters. Three were lying still, with their cloaks draped completely over them. Artorius dropped his head, knowing the men were dead. He looked to the left and saw in a completely separate area six barbarians on their knees with their hands bound behind them. Several Legionaries were standing guard over them.

Ahead of the formation the Cohort Commanders of the relief column met with the Master Centurion.

"What happened?" Calvinus of the Fifth Cohort asked.

"Ambush, text book ambush," Flavius replied. "The sortie was paralleling this ridge, when a small band of Germans jumped up and attacked with missile weapons; spears, rocks, arrows, whatever they could get their hands on. As soon as they had loosed a couple volleys, they were gone. The sortie wasn't caught completely off guard, though. Most managed to get into a hasty turtle. Then on their own initiative, the Centurions in the closest ranks gave orders to throw their javelins and counter attack. Unfortunately, the barbarians had fled before they could scale the slope."

"My guess is this will be the way they fight throughout the rest of this campaign," Valerius Proculus of the Third Cohort added. "They'll hide in the trees, up on the high ground. They'll strike, try and inflict a few casualties, and then off they go."

"I also think they'll try and lure us into an even larger trap this way," Calvinus remarked. "They hit us enough times, the lads will become so demoralized that they'll pursue too far and then end up in a world of hurt." The other Commanders nodded and muttered in concurrence.

"What about our casualties?" one Commander asked.

"Right now we have three dead, fifteen wounded, two of those serious enough to require evacuation from the front," Flavius answered.

"I see we scored a few hits ourselves," Proculus said, nodding towards the wounded barbarian prisoners.

"The range and the angle made killing shots difficult," Flavius said. "We only counted a couple of corpses up on the ridge, and I think we were lucky to hit the ones we did. We were only able to do that because they actually stuck around for more than one volley, giving us time to loose our own javelins. I doubt that they will make that mistake often."

"So about the prisoners, what do you think we should do with them?" Calvinus asked, smiling sinisterly.

As the entire column of eight cohorts marched back to the camp, Artorius looked back at the six hastily erected crucifixes set out in the open field. Their occupants moaned in pain and despair. There had been no nails available, so the prisoners had been tied to their crosses, and were then disemboweled. This would ensure that any rescue attempt would be futile, but it also allowed the coming of death to be somewhat prolonged. Artorius almost felt a tinge of remorse, but then he remembered the wounded Legionaries that they had picked up. Two of these, even if they survived their wounds, would probably never be physically able to serve in the Legions again, the same fate his Father had suffered. Three others would never go home, just like his brother. His remorse immediately turned to loathing.

Two more days of sorties produced no further results. That evening Macro called a meeting of the entire Century. As the Century formed up, Macro told them all to take a seat on the grass. Only the Centurion, Optio Valgus, Tesserarius Flaccus and Signifier Camillus remained standing. Sergeant Vitruvius lounged on the grass and looked like he was half asleep.

"Good evening, men," Macro said. His demeanor was hard, but not unpleasant.

"Good evening, Sir," the Century replied together.

"I want to talk with you for a bit about what we are doing here on this campaign, and what will be coming up soon. You all know the obvious reasons as to why we are here. We are here to avenge our brothers who perished in Teutoburger Wald. That you already know. It is my feeling that you need to know a little more specifically about whom we are fighting.

"The Cherusci are by far the largest and most warlike of all the tribes in Germania. Smaller tribes look to them for protection. They are also the ones who committed the most heinous crimes against the Roman state. For not only did the Cherusci declare war on Rome, they did so through treachery and deceit. They had supplied Varus with the bulk of his auxiliaries as well as his scouts. In the Wald, not only did the Legions have to face the attacking barbarians, they also had to face their former allies, who had suddenly turned on them. Their leader, Arminius was a close confidant of Varus. He also had at one time commanded a cavalry ala under Legate Severus. Master Centurion Flavius knew him as well. Ask them sometime if you ever want to know the full depth of his treachery." He paused to let his words sink in before continuing.

"Surprisingly, many in Arminius' own family have continued to maintain their allegiance to Rome. His brother Flavus is still serving as an auxiliary, his loyalty and bravery continuously proven. His wife's father, a nobleman named Segestes has maintained his allegiance to Rome; to the point where Arminius has laid siege to his lands. Germanicus is now en route with his column to relieve Segestes and bring him and his family back to Roman territory. Segestes was also the German who warned Varus about the intended ambush in Teutoburger Wald in the first place. We all know just how much his warning was headed," he said with a certain amount of venom in his voice.

"While this operation is in progress, we have been tasked with finishing the job of destroying the Marsi, whom we ravaged a couple of weeks ago. Our reconnaissance has located the remainder of their settlements. The Marsi were among those who took part in Teutoburger Wald, and therefore have sentenced themselves to annihilation. We also believe that they are the ones responsible for the hit and run attacks on our columns as of late.

"The settlements we will be attacking will be much larger than those we destroyed recently. Make no mistake, they will have been warned by now of our presence and they will put up more of a fight this time. We doubt that there will be anything resembling a pitched battle, however it will be more than just farmers with pitch forks.

"Men, when we engage the Marsi we must be calculated, cold, precise and thorough," his voice was like ice. "We are not a rampaging mob like the barbarians we fight. Not only are they sloppy and haphazard, they miss half of their targets because of their carelessness. We on the other hand will move with precision as well as speed. Everyone we face will die, man, woman, or child. The taking of prisoners has been prohibited on this campaign. Slaves are taken on campaigns of conquest, not retribution. Every hut we will burn and all their livestock and crops we will take or we will burn. Revenge is most satisfying when it is exacted with cold, calculated precision. Never forget that." With that he turned and walked away, the other senior Legionaries in tow. The rest of the Century sat in silence as they let all that was said sink in.

Late that night Artorius awoke, and found himself unable to sleep. He looked over at his dozing tent mates, envying them in their slumber. He got up and decided to go for a walk. He strapped on his sword belt, laced up his sandals and walked out into the night. As he walked down the row of tents, he was stopped by a roving sentry and asked to give the watchword. He gave it and continued on his way. The moon was out, and there was a slight mist in the air. It made everything seem surreal. As he walked along, he saw Centurion Macro leaning on the Century Standard outside his tent. He was breathing heavily, and though he made no sound, in the dark Artorius could tell that he was crying. His cloak was wrapped tightly around him and his body trembled violently even though it was not cold outside. Artorius watched as Macro's servant came out with a cup of steaming liquid, which he drank thirstily. It was the second time Artorius had seen his Centurion like this, only this time was much worse. Carefully he stepped backwards, afraid of being seen by his Centurion. Suddenly he was very tired and he longed for his bunk. As he lay back down he wondered what it was that haunted his Centurion. What could cause an iron horse like Platorius Macro to break like that? He then remembered an earlier conversation he had had with Magnus and he wondered if in fact he had found one of the elusive survivors of Teutoburger Wald.

CHAPTER 9

▼

DESTRUCTION OF THE MARSI

Barholden watched as his wife carried his son towards their hut. As he sat sharpening his sword, he was suddenly afraid. Not for himself, but for his family. He himself was a brave warrior, recently elevated to war chief of the Marsi. If a Roman gladius felled him, then so be it. Such was the fate and the honor of many a Marsi warrior. However, the Romans were not there to fight the Marsi warriors. They were there to exterminate the Marsi completely. His wife and his son would be no safer than he.

They had massacred and destroyed all of the Marsi settlements just east of the Rhine. Now they would try and complete their mission. Having foreseen this, Barholden had petitioned Arminius to send warriors to his aid. However the war chief of the Cherusci was too involved in a petty squabble with his father-in-law and had laid siege to his lands. So now when his allies were truly in need, Arminius was not there to support them.

Barholden had spoken to some of the few who survived the Roman massacre. They spoke of the abject cruelty to which the Romans had subjected their people to. He knew then that this was not a mere raid by the Romans. No, they were here for revenge; and their vengeance had been building over the last six years. Six years since what he had felt to be the most glorious day in the history of the Marsi.

There were a good number of warriors amongst the Marsi, however from what Barholden had been told this particular Roman army was huge. They had the Marsi warriors outnumbered as well as out trained and out equipped. He thought about how and where he would face the Romans. His warriors had conducted several ambushes on their columns already. However, now that the Romans knew the location of their settlements, the time for skirmishes would be over. The Romans would come right at them, right for their homes and families, and they would dare anyone to stand in their way. That was just what Barholden and his warriors would have to do. Evacuation was impossible, there was too little time. This day or the next, they would come.

His thoughts were interrupted as he heard his son cry happily and come running out of the hut. He ran right into his father's arms. Barholden picked the lad up and gazed at him affectionately. He was so young. "Brave boy," he said, setting the lad down. His wife, Milla, came out looking for the boy and smiled when she saw them together. He had not told her of the Romans coming; of their own impending doom and the possible extermination of the entire Marsi tribe. For that would be the price demanded by the Romans for the Marsi's role in Teutoburger Wald. "They will not get me or my family so easily," he swore to himself as he continued to sharpen his sword.

Just then a warrior came running from the outskirts of the village towards him. The man was panting and out of breath. He kneeled before his war chief, head bent.

"Hail Barholden, war chief of the Marsi! I bring news of the Romans." Barholden looked over at his wife. She was staring at him, obviously alarmed. He waived her to go inside, which she did immediately. He then stood, waiving the messenger to do the same.

"Gather all the sub chiefs and elders!" he ordered. Within the hour, Barholden was standing in the glade that separated his people from the coming Roman onslaught. With him were the most distinguished and important warriors in his tribe. All were proud men, men who had fought bravely on many previous campaigns. Most had even fought against the Romans at Teutoburger Wald. Now they all looked to him for answers to their dilemma.

"As you all know, the Romans have occupied the valley just to the west of our lands," he began. "We have all heard stories of how they have ravaged our lands in retribution for what happened six years ago. We have tried to harass them utilizing ambushes and skirmishes. This has done little to drive the Romans away. They are now within a day's march of here, and they look to destroy us once and for all. How large did you say their army was?" he asked the messenger.

"At least twenty-thousand Legionaries, plus auxiliaries," the man replied. The warriors gasped. All were brave, and none of them necessarily feared the Romans; however they were used to having the decisive advantage in numbers.

"We are outnumbered," one warrior observed.

"So what if we are," another scoffed. "We have the protection agreement with the Cherusci. Surely Arminius has warriors he can send!" Barholden hung his head low.

"Arminius is engaged in an internal dispute with his father-in-law, Segestes. Every warrior he has is now being used to lay siege to Segestes' lands. There is no help coming to us." He paused to let the words sink in. The warrior who had been confident only seconds before was suddenly filled with rage.

"You mean that after all these years, all these battles that we've fought for that man, now in our moment of need he *abandons* us?"

"We cannot hope to win this battle," another warrior observed. Barholden shook his head.

"No, we cannot. But what we can do is give the Romans such a taste of Marsi bravery, that they will never forget us!" He drew his sword and raised it high to emphasize his point. "Let us then die as warriors are meant to die; with our swords in our hands and faces towards our enemy!" This elicited a series of cheers and battle cries from his assembled warriors. He was suddenly very proud, proud to be the leader of these brave warriors. As the host returned to their homes, he was troubled once again. He would have to return to his own home, to see his wife and son for perhaps the last time.

*   *   *   *

The Legions were formed up and on the move. The Third Cohort was towards the center of the Twentieth Legion's formation, with the Second Century occupying its second rank. The elite First Cohort occupied the very center, with the Second, Third, Sixth, Seventh and Ninth Cohorts falling in on either side. The Fourth, Fifth, Eighth and Tenth Cohorts were in the second rank in reserve. Artorius was filled with excitement, as well as a little anxiety. The Legion was in Battle Formation this time, no loose skirmishing here. Shields practically linked together, javelins at the carry. Soon the wood line was in sight. They knew that there would be a gradual slope to climb, and then a straight shot to the Marsi settlements.

Sounds of fighting soon filled the air. The auxiliaries were in contact. They would be withdrawing soon, hopefully drawing all of the Marsi warriors behind them. Artorius rehearsed in his head how it was supposed to work. The first rank would throw their javelins, followed by the second and third. The first rank would stay out front and be the first to engage. *At last, a real battle!* He thought to himself. They had crossed into the woods and had just made it to the top of the slope when they saw the auxiliaries withdrawing towards them. Behind them were thousands of Marsi warriors.

"Javelins ready!" Proculus called out. Everyone hefted their javelins to the throwing position; hand up by the shoulder, placed just behind the weight at the end of the three foot metal tip.

"Quick step, march!" The pace quickened as the Legionaries closed the distance with their enemy. While there were many Marsi warriors, it was obvious that they were outnumbered. "Just save some for me," Artorius muttered under his breath. Magnus and Decimus were on either side of him. He felt reassured, knowing that he was fighting along side of these men. The auxiliaries passed through their lines, between the Cohorts. It was time, the gap was closing fast. The Marsi were a mass of men, with no semblance of order apparent. They would fight valiantly, but as individuals. None wore any protective body armor. Most had shields, though these were little more than wicker or flat wooden boards. The majority carried either spears or fire-hardened clubs, though some did carry swords. The scream of their battle cries was deafening. The Romans made not a sound, not until the very last.

"Front rank...throw!" Proculus shouted. As one, the men in the front rank sprinted a few paces and with a shout threw their javelins.

"Second rank...throw!" shouted Centurion Macro. Artorius ran forward, staying on line with the rest of his Century. He ran through the narrow gap between Soldiers in the first rank. As he passed through, he got a good look at the enemy for the first time. They were still coming at them in force, though it looked like they were starting to waiver under the storm of javelins. With no time to think, Artorius picked a target and threw his javelin as hard as he could. He watched a young Marsi warrior raise his shield in terror to block, only to have the javelin pass through his shield, as well as his forearm. The soft metal tip then bent, sticking the butt of the javelin into the ground, pulling the young man down, where he lay screaming in pain.

"Third rank...throw!" Centurion Justinian of the Third Century shouted. They ran through the front rank and immediately unleashed their javelins. Artorius was unable to see how many hit their targets, but from the screams coming from the Marsi, he knew that they were having the intended affect. He tensed up, ready for the next order.

"Gladius…draw!" came the order from Proculus. With a shout, the entire Cohort drew their swords. The Marsi were now completely unnerved.
"Advance!"

*   *   *   *

The Roman auxiliaries had broken off almost as soon as they made contact. Filled with lust and rage, the Marsi pursued them. Barholden knew that this was the Roman's intent. They would pull their auxiliaries back, and the Marsi would have to face the Legions head on. He gave a shout of encouragement to his warriors and then joined them in the chase. As the Legions came into sight, he saw the men in their first rank rush forward as one and unleash their heavy javelins. The most overly zealous of his warriors were the first to fall. As he ran towards the front of his clan, he saw a second rank of Romans run past the first before throwing their javelins. Even more warriors were skewered and ran through. Those that managed to raise their shields either ended up with their shields pinned to their bodies, or at best their shields would be stripped from their hands when the soft metal shafts bent, making it impossible to withdraw them. Barholden watched as one young warrior, perhaps no older than fifteen, raised his shield to block, only to watch in horror as the javelin passed through his shield and forearm. When the shaft bent, he was pulled to the ground, helpless. The poor lad was pulled to the ground, where he lay screaming in pain and terror.

The Marsi were rattled, their losses already starting to mount, and they hadn't even closed with the Romans yet. Suddenly a third rank loosed its javelins on them. The Romans, who had been unnervingly silent up till this point, gave a loud shout as they unsheathed their swords. The Marsi were now ready to break and run. Barholden knew he had to do something.

"Brothers, clansmen, listen to me! Take courage now! We fight for our families, for our tribe, for each other! The Romans have come to take these things from us. Do not let them take away our pride and dignity as well. *Who will follow me?*" With that, he raised his sword and charged the Roman line. It was difficult to pick out individual Soldiers, as they all moved together as one; one massive, well-disciplined killing machine.

Within seconds he had closed the gap. He did not know how he could cut through that wall of shields and swords, but he had to try. He brought his sword down in a massive slash. It impacted on the brass strip on the edge of one shield. He swung again, trying to break through, and again. As he raised his sword once more, the Roman suddenly stepped in and stabbed him in the belly. Just as quickly he pulled his gladius out and smashed Barholden with his shield. The force of the blow knocked him down. He was in immeasurable pain; his bowels ran through by the Roman's blade. Helpless and stricken, he sat back against a tree and watched as his warriors smashed into the Roman line. He was suddenly proud of them, his brave warriors. They would fight to the last to protect their homes and families. He then watched in sorrow as they were cut down in rapid succession. He saw a couple of Roman Soldiers fall as some of his warriors actually managed to penetrate their shield line. This gave him some hope. But then the Roman line suddenly held fast and the rank behind them rushed through, fresh troops smashing into the Marsi with a vengeance. Within minutes it was over. Barholden gritted his teeth in pain, blood and intestinal fluid oozing from the hole in his stomach. He took pride when he saw that not one of his warriors had run. All had stayed and fought till the end.

He winced again as pain overtook him. He wished to die, but did not have the strength to raise his sword and finish himself off. He saw other warriors similarly stricken. While the Romans' precision with their weapons ensured a high percentage of fatalities, not everyone died right away. Those ran through the abdomen took the longest to die. In spite of the horrifying pain most of the dying felt, scarcely one made a sound. Barholden knew the Romans would slaughter any warriors still alive. He hoped it would not take them long to find him.

*   *   *   *

Artorius stood and caught his breath as the reserve Cohorts passed through their lines. They would be the ones to sack and destroy the settlements. The Cohorts that had fought the battle would police up their dead and wounded and finish off any barbarians still alive. He had managed to slay one barbarian with a rapid stab underneath the ribcage. It had been all too easy. The man had been slow and unwieldy, and had probably had no real training in close quarters combat. The ferocity of the Marsi warriors' charge had caused several gaps in the line though, which they had been able to exploit and inflict casualties. He did not know yet how many in the Second Century had been killed or wounded. Details were sent out to dispatch the Marsi wounded, while others were tasked with setting up a casualty collection point, where they would bring all their dead and wounded. The Centuries that had not taken part in the direct fighting were given these tasks. As these were being accomplished, Centurions and Optios were walking up and down the lines, getting accountability of all their Soldiers.

"Artorius, are you alright?" He was surprised to see Centurion Macro standing in front of him.

"Yes Sir, I'm fine," he answered. Macro patted him on the shoulder and continued to walk down the line, checking all of his Legionaries individually. Normally the Sergeants would conduct the checks and then report back to the Centurion. Macro was the type that many times wished to check things for himself. Artorius saw that everyone in his section was alive and none seemed to be seriously wounded, though Gavius had a gash on his forearm that Praxus was applying a bandage to. He would later find out that two Legionaries from the Century had been killed, another six were wounded, including Gavius. Only one required immediate evacuation to the rear. It was hard to determine just how many barbarians fell in their storm of javelins, but from what could be gathered later from first-hand accounts, thirty-five barbarians had been killed in close combat with the Century.

"Not a bad day's work," Magnus said as they surveyed the aftermath of the battle.

Artorius laughed, "And to think you could have gotten a real job in the city."

They listened as they heard the screams and other unholy sounds coming from the settlements up ahead. With their warriors gone, the Marsi were being ravaged without mercy.

"Well, it's a start," they heard Statorius remark as he shrugged.

"Alright lads, form it up," Centurion Macro ordered. "We're going to push through and set up in reserve just short of the settlements. Once in position, we'll wait until the assault is complete, then we'll move back to camp." Without another word being spoken, the Century fell in on the rest of the Cohort and started towards the sounds of destruction. As they started to move out, Artorius watched as Macro walked over to where a German lay stricken with his back against a tree. Macro moved as if to cut the man's throat, but then changing his mind, sheathed his gladius and walked back to the line.

"Why didn't you finish him?" He heard Camillus ask.

"And grant him the mercy of a quick death? I think not," Macro answered. "That man's been stabbed through the bowels. It will take him hours to die, long, *painful* hours. They refused to grant our wounded a quick death in Teutoburger Wald, so why should we oblige them? Let him rot!"

Artorius surveyed the scene of carnage in front of them. It seemed like everything was ablaze, as far as the eye could see. Corpses littered the entire area, human as well as livestock. It looked very much like what they had done to the

other Marsi settlements, only on a much larger scale. With the river to their
backs, the Marsi had had nowhere to run to.

$$* \qquad * \qquad * \qquad *$$

Milla clutched her son tightly, shivering. She shivered not from the cold of the
waters they had just crossed, but from the pain and sorrow that crippled her
heart. She watched, tears flowing freely, as her village was plundered and
destroyed. Somehow she could not bring herself to turn away, not yet. She
watched as her friends and family were viciously cut down. The Romans were not
taking any prisoners.

She nearly smothered the young boy as she watched her aged father wielding
his old rusted sword. He gave a great cry and lunged towards one of the Soldiers.
He was brave, but grossly outmatched. The Legionary knocked him up against
the side of a building, pinning him with his shield. He then repeatedly smashed
the old man in the face and head with the boss of the shield. The sword fell from
his hand as he slid down the wall, his face a mutilated and bloody pulp. In utter
contempt, the Soldier slammed his gladius into his neck, and then spat on him.

Milla continued to watch in utter horror as her sister ran towards the river, her
own infant in her arms. She had given birth just days before and Milla knew that
even if she escaped the Romans, she had no chance of surviving the torrential current. As the young woman started to splash through the water, a Legionary gladius was thrust violently into her back. She gasped and spasm uncontrollably, the
child flying from her arms, into the river.

There were others who had taken their chances in the river. Almost all had
been swept away and sucked under the current. Milla thanked her gods again that
her father had taught her to swim from the time she was a babe. The thought
made her sob again as she saw the old man lying bloodied and lifeless. The young
men, the warriors of her tribe might have been able to make it. Most were decent
swimmers. But the warriors were all dead.

"Where's Papa?" her son asked as he clung to her. A stabbing pain pierced
Milla as she thought of her husband. As much as she had tried to hope, she knew
Barholden was dead. He would not have run. As war chief of the Marsi, he would
have fought till the bitter end.

"Papa's gone to a better place," she replied through her tears.

"Can we go see him?" the boy asked again, eyes full of hope. Milla fought back
another sob.

"Yes, we can go see him, just not yet. I promise, you *will* see your father again, but not for a long time. Don't worry, he will wait for you. He will see how strong you've grown, and he'll be proud."

The village was burning. She knew the Romans would not start burning until they had taken all they wanted and every villager was dead. Slowly she turned away from the scene of death that had been her home and her life. There was nothing for it. She would leave these lands forever; start a new life for her son. She would tell him tales of his father's bravery, and how he had died to protect them. She would find passage to the Isle of Britain. There she could raise him, away from the influence and threat of Rome.

*   *   *   *

It seemed like it took a long time for the assault Cohorts to finish their work and link up with the rest of the Legion. Calvinus walked through the carnage as his men started to set fire to the buildings. Near the edge of the village was a long line of small piles, containing gold, trinkets, weapons, fancy goblets, anything the Soldiers had decided was worth plundering. Calvinus smiled and shook his head slightly. As a senior Centurion, his salary allowed him much in the way of material comforts, negating any need or desire to plunder from the conquered. However he knew how important it was to the men, and so he allowed them the extra time necessary to gather whatever they were willing to haul back to the fort.

He almost felt a pang of remorse when he came upon the bodies of an entire family slain. A mother had lain protectively over her children, but it had been in vain. Her bowels were run through, and all three of her children had been stabbed through the heart. Calvinus then watched as a young woman was stabbed from behind as she tried to make her way to the river. The infant she was carrying flew from her arms and into the sweeping current. The Centurion's face twitched as he watched.

Uncontrollably, his mind flashed back to six years before. He had seen similar sites then as well. Only there it had been Roman citizens who had been barbarically slaughtered. He remembered seeing women who had been brutally raped and then mutilated, all while their stricken husbands had been forced to watch before they were killed. At least here all the men of fighting age were already dead. The Marsi warriors had been spared the torment of having to watch their loved ones perish in a hell of fire and steel. They had gotten off easy in the Centurion's mind. Calvinus also noted how the Romans were merciful enough to slay their victims expediently. Of course this had little to do with compassion. They were in a rush to finish the job and get back to the fort before night fell. There simply was no time for rape and torture.

"The village is cleared, Calvinus," one of the younger Centurions reported. Calvinus nodded to the man.

"Good work. Once every building is alight, conduct one last sweep through the village as we head back to our lines."

"Yes Sir," the Centurion nodded as he turned back to finish his task.

Calvinus looked into the faces of some of the men under his command as they executed their grizzly task. Many were young, no more than overgrown boys, forced to accelerate the ascension into manhood through brutality and war. He then remembered the other young faces he had once commanded. Seventy-two of his men had died in that horrible battle, six years before. Besides Calvinus, only two others had survived from his Century. Of the men he lost, he remembered in particular Metellus, the young Soldier who had saved his life. Rumor had reached Calvinus that Metellus' younger brother was now a Legionary, serving with the Third Cohort. The Centurion instinctively turned back and looked towards the glade they had passed through, which ironically was now occupied by the Third Cohort.

Calvinus never fully understood why the army had allowed him to retain his rank, moreover why they later promoted him to the command of an entire Cohort. He closed his eyes as he remembered his fallen Soldiers, his boys whom he had loved like his own sons. In that moment, any sense of remorse for what his men were doing to the village evaporated. The Marsi had taken part in the treachery of Teutoburger Wald. They had murdered his boys, and now they were paying their debts in full!

✳   ✳   ✳   ✳

The Second Century marched back towards their camp in silence. As they passed back through the woods where the battle had taken place, Artorius saw that the stricken barbarian still laid against the tree. His breathing was shallow and his complexion pale, his body and the ground around him drenched in blood and bodily fluids, but he was still alive. Artorius wondered just how long it would take for the man to expire completely. He saw that all Roman casualties and equipment had been removed from the site. Javelins would be redistributed later. The barbarian corpses would be left to rot. He saw that a pack of wild dogs were already fighting over one body. Artorius gave a nervous start when he heard a human cry come from the center of the swarm. The man the dogs were viciously devouring was still alive! Decimus let out a short, mirthless laugh as he watched the man being savagely ripped apart.

"Not exactly what he thought a warrior's death would be!" he spat.

"Such is the fate of traitors and cowards," Magnus added with contempt. Artorius remained silent, surprised at his own lack of venom at the sight.

His thoughts turned elsewhere as they reached the clearing where they first came into the woods. There he saw Severus and a contingent of cavalry riding out from another part of the woods. Severus had his sword drawn and it was covered in blood. Artorius smiled. Even though he had never met his Commanding General, he admired him. Severus was an extremely competent General, and unlike many of the soft types that infected the ranks of Senatorial Legates, he always led from the front. Germanicus had the same reputation, that if his men were in danger, so was he. The Emperor himself had been notorious for his apparently reckless lack of self preservation in battle. Such men inspired aggression and valor from even the meekest. Yes, these were definitely the sort of men Artorius wanted leading him!

*   *   *   *

Germanicus was growing frustrated, as he was sure his men were. While the Marsi had been ravaged and were out of the war completely, his primary target, the Bructeri had evaded him since the campaign began. Every time he thought he had them pinned down, they would vanish into the forests and swamps. His Legions had smashed a few settlements, but these had been rather small. As he sat at a table with the Legates and auxiliary commanders, he knew that further pursuit of the Bructeri would be in vain. The Chatti, on the other hand, he had caught off guard and devastated, though most of their warriors had also escaped being killed or captured.

"What are your orders, Sir?" one of the Legates asked.

"We will reunite with Severus," Germanicus answered. "As you know, we are not very far from Teutoburger Wald. Therefore I feel it is imperative that we go there and bury our dead." He paused to let the words sink in. There was some uneasy fidgeting from the Legates, but nobody said a word.

"I also feel it is important for us to demonstrate to the Germans that we can and will go wherever we wish," he continued. "The men also need to be taken to Teutoburger. Take them there; show them what happened to their brothers and I guarantee it will renew their fighting spirit."

"And what of the Bructeri?" another Legate asked.

"They will have to wait till another day. Further pursuit of them is completely futile at this point. Our task now is to take care of our fallen brothers. We will then turn our attention towards Arminius himself."

Just then a Soldier came running into the tent; he was obviously out of breath, having run a great distance. "Beg your pardon Sir, but you may want to come outside quick."

It was already dark, the sun having set an hour before. Germanicus and the Legates burst from the tent to see a group of Soldiers shouting and cheering clustered around something in the center of their group.

"What is the meaning of this?" he shouted as Soldiers snapped to attention and parted out of his way.

"Only this, Sir," one Legionary answered as he produced a battered but magnificent standard. It was adorned with a silver Eagle on top, and the plaque underneath read: *Legio XVII.* Germanicus gasped. How was it possible? The Eagle of the Seventeenth Legion had been found! "We found it in a gorge, Sir. Looks like it escaped capture and was simply lost. We were out on patrol when one of the lads saw a glint of something shiny. So he jumped into the hole to fetch it out, and here it is."

"Who was it that found this?" Germanicus asked.

"I did," answered a young Legionary, who stepped forward. "Legionary Gaius Clovius, Sir."

Germanicus put his hands on the lad's shoulders. "Well you are now *Sergeant* Gaius Clovius, and you shall be handsomely decorated for this!" Germanicus was suddenly filled with euphoria. It was an omen, it must be! A simple Legionary just happens to stumble upon this sacred icon in the middle of this vast wilderness? Impossible! The gods must have decreed it! Germanicus was known to be highly superstitious and was overwhelmed by what he thought was sure sign of the gods' favor. He looked to their foray into Teutoburger Wald with renewed assurance from what he perceived as divine sources.

CHAPTER 10

▼

RETURN TO TEUTOBURGER WALD

"Teutoburger Wald? Have they gone mad?" Gavius was beside himself.

"Oh come off it man," Carbo retorted. "Don't tell me you're afraid. It's a forest just like the rest of this cursed land; with some added swamps."

"And ghosts. Don't forget, it is the forest where the greatest disaster in our time took place," Gavius replied.

"All the more reason for us to go there," Artorius said, "to prove that there is nothing for us to be afraid of. Besides, I think it only right that we give some dignity and grace to our fallen, and that everyone sees just what barbarous people we are dealing with." His face was tense. He was obviously trying to quell his burning anger.

That night Artorius found he could not sleep once again. His bouts of insomnia were becoming insufferable. He looked over at his tent mates. The rookie Legionaries, namely Magnus and Gavius, tossed and turned fitfully, yet they slept. The veterans were all lost in deep, peaceful sleep.

Unable to find peace within his mind, Artorius got up and went for a walk. For reasons he could not explain, he found himself purposely walking towards Macro's tent at the end of their line. The moon was full and there was plenty of light to see by. Sure enough, the Centurion was standing outside his tent. This time he was not wrapped up in a cloak trembling. He was simply standing there, his back to Artorius. He was staring off into the distance, his hand resting on the Century's standard. Artorius was getting ready to turn and leave when Macro spoke.

"What is a Legionary doing up this late at night, if he is not on watch duty?" he spoke without turning around. Artorius was surprised that Macro knew he was there. He was suddenly afraid.

"I couldn't sleep Sir," he said, trying to not stutter or stammer.

"Then come speak with me, let me know what ails you."

Artorius walked up to where his Centurion was, not sure what else to do.

"You've been having quite a few sleepless nights," Macro observed. Artorius gasped. Did he know? Know that he'd been watching his Centurion tremble and nearly fall apart, on nights where it seemed like the very darkness would consume him.

"You've probably noticed that my nights have been less than restful as well," Macro continued.

Artorius tried to think of how to best say what was on his mind to his Centurion. What he really wanted to know was; did Centurion Platorius Macro actually survive Teutoburger Wald? And if so, could he possibly have known Metellus? It was a long shot, and Artorius knew it. Finally he spoke.

"I think there is something about this place, this campaign that troubles us both," he said slowly, "though I think that it is for different reasons. I know there are those in this Legion who are haunted by the events of six years ago, having seen it first hand. Am I right to assume that you are one of those?"

Macro continued to look straight ahead, never turning his head towards his young Legionary. "Most of us do our best to hide our little secrets about where we came from before serving with the Twentieth. I guess my secret is out. I was once a Legionary with the Nineteenth." Artorius closed his eyes, partially disappointed. Metellus had served with the Seventeenth Legion, so there was practically no chance that they would have known each other.

Macro continued, "I was one of those captured by the Germans during the battle. We watched as they sacrificed our officers on their accursed altars. We had to watch as our brothers were slowly tortured, begging as they were for death. All we could do was watch and await our turn. Three of us were placed in a wicker cage, to be burned alive. As the Germans started the fire, a fight broke out amongst them concerning some stolen weapons and armor. They ran off and started to fight amongst themselves.

"Fortunately for us, the wood was damp, and the fire did not keep. It did manage to burn most of the way through some of the rope that was holding the cage together. We forced our way out, managing to free five others who were awaiting a similar fate. We hid in the forests, ever aware of the roving bands of warriors. It was still rainy and the sky was constantly black. It would be a couple of days before we could even catch enough of a glimpse of the sun in order to find out what direction we were traveling. We immediately started moving west. It took us nearly two weeks to get to the Rhine. Two of our companions succumbed to their wounds, and died along the way. The rest of us did as best we could, subsisting off of berries and tree bark. I was nearly mad with hunger when the Rhine bridges came into sight. It was then that a roving patrol found us. They almost killed us, except that one fellow, who somehow managed to keep his wits about him, started yelling that he was from the Eighteenth Legion, and that we had survived the disaster. We were then brought to the fortress of the Twentieth Legion. Two of our men were so badly mauled from their ordeal that the patrol made them makeshift litters to carry them in on.

"We were then placed on extended leave; afterwards we were given the option of rejoining the ranks. *All* of us gladly accepted. And now you know."

"My brother, Metellus was killed in Teutoburger Wald," Artorius said. "Forgive me Sir, but I had hoped that perhaps you might have known him. He was with the Seventeenth Legion, Seventh Cohort."

Macro finally turned and looked at Artorius. "No, I did not know him," he said, "but there is somebody who might have; or at least might have known who he was. Are you on any duties tomorrow?"

"I've got sentry duty from first light till noon," Artorius answered.

"Not anymore," Macro said. "Tomorrow after breakfast I'll take you over to meet someone. Something to remember, you are not the only one who suffered loss here. While actual survivors of the disaster are few, there are others still who lost brothers or fathers." Realizing the conversation was over; Artorius snapped to attention and saluted. Macro returned his salute and Artorius turned to leave.

"One last thing Soldier," Macro said. Artorius turned back to face the Centurion. "If you ever mention our conversation to anyone, I swear by all that I consider holy, I will slash your throat and tear out your heart." His tone was non-threatening; however Artorius did not doubt the seriousness of his words.

"Yes Sir," he answered as he walked back to his tent. As he slept, he dreamed of fire, torture and death, the things described to him by Centurion Macro. These were things that he himself had never witnessed, yet he could see them so clearly in his mind.

The next day Artorius awoke feeling anxious. He could not wait for breakfast to be completed so that he could go and see this person to whom Macro was referring. Sergeant Statorius came walking towards him, looking more than a little put out.

"Artorius, I don't know what in the name of Hades you did, but the Centurion said he wants to see you."

"I'm on my way," Artorius answered as he got up and quickly walked off.

"What was that all about?" Magnus asked.

"I don't know. If he were in trouble, Macro would have told me to come back with him, but when I asked he rather vehemently told me to send Artorius and then disappear." Statorius was obviously troubled.

"Well it can't be too bad then," Magnus muttered as he went back to eating his breakfast.

Macro was standing outside his tent, his hands behind his back as Artorius approached. Artorius stepped up to the Centurion and saluted. "Legionary Artorius reporting as ordered, Sir."

"Come with me," Macro said and with that he immediately walked in the direction of the Fifth Cohort. Artorius had never dealt with anyone in the Legion outside of the Third Cohort, so he was rather surprised when he saw Macro walk right up to the Pilus Prior's tent. "Wait here," he directed as he went inside. About two minutes later he came out. With him was a Centurion who looked to be around forty. He had traces of gray in his hair, and he had a long scar on his face that ran from his eyebrow to his cheekbone.

Macro spoke first. "Legionary Artorius, this is Centurion Pilus Prior Calvinus, Commander of the Fifth Cohort. It seems he knew your brother."

Artorius went to salute, and was shocked to see the Centurion extend his hand. He fumbled with his salute and took Calvinus' hand. "A pleasure to meet you Sir," he said.

"Take what time you need. Report back to me as soon as you are done," Macro said. He turned and briskly walked away. Artorius watched him go, and then realized that he was still clutching the other Centurion's hand.

"It's a pleasure for me to meet the brother of one who saved my life," Calvinus said. He then motioned for Artorius to come inside his tent. Once inside, Calvinus pointed to a chair and asked him to sit down. Artorius was shocked. He had never been invited into a senior officer's quarters before. Calvinus handed him a goblet of wine before taking a seat himself.

"I suppose there are some questions you would like to have answered," Calvinus said.

"As a matter of fact Sir, there are," Artorius replied. "I want to know what happened to my brother, what really happened to him I mean. I also want to know what kind of Legionary he was. I was just a boy of eight or nine the last time I saw him alive."

"Your brother," Calvinus started, "was a fine Soldier. You would do well to have learned from his example. I was his Centurion in the Seventh Cohort for the two years that he served with us. He was always learning; learning the way the Century worked as part of a Cohort and how a Cohort worked as part of a Legion, how doctrine and tactics applied directly to the lowest level. He was always reading, *and* writing. I was surprised when I found out that many of the letters he wrote were being sent to his younger brother." Artorius smiled at the memory. "He did not confine himself to just military study, though. He would read anything he could get his hands on. And when he was not reading, he was strengthening his body. I remember a favorite saying of his..."

"With a sound mind and a strong body, you can accomplish anything," Artorius interrupted. "My apologies," he said immediately realizing his lapse in manners.

"I hope you took his words to heart," Calvinus said before continuing. "There was only one thing he loved more than study and physical play, and that was Rowana. I don't suppose he ever told you about her?"

"He did mention a few times about a woman that he had fallen for," Artorius answered. "It's been a while since I read his letters, but I do seem to remember him mentioning her once by name."

"Rowana was the type of girl any man would fall in love with on site. Not simply because she was beautiful, but because she was a genuinely kind and generous person. She also exuded a lot of class. She was nothing like the tramps and whores that permeate the settlements around a military post. I had the sad duty of telling her what had happened to Metellus. She left soon after and nobody's seen her again. I wonder if she's even still alive.

"I also wrote the letter to your parents, concerning his death. I wrote a *lot* of those letters." He took a long pull off of his wine and looked away for a moment.

"You mentioned that Metellus saved your life," Artorius said, trying to keep the conversation going. "Would you please tell me how?"

Calvinus looked down for a few seconds, drank some more wine and then continued. "It was nearly the end of the battle. We had fallen back to a final stronghold when the Germans broke through. There were so many of them and by this point we were in a hopeless position. Our formation had completely broken down. Metellus had been missing since the initial ambush, as had many of the other lads.

"When it seemed like everything collapsed, only I and two others that I knew of were still alive. We were in the middle of a desperate fight, when Metellus came running from out of nowhere. I was in the middle of a scrap against three barbarian warriors. Metellus lunged in and took out two of these by himself." He then told Artorius of the subsequent flight to Cassius Charea's formation, and of Metellus' subsequent mortal wounding.

"In a last desperate act to save his friends, he flung his gladius which killed a rather fleet footed barbarian who was closing fast on us. I was not aware of his presence until I heard the cry and turned to see the man fall with Metellus' blade imbedded in his spine. I saw your brother lying on his stomach just as a barbarian stabbed him in the back of the skull with his spear. The three of us who survived ran to Cassius' formation and cut our way out." He took another draught of wine.

"When we get to Teutoburger Wald, do you think you could show me where he was killed?" Artorius asked.

"I will if we can even find the place. With six years of growth and gods know what the barbarians did to the bodies, it may be impossible to identify him. However if possible, I will show you where he made his final stand. Don't worry about finding me, I will come and find you." With that he stood. Artorius, recognizing that their meeting was done, snapped to attention and saluted.

"Thank you for your time Sir," he said as he walked out.

Calvinus took a deep breath and a long pull off his wine after Artorius had left. "And so Metellus, your brother has come to avenge you. I hope he does you proud, old friend," he said as he raised his goblet in salute.

✳   ✳   ✳   ✳

Macro was not with the Century as they marched into Teutoburger Wald. Optio Valgus had been left in charge, with Camillus as his second. Macro, Calvinus and any other Soldiers known to have survived the Teutoburger massacre were sent with the cavalry to act as guides. Severus himself took charge of the reconnaissance effort. It was only then that it became publicly known just who in the Legion was a Teutoburger survivor. It seemed like all of them had taken great pains to keep their pasts a secret.

Teutoburger Wald was a forest infested with nearly impenetrable swamp and marshlands. It seemed like every few hundred meters they had to stop and build bridges and causeways through the marshes for the baggage trains to get through.

"How in the *fuck* could Varus have believed this to be a more expedient route?" Valens asked as he slipped off a rock and sank up to his knees in the water and muck. "This is by far the worst terrain we have encountered to date!"

"No argument there," Praxus said as he helped pull his friend out. He looked around at their surroundings. "He must have had a lot of trust in that bastard Arminius."

The Second Century was tasked to provide security as other units built the bridge over a particular section of the marsh. As they came to each impenetrable pass, Centuries took turns providing security and building bridges. Artorius looked around and saw that with the nightmarish terrain they were standing in, keeping close order and formation had been impossible. Praxus was fifteen feet to his left and Magnus was more than ten feet to his right. The rest of the Century had just as hard of a time maintaining a proper interval. Some Legionaries were stacked practically on top of each other in small patches of dry ground while others were spread far apart.

"You know, we could probably walk to where we're going in a day if we didn't have to build all these damn bridges for the baggage train," Carbo said.

"Hey, if you want to sleep in this crap without a tent or a cot, be my guest!" Artorius retorted.

"Hmm, I wonder if any of the locals can recommend a good bath house," Valens said as he looked at his soiled feet and legs.

"Oh sure, it's right next to that little grove where they cut your head off and offer your bowels to the forest gods. I hear Brumhilda's Whore House is just up the block from there as well," Artorius mused as everyone laughed.

"Think Brumhilda has a sister we can set Carbo up with?" Decimus asked, inciting further laughter from the section, as well as a profane insult from Carbo. Laughter was good, even if it was of the nervous kind. Everyone had been on edge since the moment they entered the Wald. It was as if the very forest would swallow them up as it had the Legions of Varus.

The next day they managed to find some drier ground to march on. This helped them to maintain formation which eased some of their anxieties about security. After a couple of hours of marching they came to a halt. A rider soon approached them. It was Centurion Calvinus. He stopped at their position.

"Can we help you Centurion?" Valgus asked.

Calvinus dismounted and walked towards Artorius. "I need him to come with me."

"Can I ask what this is about?" Valgus asked.

"There is something up ahead that requires the attention of Legionary Artorius," Calvinus answered. "It may help him in finding what he seeks here." His eyes were never off of Artorius.

"Very good Sir," Valgus said and nodded his consent to Artorius. Calvinus left his horse with Valgus and the Century as he and Artorius walked away.

"I can't be certain, but I think that this may be the place we are looking for," Calvinus said as soon as they were out of sight of the Century. "Varus' final camp is not too far from here, and I know that we fought our final action before linking up with Cassius in this area. Here we are."

They came to a clearing which was littered with skeletons. Since the Germans would have picked up their own dead, it was apparent that all of these were Roman. All had been stripped of any weapons, armor or possessions. Decay and wild animals had stripped all of the flesh away from the bones. The bones themselves were in an advanced state of decay, some were not even recognizable. There was not much else to see. Calvinus was obviously shaken. If this was the right spot, then many of these bodies had once been his Legionaries. Artorius looked to see if any of them might be his brother. Positive identification was of course impossible at this point, but still he hoped.

Calvinus continued to point out signs that made the area seem familiar to him. He saw one skull that had its face smashed in, possibly belonging to Legionary Clodius. They came across numerous skeletons that were of varying size and shape, probably some of the families and camp followers who had shared the fate of their men. It was coming together like a puzzle. Finally they saw a body off by itself that caused both men to stop dead in their tracks. It was lying face down, facing towards where Calvinus thought Cassius' formation had been. Most of the bones were scattered or missing, the work of wild dogs, mice, and other scavengers. However there was a hole in the back of the skull where a spear could very well have been thrust. Calvinus then pointed to the right femur, which was surprisingly still intact. Running sideways at an angle was a noticeable slash, one not caused by animals or decay. It was the blow of a sword; a sword that would have severed the femoral artery, wounding the man mortally.

Tears came to Artorius' eyes. There was no longer any doubt. He had found his brother. He set his javelin and shield against a tree and cradled the skull in his hands. His mind was awash in memories, happy memories of when his brother had still been alive. He remembered saying goodbye to Metellus the day he left for the army. Metellus had bent down and kissed him on top of the head right before he left. Artorius had not appreciated the gesture, which may have been all the more reason why Metellus did it.

"I want to come with you, to live the life of the Legions," he had told Metellus. His brother had laughed at the remark.

"Perhaps some day you will. Remember little brother, with a strong mind and a sound body you can accomplish anything." Those had been his last words to him. Artorius smiled through his tears and kissed the top of the skull.

"Come, I'll help you bury him," Calvinus said.

They gathered up Metellus' bones and walked to a large open field. There were still the remnants of a palisade and half-filled ditch. Here had been the place were Varus had made his final stand. The sights here were much more gruesome. Skulls were nailed to trees, ash and soot still left a residue on foul alters where the Tribunes and Centurions had been sacrificed. Signs of mutilation were obvious; even with what little remained of the bodies.

A massive hole had been excavated. Artorius was surprised to see Germanicus himself present. Without much ceremony, but with great affection he laid to rest the first of the bodies that would occupy this mass grave. Legionaries started to bring the bones of the fallen forward, laying them side by side, and eventually on top of each other. Time constraints did not allow for a more individual and personal form of burial, and the dampness prevented the traditional burning of the bodies. Artorius saw Centurion Macro and some other Soldiers whom he did not recognize off to one side. Macro saw him and nodded in acknowledgment of the burden that Artorius carried. Artorius and Calvinus took their place in line behind Soldiers bearing similar loads. As they reached the grave, they took great care to lay Metellus down gently next to his fallen brothers. Artorius ran his hand across the top of the skull one last time.

"I will bring you justice, brother."

Later that night, Artorius and Magnus were cooking dinner for their tent mates. Artorius' hand trembled as he placed some wheat cakes on the cooking pan. Magnus sat and watched in silence. Decimus and Valens walked in from sentry duty. All had seen the remnants of Varus' camp and the macabre spectacle that still existed even after six years.

"I cannot believe what we have seen today," Valens said.

"Yeah," Decimus replied. "I have no idea how many we buried. Though for most of them there wasn't much left."

"The skulls that were nailed to the trees were the worst," Valens said, closing his eyes at the thought.

"Artorius buried his brother today," Magnus said as everyone stared at him; everyone except Artorius. He just stared at the fire.

"How did you know?" he asked.

"I overheard Centurion Calvinus tell Macro. It explained why you were gone as long as you were. Besides, how often does a senior Centurion from another Cohort come and speak pleasantries with an unknown Legionary? I mean, think about how many breaches of protocol happened today between you and that Centurion." Artorius sat stone faced. He couldn't have hoped to keep this from his friends. Magnus put a hand on his shoulder.

"Artorius, we're sorry," Decimus said, grabbing his other shoulder.

"I lost an uncle here," Valens said. "I never knew him, but I saw how devastated my father was when we received word of his death. I know not whether he was one of those we buried today or not."

Artorius took a deep breath. "Well now that we've finished here, what do you think Germanicus and Severus have in mind for us now?"

"I don't know," Decimus said taking the cue to change the subject. "We've got about another month of good campaign weather before we have to start thinking about our move back across the Rhine."

"You mean we won't establish winter quarters here?" Magnus asked. "I thought it was standard practice that the army would base itself in freshly conquered territory to prevent its being retaken."

"We would, if we were interested in re-conquest," Statorius said as he walked into the fire light. "We're not here to take the Germans' land from them. As you all have seen there is nothing here we want. The ground is a nightmare to farm; the tribes are even less civilized than those of Gaul were during the conquest of Caesar. To be honest I highly doubt we will ever again expand our borders beyond the Rhine. We are here on a mission of vengeance gentlemen, nothing more."

Germanicus stood outside his tent, listening to his chief auger. The man was obviously very distraught. Germanicus stood there listening to his complaints. Though most Romans placed little real value in religion, Germanicus was one of the few who still held faith in the old beliefs.

"Sir, I don't think you comprehend how grave your transgression today was," the auger pleaded. "You are of the Order of Priests, an order which has a sacred obligation to avoid contact with the dead. In spite of this you blatantly took it upon yourself to lay your hands on the remains of those men. Do you have *any* idea of the possible repercussions of this?"

Germanicus looked at the man coldly. "Those men were sacrificed to the foul deities that inhabit these woods. It was up to me to restore to them some dignity and final grace."

The auger shook his head, still unconvinced of the righteousness of Germanicus' actions. "Your motives may not have been without merit, but your actions are still inexcusable in the eyes of the gods. I fear that in the end we may end of falling out of their favor."

Germanicus stepped close to the auger and said into his ear, "If by my actions I have fallen out of the gods' favor, then their favor I no longer want." Without another word he went back inside his tent, leaving the auger horrified at what he had just heard. Severus was waiting inside his tent, leaning on a table. He had overheard the entire conversation and had found it to be mildly amusing in a dark sort of way. The low light cast by the oil lamp showed the half smile on his face. Germanicus ignored it.

"What are your orders?" Severus asked.

"Tomorrow we will be finished with the burial mound and alter. As soon as they are completed, we will march west against Arminius. Let's see if we can get him to finally face us in open battle."

Severus smiled and nodded. "Very good, Sir."

CHAPTER 11

▼

FRUSTRATION AND THE ROADS HOME

Arminius and Ingiomerus sat on their horses, watching the scouts ride towards them. The Roman army was on the move against them. Having just come from the site of Varus' final camp, Germanicus in his fury would try and force a decisive engagement. Arminius was well aware of this. He also feared what would happen if he did face the Romans head on. He did not know the size of their army, nor what they had in terms of auxiliaries. The lead scout stopped his horse in front of them. He was stripped to the waist, carrying only a short sword and small circular shield. Arminius had always insisted that his scouts travel light.

"Hail Arminius, great war chief of the Cherusci!" the man shouted. Arminius nodded and the scout commenced with his report. "The Roman army is huge. I counted eight Legions plus a full compliment of auxiliary infantry and cavalry. Their cavalry are in pursuit of us now. They are but a couple leagues behind us."

Ingiomerus seemed shocked by the numbers, but Arminius was nonplused. "Our own cavalry will deal with them. Did you see how the Roman legions are arrayed?"

The scout nodded. "I did. They are in full battle array, five Legions in front, three in reserve. They are ready for a full-scale engagement. They know we are close, and they seem almost desperate for a fight."

"Then a fight they shall have," Ingiomerus said. Arminius turned and stared at him.

"No Uncle," he said. "We cannot be certain of victory here. I will not risk our entire army in a madcap charge head on at the Romans. That is just what they want. We will dispatch their cavalry, and then we will withdraw."

Ingiomerus looked shocked. "You mean to tell me that when we have the entire Roman army in the west at our disposal we are simply going to *run?*"

"Not run, Uncle. We will withdraw for the time being. It is late in the campaigning season for the Romans. They will have to withdraw to their fortresses across the Rhine sooner or later. And when they do, we will pursue and hunt them down." Ingiomerus looked aggravated and disappointed, but he did not argue. They looked over to see their cavalry and massive numbers of warriors awaiting the approach of the Roman auxiliaries. Soon they saw the shapes of men and horses approaching. As they approached, Arminius was shocked to see that there was no infantry with them. They should have been in sight. Arminius smiled. The cavalry had pushed too far ahead of the main column. They had left themselves exposed and without support. He nodded to Ingiomerus as the first wave of horsemen approached the woods where they sat. Ingiomerus raised his sword, gave a loud battle cry and the Cherusci charged.

*   *   *   *

Artorius was growing impatient. They had been on the march for several hours. They had deployed into battle formation nearly an hour before, anticipating a clash with the Cherusci at any moment. He scanned out ahead as far as he could see. The cavalry and auxiliary infantry were nowhere in site. Something wasn't right. The auxiliaries were supposed to maintain visual contact with the Legions in case they got into trouble. Suddenly he saw cavalrymen riding towards them. They were scattered and in disarray. This was no passage-of-lines; these men were riding for their lives. *What had happened out there?*

"So few," Gavius observed quietly. Just then they caught site of the auxiliary infantry. They were obviously spooked. There numbers looked to be intact, but they were running from whatever it was that had attacked the cavalry.

"Javelins ready! At the quick step…march!" The order was echoed up and down the lines.

"At last," Artorius muttered as he shouldered his javelin, ready to throw. Suddenly the Germans were in site. There was a massive hoard of them, shouting and waiving their weapons. Artorius had no way of guessing their actual numbers. He just knew that there were probably more of them than there were Romans. The gap started to close between the two armies. His heart pounded in his chest, a trickle of sweat forming on is brow. *Come on,* he thought to himself. *Just a little closer.* His Century was in the fourth rank of the Cohort, but he knew that there would still be plenty of killing to do before the day was done. Then suddenly without warning, the Germans turned around and started running the other way.

What is this? Artorius thought. It was not possible! Here they were, ready to at last close in on the Germanic hordes and they were running away! The Romans maintained their steady pace, their discipline not allowing them to get hot headed and chase after the barbarians. Soon the Germans were out of site. Artorius let out a groan of frustration.

"Javelins at the carry! At the walk...march!" It was over. The battle that they were all hoping for had not taken place. The Germans had mauled their cavalry and then come out to taunt them! Artorius seethed with frustration. He looked around to see that all of his companions were feeling the same way. No one dared to say anything, though. Now was not the time for emotions to run amok. Soon the order was given to stand down and set up camp for the night.

Offensive operations for the campaign were over. Germanicus knew this. The time it would take to try and draw Arminius into a decisive engagement would draw them too close to fall and winter. Arminius had no intention of forcing a major battle, which was made obvious by the day's actions. Even more frustrating was the losses inflicted upon their auxiliary cavalry. Germanicus had given the survivors a severe tongue lashing for their blatant disregard for safety and failure to maintain proper interval with the infantry. He'd intended to relieve the cavalry commander and then have him flogged; only the man was dead. Germanicus and Severus walked the inside perimeter of their camp as they discussed these things.

"Today was a frustrating day for the lads," Severus observed, "especially with having just come from the site of Varus' final resting place."

"Arminius is deliberately trying to frustrate us and cause disarray," Germanicus replied. "I believe that he realizes the futility of engaging us openly. Therefore, he settles for skirmishes, ambushes, and open acts of taunting as he did today. However, while he understands the benefits of his psychological war against us, it is highly doubtful that his fellow war chiefs feel the same way."

"I agree," Severus said. "To them it is both honorable and glorious to face their enemies head on. These hit and run tactics may actually seem like cowardice to his warriors. I think his little display today may have had more of a negative impact on his warriors than it did on our Soldiers."

"Well, it would have had the cavalry not blundered the way they did. That's the problem with auxiliaries, no matter how much we work with them they always lack true discipline and they don't think about the repercussions of their actions. Our Legionaries would never have allowed themselves to be left so obviously out in the open and unprotected!"

"Yes, but unfortunately most Legionaries can't ride a horse to save their lives," Severus replied. "Rome has the finest infantry fighters in the world, yet for some reason most of us lack basic horsemanship skills."

"So what are your recommendations?" Germanicus asked.

"From what I see we've got a massive number of men to get back to our strongholds across the Rhine. To move the entire army as one unit will be cumbersome. We have two routes we can take. We can both go north and take the sea back to friendly territory, or we can travel south to the Ahenobarbi bridges and cross there."

"The bridges are in disrepair and need work done on them," Germanicus observed. "I'll send you with your Legions to repair the bridges before crossing. It is doubtful that in their current state they will hold up under the baggage trains. I will take the remaining Legions to the sea route home.

"One thing to keep in mind, Severus; the route to the Ahenobarbi bridges is well traveled. It may seem obvious to Arminius that this will be our course of action. Also the area around the bridges is mostly marshland. Be extremely careful. I foresee Arminius trying something while you repair the bridges."

"We'll be careful," Severus answered. "I can detail Soldiers to fix the bridges, build the necessary fort, and provide security easy enough. I worry more about your choice of traveling by sea at this time of year."

They continued their walk of the perimeter, stopping to talk with individual Soldiers on sentry duty.

*   *   *   *

"You're certain that this is the route they are taking?" Arminius asked his chief scout.

"Absolutely, oh Great War Chief," the scout replied. "I saw the standards of four Legions, the First, Fifth, Twentieth and Twenty First. They are all headed south, straight for the Ahenobarbi bridges."

"What of the other Legions?" Arminius asked.

"We're not sure. We saw them heading north, though their exact route is unknown."

Arminius paused for a minute and then turned to Ingiomerus. "You see, Uncle? They are heading just where I thought they would. We do not have the forces necessary to attack both elements; however we have more than enough to inflict serious losses upon those heading towards the bridges." He took his sword and drew on the dirt. "We will follow them, maintaining about half a day's distance away, in case they turn back and try to force us into an open battle. They will have to do major repair work on the bridges in order to get their wagons across. We will strike at them as they do so."

"The marshy terrain will work to their disadvantage," Ingiomerus observed. "Their heavy armor and weapons will slow them down and hinder their mobility."

"It will get even worse by the time we've prepped the area," Arminius said as he continued to draw his diagram on the dirt. He then signaled to one of his sub chiefs. "Take your men and start digging a runoff from this tributary here. Once the water is sufficiently diverted, it will increase the water levels in the marshlands, hindering the Romans that much more. Once they are sufficiently incapacitated, we will launch our strikes against them." The sub chief smiled yelled orders to his men and soon vanished. Arminius looked up at his uncle. "If we do this right, we may add four more Legions to our list of the vanquished." Ingiomerus smiled and laughed a dark and sinister laugh.

CHAPTER 12

▼

AT THE AHENOBARBI
BRIDGES

"This is absolute *shit!*" Valens bickered as he sank up to his waist in water and muck. The marshes surrounding the Ahenobarbi bridges were unusually flooded, which made working on the bridges themselves an even bigger chore.

"They don't pick the best terrain for us to travel, now do they?" Magnus mused as he handed Valens a piece of timber to replace a sodden brace on the underside of the bridge.

"This is worse than that crap we had to slog our way through in Teutoburger," Valens continued, taking the timber support from Magnus.

"What I don't get," Artorius said as he waded through the marsh with a coil of rope over his shoulder, "is the rivers are not swelled above their banks. There hasn't been an excess amount of rain this summer, so there is really no reason for the area to be this swampy."

"I know, it's like we're walking through a damn lake," Praxus said as he and Decimus brought more timber up. They looked over to see where the sentries were posted. They were nearly up to their knees in water, and all looked nervous about their predicament.

Praxus shook his head. "If we come under attack here, we'll be in serious trouble."

"Well if we do, I hope it comes after the fort is done," Valens said, looking across the river to where other working parties were digging the ditches and building the palisades. They continued to work on the supports underneath the bridge until they ran out of supplies. As they crawled out from underneath the bridge a war horn sounded in the distance. All paused, as if stricken.

"You have got to be kidding," Magnus said. The horn sounded again, this time accompanied by the sounds of battle cries.

"Afraid not," Artorius said, as he reached for his helmet, javelin, and shield. All Soldiers had stacked their arms by sections where they could quickly be reached. Unfortunately, there was no dry place for them to do this, so most of their shields were soaked through the bottom half by the time they picked them up.

"*Everybody online, two ranks!*" Centurion Macro called out. In spite of the difficulty in slogging through the swampy water, all Soldiers were soon formed up, shield to shield, one rank directly behind the other. Artorius stood behind a Soldier from Sergeant Ostorius' section. He knew that in a defensive engagement, if the enemy used missile weapons, his job would be to provide overhead cover for both himself and the Soldier in front of him. The Soldier in front would provide frontal protection.

Suddenly the Germans were in site. They mostly carried slings, throwing spears and a few bows. All were stripped practically naked. This was a harassment attack. As they surged forward, they unleashed a torrent of sling stones, arrows and spears.

"*Down!*" Macro shouted. As one, the Soldiers in the front rank dropped to one knee, keeping their shields in front, linked together. The Soldiers in the back rank raised their shields overhead, dropped to one knee and placing their shields over their own heads, as well as those of the Soldiers in front of them. As Artorius dropped down, the water level was up to his chest. He listened as stones and arrows skipped off their wall of shields. He looked to his right and saw other units similarly engaged.

"*Up! Javelins ready!*" As the Century rose to its collective feet, the Germans turned and ran back out of range.

"Damn!" Artorius heard Macro mutter under his breath. He then heard his Centurion call out, "Is anybody hit?" Sergeants immediately checked their men before replying back.

"We're alright!"

"We're good!"

"Nobody's hit!"

"Here they come again!" Optio Valgus called out. Another wave of missile throwers came at the Century.

"Javelins ready!" Macro shouted. The Germans were closing fast. It would be a matter of timing. Release their javelins, and drop back down behind their shield wall before the Germans could unleash. The swampy terrain had to be factored in as well, since it would impede movement and their javelin throwing abilities. Macro thought about all of these things in the few seconds he had before the Germans were within range of their javelins.

"Front rank...throw!" He shouted. The men in the front rank raised their javelins and stepped forward as they threw.

"Down!" Macro yelled as the Germans loosed their own volley. There was no time to see if their javelins struck home or not. The Romans had barely dropped down and raised their shields as the German missiles rained down upon them. Artorius heard a cry of pain from somewhere to his left. Somebody had been hit! There was no time to think about it. A second rank of barbarians, all carrying spears and shields charged past their companions with the missiles.

"Up!" Came the order from their Centurion. *"Second rank...throw!"* Artorius slogged through the marsh past the Soldier in front of him, quickly picked out a target and threw his javelin. The Germans were right on top of them. His javelin flew in a short arc, scoring a precise hit on a warrior not fifteen feet in front of him. The javelin had pierced the man's heart, and he was dead before he hit the water. Artorius barely had time to draw his gladius before the Germans collided with their lines.

A burly German crashed into his shield, trying to knock him down. His balance was completely off as he struggled in the marsh. The bottom of his shield dragged through the water, making it nearly impossible for him to punch his opponent. He rapidly jabbed with his gladius, but the barbarian was keeping his distance, and his weapon skipped off the man's shield. All up and down the line, Legionaries were having similar difficulties. A barbarian slammed his body into Carbo's shield, knocking him down. Fortunately, it also offset the German, and a Soldier in the second rank quickly stepped forward and stabbed the barbarian in the throat. Then as suddenly as it began, the Germans retreated. The Romans watched as the barbarians formed up in the tree lines and started waving their weapons and shouting insults that the Romans could not understand.

Artorius stood panting and frustrated. Three Soldiers had been wounded in the exchange. Macro quickly gave orders for them to be evacuated across the bridge to the fort. The ground over there was relatively dry and even; a much better place to fight a battle, if only they could get their damn wagons across! He looked around, wondering who was hurt. Then he heard a voice call out, *"Valgus is down!"*

Statorius and Vitruvius struggled to lift the wounded Optio out of the murky water. He had been relaying orders and had himself been too slow in dropping down behind his shield. A spear had plunged into his hip and he was bleeding badly. He groaned in pain as he fought to remain conscious. As they lifted him up, one overzealous barbarian ran forward in attempts to finish off the Optio. As he did, Vitruvius growled in rage. He wrapped an arm in a choke hold around the German, and with a horrific jerk snapped his neck.

"Get him to the fort!" Macro ordered.

"Sir!" Statorius acknowledged. Vitruvius and Statorius took their sections to act as escorts as they bore the wounded away. Valgus was by far the worst off. As they got to the fort, doctors were already setting up tables and had their instruments ready. Valgus had passed out, and his skin was pale and clammy. The doctors worked frantically to stop his bleeding. Artorius stood watching as Statorius grabbed him by the collar.

"Come on!" the Sergeant yelled. "We have to get back to the line!"

The rest of the morning passed in relative quiet as the Romans quickly tried to finish the work on the bridges while the Germans watched and taunted. Soon orders were given to form the entire army up into a hollow square. First Legion was to take the front, Fifth and Twenty First the flanks, the Twentieth was to take the rear. All wagons were placed in the center. Slowly the massive formation started its move towards the bridges. On the other side, the fort awaited their occupation. Artorius watched as the Germans slowly started creeping towards them. By the gods there were a lot of them! More than twenty thousand Legionaries were formed up in the hollow square, yet Artorius could not help but feel that they were hopelessly outnumbered.

Without warning, Cornicens on the flanks sounded the call to double-time. All of the sudden, both the Fifth and Twenty First Legions started to take off at a run towards the bridges. Their move was very deliberate and organized. Artorius wondered if there had been a mix up in the orders.

"What the hell are they doing?" Magnus swore.

"They're leaving the baggage trains exposed," Praxus replied.

"Not to mention our backsides!" Artorius observed. War horns sounded and the Germans charged. Legate Severus was riding amongst the baggage trains, trying to restore order. Artorius looked in horror as their Commanding General was suddenly swarmed by the enemy. Quickly Master Centurion Flavius rode up on his horse.

"First, Second and Third Cohorts, to the Commander!" He shouted as he drew his gladius. With a loud cry, the three Cohorts formed up in battle lines and rapidly advanced towards the Germans attacking their Legate. The barbarians, upon seeing the Romans bearing down on them, gave up their assault on the Legate and his bodyguard cavalry, and instead quickly grabbed what they could from the supply wagons, killed the pack animals and fled.

As they approached their Commander, Artorius saw that Chief Tribune Strabo was with Severus. His face and his sword were covered in blood and he was breathing heavily. Severus nodded in thanks when Flavius rode up to him.

"We cannot save the baggage trains," he told Flavius. "Get your men across and over to the fort. Thankfully most of the rations, as well as all of the artillery made it across. We just may end up sleeping on the ground tonight."

"Yes Sir," Flavius answered.

As they marched into the fort, everyone knew right away where to head to. The layout of a Legionary fort was always the same and every Soldier from the Legate down to the lowest Legionary knew exactly where his place was within her. This time there was a conspicuous lack of tents and other baggage. The barbarians had taken full advantage of the time they had been given to make off with much of the Romans' supplies and equipment.

It's going to be a long night, Artorius thought. He looked around and saw that most of the Legionaries were obviously distraught, though he doubted that it was because they would be sleeping on the ground without a tent. No, there was something more to it.

"Dear gods, did you see how many of them there were?" Carbo said, staring at the ground.

"I didn't know there were that many souls in this entire festering hell hole of a land!" Valens added. Just then Flaccus came walking up to talk with Statorius and the other Sergeants. With Valgus down, it fell upon Flaccus to temporarily take over his duties. Even though Camillus was technically senior to the Tesserarius, his position as Signifier was too crucial for him to vacate. It was still understood that should Macro fall, he would take command of the Century. Artorius heard them talking about how no fires would be permitted that night, and that noise discipline was to be enforced to the utmost.

"Well I guess we get to eat our supper cold tonight," he muttered.

"I guess no fireside banter either," Carbo mused.

"Like we need to hear more stories about tavern wenches and their mythical sisters," Gavius scoffed.

"Alright, everyone gather around," Statorius said. "As you have already heard, no fires tonight, and absolute noise discipline will be enforced. You can bet that the Germans will be making all sorts of racket tonight to try and unnerve us. That is fine, let them. In the morning, we will lay a little trap for them. Macro is getting all of the details right now. Suffice it to say, I think we may soon get the chance to inflict a little payback on these bastards." Artorius smiled at the thought.

"How's Valgus?" he asked.

"The doctors think he'll live," Statorius said, "but with the extent of his injuries, and the sheer loss of blood alone, I doubt that we'll be seeing him back." The thought of their Optio lying in a pile of rags soaked in his own blood and fluids, barely clinging to life left a somber attitude on them. It was a sight the contrasted greatly with that of the strong, confident man who had drilled them through recruit training.

Vitruvius went to visit his old friend that night. Valgus lay on a cot, one of the few that had not been taken by the barbarians when their baggage trains got raided. He had fresh bandages on his wound, a change from the blood soaked rags from earlier. He was awake and in obvious pain. He smiled at the sight of Vitruvius when the Sergeant came walking up. Valgus reached out a hand and clasped Vitruvius' with surprising strength. There was still a lot of fight left in the Optio.

"How are you, Valgus?" Vitruvius asked.

"Given that that cursed spear missed my balls by a matter of inches, I'm doing alright," Valgus replied. He started to laugh, but then clenched his teeth as pain shot through his hip. "Damn it I should have known better." He shook his head, obviously upset with himself.

"We were in a bad spot. You did the best you could."

"And now the war is over for me," Valgus replied. "Hell, my whole damn career is over, even if I do survive this." Tears of frustration were starting to show in his eyes.

"Would you rather we had left you to drown in the marsh back there?" the Sergeant asked. "Vitruvia would have killed me!" Vitruvius was referring to his sister, whom Valgus had grown close to over the last couple of years, to the point where she now lived in the small community outside the fortress in order to be with him. He had intended to make their union official once he had either risen to Centurion or retired. Valgus smiled at the mention of the woman he loved. He would stay alive, if only to see her again.

"Just do me a favor," he said. "Don't get overrun tomorrow. If I plan on seeing Vitruvia again, I can't very well do it if you guys get wiped out."

Vitruvius smiled. "You got it. Just don't go getting gangrene and dying on us either then!" Both men laughed, though there was no mirth in it.

As Vitruvius left the hospital area, he wondered whether or not they would get overrun on the morrow. He felt like a rat trapped in a cage. For the first time in many years, the invincible Sergeant was afraid.

*   *   *   *

The warriors tore through the Roman supply wagons, each man trying to carry off as much plunder as he could. Arminius looked on amused at the spectacle. He then turned to the council of war chiefs that he had summoned. There were many of them, all gathered around in a circle, awaiting the orders from their supreme commander. Many were older than Arminius, and these bore the scars of previous campaigns against the Romans; campaigns that before Arminius had been fought with little to no success.

"Friends, brother warriors," he began. "As you can see once again we have the Roman Army on the run. They have walked into our trap, and will soon be at our mercy. As soon as they move out from their camp we will hunt them down and destroy them."

"Why should we wait for them to leave their camp?" Ingiomerus asked. "They are already within our trap. If we attack now, there is little chance of any of them escaping. Brother warriors, we have already won this battle! Let us strike now and take what plunder there is to be had while it is all in one place!" Many of the war chiefs nodded and muttered in agreement. Arminius turned to his uncle.

"The Romans are headed back to winter quarters; it is unlikely that they will stay in their fort for very long. It would be better if we ambushed them in route rather than attack a fortified position."

"We do not fear death, nor do we fear the Romans any longer," one of the war chiefs said, standing up. "An attack on their fort will show that they can neither run nor hide from us!" All the war chiefs were now standing and chanting for an attack on the Roman fort. Arminius was troubled. Yes, the Romans were reeling from the skirmishes of that day, along with the loss of their baggage trains. He also knew that they were far from beaten. A direct assault on a fort containing four Legions would be suicidal. Many would perish for sure. He looked at the faces of his brother war chiefs. These men were brave, but they were also reckless.

He also realized that they were determined to go through with the attack. He would have no choice but to relent.

"Very well," he said. "We shall attack the Roman fort tomorrow at first light. Tonight we celebrate our pending victory. There shall be much in the way of celebration and the beating of war drums. Let us deny the Romans any sleep, and let their last night on this earth be spent cowering in fear!" The war chiefs all shouted in exultation and waived their weapons in the air.

"A word, Uncle," Arminius said as he and Ingiomerus walked away from the jubilant crowd. "By the gods, have you lost control of your senses? Do you realize that by your actions you have sent a large number of these warriors to their deaths? This war does not end with this action. If our losses are heavy tomorrow, then we will be hard pressed to continue in this campaign."

"You still continue to deny these brave men the fruits of their labors," Ingiomerus replied. "These hit and run tactics of yours, while affective, are causing you to lose credibility amongst the other war chiefs. There have been mutterings amongst many of them that you have lost your warrior spirit and that you have lost your will to fight. These men need a real battle."

Arminius looked his uncle in the eye. "Then you shall lead them tomorrow. Let the glory and honor be yours," with that he walked away.

*   *   *   *

Artorius stood on top of the wall, staring at all of the campfires in the distance. Suddenly he was cold, and he wrapped his cloak around him. He did not really mind being on sentry duty, since sleep would be impossible to come by on this night. The drums and war chants could be heard clearly. He wondered what it was exactly that they were saying.

"How many do you think there are?" he asked Magnus.

"I don't know. A lot more of them then there are of us, I'm certain."

"I just hope Severus has a plan to get us out of this. To be honest I've been wondering if this is how Varus' men felt, when they knew they were cut off and surrounded."

"Yes, but they didn't have Severus leading them," Magnus said. They looked back to see Scorpion crews unpacking their wagons.

"About time we got some use out of them," Artorius observed, averting his gaze back to his front. The war chants were growing louder, though it did not look like the Germans were getting any closer.

"Think there's any chance of them attacking us tonight?" Magnus asked.

"I doubt it," Artorius answered. "They'll wait until daylight. These barbarians love to put on a show for all to see. Besides, even well disciplined armies have difficulty fighting at night. They would all get lost and probably end up killing each other." Magnus laughed quietly at the last remark. Praxus and Decimus came walking over to their position. Though they were not on duty, it seemed that curiosity had gotten the best of them.

"I wish those guys would shut up already," Decimus bickered.

"Yeah, it's not like we don't know they're here," Praxus added. He surveyed the vast numbers of campfires and torches in the distance. He whistled softly as he took it all in.

"By the gods, there are a lot of them."

"Well, there will be a lot fewer after tomorrow," Decimus retorted, smirking. The others looked at him in curiosity.

"Know something we don't?" Magnus asked with his eyebrows raised.

"Oh yes," Decimus replied. "I overheard that Severus has a plan to trap the bastards tomorrow. The reason why we are prohibited from making fire and any kind of noise is because that is part of the bait."

"Lure them in, thinking we are docile and ready for the slaughter and them hit them with everything we have," Artorius observed, gazing into the lights in the distance.

"Well I hope dawn comes soon, because I'd just as soon get it over with," Magnus replied as he yawned and stretched. "Not that we'll be able to get any sleep tonight as it is."

Just then they heard a great commotion as dozens of men made a mad dash to the main gate. They were in an utter panic, and some could be heard shouting that the barbarians had breached the wall and that they had been overrun.

"What the hell is wrong with those guys?" Magnus asked, extremely irritated. "We haven't been overrun!"

"Well something sure as hell has spooked them," Artorius observed. As the frightened Soldiers closed on the main gate, Severus could be seen running from the other direction and diving onto his stomach in front of the mob.

"Surely none of you will trample over your commander!" they heard him shout. The mass of men stopped in their tracks. Even their overwhelming fear would not allow them to commit such a travesty. As everyone waited to see what would happen next, a voice could be heard shouting, "It's just a damn horse that got loose!" At that moment, a Centurion ran in between the Soldiers and their commander. He was in a rage and was swinging his vine stick violently.

"*What the hell is this?* You bloody cowards run from a *horse?* By the gods, I'll give you something to be afraid of!" A wave of profanity spewed forth from his mouth as he beat and chastised those unfortunate enough to in range of his blows. The Soldiers who had fled started running back to their camps, ashamed and humiliated by their conduct. Severus had gotten to his feet and caught up to the enraged Centurion. He grabbed the man by the shoulder before he could pursue the fleeing Legionaries. The men exchanged a few words, and the Centurion seemed to have calmed down some. He gave Severus an affirmative nod as the Legate gave him a good-natured smack on the shoulder and walked back to his tent.

"Well there's something you don't see every day," Magnus observed. Artorius snorted at the remark.

I just hope those guys don't up and panic tomorrow when we do have a real fight on our hands," he replied, irritated.

CHAPTER 13

▼

THE TRAP IS SPRUNG

Dawn finally came. As it did, Severus called a meeting of all of the senior officers in each Legion. All Cohort Commanders were present. He sat mounted on his horse as he gazed into the faces of his men. He saw weariness in their eyes from lack of sleep, but also a fierce determination. The embarrassing events of the night before were forgotten. Severus swore that he would never mention it in front of his men, especially when at that moment they needed inspiration.

"Today the hordes of our enemy Arminius will try and do to us what they did to Varus. However, we will not share their fate. I predict that the Germans will figure us to be beaten and cowering in fear. I look at you, and I look at your men. I see no cowards here. I see men ready to face the barbarians, and ready to send those bastards straight to Hades' door!

"Each Legion will take a side of the perimeter. We will offer only token resistance from our archers, allowing them to think that they do in fact have us beaten. Once they close on the wall, we will withdraw our archers. Each Legion will have Cohorts designated for assault and javelin throwers. As the barbarians come over the walls, we will hammer them with as many javelin volleys as we can. Scorpions will be placed directly behind each gate. Once the barbarians have been beaten back from the walls, the assaulting elements will open the gates, fire two volleys from the Scorpions, and attack. Our best equestrians will lead the attack, which they will execute in wedge formation, breaking the German ranks and allowing the infantry time to form up. All officers are hereby ordered to give their horses to the equestrian ranks. To show that I myself will not flee from the battle should things go wrong, I will be the first to hand over my horse." With that he dismounted and handed the reigns of his horse to a waiting Soldier.

"Whatever happens today, I will share your fate."

*   *   *   *

Ingiomerus stood at the head of the hoard. All were tensed with anticipation. The Roman fort seemed small and insignificant compared to the sheer might of his warriors. He looked over at the mass of men that he commanded. Most carried wicker or wooden shields with spears or clubs as their primary weapons. Only a few of the more wealthy, like him, carried swords. His was a two-handed broadsword. It was heavy, which he hoped would help him crack through the Roman shields and armor. While his warriors were not as well equipped as their enemy, they were brave and would not waiver.

The Romans, on the other hand, were already beaten. There was not a sound coming from their camp. It was as if it were already a tomb. Their hastily thrown up earthworks would do little to slow down the Cherusci and their allies. A few archers could be seen on the walls. They would be but flies to be swatted away. Ingiomerus raised his sword high and turned to address his warriors.

"The Romans, in their arrogance and recklessness have returned to the land of the Cherusci! Today they will join the Legions that we vanquished six years ago! Your courage and your strength will carry you today, much plunder and glory will you reap! Destroy everything, leave no one alive!" The Cherusci erupted into a series of battle cries as they beat their weapons against their shields in a frenzy of berserker rage. Ingiomerus turned back towards the fort, and with a cry of his own started to run. He was older than most of the other warriors and was therefore slowed down. It mattered not. Though many of his warriors surged past him, his purpose had been served. He had rallied the Cherusci and whipped them into frenzy. They would surge over the walls of the Roman fort, and annihilate their presence once and for all.

Arminius sat on his horse, watching from the wood lines on the ridge well behind the mass of warriors that were now rushing towards the fort at a dead run. "And so Uncle, how many will perish today because of your recklessness?"

*   *   *   *

Artorius stood waiting with anticipation. The Twentieth Legion occupied the west wall of the fort and the Third Cohort had been designated to be part of the assault element. They had been directed to give their javelins to the Soldiers behind the ramparts. With the sheer number of barbarians attacking the fort, they would need all the javelins they could get. Artorius could hear the beating of drums and the chants of the barbarians. They were getting close. He fumbled with the pommel of his gladius.

The cavalry was formed up to their direct front, with a dozen scorpions lined up in front of them, about thirty feet from the gate. Pilate and Dionysus were pacing back and forth behind their machines, which were loaded and ready to fire.

The sound of the approaching hordes grew even louder. Artorius tried to visualize in his mind the site of their sheer numbers, waves of men, coming at them like a tide, a tide that would soon break on the rocks of their shields and swords.

"Archers...draw!" He looked over to see the archers pull back on their bowstrings. On command, they all loosed their arrows.

What a site it must be from their vantage point! He thought. Twice more they unleashed their arrows. Artorius wondered how many barbarians had fallen already. It was impossible to know. The noise of their attack was becoming deafening.

"Archers, fall back!" The command was given as throwing spears and the occasional arrow started to fly from the German ranks. The archers quickly dismounted the rampart and fell back to their supplementary positions behind the infantry. Several were not fast enough and were felled by the German missiles. Artorius watched as one poor fellow fell off the wall with a spear running clean through his back and coming out of his chest. The shouts of the barbarians were almost deafening. He could hear the loud clambering as they stumbled through the ditches and scrambled up and over the rampart.

"Javelins ready!" He heard the command echoed from the Cohorts behind the wall. The Legionaries gave a loud shout as they hefted their javelins. It was the first audible sound they had made since coming to the fort. As the Germans came over the rampart, many froze in their tracks at what they saw. Instead of being cowed and frightened, ready for the slaughter, here was an entire army ready to fight. The warriors were suddenly struck with fear as they looked at the wall of armored Soldiers, all with javelins ready to unleash. A general panic ensued as the warriors in the back pushed the ones up front forward to their doom.

"*Front rank...throw!*" The first volley flew straight into the swarm of barbarians on the wall. They were so densely packed together that it was impossible for any of the javelin throwers to miss. Jubilant battle cries were replaced by screams of agony and terror as the first mass of warriors fell skewered on the Roman javelins.

"*Second rank...throw!*" Another volley flew home, killing or maiming another wave of barbarians.

"*Third rank...throw!*"
"*Fourth rank...throw!*"
"*Fifth rank...throw!*"
"*Sixth rank...throw!*"

As each successive wave of barbarians pushed their way to the front, a volley of javelins quickly cut them down. Bodies started to pile up on the wall, many of the stricken falling off the wall and into heaps on the ground. Seeing the fate of their fellows, the warriors on the wall tried to force their way back through the waves following behind them. Those attempting to smash through the gate were equally confused and dismayed by the repulse of the warriors on the wall. They were completely shocked when suddenly the gates were thrown open.

*   *   *   *

Ingiomerus could not see what was happening in front of him. The shouts and cries of his warriors sounded different. No longer did they sound confident and assured of victory. Instead they sounded frightened and shocked. There were cries of pain and anguish as well. As he closed on the rampart, he stumbled into the ditch the Romans always dug around their fortifications. He watched as his warriors continued to surge forward, yet there was definitely something wrong. They seemed to be stalled on the rampart itself. He began to see some fall from the wall, having been stricken by Roman javelins.

"What is happening in there?" he asked himself as he climbed out of the ditch. As he started up the wall, he was knocked down when a body of a warrior fell on top of him. The man was still alive, though he was ran through the stomach with a javelin. He clawed at the javelin as bile and blood seeped from the wound. Blood erupted from his mouth as he tried to cry out in pain. Ingiomerus was filled with rage. He could not believe that the Romans were mounting any kind of resistance. It did not seem possible. He *had* to get to the top! He pushed the dying man off of him and started to scramble up the slope. He watched horrified as an entire waive of men were suddenly cut down by a volley of javelins, not ten feet in front of him. Most fell forward into the fort; others collapsed onto the wall or fell back down the slope.

"No!" he cried as he saw his warriors starting to waiver. It seemed like every time a group reached the top, they were immediately slaughtered. With a cry of rage, he raised his sword and surged to the top. As he gazed over the rampart, the sight was unbelievable. The Romans were anything but beaten. They were formed up in six ranks, all bearing javelins, all looking for a fight. He watched in horror as an entire rank threw their javelins as one. Unable to move, he watched as a javelin came right at him. Suddenly he felt a stabbing pain in his side as his flesh was pierced. Warriors fell all around him. He dropped his sword and grabbed the javelin, knowing that if it were allowed to bend, his side would be torn open. Suddenly he lost his footing and fell down the slope.

The javelin had not gone completely through. Knowing that it would make the wound worse, but not knowing what else to do, he tore it from him. Ingiomerus howled in pain as his side was torn asunder. Before he could do anything else, another slain warrior collapsed on top of him, pinning him to the ground. Helpless, he watched as the nearby gates were flung open.

$$*\qquad*\qquad*\qquad*$$

"Scorpions fire!" Pilate shouted. Twelve Scorpions fired as one, their bolts slamming home into their hapless victims. *"Reload!"* With rapid precision, the crews quickly wound the cranks on their weapons and loaded bolts into the feed groves.

"Fire!" Pilate ordered as soon as he saw that all weapons were reloaded. The barbarian charge was already broken, this next wave of Scorpion bolts only emphasizing the point. *"Cease fire!"*

"Cavalry...advance!" Master Centurion Flavius called out. The cavalry moved at a gallop, immediately falling into a wedge formation once they had cleared the gate. They crashed into the barbarian ranks, slashing and stabbing with their swords, trampling many underneath the hooves of their horses.

"Gladius...draw!" Centurion Macro shouted. As one, swords were drawn from their scabbards, Legionaries giving a loud shout as they did so.

"Infantry...advance!" The Master Centurion ordered. The infantry ran out the gate, keeping together, Centurions and Optios ensuring that formations stayed intact. Once through the gate the Cohorts formed up on line, three ranks deep. Artorius gasped at what he saw. There were literally thousands of barbarian war-

riors in front of him, no more than a few dozen meters away. He saw volleys of arrows come sailing from the walls of the fort as the archers reoccupied the ramparts. The arrows impacted deep within the German ranks, making it impossible to see the full effect they were having.

The cavalry had created a large enough gap to allow the infantry room to maneuver and form up online. They had left many German bodies in their wake. A small number of cavalrymen had been slain as well, their bodies bludgeoned and mutilated by the barbarians. The cavalry then peeled off in each direction, riding in file around the infantry and forming up behind them. Though the barbarian numbers were massive, their spirit to fight seemed to be broken. There was mass confusion, as they did not know whether to retire or to attack. The Romans made the decision for them.

"At the double-time…march!" Cohort Commanders echoed. Within seconds, they had closed with the barbarian ranks. The Second Century was in the first rank, along with the First Century. With drilled precision, shield bosses slammed into barbarian warriors, followed by rapid stabs with the gladius.

Artorius first faced an incredibly tall barbarian. The man was too tall for Artorius to smash in the face, so he settled for slamming his shield boss into the barbarian's stomach. He was surprised that the ferocity of his attack actually knocked the giant down. He quickly stepped in and thrust his gladius underneath the German's jaw, the point of the blade exciting just beneath the skull in the back. His stab and withdrawal was so rapid that he managed to get his blade free before the gushing blood could stain the pommel of his sword or his hand. He stepped back and quickly looked to his left and right. Decimus and Magnus were both engaged. However, they seemed to have a handle on the situation as their opponents were quickly cut down.

Artorius then focused on his front, awaiting the next challenger. He only had to wait a few seconds, as a burly barbarian with an axe came running at him. Artorius smiled. The barbarian's course of action was all too predictable. Artorius instinctively dropped to one knee as the barbarian swung his axe overhead. He allowed the German to hook his shield with his axe. Once the German hauled back on his axe, he pulled his shield in with his left hand and stepped out. A quick stab to the groin and it was over. He rapidly recovered to his feet and took a step back.

*   *   *   *

Ingiomerus slowly pulled himself from underneath the corpse that had pinned him down. As soon as he was free, he gasped as he felt the pain erupt from his wound. It was a fearful mess, however it looked as if the blood had sufficiently clotted and he was no longer in danger of bleeding to death. He lay back and tried to catch his breath.

He was then suddenly aware of the battle going on outside the fort. The Roman counterattack had caught his warriors completely off guard. They were now being cut down in rapid succession as they fought to maintain some semblance of an offensive. The old warrior looked up at the rampart he had just fallen from. Roman archers had reoccupied it and were firing volleys of arrows over the heads of their infantry into the ranks of the Cherusci. So focused were they on the battle taking place out there that they were totally oblivious of his presence. Slowly he looked around to see if there was anyone else still alive amongst the heaps of corpses where he found himself. Only a handful stirred themselves in the last throes of death. The Roman javelins had been extremely accurate, and those who were not immediately killed would soon die from the fearful wounds they had suffered.

Slowly Ingiomerus crawled down the slope. He rolled into the ditch and lay there for a minute. He looked up as another volley of arrows passed in a high arc over his head. He closed his eyes, cringing at the pain and suffering these would cause. There were only small pauses between waves of arrows, just enough time for the archers to re-notch, draw and fire. He looked over the side of the ditch to see how the battle itself was faring. It did not look good. The Romans, though grievously outnumbered, were slowly pushing the Germanic hoards back. It would not be long before the battle was decided.

*   *   *   *

"Set for passage-of-lines!" Centurion Proculus shouted. Macro and the Optios quickly echoed the command. All Soldiers in the front rank stopped in place, keeping their shields at the defensive. Soldiers in the second rank set into their fighting stances, ready to spring. The barbarians actually paused in their attack, morbidly fascinated by the precision drill that the Romans were about to execute. They stood frozen, as if waiting for the next wave of doom to approach.

"Execute passage-of-lines!" On command, the second rank lunged forward together, passing in between the Soldiers in the front rank. Artorius watched as two Legionaries passed on either side of him, slamming their shields home, following up with rapid stabs with their swords. Immediately they checked for any friendly dead or wounded and proceeded to pass back through the Soldiers in the third rank.

Everybody caught their collective breath as they formed up at the rear of the Cohort. Remarkably, nobody had been killed or injured in the exchange. They advanced slowly, watching the melee continue to unfold in front of them. Within minutes, as the Cohort executed its next passage-of-lines, the barbarian ranks completely broke. There was no order to be had. They panicked and started to run, the Romans in pursuit. Cornicens sounded the charge. On cue the cavalry rode past them, intent on cutting off and slaughtering as many barbarians as they could.

The Romans chased the barbarians for some time. As defeated warriors stumbled or fell behind, they met their fate quickly as the Legionaries slew them. A number became trapped between the Legions and the river. Chief Tribune Strabo, who had led the cavalry attack, watched as many jumped into the rushing current to try to swim away. A wall of shields quickly smashed those that hesitated, as the Legions stormed forward. It did not take long for them to finish the job.

"Archers, javelins forward!" He shouted. Within minutes, the javelin throwers and archers were online, facing the river. It became something of a sport to them as they loosed their weapons on the helpless barbarians, trying to swim to safety. Arrows and javelins cut down most of the warriors, who did not drown in the current. Strabo smiled gleefully at the sight. He turned to his left and watched in the distance as the remaining hordes disappeared amongst the woods on the horizon. Though many had perished, in reality the majority had survived to fight another day. The barbarians had been dealt a vicious defeat, but he knew the war was far from over. It was getting late, and the army needed to reform back at the fort soon.

"Sound recall," he told the Cornicen mounted next to him. The young man raised his horn and sounded the notes that signaled the army was to return to the fort.

Horns echoed the commands and soon the Legion was marching back towards the fort. All were exhausted from not having slept the night before, then having to fight a battle all day. In spite of this, all marched with a sense of energy and purpose. Artorius relished the extreme adrenaline rush that he felt. It was an almost euphoric feeling. He observed the landscape, which was strewn with bodies. There were many Germans stricken with severe wounds, who were trying to crawl away. Occasionally a Legionary would step off and finish one with a rapid thrust of his sword. This in turn would bring a severe chastising from their Centurions, who would then tell them to, "Let the bastards suffer and rot!"

After they reached the fort, all Cohorts held immediate formations to determine any losses and to account for any wounded. The counterattack was executed with complete surprise and precision, to the point that casualties were remarkably light. Six Soldiers in the entire Cohort had been wounded, none of them seriously, and none coming from the Second Century. This only added to Artorius' feelings of euphoria. It was as if a huge weight had been lifted off his shoulders. The continuous disasters, combined with the enemy's refusal to engage them in open battle had done much to rupture their spirits. The enemy had fallen completely into their trap and had left thousands dead as a result. Artorius prided himself that he had killed three, two during the battle and one more during the pursuit.

"I saw that little fancy move you pulled on the barbarian with the axe today," Statorius said to him after Proculus had dismissed the formation. Artorius thought his Sergeant was going to chastise him for his unorthodox way of fighting, but he saw that Statorius was smiling. "It takes most Legionaries years of drill, practice, and actual fighting to learn to fight with the speed and precision you possess," he continued. "Obviously your little sparing sessions with Vitruvius are paying off."

Artorius smirked at the remark and shook his head. "Sergeant, he thrashes the shit out of me every time I face him."

"Well obviously he's taught you *something*," Statorius countered. "You have a lot of potential, Artorius. I see you going places within the Legion. I may have a few things to add to your development once we get back to winter quarters." With that, he slapped Artorius on the shoulder and then walked back to their section's campsite, devoid as it still was of a tent.

That night, wrapped only in his cloak and using his pack as a pillow, Artorius slept a deeper sleep than he had since the campaign began. He dreamed of home, of his father, Juliana, and Camilla. He dreamed of his mother and his brother. Something inside his soul told him that he was finally bringing them justice, one battle at a time.

The young Legionaries were not the only ones ecstatic about their victory that day. Severus was quite exuberant as he addressed his Legates and other senior officers.

"Men," he said, "today we have dealt the enemy a horrific blow. They thought they could finish us in the same manner that they had finished Varus. There were no sacrifices to their foul gods today, no Legionaries were tortured or mutilated. The few we did lose died valiantly, fighting as Romans! Mark well the deeds of your men. I will want full details on those you wish to recognize individually for their acts of valor, once we return to the fortress. I only wish I had wine to offer you, but sadly, our stores were taken yesterday during our debacle across the bridges." The Legate and senior officers of the Fifth and Twenty-First Legions looked down, embarrassed.

"In spite of our victory," Severus continued, "I want everyone to be warned. Though we dealt the enemy a nasty defeat, they are far from destroyed. Their losses, while extremely heavy, were not catastrophic. The Cherusci are still a viable threat, and the war is still far from over. I want everyone to maintain vigilance and security on the remaining march. Let us not allow our men to fall into lethargic carelessness, thereby spoiling our victory."

*　　*　　*　　*

Ingiomerus held a blood soaked rag to his side as he sat by the fire. Though his wound had bled profusely and he was in extreme pain, it would not be mortal if he could keep an infection from setting in. He had slunk away during a lull in the fighting, while the majority of the Romans had been in pursuit of his fleeing army. By the gods, the Romans thrashed them! In spite of his sheer hatred for all things Roman, he almost had to respect them for the way they had fought that day. Not one of his warriors had managed to get over the wall without a javelin striking him down. The subsequent battle had been completely one-sided. His warriors had lost their nerve when they saw their companions routed on the walls. Other warriors sat around his fire, many of them bearing wounds from the day. They were discussing the events of the battle. Arminius sat in the background, his arms folded across his knees, and watched in silence.

"The Romans were waiting for us. We never had a chance," a warrior named Ietano said.

"No," Ingiomerus countered, "we lost our nerve. Had we maintained the attack, we could still have easily overwhelmed the Romans. Simply put, our warriors lost their nerve at the first sign of difficulty. It will not happen again."

"You saw the carnage they inflicted," Ietano said. "These men are nothing like the ones we smashed in Teutoburger. When cornered, these lash out like demons."

"You are a coward, Ietano!" another warrior named Haraxus said. "You, who are devoid of any wounds from the day, were probably one of the first to run!"

"That's a lie!" Ietano shouted, rising to his feet.

Haraxus scoffed. "Is it? Ingiomerus is right. Had we maintained our attack, we would have smashed the Romans into dust!" Other warriors started to voice their consent. "We will regroup and destroy the Romans before they can retire across the Rhine!"

"We will do no such thing," Arminius finally spoke. "We will regroup, we will reform, and we will destroy the Romans, but not today. They are fresh from their victory; oh yes, theirs was a decisive victory today; and any attacks made by us will be met with renewed vigor. No, we will retire to winter quarters ourselves. We will reform our armies into one. We will only fight the Romans once we have the decisive advantage. And I will not be second guessed again." He stared at his uncle, coldly.

▼

CHAPTER 14

WINTER QUARTERS

Fortress of the Twentieth Legion, Rhine Frontier
October A.D. 15

As the Legionaries grounded all of their gear in their barracks room, Artorius noticed a number of letters and parcels on everyone's bunks.

"Ah, I see the post has finally caught up to us," Decimus said wryly. "Time to catch up on the last six months of gossip and news from back home."

"*After* you've cleaned and inspected all of your gear, Trooper," Statorius replied.

Once Artorius had packed away the last of his equipment, he sat on his bunk and looked at the letters he had received. There were three of them; two were from his father, the other from Camilla. It was dated from three months before. He quickly tore this one open and started to read.

My dear, sweet Artorius,

I am sorry that it has been so long since I last wrote to you. My life has been an absolute whirlwind of activity, that I have not had time. I hope that you will not be upset, but will be happy for me when I tell you that I got married recently! His name is Marcellus; he is the son of a local magistrate, and we live very well. He is a nice man, though to be honest I find it difficult to love him. I married him more for the social advancement and the need to marry, rather than love.

I still think of you with much affection, Artorius. Though another man may be my husband, you will always be my lover. Please continue to write to me. I still worry about you, and care for you deeply. Yours affectionately,

Camilla

It was Thursday. Artorius stood face to face against Vitruvius. Gradually he was starting to last longer in his sparring sessions against the Chief Weapons Instructor. The result was always the same, though. Perhaps today would be different. Vitruvius *had* to have some weak point. No man was invulnerable, though you could try telling that to Vitruvius. During their last battle against the Cherusci, he had personally killed eight enemy warriors, and once again had come away without a scratch. Artorius wondered just how many people Vitruvius had killed in his lifetime.

"Ready to do this?" Vitruvius asked.

"Yeah, let's do it," Artorius answered as he hefted his practice shield and gladius. Both men came at each other quickly, punching with their shields, looking for openings to strike what with service weapons would be a fatal blow. Vitruvius stabbed towards Artorius' flank, the young Legionary quickly swinging his shield arm in a backhand swing. Vitruvius immediately lunged forward, punching with his shield. Artorius swung his shield back around, hooking the Sergeant's shield on the inside. As Vitruvius pulled back on his shield, Artorius lunged forward, punching the Sergeant with his shield. Vitruvius stumbled back. Artorius was suddenly ecstatic. He had found a weak point. He lunged forward, stabbing with his gladius. As he did so, Vitruvius rocked forward onto the balls of his feet and brought his own sword down in a hard slash onto Artorius' forearm. Artorius yelped in surprise and pain, dropping his gladius. Vitruvius then ducked down and brought his sword back in a quick stab to the sternum. Artorius dropped to his knees, the wind knocked out of him. So much for having found Vitruvius' weakness!

"You're improving, slowly but surely," Vitruvius said. Artorius could only gasp, clutching beneath his chest. Vitruvius smiled and helped him to his feet. "I daresay you'd be a match against any Soldier within the entire Third Cohort!"

"Anyone except you," Artorius said between gasps. There was a bit of frustration in his voice. He had been sparring with Vitruvius for months now. Granted he had learned many things from the Chief Weapons Instructor, however he thought that by now he would have beaten the Sergeant at least once.

Vitruvius patted him on the shoulder and started to walk towards the door. "See you next week," he said as he left.

Once he had fully gotten his breath back, Artorius stowed his training shield and gladius and walked out of the training hall. It was a cold but sunny day. There was just a trace of snow on the ground. Damn, but he hated the cold! He failed to see how anyone could stand to live in such a frigid, damp environment. He was sweaty from his exertions, and this combined with the cold air made him tremble badly. He needed to dry off and warm up or he would surely catch a chill. After a short stint in the bathhouse, he headed back to the Second Century's barracks.

As he walked into the main hall, he saw Statorius and the rest of their section looking at a large piece of parchment on a table. He recognized the Soldiers from Sergeant Vitruvius' section as well, though the Sergeant himself was not present. Flaccus was pointing things out to them on the parchment and answering questions.

"Artorius, back from your weekly thrashings I see," Statorius remarked. "Come here and take a look at this." Artorius walked up to the table. On the parchment there looked to be plans and building diagrams.

"What is this?" He asked.

"This is something you will become very efficient at building over the next couple of months," Flaccus said with a smile. "These are plans for costal barges. Each can carry approximately twenty men. The army has orders to build a thousand of these by the time we start our next campaign."

"Meaning our next campaign will involve an amphibious assault," Artorius observed.

"Correct," Flaccus replied.

"And since approximately twenty men can fit onto one of these, every two sections in each Century gets to build one," Statorius said.

"Top that off with the privilege you get of riding all the way into the heart of Germania with me," Vitruvius said as he walked in the door.

"Nice of you to join us," Flaccus said dryly. "Now as you can see these things are not that difficult to construct. There will be a massive amount of supplies needed to construct a thousand of them. We have ample timber available; it will be just a matter of collecting enough to start construction. In addition, in order to protect our building site, a wall will be constructed on either side of the fortress leading to the river. Yes, this will mean extra work details along with extra sentry duty. Right now, the Eighth and Ninth Cohorts have been tasked with building the walls while we start work on our barges. You can bet that once we get finished with our boats, we'll be the ones guarding the outer walls while they finish theirs."

The afternoon was spent foraging lumber from the nearby forests. In spite of the cold, Artorius felt good, the exertion from swinging the axe and felling trees keeping him warm. Once each tree was cut down, they stripped it of its branches and bark, tied towing ropes to it and dragged it back to the construction site down by the river. Soldiers from other Cohorts were providing security and building the rampart extensions. Positions were laid out along the river, with mooring locations marked for every each Cohort's barges. Since it would be impossible to have every single barge moored along the river, each Cohort built theirs leading back towards the fortress. When time came to launch, each crew would have to tow their barge to the river. Artorius and his section found the site allocated for their barge.

That night Artorius sat at a small table in the main hall. He had a small oil lamp and some parchment. On it, he wrote:

My Dearest Father,

It has been a while since I was last able to write to you. I am doing fine. The only thing that troubles me is that you did not tell me that Camilla had married. To be honest, I'm not surprised. Though I will always have fond memories of her, she was and still is little more than a girl. She saw the need rather than the desire to marry, and in her mind I was not worth waiting for. I have decided not to write back to her. Congratulate her for me, if you would, then allow me to become nothing more than a memory to her.

We are established in winter quarters, preparing for the spring campaign. We keep hearing that this will be the last campaign of this war, that by whatever means necessary it will end with this. Currently we are building a massive fleet of boats and barges that will take us deep into enemy territory. I look forward to ending this conflict. The barbarians paid a heavy toll during our last campaign; hopefully this next one will finish things.

I am proud of the men I am serving with. Magnus, the Legionary I told you that I came up through recruit training with, has been as good of a friend as any could expect. He is strong and a good fighter. Sergeant Statorius is a competent section leader, and I am glad to be working with him. Centurion Macro is still a bit of a mystery. I do know that he is a survivor of the Teutoburger disaster. Given my position, I rarely have direct contact with him. One individual that I have had a lot of contact with is Sergeant Vitruvius, our Chief Weapons Instructor. I have been sparring with him weekly, and he has taught me a lot, including how to take a good thrashing! He says I have a lot of potential, and Sergeant Statorius has even said that I have already demonstrated a lot more skill in close combat than many in the Legion.

During our last campaign, we journeyed into Teutoburger Wald. I curse that bastard Varus for leading his men into that gods' forsaken place! It was an absolute nightmare just trying to get to the place of their final battle. I met a Centurion Pilus Prior named Calvinus. You may recognize his name. He was Metellus' Centurion. He told me the story of how Metellus died, that he died fighting like a Roman! You would have been proud of him, Father. He saved the lives of several of his companions before he was killed. Calvinus took me to the spot where they had made their last stand. Though there was little left of the bodies, just a few bones and skulls, I found what I am certain are the remains of Metellus. The identifying wounds, the location of the bones, all matched Calvinus' story. The greatest honor that I have had is that I was able to lay my brother to rest.

I hope you are doing well, and please give Juliana my best. With deepest affection, your son,

Titus Artorius Justus
Legionary, XX Legion Valeria

He finished writing, rolled the parchment up, and placed it into the bin where Camillus took care of all dispatches and mail and stepped outside. It was a cold and cloudless night. He walked just out from underneath the overhang and looked up at the stars. He wondered if perhaps his father were doing the same at that moment. He wondered how he was doing. Had he finally taken the next step with Juliana? He smiled at the thought. Juliana had done more to help his father than he realized. Had they not had each other, perhaps both would have followed their families to the grave.

Artorius gave a deep sigh. With the army in winter quarters, there was not as much to occupy their time with, outside of the usual training and now the building of the coastal barges. His interests lay not in gambling, unlike so many of his fellows, and he often found his mind wandering. He truly missed home, his father, Juliana, all his friends who had not joined the Legions, and the young girls whom he used to woo with his feats of strength and intellect. He then started to miss Camilla as well, but then quickly dismissed the notion. What he did miss, though was the climate! Winter in Germania was miserable to say the least. He knew that a decisive victory over Arminius and an end to the war would almost certainly mean a triumph in Rome. That would give him the opportunity to see his father again. He also longed to see the old city once more. Though his home in Ostia was very close to Rome, they rarely ventured there. He was just a boy the last time his father had taken him to the capital itself, the heart of the Empire. A cold wind brought him back to the harsh reality of where he was. He was not in Rome, he had elected to leave home and join the army, and his focus needed to be on just surviving the next season's campaign. Triumphs would wait until another day.

"The barges are coming along on schedule," Chief Tribune Strabo reported.

"Very good," Severus observed. "And how are the training regimes for the upcoming campaign coming?"

"With our casualties having been so light, we've had only a handful of recruits and replacements to train up," answered Master Centurion Flavius.

The three men sat alone in Severus' quarters. All lounged comfortably, sampling dates and nuts and sipping on wine. This was an informal meeting to say the least.

Severus sat up briefly and stretched out his lower back and neck. He was slowly starting to feel the affects that age and years of campaigning were having. Though he looked young in appearance, his body told him otherwise on a daily basis. Yet he could not allow himself to sit back and watch the battles unfold before him without his direct involvement. His habit of leading from the front was something he had picked up from campaigning with Tiberius. Though the Emperor often said that he learned to do this from Severus, the old General wasn't so sure. He took a deep breath at the thought of how many years ago that was. He hoped that this would be his last campaign. Germanicus had become a fine Commanding General and there was little more Severus could teach him. He had therefore written to the Emperor, asking that he at last be allowed to retire once Arminius was destroyed. He looked over at his two subordinate commanders.

Strabo was developing into a fine officer. His tactical decisions were usually sound, his care for the men genuine, and he was not afraid to get his hands a little bit dirty, or bloody, as was often the case. Like most Chief Tribunes, he was a young man of the senatorial class, destined to become a Legion Commander himself some day. Of course, there would be years of politicking and other less exciting, albeit necessary positions to fill along the way. Once his required time as Chief Tribune was complete, it would be years before he would wear the uniform again. Strabo was not looking forward to it and he therefore relished his time with the Legion.

Flavius was everything one would expect a Master Centurion to be. A professional Soldier with over thirty years in the army, he was hard as iron, both in body and spirit. Like all Centurions, he had come up from the ranks, slowly making the climb up the ladder of the Centurionate, until he was finally awarded promotion to the First Cohort. Five years before, he had been selected to be its Commander. In and of itself, command of the First Cohort was not difficult. All Soldiers within the First were handpicked veterans who required little to no direct supervision. Its Centurions were the elite of any Legion and were there for technical and tactical advice, along with directly leading their men in battle. The Centurion Primus Pilus or "First Spear" was the elite of this class of fighting men. He truly was a *Master* Centurion. Beneath his hard exterior, Flavius was a compassionate man, both towards his men as well as his own family. Many Soldiers within the Legion found it hard to believe that he even had a family. Yet he did in fact have an adoring wife and two grown sons, one of whom was serving with Legions in the east. His other son had taken the path of poet, historian, and philosopher. To many this seemed like an odd path for the son of a Master Centurion to take. And yet, if one were to look into his private quarters, one would find numerous copies of his son's works sitting on Flavius' desk and bookcases. He was equally proud of both of his sons, and appreciated their diverse paths in life.

The First Cohort was in many ways its own entity apart from the rest of the Legion. The Soldiers lived in oversized barracks that were separate from the other Cohorts, and their Centurions lived in actual two-story houses instead of one room barracks's. Their sole purpose was to train to fight, so aside from those tasked to supervise the armories and other shops, they had little interaction with the rest of the Legion. Flavius had therefore paid little heed to the growing troubles that had led to the mutiny two years before. The First Cohort had been performing well. From what he had gathered there were no issues concerning duty performance from the other Cohorts, so he had let things develop without any real interaction with the other Cohorts. What a fool he had thought himself when all of the allegations became known! He had considered himself directly responsible for the disaster, and had asked that he be relieved of his position and forced into retirement. Both Severus and Germanicus had vehemently denied his request. Though they acknowledged that he needed to keep a tighter reign on the Centurions in other Cohorts, he was an officer with too much tactical experience and could not be spared. Besides, his record was exemplary. Flavius had since taken a closer look into the workings of all the Centuries within the Legion, especially since young and less experienced Soldiers had filled many of the vacancies left by the cashiered former officers. He especially kept a close working relationship with the Cohort Commanders.

"Well, I'm sure you're both wanting to know what Germanicus has in mind for the next campaign; the specifics I mean," Severus said. He knew that practically the entire army had figured out that the building of boats and costal barges meant a deep waterborne strike into the heart of Germania. Barbarian scouts had seen the work going on and had probably figured this out as well.

"We are all pretty sure *what* we will be doing Sir, the only question is *where*," Strabo replied.

"I'm sure that's the question on Arminius' mind as well," Flavius said, smirking.

Severus smiled. "Our boat building operations are no secret to anyone, nor do we want them to be. I daresay that our little project will draw some of the more, shall we say *adventurous* barbarians to try to disrupt them. That is why one of our tasks will be to set up ambush sites along known avenues of approach to the docks." He grabbed a handful of nuts and downed some wine before continuing.

"The main reason for an amphibious assault is there will be little the Germans will be able to do to stop us from going wherever we please once we depart. A lengthy ground movement will only elicit ambushes and skirmishes along the way. If we move by water, they will be able to do little more than throw some harassing skirmishers and slingers our way. And we'll use Scorpions to keep them at bay. An amphibious strike deep into the heart of Germania will upset most of the tribes who have felt little of the shock of this war. Nobody will consider himself safe anymore, and Arminius will have to fight us in a major battle. Otherwise, he will be finished. He cannot afford to lose face in front of his warriors, and avoiding battle with us in the very heart of their land will cause just that. I believe Arminius is rattled after his defeat at the Ahenobarbi bridges. However, our victory was marred by the constant disasters, as well as complete communications breakdown with the Fifth and Twenty-First Legions. I myself bare full responsibility for this, and I assure you it will not happen again."

"So where exactly are we going Sir?" Strabo asked.

"That I don't know," Severus answered. "I'm certain we will find out soon enough. Germanicus is scheduled to arrive here in the next couple of weeks to check on us and our progress. He has told me that he will divulge his entire plan then."

Just then there was a knock at the door and a sentry stepped in. "Excuse me Sir, but Commander Flavus from the auxiliary corps is here to see you."

"Ah, very good! Send him in," Severus answered, standing up. A big German was ushered in. He was wearing a leather cuirass, and he carried a Legionary helmet under his arm. While most barbarian auxiliaries maintained their traditional standards of grooming, Flavus kept his hair cropped short and was clean-shaven. A patch covered his left eye, where a hideous scar ran from his eye to his ear.

"Who is this guy?" Strabo whispered to Flavius.

"Arminius' brother," Flavius replied. Strabo looked at him horrified. Flavius just smiled.

"Don't worry," the Master Centurion consoled, "Flavus has repeatedly proven his loyalty to Rome, I mean *really* proven his loyalty. He is an asset that will also help us to draw out Arminius."

"Please, come and join us," Severus said, waiving Flavus to the couches. He handed him a goblet of whine.

"Thank you, I am thirsty from my ride," the German said, with only the slightest hint of an accent in his voice. He drained the goblet, unbuckled his cuirass, and set it in a corner, after which he refilled his goblet. Strabo and Flavius stood, and Flavus extended his hand to each of them.

"This is Gaius Strabo, my Chief Tribune," Severus said as Flavus took his hand. Strabo still looked puzzled and troubled. "And this is Flavius Quietus, the Master Centurion."

"A pleasure," Flavus said as they returned to their couches.

"So tell me, my friend, what news from across the Rhine do you have for us?" Severus asked.

"My brother is definitely under a lot of pressure, and it is getting to him. The war chiefs are united in the opinion that Arminius is growing soft and needs to exercise some decisive authority quickly, or else he may be replaced. Our uncle, Ingiomerus is at the lead of this. He himself does not want to be Supreme War Chief, though. He simply wants to watch Arminius smash us into dust like he did Varus."

"You say *us* but is this not your own family we are fighting?" Strabo asked.

"Arminius may be my brother, but he has betrayed me, just as he betrayed you. We both swore an oath to serve Rome. I valued my oath, he did not. He has brought my former tribe nothing but misery and despair. They talk of glory and fame to be had in battle, yet there is nothing tangible in this. Rome has been good to me, *very* good in fact." He took a pull off his wine. "I have a home. My family is safe and well taken care of. My children have a future. The children of Arminius will have no future."

"That's not entirely true," Severus said.

"What do you mean?" Flavus asked.

"As you know, Segestes, your brother's father-in-law, has also remained loyal to Rome. So loyal in fact that Arminius laid siege to his lands. Segestes asked for our help. Germanicus did not have the forces necessary to save his lands; however he managed to liberate both Segestes as well as his daughter, who is pregnant with Arminius' child."

"Where are they now?" Flavus asked, obviously excited by the news.

"On their way here," Severus answered. "They should be here within a couple of weeks. Afterwards they will journey back to Rome. At least one of Arminius' children will have a future, a future devoid of any knowledge of who his father was. And if simply his prestige as a war chief is not enough to convince Arminius to fight us, the fact that we have his wife and unborn child should."

Flavus smiled, stood up, and raised his wine goblet. "My friends, to the future of all children who grow up free of the influence of Arminius and his kind!"

"I thought you were their kind," Strabo muttered under his breath as he took a swallow of wine.

"Easy there, Tribune," Flavius said, laughing as he took a drink off his own goblet.

CHAPTER 15

▼

AMBUSHING THE RAIDERS

The Century was on ambush duty that night. Artorius dreaded the task, simply because it was cold enough when they were moving about during the daytime. Having to sit in one spot all night was tedious and miserable. They had pulled three ambushes already and had failed to come into contact. Centurion Dominus and the Fourth Century would be with them that night. Artorius stepped into his cold weather leggings, cringing at the idea of spending all night lying in the cold snow.

"Alright, let's go!" Flaccus said, sticking his head in the door. He was walking down to all the section rooms, getting everyone to expedite their move. Quickly everyone was outside, the Second and Fourth Centuries ready to move out. It was already dark by the time they left the fortress. Torches were completely forbidden, so their pace moved at an absolute crawl. The ground was covered in hard packed snow, and it crunched between the Soldiers' feet. It was a cloudy night, and there was no illumination with which to see. After what felt like a couple of hours, though in reality it had been much less, they arrived at their assigned position. Artorius had no idea how Macro knew where to go. Each Century formed up on line on either side of the road. There was a small embankment on the one side where the Fourth Century was, and a grove of trees where the Second Century was placed. The Second Century carried their javelins, which they would use to drive the enemy towards the Fourth Century who would attack them from behind. Cavalry were in a reserve location, waiting to cut off any escape attempts. A Cornicen had been assigned to the ambush element in order to relay the signal.

Artorius lay freezing on the ground, his shield and javelin held close. His cloak was wrapped around him, but was unfastened in case he needed to throw it off in a hurry. It seemed to do him little good anyway. He lay shivering in the snow and time seemed to practically stand still. He could just make out Magnus and Decimus on either side of him. They seemed to be fairing better in the cold, though not by much.

After what seemed like an eternity, he saw the faint glow of the predawn. It was at this time that the barbarians were thought most likely to strike. Artorius scoffed at the thought. They were still licking their wounds from the thrashing they received at Ahenobarbi! As he thought this, he saw a flicker in the distance off to his right. He thought that he must be dreaming, but then he felt a stir coming from amongst the ranks. Everyone else had seen it as well. Several more flickers could be seen moving along the path. The barbarians were coming! They would use torches to guide their way to a staging point, just before the docks would come into sight. Then they would extinguish all light and attack just as the rising sun shown in the eyes of the Roman defenders. Or so was their intent.

Artorius lay low as he saw the line of torches moving laterally towards them. It was hard to tell just how many there were, a couple of hundred maybe. Raiding parties like this relied on speed and stealth rather than numbers. He held his breath as the first barbarians passed by him, about twenty feet in front. It was difficult to see them, and he was certain that he and his companions could not be seen, though subconsciously he was convinced that he would be spotted at any moment. More raiders passed in front of him. They were fairly silent except for the occasional grunt, grumble, or curse muttered. His own breath was coming rapidly. It wouldn't be long.

"*Up! Javelins throw!*" Macro shouted. The Cornicen sounded his horn as the entire Century rose up, the stiffness and cold forgotten. Artorius let his cloak fall as he raised his javelin and threw it towards a point of light. Screams of surprise and pain were heard as the barbarians not hit by the javelin storm turned to face them. Some panicked outright and ran. As the brave charged towards Artorius and the Second Century, the Legionaries of the Fourth Century rose up silently, drew their swords, and attacked the raiders from behind. Only when they were ready to strike did they make a sound. More screams could be heard as the barbarians were slaughtered from behind by their unseen foe. As they turned to face this new threat, the Second Century attacked.

Artorius saw one German directly to his front, carrying a club and shield. The man had just turned his head to see what was happening to his friends behind him when Artorius slammed his shield boss into his face. The German was knocked to the ground, senseless. A quick stab from his gladius into the man's heart ended it. There was the now almost familiar feeling of warm blood spurting onto his hand. With his hand practically numb from the cold, the warming sensation felt good. As Artorius withdrew his gladius, the remaining Germans had panicked and run back the way they had come, dropping their torches as they did so. The sun was starting to rise and was shining in their faces. They were unable to make out the line of cavalry that was riding towards them, cutting off their escape. Only a small handful managed to escape the impending slaughter.

Artorius wiped the blade of his gladius off in the snow. His hand was still covered in warm blood, which he attempted to wash off in the snow as well. The adrenaline rush from the skirmish was starting to fade, and he was once again growing cold. He searched for his javelin and was shocked when he saw one buried directly in the eye socket of a slain warrior. He had no way of knowing whether or not it was the one he had thrown, but he wouldn't have been surprised. He had after all thrown it directly at the torchlight he had seen. Regardless, he tore the javelin loose and walked back to where he had dropped his cloak.

"Everyone alright?" Macro called down the ranks.

Artorius felt Statorius smack him across the back. "Hey Artorius, you alright?" the Sergeant asked.

"I'm fine," Artorius answered as he draped his cloak over his shoulders. Statorius walked up to all of his men, checking each in turn before reporting to the Centurion that everyone was alright. No losses had been suffered by either Century. It had been a text book ambush, and had been executed perfectly. A detail was sent to cut the throats of all the barbarians still alive. The corpses were left where they had fallen as they fell back into formation and marched back to the fortress. Artorius longed for the warmth of the bathhouse. Along with the warmth was being able to thoroughly wash the blood from his hand, which had cooled and started to dry and flake off.

Proculus was waiting for them at the gate as they marched in. The cavalry had already reported back what had happened. He clasped the hands of both Macro and Dominus. "Well done," Artorius heard him say. The Centurions all walked towards the Cohort Commanders quarters while Optios briefed the Legionaries and dismissed them. Valgus had not been replaced yet, so Flaccus was filling in temporarily.

"Sergeant Vitruvius!" he called out. Vitruvius stepped out from the formation and stood in front of the Tesserarius. After a few whispered words between the men, Flaccus turned and left. Vitruvius then faced the men.

"Well done, lads," he said. "Go get yourselves warmed up, and then check your equipment. All section leaders will report to me once all equipment has been inspected and stowed. After that, you are released for the day." This elicited a serious of shouts and cheers from the Century.

"What was that all about?" Gavius asked as the section headed towards their billets.

"I don't know," Praxus answered. "It does seem a bit odd that Flaccus would defer to Vitruvius to address the Century."

"I wonder if this means Flaccus is not to become our next Optio," Artorius wondered aloud.

Proculus handed Dominus and Macro each a goblet of warm cider. Macro clutched the goblet, allowing its warmth to penetrate his frozen hands.

"A classic text book ambush," Proculus said as he raised his goblet to his fellow Centurions. "How many of the bastards did you net?"

"We counted approximately sixty corpses in the immediate vicinity of the ambush," Macro answered as he took a seat. Dominus greedily downed his beverage and waived a servant over to refill his cup.

"The cavalry reported that an additional thirty were slain during the pursuit," Proculus added, leaning back in his own chair.

"Well that's almost half of what we estimate had been there," Dominus remarked.

"More importantly, neither of you suffered any losses," Proculus observed. "I know we took a risk in sending you out like that, especially at night and under these conditions. It was a difficult task, and you performed it well."

"I wouldn't say it was difficult," Dominus answered, "I just froze my backside off is all."

"Doubtless the barbarians will be ready for us next time," Macro remarked.

"I kind of doubt it," Proculus replied. "These roving bands lack central organization. Given the careless and haphazard nature of their attempted raids, I do not think that Arminius ordered them to cross the river to try and harangue our boat making efforts. He knows the risks, and the potential loss of life. It's just not a productive use of his resources. No, these men acted on their own, and it cost them. I highly doubt they will be back anytime soon. Besides, the ramparts leading down to the docks have been completed, so our boats are relatively safe.

Therefore, all future ambushes are cancelled." Dominus and Macro both breathed sighs of relief. Proculus smiled at their reaction. "I didn't think you guys would be too terribly disappointed. I also want you to suspend all work details for the next two days. Let your men know that they performed well, and that they deserve a couple of days off."

"That'll give them a chance to get the feeling back in their limbs," Macro observed as he tried to work some feeling back into his own hands.

"You know, if the Germans were smart, they would try and draw us out during the winter," Dominus remarked. Proculus frowned and nodded at the remark.

"Too true," he replied. "They are much better suited to this climate than we are. Even our men who've been on the frontier for a long time have never gotten used to this accursed weather. Thing is, they lack any kind of logistics system. There is no way they could keep any sizable army fed and supplied during the winter months."

"Thank the gods for that," Macro replied as he raised his glass.

"So have you chosen your new Optio?" Proculus asked, changing the subject.

"I have," Macro answered. "I have a Sergeant, who's also my Chief Weapons Instructor." Dominus started to laugh.

"You're talking about Vitruvius, aren't you?" he asked.

"He's been trying to avoid getting promoted for years," Macro continued. "Well, I'm not giving him a choice this time. He's declined promotion enough times to satisfy his vanity. I feel that it is time he started stepping up and that we take a hard look at him in the future for further promotion."

"You think he'll be ready for the Centurionate that quickly?" Proculus asked with a raised eyebrow. Macro took another drink before answering.

"I dare say, he's ready for it now," he replied. "I think once Vitruvius stops obsessing about his role as Chief Weapons Instructor he will rise through the ranks rather quickly. I daresay he may even become a Cohort Commander one day."

"Quite lofty expectations for one of your men who is still a Sergeant," Dominus remarked.

"You know Vitruvius by reputation only," Macro answered. "If you knew him as well as I do, you would not hesitate to agree."

"Well that settles it then," Proculus said, setting his cup down. "Get the orders drawn up and start putting him to work where he belongs."

"Already been done," Macro responded.

"Well I guess they won't be attempting to mess with our boats anytime soon," Magnus said as he and Artorius walked into the barracks. The bathhouse had been a blessing, and had thoroughly rejuvenated them.

"At least they won't try from that avenue of approach," Artorius replied. He sat down on his bunk, took out a cloth and some oil and started to wipe down his gladius. His armor would need some oiling as well. Too much time had been spent in the wet snow, and it would soon start to rust. Magnus was taking a hammer to his javelin, attempting to straighten out the metal tip. The rest of the men in the section either slept or were still at the bathhouse.

"How many do you think we killed today?" Magnus asked.

"I don't know. I've stopped paying too much attention to those kinds of things," Artorius replied. "What I look forward to is the decisive battle which will finally end this thing."

"If Arminius can be convinced to face us out in the open," Magnus said.

"Something tells me he will," Artorius answered. "He cannot continue to allow us to ravage his lands, while only offering token resistance. His influence will fade with his own people. No, he'll have to fight us sooner or later. I think that by us invading so deep within his territory, that it will come sooner."

*   *   *   *

Arminius sat in his chair, with his chin in his hand. He was deeply troubled, and even more deeply angered. While his siege of Segestes' lands had been carried successfully, his father-in-law himself had escaped. What was worse was that Segestes' daughter Thusnelda, Arminius own wife, had been spirited away as well. Arminius knew that Thusnelda carried his child, a child that would be raised by the Romans! It would be better if the child had been slain!

The attempted raids on the Roman docks had been for the most part unsuccessful. A couple had inflicted some loss on the Roman boat building efforts, however the raiding parties had paid a heavy toll for this. Other groups had been ambushed and destroyed before they had even reached the docks. The Romans could replace their burned ships a lot faster than he could replace dead warriors. He had ordered a stop to the raids in order to not suffer any more unnecessary loss. This of course had been met with opposition. Any time he had ordered anything less than a head on attack, the other war chiefs would voice their disapproval.

So the Romans would finish their boat building. Then what? It was obvious that they intended to strike deep into Germania and force him into a decisive engagement. The Cherusci lands for the most part had gone unmolested, but now they would no longer be safe. He would *have* to finally face the Romans and end this war once and for all. Since Teutoburger Wald, he had prayed nightly to all that he believed in that he would never have to face Tiberius on the battlefield. Now he faced another Tiberius. Germanicus had learned the lessons of his uncle well. That hateful bastard Severus, whom Tiberius had sent to aid Germanicus, was proving to be a nightmare to face as well. Though he was advanced in years, the old mentor of Tiberius had lost none of his tenacity, cunning, or sheer ruthlessness. This had been made very clear at Ahenobarbi.

Very well, if a confrontation with the Romans was inevitable, then at least he would choose the ground. He rose and nodded to the guard at the door to his chamber. The guard left and was soon accompanied back in by a host of warriors, great chiefs and influential fighters who would help Arminius in his final campaign against Rome. All looked solemn, and some more than a little anxious. Arminius knew that if he did not act decisively on this campaign, then he was in grave danger of losing all influence amongst his fellow warriors. Sadly, not one of them could tell the difference between a Valgus and a Germanicus. To them a Roman was simply a Roman. If they had been so successful in Teutoburger Wald, then why had they not been for the last few years? Arminius realized that he *had* to give them a victory.

"Friends, allies, fellow warriors," Arminius said when all had been seated, "we all know of the Roman ship building that has been going on since the end of the campaign season. They are intent on striking deep into the heart of our lands. They have a huge army with which they hope to destroy us. Therefore, if we are going to face them in battle, we will need every warrior you can muster. None must be allowed to remain back. We gamble everything on this. Everything we fought for and won in Teutoburger Wald must now be defended to the last.

"There is a place called Idistaviso, it is towards the end of the Weser River. There we will make our stand against Rome. They will be miles from home, alone and cut off from any hope of support. We, on the other hand, will have mustered every fighting man from every last tribe within our lands with which to finally exterminate the Roman presence in the west!"

A loud cheer erupted as warriors stood, shook their fists in the air, slammed the table, and clambered for the head of Germanicus. Some even called to make Arminius king of all the united tribes of Germania. When they had left, Arminius was left alone to stew over his decision. Though he had been goaded into this by practically everyone, his uncle, his fellow war chiefs, the Romans themselves, he still bore full responsibility for the outcome. All he had told them was where they would be fighting, yet they had not so much as even come up with a rudimentary plan of attack. He walked out with much on his mind.

CHAPTER 16

▼

THE NEW OPTIO

Germanicus watched concerned as Soldiers practiced launching their barges into the river. They seemed to leak excessively, and he worried about the possibility of them sinking once fully loaded.

"I wouldn't be too concerned Sir," a young Tribune at his side said. "They generally only draw a couple inches of water and then they're good."

"Tribune, are you planning on riding into Germania on one of these barges?" Germanicus asked.

"No Sir, staff officers are supposed to ride on one of the Triemanes," the Tribune answered.

"So *you* won't have to spend weeks sitting in a couple inches of water, all the while wondering if your whole ship will up and sink." Germanicus looked at the Tribune sternly. "Get as much tar and sealant as you can get your hands on, and seal up all the seams in these damn barges!"

"Right away Sir!" with that, the Tribune left in a hurry.

The tavern was packed with Soldiers, as was the norm when the Century was given leave time. The weather had started to improve. The snow was off the ground and the air had started to warm. For Artorius it actually felt good to stand outside in the open air and enjoy his wine. A young Gallic woman had been vying for his attention for some time. He was about to oblige her when he saw Vitruvius arguing with Flaccus by the corner of the tavern. He had seen Flaccus point his way a couple of times. He wondered if their argument was in regards to the rumors they had heard about Vitruvius being selected to replace Valgus as Optio. It was well known that Vitruvius did not want the position. It was also known that the higher command had been pushing Vitruvius to take a promotion so that they could groom him for the Centurionate. Whether he wanted it or not, Artorius had a feeling that Vitruvius would now be on the move up through the ranks. He was the type that would occupy the Optiate only long enough for a Centurion vacancy to come open.

While he watched the unfolding debate, of which he couldn't hear a word, he felt a touch at his elbow. The young Gallic wench was standing there, with her arm looped through his. She was a pretty thing, blonde hair flowing about her shoulders, pretty lips, and a full set of teeth. He had to laugh to himself, remembering the semi-toothless woman from the butcher's shop that had struck Valens' fancy a while back. This one looked so sweet and innocent. Ha! "But you're not so innocent, are you?" he said aloud.

"Why don't you come with me and find out?" she replied wryly. He looked back at the two Soldiers still arguing. Well, whatever it was, it really wasn't his concern, and besides there would be time to find out later. He smiled back at the young woman, placed his arm around her, and walked off into the night.

"Damn it Flaccus, you're the Tesserarius and are therefore senior. It should be *you* who replaces Valgus!" Vitruvius was obviously shaken.

"Vitruvius, you have been ducking this promotion for years," Flaccus replied calmly. "Though I may be older, and have been in the army much longer, you were a Sergeant well before me. And let us not forget that you've been offered the Optionate three times already! You need to understand there is more to being a great leader than just teaching Soldiers how to fight with a gladius and javelin. You have a way with the men, and as much as it pains me to admit this, you are a better leader than I am. For the good of the Century, you *must* take this position."

Vitruvius sighed audibly. "Then who will take over as Chief Weapons Instructor?" he asked.

"Find a replacement," Flaccus replied, looking briefly over to where Artorius had stood moments before. "Otherwise I suppose you could pull double-duty as both Optio and Chief Weapons Instructor. Either way, it doesn't matter. You know Macro's not giving you a choice this time."

"I know," Vitruvius hung his head for a second. "Alright then, for the good of the Century I will occupy both positions. Chief Weapons Instructor is an additional duty anyway. I can make time for it, until I find a suitable replacement."

"And when will that be?" Flaccus asked smiling.

"When I finally find someone in this damn army who can beat me in single combat," Vitruvius answered.

"You think too much of your abilities," Flaccus remarked, "Though not entirely without merit, I admit." Vitruvius smiled and looked away.

"All I've ever wanted was to be on the line, where the action is. This just doesn't feel right to me. After all, you and Camillus both are senior to me. I still think one of you should take the position."

"You've got to remember," Flaccus replied, "that the term 'Optio' literally means 'chosen one.' You are the one Macro chose. It could have been anybody, but he selected you. And just so you know, Camillus feels the same way I do. Accept your destiny, old friend."

∗   ∗   ∗   ∗

"Come on, Artorius! You've gone soft today!" Vitruvius said as Artorius lay on the ground, gasping from where the Sergeant had knocked the wind out of him. It had just been a bad combination of events. His night of fun with his lady friend had run late, he was mildly feeling the effects of her frolicking, as well as a little too much wine. Combine that with the fact that Vitruvius was extremely irritable after the events of the night before, and was looking for someone to thrash for it. Why had all of this had to have happened the night before their weekly sparring sessions?

"What, did that little hussy drain all of your manhood out of you last night?" Vitruvius asked dryly.

"Something like that," Artorius said as he staggered to his feet.

"Well come on, man. A few more good thrashings will purge her venom from your veins!" Artorius came at him, punching hard with his shield, and jabbing with his gladius. He knocked Vitruvius' shield up, lunged down and stabbed the Sergeant in the foot. Vitruvius yelped in pain and brought his own gladius down on top of Artorius neck. The after affects of the night had slowed him down and he was unable to pull back and defend against the Sergeant's onslaught. Artorius lay groaning on the floor while Vitruvius limped around the training hall.

"Better, much better!" Vitruvius said through clenched teeth. Artorius just lay on the floor groaning. Vitruvius walked back to him and poked him in the ribs with his training gladius. "So was she worth it?" he asked, laughing.

"Yeah," Artorius moaned as he worked up to his hands and knees, "I would say so."

"Well then, no harm done!" Vitruvius laughed and pulled the young Legionary to his feet. "You're still improving, even after a night of playing with the harlots! Just don't make a habit of it right before we spar! See you next week."

Artorius made his way to the bathhouse. He was sore, sweaty and remembered that he had not bathed since the day before. He saw Praxus walking in just ahead of him.

"You're catching up to Vitruvius," Praxus remarked. "I saw him come limping by here just a while ago. He was trying to hide it of course. It looks like he still got the best of you, though."

"You have no idea," Artorius said. His body hurt all over and he just wanted to get cleaned up and soak in the hot water. As they lay on the tables where slaves rubbed them with oil and scraped the dirt away, Praxus continued their conversation. Artorius found he was only half conscious.

"The weather's improving," Praxus observed. "We should be readying ourselves for the spring campaign before too long."

"Probably," Artorius muttered.

"The boats are all done," Praxus continued, "Everyone's been conducting amphibious assault rehearsals, along with all of the usual drill and weapons practice, some of us more than others." He reached over and punched Artorius on the shoulder as he said that. Artorius simply groaned. The cold plunge bath revived Artorius, and the time in the heated pool relieved his aching joints and muscles. He felt much better as he and Praxus walked out of the bathhouse.

"Can I ask you something?" Praxus asked, not waiting for an answer. "Why do you go through those weekly sparring sessions with Vitruvius? I can understand wanting to be a good fighter, but you're not a gladiator, Artorius. Very few of us have skills even close to those of Vitruvius, yet we still succeed in battle. We work together. Eight men working as one unit can be more effective than a hundred fighting as individuals. Your body pays a heavy toll every week with the beatings he gives you. Remember, you're not going to win this war by yourself."

"I know that," Artorius replied. "I just think it would be better if those eight men you speak of all fought as well individually as Vitruvius. I'll be honest with you, Praxus. I have no intention of spending my career as a simple Legionary. I know I've only been serving for a little over a year, and that any type of promotion takes time. I know that it is not uncommon for veteran Soldiers to retire at the same rank held when they first entered the Legions. I just feel that if I were the best close combat fighter in the Legion, I might someday be able to take Vitruvius' place."

"If you can beat Vitruvius, you *will* be the best in the Legion, probably in the entire army," Praxus remarked.

"It's also a challenge to me," Artorius said. "I've heard he is unbeatable. I've seen how all the veterans continue to get scarred in battle. His body remains conspicuously devoid of any injury, yet he kills more than anyone whenever we engage with the enemy. Something inside of me yearns to beat him, to be the best there is. Besides, I'd rather take my beatings from him than from a barbarian with an axe!"

That day the Century stood in formation, all dressed for parade. Centurion Macro stood in front of the formation. In his hands he held a parchment bearing a set of orders, along with the three-foot staff normally associated with the rank of Optio.

"The rank of Optio comes from a term meaning 'chosen one,'" Macro stated. "The Optio of a Century is hand picked by the Centurion to act as his right hand. He is subordinate only to the Centurion himself, having been selected for promotion ahead of his peers. In the absence of the Centurion, it is the Optio who assumes command.

"The staff carried by the Optio has the practical use of keeping Legionaries in formation during the heat of battle. Many a battle has hinged on the abilities of such chosen men to keep their Soldiers focused and disciplined when it was most crucial. The staff is also a symbol of his rank, and of his newly granted authority." Macro paused for a moment before unrolling the document he held.

"*Sergeant Vitruvius, post!*" he barked. Stone faced, Vitruvius marched to the front of the formation and stood facing the Centurion. Macro then read the order.

"Sergeant Vitruvius, as a testament to your abilities as a leader of men and of your unfailing loyalty to the Emperor, the Senate and People of Rome, and your unwavering fidelity to your Legion, you are hereby promoted to the rank of Optio." Vitruvius was very stern faced as he took the parchment bearing his promotion orders, along with the three-foot staff that signified his office. He still walked with a very slight limp from where Artorius had stabbed him in the foot with a training gladius, as he took his place at the center, behind the formation.

A Soldier named Sextus was subsequently promoted to Sergeant to replace Vitruvius as section leader. Three new recruits had sworn the oath of allegiance that day as well and were entered into the rolls of the Legion. Artorius had remembered what it had been like when he had finally been allowed to swear the oath and join the ranks. Had it been only a year? It felt longer, almost a lifetime since he first swore the oath of allegiance to the Emperor, Senate, and People of Rome. He did not know the new men, since they were assigned to different sections. Still he made it a point, along with just about everyone else in the Century, of clasping each on the shoulder, shaking their hands and welcoming them to the Legion.

*   *   *   *

The journey had been very disagreeable for Thusnelda, especially in her condition. She knew that it would not be long until she would go into labor. Her child kicked, causing her to wince.

She hated that she was caught in the middle of this feud between Arminius and her father. And now with the Romans involved, it only made things worse. The Romans had taken her to one of their Legionary fortresses, west of the Rhine. Her father had assured her that everything would be alright. Yet in spite of his reassurances, she still felt uneasy. The fortress was huge, unlike anything she had ever seen before.

The Romans had treated her cordially enough. They had offered her a comfortable bed to sleep in, and had offered their own doctors to assist her when the time came for her child to be borne. She was reluctant to accept their offer, however she was pretty much choice less at this point. Her father came walking into the room.

"How are you holding up, daughter?" Segestes asked. Thusnelda placed a hand over her swollen belly.

"The little fellow is kicking hard. I think he wants to come out and play," she answered. Segestes smiled. As much as he hated Arminius, and the fact that his daughter bore that man's child, he still deeply loved his daughter. Though she tried to outwardly remain cheerful, Segestes could easily see the confusion and sadness that gripped her.

"You know I did what I thought was best for you," he said.

"I know," she replied, slowly running her hand over her stomach. "I never wanted to leave with Arminius in the first place. He practically kidnapped me! But then, all that time I spent with him, I did start to grow fond of him…"

"He stole you away from your family!" Segestes snapped. "And let's not forget, he is the one who betrayed the Romans, thereby sealing the fate of many of our peoples."

"I don't know why he betrayed the Romans," the young woman replied. "I had never met one before this whole nightmare began. He always told me that he was looking to make Germania independent, united. Given the nature of our people, that may be little more than a dream. However, in that one moment when he struck down three of Rome's Legions, he actually brought all of the tribes together in one common cause." She looked away, dreamily. She immediately snapped back when she saw the look of concern on her father's face. It was he after all who had warned Varus of Arminius' betrayal and the pending disaster.

"Rome has been good to my family and to my people," he said softly. "And now Arminius has our lands. The Romans will ravage them in retribution for what he has done. Many of the sub tribes that Arminius rallied to his cause have already paid a heavy price. The Chatti have been smashed, the Marsi practically exterminated." Thusnelda closed her eyes at that. She had many friends amongst both tribes, and she feared greatly for their safety. Yet she also knew that her father's statement was no exaggeration. She shuddered at the thought.

"He cannot hope to win this war," Segestes continued. "So many have died already, and yet I fear that this pending campaign will be even worse. Arminius' dreams have lead to nothing but excessive suffering and bloodshed."

"And what of us now, Father?" Thusnelda asked. "Are we little more than political prisoners for the Romans?" Segestes looked puzzled.

"How can I be a prisoner when I asked the Romans for help in the first place?" he asked. "No, my daughter, we are the Romans' *guests*. And I have decided that we will be done with Germania forever. We will travel to Rome, and there life will start anew."

"And what of my child, Arminius' child?" Thusnelda asked.

"The child will never know his true lineage. He will have a future completely devoid of any knowledge as to who his father really is. That in and of itself will cause Arminius to seethe. What will become of him after he is born, I really do not know. The Romans will see any seed of Arminius as a threat, however I do have the promise of Germanicus that your child will be allowed to live."

"As a slave, you mean," Thusnelda replied, a tear coming to her eye. Her father sighed and lowered his head.

"It's still the child of Arminius. I don't know what the Romans plan for him, or her as may be the case. Just be content that your child will live."

*   *   *   *

Orders had come through, and everyone was in frenzy, trying to get all equipment packed and loaded onto the transports. In addition to each barge carrying two sections with all of their gear, a Scorpion was placed up front, able to fire at targets attacking either side of the barge. The barges had been placed on rollers, so that they could be more easily moved into the water. Artorius was awestruck by the site. There were several Triemenes carrying most of the baggage, as well as the senior officers. Most of the men rode in the smaller barges. Even Flavius, the Master Centurion, had elected to ride on a barge with the men instead of on a ship.

He watched as each Cohort in turn rolled their barges into the river, the crews fighting to keep them in formation. Soon it was their turn, and their section, along with Sergeant Sextus' section rolled the barge into the waiting river. The water was cold as Artorius waded up to his crotch to get the barge underway.

Once everyone was on board, the designated oarsmen pushed off and rowed out to their place in the massive formation. He watched as the fortress slowly disappeared over the horizon. It would be another full campaign season before he returned to the place he had come to call home. He hoped that when he did see her again, it would be as part of a triumphant army, having just vanquished Arminius and his demonic hordes.

*   *   *   *

"The Romans have left their winter quarters," the Scout reported. Arminius immediately sat up. He had been reclining on his bed, contemplating the events of the previous campaign and the loss of his wife.

"Where are they at now?" he asked.

"Somewhere along the Frisian coast," the scout replied. "Some local tribes have thought to organize sorties against them, however these would be ill advised. The Roman barges all have their cursed artillery weapons on board."

Arminius was vexed. He did not know where the Romans would land and launch their invasion from, though he knew it would come deep within their territory. What he needed now was time to organize and muster his forces. He had kept all the war chiefs as his guests throughout the winter, in order to keep them close at hand when the moment came. He stepped outside. It was a warm day. He watched as huntsmen returned with their game, foresters returning with loads of lumber. All these men would soon throw down their labors and rally to their true calling. These men were Cherusci, warriors without equal in courage and tenacity. They would all be needed in order to repel the Roman invaders. Ingiomerus came walking over to him. The tenacious old warrior had almost fully recovered from the fearful wound he had suffered at Ahenobarbi just a few months before.

"Well?" he asked. Arminius turned to face him.

"It is time," he replied. Ingiomerus smiled and turned to go find the other war chiefs. Soon all were gathered around their leader. In spite of their hardheadedness and reckless abandon, Arminius truly loved these men. They were after all his people. They had faced the Romans time and again, and would continue to do so until the issue was decided for good.

"Where shall we face the Romans?" Haraxus asked. He had been among the most fanatical and devoted of all the warriors Arminius had. With him was his young son, eager to join his father in battle. Arminius smiled at the lad and immediately thought about his own son. He sighed. His son, if it was a son, had to have been born by then. Would he ever see him, and would he ever know his father? It was highly unlikely. Arminius shook his head. He could not focus on such things if he was going to lead his people to any kind of military success against the pending invaders.

"Our warriors are brave, but I believe they are a bit shaken since last season," he began.

"Arminius, your warriors will follow you into hell itself!" Haraxus retorted. The rest of the council muttered and nodded in agreement.

And that's just where I'm taking them, he thought to himself.

"The Romans will fight us wherever we mass," he said aloud, "so anxious are they for battle. There is a place where not only will they have the courage and the valor of our warriors to deal with, they will also have the gods themselves to face! It is there that we will bring every warrior from every tribe in our alliance. There we will give battle. That place is called Idistaviso."

CHAPTER 17

▼

INTO THE HEART OF GERMANIA

Off the coast of Germania, near the Ems River
May, A.D. 16

Artorius watched as the coast slowly passed by. It was his turn to man the Scorpion, along with Magnus. Every time he had to man the Scorpion, he hoped he would see barbarians on the coast, trying to harass their movement. So far it had been quiet. Only one time had they been harassed, and he had been on oar duty at the time. Gavius and Valens had succeeded in killing one enemy assailant with the Scorpion before the others fled. Today it did not look like Artorius and Magnus would get to see any action.

Everyone was a little bit on edge, since they were approaching the heart of Germania. They had a feeling that Arminius was simply waiting for them to get to a tight spot on the river, and then spring his trap. They could feel the eyes of barbarians watching them as they floated quietly along the coast.

Artorius looked around. The fleet of ships had gotten huge by the time the other Legions, plus auxiliaries had linked up with them. He could see neither the beginning nor the end of the formation. "And against us the Germans will throw every warrior in the entire damn land," he heard Magnus mutter.

"Let them," Artorius said. "I hope they do come at us with everything they have. Then we can kill them off once and for all!"

Magnus smirked. "Still haven't quite lost your lust for revenge, eh?"

"Oh no," Artorius answered, "Just a little more focused is all."

"You know, the only thing I really lust for…" Valens started to say as Decimus lifted his oar out of the water and smacked him on top of the head.

"We *know* what you lust for!" Decimus said. Valens threw down his oar, turned and jumped on top of Decimus. He picked the other Legionary up and threw him into the water. As Decimus pulled himself back onto the barge, Statorius grabbed his gladius, still in the scabbard, and smashed them both across the ears.

"Enough!" he shouted. "I will not have my Legionaries acting like a bunch of fucking vagabonds! One more stunt like that and it will be the Centurion's vine stick for the both of you!"

"Could you guys *please* not rock the boat!" they heard Carbo shout from the back of the barge. He was squatting off the back, holding on to a piece of timber, while trying to relieve himself. Any sense of modesty was completely overwhelmed by the needs of nature.

"Tension's starting to get to everyone," Magnus whispered.

"Yeah, well we've been on this barge for two weeks already," Artorius replied under his breath. "I think boredom is starting to set in."

"It set in a couple of days into this damn voyage," Magnus said.

"Could be worse," Artorius said. "We could be facing skirmishes, ambushes and building damn bridges through the swamps of that cursed land like last time."

"I can't *believe* no one thought to put a damn privy seat back here," Carbo muttered, causing everyone to laugh at their friend's plight.

Germanicus watched the fleet coast along from his vantage point in the flag ship. He was awestruck by the sheer power that he wielded. This was the most impressive machine of war assembled in one place. His eight Legions alone numbered roughly forty-thousand men. In addition to these were auxiliaries, cavalry, archers, and over four-hundred pieces of artillery awaiting his orders. Communication and coordination were an absolute necessity. As huge as his army was, he knew that the forces mustered by Arminius would be much larger. It didn't seem possible as he watched the ships as far as he could see. The Ems River was soon in sight on the horizon to the east. A few days travel down the river, find where Arminius had massed his forces, and it would hopefully be over soon afterwards. They had dealt Arminius a blow the year before, however they were far from having avenged the tragedy of Teutoburger Wald. After three days of sailing down the Ems River, the army disembarked and started setting up its massive camp.

The camp was absolutely huge. Lumber was plentiful in the heart of Germania, but the labor involved in erecting such a massive fortification as to house such an astronomical number of men had been astounding. Artorius stood his post on sentry duty, marveling at his own small role in everything. Decimus stood the post with him as well, the rest of the section either working on personal equipment issues, or catching up on sleep.

"How long have they been gone?" Artorius asked, referring to the flying column that had left to go ravage the newly rebellious Angrivarii tribe.

"Four days maybe," Decimus answered.

"I'm kind of glad we missed out on that little operation," Artorius replied, looking off into the distance where he knew the Angrivarii were being sorely punished for their misdeeds.

"Serves them right," Decimus said. "Though I admit that thrashing farmers and destroying land is not one of the more enjoyable tasks a Legionary performs."

"What are some of the more enjoyable tasks?" Artorius asked, trying to make for an interesting conversation.

"Whoring, drinking, gambling, sport, and I suppose whoring some more...with a little bit of plunder thrown in!" Decimus shouted boisterously.

Artorius laughed. "Sounds like the life of Sicilian pirates!" he remarked.

"Except we're more efficient at it. Plus we get paid more, oh yeah and we don't like the sea very much."

The wind was blowing warm and gently. It felt good to Artorius. He still cringed from the cold winter that they had had to endure. He hoped that next winter would be spent mostly indoors and not out on ambush duty or building boats. The grass was green and everything was in full bloom.

"With days like today, it's hard to believe that there's a war going on," he remarked.

"I know," Decimus replied. Just then they caught movement out in the distance. There were several horsemen at the front of a large number of men. Some of the horsemen were carrying Roman standards.

"*Column's returning!*" Artorius shouted over his shoulder. This was echoed by the other sentries. He watched as several men rode on horseback from the center of the camp. With the camp being as large as it was, it was impossible to move from one end to the other at any decent speed without a horse. He recognized two of the men as Germanicus and Severus. They met with the column and its Legate as they rode in through the front gate.

"Looks like they had a profitable time," Artorius remarked, looking at the weighted bags of plunder the infantry carried with them.

"Yeah, I guess it's too bad we didn't go on this one," Decimus replied. "Looks like the Angrivarii were quite the prosperous tribe."

"That's just it. They *were* a prosperous tribe," Artorius retorted as he turned back to watch his sector and enjoy the warm breeze and the smells of the open fields. The paradox was not lost on him. He contemplated the gorgeous and peaceful view that calmed his senses, with the fact that here he was, an armed, professional killer in the midst of it all.

The gods have a sick sense of humor, he thought to himself.

At the same time that the flying column had returned from ravaging the Angrivarii, reconnaissance cavalry had also returned from the east. They had a full report to give to the Commanding General. Germanicus had therefore called for a meeting of all his senior leaders within the army. Everyone from the rank of Centurion Pilus Prior and above sat or stood in a circle as the lead scout drew out the known locations of the enemy onto the ground.

"You were correct Sir," the scout began, "Arminius does intend to finally face us in open battle. Our operations against the Angrivarii have given him time to muster his minions."

"How many does he have?" Gaius Caetronius, the Legate of the First Legion asked.

"It is impossible to tell for sure how many he has. Suffice it to say; with what we were able to get eyes on they outnumber us significantly. Though the Cherusci themselves have amassed the largest number of warriors, there are in fact at least twelve tribes who have joined forces with Arminius. And it looks like each has committed every warrior they have."

"Where have they massed their troops?" Gaius Silius, the newly appointed Legate of the Fifth Legion asked.

"They're massing at a place called Idistaviso. It is on the eastern side of the Weser River."

"That place is very sacred to the Cherusci," an auxiliary Commander named Chariovalda said. "It is next to a grove that they have dedicated to a god not unlike your Hercules."

"So they feel that they will have their gods to support them," Severus scoffed.

"The Weser is a wide, turbulent river," the scout continued. "There are several places where cavalry will be able to cross fairly easily. However, we will need bridges for the infantry to cross en mass."

"That can be done easily enough," Severus said, "provided we can keep the bastards from attacking our working parties."

"Is the river too wide for artillery to be affective?" Germanicus asked.

"I'm no expert Sir," the scout said. "However I can surmise that at max elevation, artillery should at least be able to have some impact on whatever forces may oppose us on the opposite bank."

"Pilate, sounds like you have your work cut out for you," Severus said.

The young Tribune nodded confidently. "We'll make it happen, Sir."

"We have nearly four-hundred pieces of artillery, to include Scorpions and Onager catapults," Germanicus observed. "I intend to use all of them to suppress the enemy. In addition, I intend to send a cavalry contingent across to harass and create a diversion." He looked over at Chariovalda, who in addition to being an auxiliary commander was war leader of the allied Batavi. With him was a Roman cavalry officer named Stertinius and a Centurion Primus Ordo named Aemilius.

"You, my friend will lead your cavalry across the fording site and start harassing the near enemy flank," Germanicus said. The war leader stood with his arms folded across his chest and nodded. "Two wings of our own cavalry, led by Commander Stertinius and Centurion Aemilius will cross behind you, swinging out in a wide arc and penetrating deeply into the enemy flanks. They will act initially as a diversion, as well as your reserve, should you get into trouble. While this is going on, Tribune Pilate will oversea placing our artillery along the western side of the river. We will keep up a sustained rate of fire with the Onagers, using fire on their formations and suspected hiding places in the woods. Scorpions will be used for precision shots, and will suppress the enemy archers and slingers.

"This will all provide cover for our working parties who will build eight bridges across the Weser, one for each Legion. I want each wide enough for a section to walk abreast. Once the infantry is across, artillery will collapse on the bridges and cross in turn. From there we will establish a new camp and prepare for battle."

As the meeting broke up, Germanicus motioned for Chariovalda. The Batavi leader came forward. He was a well built German, still maintaining his long hair, yet his face was clean shaven. He was a master horseman and was well respected by both his own warriors as well as his Roman allies. The Batavi that he led were an offshoot of the Chatti tribe. While their cousins the Chatti had sided with Arminius, the Batavi had remained fiercely loyal to Rome. Were Germania a unified country, the conflict would have resembled a civil war as much as anything. Stertinius and Aemilius had grown rather fond of their auxiliary counterpart, and a strong bond of friendship had grown between the three men. Germanicus placed his hands on the war leader's shoulders.

"This is a difficult and dangerous mission I am assigning to you," he said. Chariovalda only nodded.

"The honor is mine to serve underneath a leader such as yourself, Germanicus Caesar!" he replied.

"Your men are brave, but I do not want you to be careless with your lives. I know the hatred that exists between your people and the other tribes of Germania, particularly your cousins the Chatti. I only need you to engage and keep them distracted for a short time. I'm sending what cavalry we have to support you in case you run into trouble. Be careful old friend." With that, Germanicus clasped the Batavi leader's hand and then in what many would consider a severe breach of protocol, raised his hand in salute. Chariovalda returned the salute and mounted his horse, smiling all the while.

"Rome has been good to me and to my people," he said as he turned to ride away. "I am honored to do my duty to protect her."

CHAPTER 18

▼

THE WESER RIVER

Centurions and Options mounted their horses and surveyed their troops. Legionaries saddled their packs, and hefted their javelins and shields. Macro and Vitruvius looked on, pleased at the site of their Soldiers.

"These are good men," the newly promoted Optio said. "They will do well."

"They should; you trained almost all of them," Centurion Macro replied.

"Cohort!" Centurion Proculus shouted.

"Century!" Macro and the other Centurions sounded off.

"Advance!" As one, the men of the Third Cohort, as well as those of the entire army, started their march towards the Weser River. As they marched, Artorius surveyed the sea of armored men surrounding him. The army marched in step, the ground practically shaking with the force of their march. Shields and sword belts bumped leisurely against their armor, sounding almost like a cadence of its own. By the gods, how could Arminius even hope to achieve victory against such a force? Artorius had full confidence in his own ability to fight. Yet here were tens-of-thousands with similar skills and abilities. Moreover they were tens-of-thousands that were working together as one. Praxus had been right; the strength of the Roman army lay not in the skill of its Soldiers as individuals. Their strength lay in their ability to work together, to fight as one man. The Germans may have had them outnumbered, but Artorius never once doubted the final outcome of the pending battle. Just getting to that battle was a maddeningly slow process.

Artorius had not fought a German since their successful ambush against the raiding party the winter before. His sword arm twitched, almost as if it were suffering from a hunger that could only be satisfied by slaying as many barbarians as it could. He then looked at the meadows and woods they passed. The serenity contrasted with the mass of men and metal that bore through her.

*   *   *   *

Arminius sat on his horse, hidden in the woods, yet able to survey the river below. In spite of his warnings, warriors stood in large numbers at the edge of the water, shouting insults and waiving their weapons at the Romans who were massing on the opposite bank. The enemy were lined up in neat rows, shields together, javelin butts resting in the ground.

"So they have come at last," he muttered to himself.

"A blessing to finally be able to vanquish the Romans once and for all," Haraxus said as he rode up beside him. Ingiomerus was with him. They watched as the Romans started to unload wagons that they had parked near the edge of the water. Arminius' eyes grew wide. An artillery barrage would be devastating to the warriors on the bank below. Why did they never listen? To them it would almost be like a sport to try and dodge the Roman missiles.

"Some lessons the stubborn will only learn through pain and hardship," he muttered to himself.

"What was that?" Ingiomerus asked.

"Nothing," Arminius replied. "Give it few minutes and we'll see if we cannot get those fools to pull back from the river bank."

*   *   *   *

"Scorpion crews ready!" a Centurion reported to Pilate.

"Onager crews ready!" another shouted.

"Make any last minute adjustments to tension and elevation," Pilate answered.

"Already been done," Dionysus said as he walked back from the line of artillery weapons. Pilate smiled. He drew his gladius and raised it in the air. Onager crews ignited their payloads. As Pilate brought his gladius down in an arc, almost simultaneously the command was shouted by all section leaders. *"Fire!"*

A wave of fireballs sailed towards the opposite bank. Most crashed into the trees, starting small fires. A few landed right in amongst the barbarians on the opposite bank. Pilate watched one burning pot hit a warrior directly on top of the head and explode. The man screamed as he was covered in burning oil. His companions nearby were also doused in fire. Pilate nodded to Dionysus.

"*Scorpions fire!*" the Centurion shouted.

A volley of Scorpion bolts flew in a low arc at their enemies. A few landed short or sailed too high, though most managed to strike home amongst their intended targets. Screams could be heard as men fell stricken and dying. Another volley from each weapon system and the barbarians were running towards the tree lines behind them. The beach on the German side of the river was littered with corpses, some of which still burned. The smell of burning flesh and hair assailed Pilate's nostrils. It was repugnant and yet exhilarating at the same time.

"Onagers, maintain harassing fire on the wood lines! Scorpions, precision shots only! Watch your sectors and keep your eyes open for any threats to our working parties!"

"Sir!" the section leaders replied in unison. Pilate turned and nodded to Severus, who in turn nodded his approval. The Legate then waived a hand towards the riverbank.

"*Working parties forward!*" a Centurion shouted. Soldiers immediately came forward bearing lumber and tools and started to work on the Legion's bridge. Up and down the river Artorius was certain that similar episodes were being played out by the other Legions. The Third Cohort had not been assigned to a working party. Instead, they would provide close security, as well as being among the first across the river once the bridge was complete.

*   *   *   *

On another section of the river, one that was too wide for the Roman artillery to be affective, two brothers stood on opposite banks, facing each other. Chief Tribune Strabo and Master Centurion Flavius were among those sent to accompany their ally Flavus to his meeting with his hated brother. They sat back and watched the spectacle, while an auxiliary from Flavus' unit translated the dialog for them.

"So my brother has come home at last!" Arminius shouted. "It is too bad that he has returned as nothing more than a whipped lapdog of Rome!"

"At least I maintained my oath, *Brother!*" Flavus answered. "You speak of being whipped, yet it is you who are whipped. You claim to be a great war chief, yet you are the one who is a slave. You are a slave to your warriors and their lust! You are nothing but a figurehead, you have no real power!"

"I am loyal to my tribe and my family! You my brother are loyal only to how much the Roman pays you!" All the while, Arminius could not help but stare at the scar on his brother's face, and the fact that he was missing an eye.

"Do tell, Brother," he said at length, his voice softening slightly, "when was it you received such a fearful wound to your face?"

"Several years ago, while serving under Tiberius. I took a spear to the face while saving the life of one of my wounded troopers."

"And how did the Romans compensate you for such disfigurement?" Arminius found himself intrigued to hear the story of his brother's plight.

"I have since been promoted to command of an ala of cavalry, with a significant increase in pay. I received the Silver Torque for Valor for my actions that day. And for saving the trooper's life, I was awarded the Civic Crown."

"A crown of oak leaves?" Arminius scoffed. "*That* was your reward for being permanently disfigured? What a paltry recompense for having enslaved yourself! You are certainly one to be envied!" [1] The sarcasm and disdain ran deep in his voice.

"As is your wife," Flavus retorted. "She has been treated well by the Romans; as a guest rather than a conquest." He watched as Arminius' face twitched and his complexion reddened at the mention of Thusnelda.

"Rome is the light in the darkness of this world!" Flavus continued. "Mercy and a return to friendship await those who surrender and repent of their crimes. Only death will you bring to those who stand by you in defiance of the Empire! The Romans seek neither plunder nor slaves, only revenge. You *know* this. They will spare nothing and no one. All will be burned in their wake, every last person slain. Such is the punishment of vanquished traitors!"

"You dare speak of traitors?" Arminius retorted. "You betrayed our fatherland, our very ancestral freedom, and the gods of the homes of Germania! Our mother has shared my prayers that you might not choose to be the deserter and betrayer. Rather that you would become ruler of our kinsfolk and relatives, and indeed of our own people. [2] I see that such prayers were in vain! Rome has corrupted your soul. This is your home no longer, and these are no longer your fellow tribesmen. You are no longer Cherusci, you are Roman!" He spat on the ground to emphasize his point.

An evil smirk crossed Flavus' face. "Do you want to know who else in your family is now a Roman? *Your son!* Oh yes, Thusnelda bore you a son, a son that will never know his lineage to you! He bears a Roman name, has been given Roman citizenship, and will grow up to be a Roman! And unlike his father, he will have a future, one with promise and hope. You my brother, and whatever other bastards you may spawn, will have nothing!" Flavus knew he exaggerated when speaking of Arminius' son. Indeed, he knew the boy would be lucky if he were even allowed to live.

Arminius flew into a rage. "How dare you call me your brother! You are no kin to me! I have no brother!"

"And you no longer have a son!" Flavus called out as he drew his sword. Arminius sneered at this gesture.

"Come to me, Flavus and let us end this! The current here is not so swift, nor the river so deep that you cannot cross in safety. Safe passage I will give you to cross to this side, that I may slay you as a man does!" He brandished his own sword as he spoke. Flavus smiled wickedly.

"I'm going to kill you, Arminius! I'm going to rip your guts out and feast on them!" He started to move towards the river, when Stertinius, who had also accompanied Flavus, seized the reigns of his horse.

"Not this way!" he shouted. "Listen to me, Flavus. He will only lure you across so that he can ambush you like he has so many others. Look, and see for yourself!" He pointed across the river to where indeed a number of mounted barbarians were stirring anxiously amongst the trees. Flavus exhaled audibly through his nose, nodded and sheathed his sword. Arminius gave a great cry, which was echoed by the warriors who had accompanied him. His face was red with rage, which was boiling over. Flavus had regained his composure, and calmly turned and rode away.

"See, I told you he had proven his loyalty to us," Flavius said to Strabo as they watched Arminius ride away in fury.

*   *   *   *

The next morning Stertinius and Aemilius accompanied the Batavi to the Weser River. The water was cold and swift as Chariovalda swam his horse across. Like all great warrior leaders, he was always the first to cross into hostile territory. He also made it a point to be the first to directly engage the enemy once in contact. The woods were dense on the other side. He could not tell if the Cherusci were waiting for them or not. He was certain that they would be distracted by the Romans on the other bank. As he stepped onto the soft dirt of the river bank, he quickly mounted his horse, drew his long sword and looked back to see how the rest of his warriors were faring. All were experienced at fording rivers, so it was not a great ordeal to them. The Roman cavalry, on the other hand, were struggling in the current. As soon as the last of his warriors had crossed, he signaled for them to move out.

As they made their way through the dense woods, he saw a party of enemy warriors running their way. They were confused and looked as if they were running from something. Since they were still fairly close to the river bank, Chariovalda assumed that they had just felt the wrath of the Roman artillery.

"*Yah!*" he shouted as he kicked his horse into a full gallop. His warriors were close behind him, all shouting and waiving their swords. As they came upon the surprised mob, Chariovalda swung his sword in an underhand swing. The sharp blade made contact with one warrior's neck, severing his head from his shoulders. The rest of his cavalry crashed into the ranks of the Cherusci, causing those they did not kill outright to scatter. One barbarian made a half-hearted attempt to attack Chariovalda with his spear. Chariovalda grabbed the spear with left hand and then plunged his sword deep into the man's chest, right below the throat. Blood erupted in a geyser from the barbarian's mouth as it gushed from the wound.

The Batavi warriors shouted and raised their weapons in triumph. Most cared little about the conflict between Arminius and Rome. The Batavi were involved in an inter-tribal war, and Rome was their means to winning that war. Now they had spilled first blood against their hated neighboring tribes.

Chariovalda looked around. It seemed that a number of Cherusci were running away from the battle together, a perfect target. "With me!" he shouted and waived his warriors towards their fleeing enemy. As they closed, he swung his sword hard across the back of one unsuspecting foe. He heard the vertebrae and spine split underneath the force of his blow. The barbarian screamed and fell to the ground.

The Batavi were in the midst of another massacre of their enemy when suddenly a throwing spear flew through the air, impacting the chest of a warrior riding next to Chariovalda. He looked in the direction it had come and saw a number of Cherusci regrouping ahead of them. He looked to his left and right and saw even more of them massing on him. Another throwing spear felled one of his warriors as the Cherusci gave a great cry and charged. A volley of darts and arrows showered the ranks of the Batavi, who raised their shields to protect themselves. Cries of shock and pain could be heard as horsemen were stricken from their mounts.

Centurion Aemilius ran his sword through the back of a fleeing barbarian. His men had caught a small band of Cherusci completely off-guard and had slaughtered them without loss. He then heard the commotion coming from where he knew Chariovalda was in contact. He turned his gaze to his front and saw that a large number of Cherusci warriors were rushing towards the sounds of battle. He grimaced, knowing full well that Chariovalda was in trouble.

"Cornicen, sound recall!" he shouted, turning his horse about. Stertinius, alerted by the trumpet's sound, immediately brought his own contingent about, rushing to the aid of the Batavi.

"To me, my brave warriors!" Chariovalda shouted, raising his sword. His warriors, realizing their plight, quickly rode to their leader, forming a circle with their shields facing out. The Cherusci now had them completely surrounded, and were attacking in massive numbers. As they clashed with the Batavi, many were initially cut down by the better equipped horsemen, who had the advantage of being mounted. Gradually however, the Batavi circle started to break. Warriors succumbed to fatigue and were struck down. Others, overwhelmed by the sheer numbers of Cherusci, were pulled from their mounts and hacked to pieces. Realizing their desperate situation, Chariovalda rode straight at what he thought to be the weakest point in the Cherusci mass.

"Follow me to freedom!" he shouted as he brought his sword down on the skull of one Cherusci warrior, with a horrific crunch. Suddenly a spear skipped underneath his shield and pierced his side. He gasped in pain as his breath was suddenly taken from him. The spear was wrenched from his side, causing the wound to bleed profusely. A volley of darts ruptured his flesh, sending him reeling. As he fell from his horse, he saw his warriors riding around him, hacking and stabbing away at the hated Cherusci. His vision started to fade as he saw the Roman cavalry coming to their aid at a dead charge. The shock of their impact caused the Cherusci to reel temporarily. Chariovalda felt the strong hands of his warriors as they lifted him onto the back of a horse. As they rode away from the battle his vision faded and he breathed his last.

Aemilius watched in horror as Chariovalda and a number of his warriors fell under a storm of darts and arrows. He grimaced in rage. Stertinius could be seen approaching from their left, his contingent looking to envelope the Cherusci. Aemilius decided then to drive the barbarians into them.

"Wedge formation, keep it tight!" he shouted to his men. *"Charge!"* The Cherusci immediately panicked and started to flee in the wake of his onslaught. Still, his cavalry managed to slay and trample a number of them under the hooves of

their chargers. They came to a halt soon after having pushed past the Batavi, who were gathering up their dead and wounded.

Aemilius dismounted his horse and walked over to where Chariovalda lay slumped across the back of one of his warrior's mounts. The dead chief's eyes were open, yet lifeless; a trickle of blood ran from the corner of his mouth. The Centurion removed his helmet and reached up to close his friend's eyes.

"With your permission," he said to the warrior on the horse, "I would like to carry him back myself." The exhausted warrior could only nod his consent, too tired as he was for words. Carefully Aemilius lifted the Batavi chief into his arms and laid him across the back of his own mount, all the while ignoring the blood and gore which smeared all over his armor in the process.

✳   ✳   ✳   ✳

It was late, and construction on the bridges had stopped for the night. They would finish up in the morning, allowing the Legion to cross in force. Onagers had continued to fire sporadically into the tree lines on the opposite bank. Not only was this to disperse any would be attackers, but the fires left behind would case enough light for Scorpion crews to fire on anyone trying to dismantle the half complete bridge.

Artorius sat next to a small camp fire, unable to keep his eyes off of the opposite bank. Flanking units had set up the standard palisade and ditch leading down to the river. The river itself served as a natural obstacle, so there was no need to further reinforce it. His half sleep was disrupted by the sounds of a Scorpion firing.

"Got you, you bastard!" he heard the gunner shout. "Did any of you see that? Ha ha!"

"Shut your mouth and reload!" the section leader shouted. He couldn't help but smile as he saw in the dim light a barbarian lying twitching in the sand with a bolt protruding from between his eyes. It *had* been a pretty good shot!

"I wonder what must be going through Arminius' mind right about now," Artorius mused as he leaned back and watched the spectacle. For not having his tent or a cot to sleep on, he found he was surprisingly comfortable. The dense woods and uneven terrain had prohibited their setup.

"Probably soiling his loin cloth," Valens thought aloud.

"Either that or he's making some unholy sacrifice to their foul deities that they might be delivered from our vengeance," Magnus said.

"What kind of sacrifices do they make?" Gavius asked.

"They place an ox on a burning alter, cut its throat and then shag it before it stops twitching," Decimus, answered.

"Dear gods, do they really?" Gavius asked. Everyone started laughing.

"I don't know. I just made that up!" Decimus replied.

"That does sound about right, though," Valens said through a mouthful of wheat cakes and bacon.

"This coming from a guy who will go to bed with anything that moves and is still breathing," Praxus muttered. Valens picked up a rock and threw it at him. It skipped away harmlessly as Praxus laughed to himself.

"I think he is planning on making as much of a stand against us as is possible," Artorius said. "Whether he can beat us or not, I think he plans on making this pending battle as costly for us as he possibly can."

"Which is where discipline and training will pay off," Statorius said. He sat back from the fire, listening to his Soldier's conversations as he often did. "If we stick together, do what we know how to do and watch out for each other, we'll be alright." He took a bite of his supper and a long drink from his water bladder.

CHAPTER 19

▼

CALM BEFORE THE STORM

The next day the Legion crossed unmolested. Artorius and many of the others nearly gagging as they passed the German corpses that were starting to rot and bloat. Vitruvius rode past them, seemingly impervious to the repugnant site and stench.

"Just think lads, there will be many more of them to stink up this cursed land!" he shouted. Artorius laughed and then gagged again as a fresh breeze blew the smell right into his face.

"Personally I think they smell almost as bad when they are alive," he muttered.

A hard day's march brought them to the edge of the land known as Idistaviso. There the Romans quickly erected their forts. As night fell, Germanicus rushed to the gate where the cavalry was returning from their long, harrowing ordeal. The Batavi looked to have taken the worst of it. There were a lot fewer of them then there were before, and those that remained looked haggard and weak from fatigue and injury.

Germanicus' face fell when he saw the sight of Centurion Aemilius. In his arms he bore the ravaged and bloodied corpse of Chariovalda. With him was a younger Batavi named Halmar, who Germanicus knew to be the slain chief's brother. With great reverence, Aemilius placed Chariovalda's body at the feet of Germanicus. The Centurion fought hard to mask his sorrow.

Severus walked up as Germanicus kneeled down and placed his hand on the dead chief's shoulder. The Legate gave orders to have the surgeons sent for immediately, and that fresh wine and food be brought for the survivors.

"He died saving his men," Aemilius said quietly. Germanicus barely heard him. He couldn't help but marvel in that in spite of his fearful wounds and being doused in blood, Chariovalda's face looked somehow serene and tranquil.

"Here has passed a brave man into eternity," he said as he rose to his feet. His gaze then fell upon Halmar, who stood trembling in what Germanicus knew to be a combination of hunger, fatigue and sorrow. He stepped forward and placed a hand on the Batavi's shoulder.

"You must lead your people now," he stated. Halmar nodded in reluctant ascent. "Know that your valor will not be forgotten. You allowed our Legions to cross the Weser in safety. The actions of your men saved the lives of hundreds, if not thousands of Roman Soldiers. Your people have done their part in this war. Therefore, I release you to return to your homes in honor." Halmar shook his head at this last remark.

"My brother would have wished for us to finish what we started. We may be fewer in number, but my men have lost none of their resolve. We will stand by you, Germanicus Caesar, and we will fight till the bitter end of this war."

"You are a worthy ally," Stertinius said as he approached the pair. "With the General's permission, I would like to send my contingent to fight beside our friend, Halmar in the upcoming battle." Germanicus nodded his consent and the dismissed the pair, who then carried Chariovalda's body away.

"Severus," he called to the older Legate who had been standing in the background, watching everything unfold.

"Sir?"

"I need to get a feel for the men's morale with the climatic battle of this war at hand." He turned and faced Severus, his arms folded across his chest. "I could call for a meeting of the Tribunes and senior Centurions. However, I feel that in spite of their best intentions they may be apt to tell me what they think I want to hear." He paused for a minute in deep thought before making his decision. "Take me to the Aquilifer of the Twentieth Legion. He may be able to help me."

"Yes Sir," Severus replied with a grin, suspecting what Germanicus had in mind.

*   *   *   *

Artorius and his section were sitting by their fire when a Signifier walked up to them. Though all of them had dropped their body armor and equipment, this man was still fully dressed in armor and animal skins. Upon closer inspection they noticed that he was wearing a lion skin over his helmet and shoulders. This signified him as the Aquilifer who bore the Eagle of the Legion. The sheer honor and prestige of this position was enormous. An Aquilifer's pay was considerable, his rank equivalent to that of a senior Centurion.

"May I sit and join you this evening?" he asked.

"Of course, friend. Come, sit down," Statorius said as he waved the man over. "So what brings you so far from your headquarters duties?"

"I only wished to get away from there for a while. It has been a long time since I was in a Century on the line. While mine is an honorable position, I still miss being out front sometimes," the Aquilifer answered.

Statorius signaled to Gavius, whose turn it was to cook supper. Gavius grabbed a mess tin and filled it with cakes and sliced meat. He handed it to the Aquilifer, who readily accepted.

"Thank you, my friends," he said as he ate. "I admit that I am curious as to how Soldiers in the ranks perceive this mission and our Commander."

"Our Commander is a good man," Praxus said. "A bit superstitious, maybe, but there is none other I would rather follow into battle."

"True," Statorius replied. "I have served with many Commanding Generals and I have to say Germanicus is among the best I have ever seen."

"What is it that makes him so special to you?" the Aquilifer asked.

"He is tactically sound, and he leads from the front," Artorius piped in. "I saw him after an engagement. A couple of infantry Cohorts were more than able to handle the situation, yet there he was, taking the lead himself. I saw his sword covered in blood at the end of the battle. He is as brave as any I have ever seen."

"There's only one other I would rather serve under, and that is the Emperor himself," Magnus said.

"Magnus you weren't even in the army when Tiberius was still in the field!" Decimus retorted.

"Still, his reputation precedes him," the Aquilifer replied calmly. "Tell me, do you think Germanicus learned well from his uncle?"

"I served with Tiberius," Praxus said. "I can tell you that both men are about equal when it comes to tactical savvy and personal courage. The only difference that I could ever tell is that aside from having the advantage of experience, Tiberius seemed almost reckless when it came to his personal safety. Yet both men would willingly trade their safety for that of their men. I am truly honored to have served under them."

"As am I," Statorius added as he stared into the fire.

They caught a hint of a smile in the Aquilifer's face, concealed as it was in the shadows of his garb. "Thank you for your time and hospitality, my friends," he said as he rose. He handed Gavius his mess tin. "We shall meet again." With that he left.

The Aquilifer made a number of rounds to other campfires that night. Well past midnight he walked back to his tent. He saw Severus standing outside, drinking a goblet of wine.

"How did it go, Germanicus?" Severus asked. "Did you find the answers you were looking for?"

"I found them, and then some," Germanicus said as he removed the animal skins and helmet. He handed them to the Soldier who was standing next to Severus, also drinking a goblet of wine. "Thank you," he said.

"You're welcome Sir," the Soldier answered, smiling.

Early the next morning, Artorius and Magnus were on sentry duty. As the sun broke the horizon they saw a lone rider coming towards them. His unkempt appearance and lack of helmet or armor showed him to be a German. He carried a banner of truce.

"What in Hades does this guy want?" Magnus asked.

"Rider approaching! Enemy from the looks of him!" Artorius shouted. Soon other Soldiers were on the wall. Centurion Macro had joined them as well as their Cohort Commander, Centurion Proculus. The rider approached and stopped about thirty meters short of the rampart.

"Fellow warriors!" he shouted in perfect Latin. "I bring an offer from Arminius, supreme war chief of the Cherusci. He asks that you lay down your arms and walk away from your forts. For each Soldier who accepts, we offer him twenty five denarii per day until the end of the war. We know that the average Soldier only makes two hundred and twenty-five denarii per year, so this will be a handsome gift. We will also give you a plot of land to call your own, and a beautiful German wife!"

"Think it's a ruse?" Magnus asked.

"Does it matter?" Artorius retorted. "Their wives and land are ours for the taking. Why else would they make this offer if they weren't so close to breaking?"

"Then why don't you let him know that?" Macro asked, nodding towards the messenger.

"Sir, Proculus is the senior officer present. Shouldn't he be the one to parlay?"

"No, I think it would be just fine if a Legionary from the ranks gave our response," Macro answered.

Artorius cocked a half smile and turned towards the German messenger. "Tell Arminius that we will take his lands and his women with or without his permission!" he shouted. "Let daylight come, let battle be given! The Soldiers will possess themselves of the lands of the Germans and will carry off their wives. We hail the omen; we mean the women and riches of the enemy to be our spoil. [1] How *dare* Arminius think that we would betray our own? We will ravage your lands and your wives at our leisure! All of you will burn in vengeance for his betrayal!" With that he spat at the German, causing the rest of the Soldiers on the wall to erupt in a torrent of insults and profanity. The German hardened his face, threw down the banner of truce and rode away.

"If that's not a good sign of things to come, then I don't know what is," Magnus remarked.

"Does this mean I can actually get a piece of one of those Germanic beauties once this is over?" Valens asked. This caused Macro to sigh audibly while everyone else stifled their laughter.

"Yes Valens," he replied, "you can have as many Germanic whores as you want once the fighting is over."

*   *   *   *

"High ground to our front, tree lines beyond that," Severus observed, gazing at a terrain sketch one of the scouts had made. "No doubt they will use the terrain to build up momentum against us. Wait until we get close to the slopes and then try and roll over us with their superior numbers."

Germanicus sat with his legs crossed and his chin in his hand, contemplating. He had an enormous army which he needed to be able to deploy rapidly. Combine that with the fact that he was horribly outnumbered, with the enemy on the high ground, he had a lot to think about.

"The terrain looks wide enough for us to deploy four Legions on line, with four more in reserve. This may very well work to our advantage," he said at last.

"Yes Sir," Severus agreed. "One thing they may attempt is to remain in the woods and fight us there. The trees would break up our formations and perhaps even the odds in their minds."

"Then we smoke them out like vermin," Germanicus countered. "Once we have all of our assaulting elements arrayed, we'll pound the tree lines with artillery. They'll either have to face us in the open, or they can slowly burn to death as we torch their sacred groves. That in and of itself should draw them out." Severus smiled at the thought.

"Very good," he replied. "And I take it you'll want the auxiliary infantry out front to act as a screen line?"

"Yes," Germanicus nodded. "They can act as a delaying force in case the Germans decide to advance prematurely. Plus we can use them to stall the enemy's momentum long enough for the Legions to engage. Just make certain that they maintain visual contact this time!" He scowled at the thought of the auxiliary's debacle the year before.

"That's already been taken care of," Severus said with a half smile. "Trust me; there will be *no* mistakes this time."

"And how are you so sure of this?" Germanicus asked, curious as to how his second was so certain.

"Simple," Severus shrugged. "I told the auxiliary commanders that if there were any lapses in discipline this time, I would personally crucify the lot of them." Germanicus nodded. That would do it, alright.

"I myself will take the cavalry," Germanicus continued. "Once the battle is fully engaged, we will work to encircle the enemy, harassing the flanks and rear. We'll also try and lure their cavalry into the center, negating their maneuverability. I'm going to leave it up to you when you want to deploy the reserve Legions. Just make certain you do it before the ones up front become too beaten down. We'll still need to use them as a reserve once the Legions in the rear commit."

CHAPTER 20

▼

IDISTAVISO

A red sun dawned. Blood would be spilt that day. The sun cast its light over the ground as the Legionaries went about readying themselves for the coming battle. For the huge number of men assembled, it was unnervingly quiet, at least to the outside observer. Every Soldier was very calm and deliberate as he made his preparations. Unlike their barbarian adversaries, the Romans found it pointless to dance about, making all sorts of noise before a battle. All that would do is lead to anxiety and allow for breeches of discipline. Only at the last, when they were about to directly engage the enemy, would the Romans come alive audibly. Until then, all would be quiet, a silence that would soothe their Soldiers and rattle the enemy more than any battle cry ever could.

Meticulously, Artorius inspected every piece of equipment he would be using that day. He made it a point of donning a fresh tunic. He checked the straps and soles of his shoes as he strapped them on. With an oil dampened cloth he wiped down his armor, checking every rivet, band, and strap for serviceability. He then did the same with his helmet. He donned both, tugging on straps and making certain that everything fit right. He followed this up with a quick check of the brass strips and handle on his shield. He then looked down the shaft of his javelin, ensuring that it was straight and the point honed sharp. Lastly, he drew his gladius and gave it a quick wipe down with the cloth. Artorius smiled to himself as he examined the blade. As always, it was razor sharp. Once everything was done, he removed his helmet and stood by, leaning on his shield.

Sergeant Statorius walked over and checked his Soldiers one by one. Very little was said as he checked their armor and weapons. When he came to Artorius, the Sergeant nodded for him to don his helmet. He did a quick visual inspection, checking all of his Soldier's equipment for serviceability and wear. He then held out his hand. Artorius drew his gladius and handed it to the Sergeant, who smiled as he hefted the weapon.

"You've taken good care of this," he said quietly, running his fingers over the blade and pommel. "One would never guess as to how much action it has already seen. I daresay, one would think this weapon was brand new off the armory's rack."

"Thank you Sergeant," Artorius replied. Statorius then handed the weapon back to him handle first.

"She'll serve you well today," he said as Artorius placed the weapon back in its scabbard. Statorius then gave him a friendly smack on the shoulder and went about checking the next man.

Macro, Vitruvius, and Camillus stood off to the side, watching as the Sergeants finished the last minute checks of their men. Camillus wore the traditional wolf skin over his helmet and shoulders. He had both hands wrapped around the Century's standard, which he leaned against. Macro and Vitruvius were fully armored, each carrying their helmets under their left arms. Flaccus stood over by where the inspections were being conducted, each Sergeant reporting to him when their section was complete. Finally, he turned and walked over to Macro and reported.

"All sections are ready," he said. The Centurion nodded his approval and the Sergeants gathered around their Commander.

"Get all sections on line, and then have them stand easy," he ordered. His voice was strong, but very calm and relaxed. "Once the order is sounded, we will fall in directly behind Proculus and the First Century." He nodded to where Soldiers of the First Century stood a few yards ahead of them, going through a similar ritual with their officers. He then continued in his speech.

"As you all know, the Twentieth Legion will be among the first to engage the enemy today. Keep an eye on your men. Make sure they keep an eye on each other. If someone goes down, whether they are on our line or the one in front of us, pull him off immediately. Our armor will protect us against most of our enemies' blows. Don't give them the opportunity to finish us should we fall. Only together can we hope to survive this day and achieve victory. You all know what to do. Know that every Soldier in this Century has my utmost faith and trust. Now, let us show the Cherusci why we are known as 'The Valiant!'"

✳   ✳   ✳   ✳

Arminius rode through the glade, which was difficult given that it was packed with Cherusci warriors, most of who stood shoulder to shoulder. Many cheered as their war chief rode past; warriors waived their weapons in the air and banged them against their shields. There was an air of confidence and anticipation as they waited for the Romans to come.

Arminius reached the top of the hill, overlooking the valley below. In the distance, he could just make out the first signs of the Roman army's approach. As the shouts and cheering died down, everyone could hear the soft cadence of men in step, marching towards them. The sound grew louder as the Legions advanced. Gradually the blurry mass took on shapes. The Roman auxiliaries screened their front in four ranks, with the Legions behind them. Arminius was just able to make out wagons to the very rear of the Roman army, wagons bearing their hated artillery. No other sound came from the Romans except for their footsteps, and the soft beat of their sword belts bouncing against their armor, in cadence with their steps.

"Their footfalls come as the steps of doom," Arminius whispered. Though he maintained a calm expression on his face, his knuckles were white as he held the reigns of his horse in a death grip. He took a deep breath and suddenly took heart. He knew that all would be settled on this day. It was up to him to drive his warriors to final victory over the hated Legions. He turned and faced his men giving as stirring of a speech as any he had given before.

"These Romans are the most cowardly fugitives out of Varus' army, men who rather than endure war had taken to mutiny! Half of them have their backs covered with wounds; half are once again exposing limbs battered by waves and storms to a foe full of fury, and to hostile deities, with no hope of advantage. They have, in fact, had recourse to a fleet and to a trackless ocean, that their coming might be unopposed, their flight un-pursued. But when once they have joined conflict with us, the help of winds or oars will be unavailing to the vanquished. Remember only their greed, their cruelty, their pride. Is anything left for us but to retain our freedom or to die before we are enslaved?" [1]

Ingiomerus paced back and forth amongst the warriors in the trees. He walked over to the edge, where the area opened up onto the plain below. Through the mass of warriors surrounding and in front of him, it was difficult to make out the Legions in the distance. From what he could see, they seemed small, insignificant. Though he could not see them very well, he could hear the cadence of their march growing steadily louder. He decided to drown out that despicable sound.

"Brother Cherusci!" he shouted, with his sword held aloft. "The Romans have at last come to make battle with us. And what a battle we shall give them! Their arrogance, their vanity, and their air of superiority will avail them nothing!" Cherusci warriors started to shout in agreement.

"So let the Romans know that we are here! Let them know that it is the Cherusci who will send them to hell's door!" With that the warriors went into frenzy. The forest itself seemed to come alive. Ingiomerus was certain that their battle cries could be heard to the ends of the Earth.

*   *   *   *

The army was arrayed in battle formation. Everything was set. Germanicus looked proudly towards his army. He thought briefly back to the speech he had given to his men before the order to advance was given.

"It is not," he had said, "plains only which are good for the fighting of Roman soldiers, but woods and forest passes, if science be used. For the huge shields and unwieldy lances of the barbarians cannot, amid trunks of trees and brushwood that springs from the ground, be so well managed as our javelins and swords and closefitting armor. Shower your blows thickly; strike at the face with your sword points. The German has neither cuirass nor helmet; even his shield is not strengthened with leather or steel, but is of osiers woven together or of thin and painted board. If their first line is armed with spears, the rest have only weapons hardened by fire or very short.

"Again, though their frames are terrible to the eye and formidable in a brief onset, they have no capacity of enduring wounds; without any shame at the disgrace, without any regard to their leaders, they quit the field and flee; they quail under disaster, just as in success they forget alike divine and human laws. If in your weariness of land and sea you desire an end of service, this battle prepares the way to it. The Elbe is now nearer than the Rhine, and there is no war beyond, provided only you enable me, keeping close as I do to my father's and my uncle's footsteps, to stand and conqueror on the same spot." [2]

Preparations had been meticulous. The auxiliary infantry were out front, supported by archers. They would bloody the Germans and fix them in place. Four Legions were behind them, along with two Cohorts of the Praetorian Guard that Germanicus had hand picked to take part in the attack. Germanicus himself rode in the center of this formation, along with selected members of the cavalry. Behind them were the four Legions in reserve; behind these were mounted archers who acted as a rear guard. At the very back was a line of Onagers. Pilate had ordered his crews to overshoot rather than under. Germanicus wanted to use the artillery to hammer the enemy rear, thereby driving them into their waiting swords. As the army slowly advanced, Germanicus looked up and was shocked to see eight eagles flying in the direction they were traveling. They were arrayed in exactly the same type of formation that his Legions were in, four in front, four behind. Surely it was another omen; eight eagles, one for each Legion. Any doubts he may have had about the pending battle evaporated in an instant.

"My brothers look!" he shouted, pointing to the heavens. "The gods favor us this day! The eagles of our Legions fly towards destiny and victory!" A shout sounded from those who looked up and saw the eagles. Germanicus' heart soared.

The Twentieth Legion Valeria advanced on the right-hand side of the formation. The Second Century occupied the second rank in the Third Cohort. Artorius could see the auxiliary infantry and archers to his front. They were maintaining discipline and visual contact. There would be no mistakes this time.

The barbarian hordes were massed on the high ground to their front. The hills sloped downward, converging on the plain where the Legions now advanced. By Hades there were a lot of them! The entire horizon was literally covered with barbarian warriors. How many were there, tens-of-thousands, hundreds-of-thousands? There was no way of knowing for sure. The ridge was covered in woods, the sacred groves of their foul god whom they had the audacity of comparing to Hercules. Thousands more stood hidden in these groves that they thought would give them divine protection. Ha! Their sheer numbers and even their gods would be no match for the might of the Roman war machine!

"We move as the Hammer of Vengeance," he uttered to himself.

"Set for max elevation!" Pilate shouted.

"Elevation set!" Dionysus called back.

"Onagers ignite!" Crews lit the ammunition placed in the baskets of the catapults.

"Catapults ready Sir!"

Pilate took a deep breath and wiped his forearm across his brow before issuing the next order.

"Fire!"

*   *   *   *

Dozens of flaming missiles sailed through the air, over the heads of the advancing Legions, impacting amongst the trees near the rear of the German ranks. The trees only enhanced the devastating effects of the fire bombs. Upon impact, each ball would literally explode, spraying fire everywhere. The dry timber easily caught fire, adding to the havoc. Some unlucky warriors were doused completely and soon consumed in the blaze. These ran about in utter panic before they succumbed to the effects of the fire. It was terrible! It seemed as if hell itself were spitting flaming death at them. More fireballs smashed into the trees at higher levels, spraying their fury onto even larger numbers of barbarians below.

The Germans started to panic. Though Arminius had forbidden them from attacking before the signal was given, they hated the thought of standing by helpless while the Romans rained death upon them.

"We cannot just stand here and take this!" one warrior shouted to Ingiomerus.

"Steady lads! Keep your courage!" Ingiomerus called to his warriors. "We must not falter. We must stick to the plan!"

"If this keeps up, there won't be any of us left to execute the plan!" another warrior cried out as a fireball exploded in the trees above them. Ingiomerus looked around. Though they were being tormented and were taking casualties, the warrior's assessment was absurd. Yes, a number would be consumed by the flames; however their casualties would not be catastrophic. The Roman barrage was meant to harass them; to try and force them to execute their attack prematurely. That way they could be caught out in the open, where the Legions would have the advantage.

As he contemplated this, Ingiomerus felt a searing pain as red-hot embers scorched his face and arms. The hair of a warrior next to him had caught on fire, and the man was running about in utter terror, screaming at the top of his lungs. Suddenly he too panicked. Not realizing fully what he was doing, he raised his sword, and started to run towards the enemy.

"With me, my warriors! Who will come with me?"

The warriors all gave a shout and surged forward with him. Those in front of the groves of trees mistook this to mean that the attack had commenced. A deafening cry erupted and they charged. Arminius lowered his head. He had done all he could. Everything now depended on the ability of his warriors to carry their charge, a charge they had executed prematurely.

"Archers draw!" The archers in front of the auxiliaries quickly drew back and unleashed a shower of arrows that rained down upon the Germans rushing towards them. So closely packed were the barbarians that few missed their marks. Some held their shields overhead in hopes of protecting themselves from the rain of death. With no discipline, nor any mutual support, their efforts were largely in vain. Shields would absorb a few arrows, but more would find flesh, muscle and organs. In spite of this, the charge lost none of its momentum. As warriors were shot down, they were roughly shoved aside, tripped over, or tossed out of the way. The Roman auxiliary infantry kept up their advance as the archers paused and unleashed yet another volley. Soon the gap closed.

In his frustration, Arminius drew his sword. "Our warriors charge bravely. We go to join them. *Cherusci forward!*" With a shout, the cavalry surged from the hilltops towards the center of the fray. He led them straight into the Roman archers as they fired again. Their officers saw this new threat approaching them.

"Aim for their cavalry!" One ordered. The archers drew their bows, decreased elevation, and fired into the ranks of the Cherusci cavalry. Men and horses fell in heaps to the earth, yet still they came. Arminius spurred his horse with renewed vigor as a warrior next to him was shot clean off his mount.

"Archers fall back!" As they withdrew, the barbarian hordes crashed head on into the ranks of the auxiliary infantry. A violent melee ensued. Most auxiliaries carried metal spears and oblong shields. They wore Legionary style helmets and mail shirts. Though better equipped and trained than their enemies, they were no Legionaries. The Germans started to fall, yet they continued to surge forward. They had a decisive edge in numbers, and they quickly started to overwhelm the Roman auxiliaries. Men stabbed, slashed, and hacked away at each other, opening up fearful wounds whenever a blow found its mark. Men screamed in rage and pain as they sought to disembowel each other.

As the Cherusci cavalry smashed into their lines, the auxiliaries, in a move learned from their Legionary brothers, dropped to one knee, braced behind their shields, and set the butts of their spears into the ground, the points facing their foe. Each man braced himself hard against his shield, clutching his spear for all he was worth. They were formed up in looser array than Legionaries, which lessoned the affects of their defense. Still many cavalrymen fell to the auxiliary spears. Some horses instinctively came to a halt, refusing to ride into the wall of spears.

Their riders were thrown by the momentum and sudden stop. Yet still many more smashed over the Roman auxiliaries, trampling them underfoot. The fighting soon became even more brutal and fierce. The Germanic tribesmen fought with rage and fury, knowing full well that the auxiliaries they faced were mostly of Gallic and Germanic origins. The thought of being betrayed by their own kinsmen enraged them. The auxiliary lines started to give, their casualties mounting and the sheer force of the barbarian charge pushing them back. The Cherusci gave a triumphant cry. Yet they almost forgot that eight Legions of Rome's best infantry were directly behind the auxiliaries and coming up fast.

Arminius swung his sword in fury, smashing an auxiliary helm. Suddenly an arrow struck him across the face, opening a fearful wound. A stab from an auxiliary spear knocked him from his mount. He looked up to see a man with a spear pointed directly at his heart. The man was a Chauci, one of those who fought his own kinsmen on this very battlefield in the name of Rome. The auxiliary paused, suddenly realizing who he had struck down. He then ceased his attack, lowering his spear and his head. Arminius struggled to his feet. The auxiliary motioned with his head for Arminius to leave. The Cherusci war chief nodded and with painful effort remounted his horse. He looked over to where the Legions were advancing. Suddenly he was fearful. While his warriors had almost broken the ranks of the Roman auxiliaries, they had yet to contend with the Legions. He smeared blood all over his face, hoping to mask his identity and rode away. The wound to his abdomen was bleeding badly. He was starting to feel faint. There was no reason for him to stay on the field any longer. The battle would be decided without him.

"Cease fire!" Pilate shouted. The command was echoed by the section leaders. As quickly as they had began, all Onager crews abruptly halted in their labors. They stood by their weapons, sweating and breathing heavily. Though smaller than the siege engines used for bringing down a city or fortress, the Onagers still demanded a lot of exertion from their crews. They watched as the infantry marched with purpose towards its destiny. The artillery had done all they could. Now they would become observers to the battle. All of them hoped that their labors had not been in vain.

"Check your weapons!" Pilate ordered. Crews immediately stopped watching the battle to their front and systematically started checking all the components of their catapults. A number of concerned section leaders starting talking frantically with their Centurion. He nodded and walked over to Pilate.

"Seems like these weapons have taken a real beating," Dionysus told the Tribune. "They aren't exactly the most soundly designed siege engines either."

"What's the problem?" Pilate asked. The Centurion took him over to one machine.

"It's the tension ropes, mainly," he said, pointing to where some sections of the ropes were starting to fray and come apart. "Plus the very nature of these machines makes them prone to fly apart after prolonged use. And let's face it; we've used the hell out of these things, with little to no time to conduct proper maintenance and replacement of worn parts."

Pilate tugged on one of the tension ropes. It was frayed, but it still held. The beams in front, where the throwing arm impacted were starting to split as well.

"Well at least they did their job today," he observed. "Do what maintenance you can. I know we have a shortage of parts; however we must make certain that these weapons are as serviceable as can be. We may or may not need to use them again before this campaign is over." As Dionysus started to oversee the repairs, Pilate turned and walked away. He was starting to grow concerned over his machines. They had taken a severe punishing. The Scorpions had seen less use, and were more reliable anyway. If all else failed, he could still utilize them. He took a deep breath and turned back to watch the battle to their front as it unfolded.

"Javelins ready! At the double-time...march!" Proculus shouted. Everyone knew what to do. It all came instinctively now. Artorius hefted his javelin to throwing position and started to move at a jog, all the while keeping in tight with the rest of his Century. He was comforted by the fact that two of his friends, Magnus and Decimus, were on either side of him. The auxiliary infantry was heavily engaged. More were falling with the continuous onslaught of the German hordes showing no signs of letting up. Timing would be crucial; give the auxiliaries enough time to withdraw and allow the Legions time to unleash their javelins before engaging. Suddenly a Cornicen sounded the order for the auxiliaries to withdraw. Quickly they turned about and ran back through the ranks of the Roman infantry. Artorius watched as one dazed and battered auxiliary Soldier ran directly at him. The young fighter veered at the last second and avoided colliding with the Legionary. The Germans paused for a split second, as they seemed almost shocked to see the Legions bearing down on them. The timing was perfect.

Ingiomerus took heart as he watched the ranks of auxiliaries turn and run. The fighting had been fierce, with both sides leaving many dead and dying on the field, yet the Cherusci and their allies had triumphed! He was breathing hard as he watched his warriors surge forward to finish off their enemy. Suddenly the entire army stopped dead in its tracks. The auxiliaries seemed to disappear and in their wake was a mass of armored men, bearing red and gold painted shields and those hated javelins! In step they marched, with their javelins ready to throw. Instinctively, Ingiomerus clutched his side, the wound from the previous year seeming to cry out in fresh agony.

"*No!*" he shouted, though his voice was completely drowned out by the noise surrounding him. He immediately started to backpedal, his heart filled with fear. He gazed to his left and saw a Centurion shouting an order. Hell was soon unleashed.

"*Front rank...throw!*" Proculus shouted.

"*Second rank...throw!*" Macro ordered before the first rank had even finished throwing its javelins. Artorius threw his without even picking out a single target. He had just enough time to watch his javelin sail low and strike a barbarian in the thigh before the third rank passed him and disgorged their javelins. Almost a continuous volley of javelins rained down on the barbarians as all six ranks unleashed. An entire wave of Cherusci fell with each successive volley. There were cries of anguish and pain as they fell stricken and dying. Warriors directly behind them were sprayed with blood and gore. Yet they were unnerved, and they moved to face this fresh wave of Romans. It was one thing to fight auxiliaries, now they would spill their wrath onto the hated Legions.

"*Gladius...draw!*"

"*Rah!*" the Legionaries all shouted as one. The advance never ceased and they continued to close with their foe. The Germans, many still reeling from the lashing they had received from the javelin storm, gave a great battle cry of their own and charged. It was the massive, brave, and yet undisciplined horde, versus the host of iron men, fighting with cold discipline, moving together as one.

Ingiomerus once again took heart when he saw that his warriors had not faltered. The more men that fell to the Roman javelins, the stronger their resolve became. They would not break this time! Those who had been sprayed with blood from the stricken rubbed it into their faces with lust and zeal. Some even licked it from their lips, relishing in its flavor, drawing strength from the fallen. This only increased their berserker ferocity. Quickly they stepped on and over the dead and dying. There was no time to pay reverence to the dead. That would come once the hated Legions were destroyed. Like a host of demons, they cried out and renewed their charge. The Romans were ready for them.

Barbarians smashed into the Roman ranks, only to be cut down in rapid succession. As they fought to make holes in the Roman lines, Legionaries punched them with their shields and stabbed away with their swords. The Cherusci made a great show of jumping about, swinging their weapons wildly. Desperately they tried to use their superior size and brute force to overwhelm their opponents. In contrast, the Roman Soldiers' techniques were simple and anything but flamboyant. Each blow was executed with precision, speed and power. In desperation many warriors flung their bodies into the Roman lines, hoping to knock the Legionaries down. The Romans' superior balance and technique negated much of this. A German would throw his bodyweight into the shield of a Roman Soldier, throwing himself off balance before he was quickly stabbed by one of the Soldier's companions. As Legionary and Warrior smashed, hacked and stabbed at each other, most individual battles were completely one-sided. It was nearly impossible for a warrior to find a gap in the Roman defense. Yet still they came. Sooner or later the Roman lines would wear down and break. Then they would have them!

CHAPTER 21

▼

FOR WRATH, FOR VENGEANCE

Artorius watched as the front rank engaged the enemy in as fierce a combat as he had ever witnessed. He had never seen men fight with such fury. He knew that in a battle of this magnitude, passages-of-lines would come rapidly. It was crucial to keep fresh troops out front, as the tempo of this battle would cause Soldiers to expend energy at an alarming rate. Artorius sighed. He knew this would be an exhausting day. The sun was out, and it was starting to get warm. The Germans were taking a severe punishing, there were just so many of them. Occasionally a Roman Soldier would fall as well. Artorius watched as one poor fellow was stabbed in the abdomen, his armor buckling as barbarian attempted to penetrate with his spear.

"*Get him off the line!*" Sergeant Ostorius shouted as two men grabbed the injured Legionary and dragged away from the fighting. They handed him back to Soldiers in the third rank, who would get him to the litter bearers.

"*Set for passage-of-lines!*" Proculus shouted. Artorius settled into his fighting stance. He smiled sinisterly, rage in his eyes. Everything would be settled here!

"Stay together lads! Watch out for each other!" he heard Centurion Macro say at the end of the line.

"Precision strikes, nothing fancy, make every blow count!" Optio Vitruvius called out at the other end. "They're big, but they can't stand being hurt!"

"Now my friends," the Centurion said, his voice rising, "for wrath, for vengeance and for the souls lost in Teutoburger Wald!"

"Execute passage-of-lines!"

The Second Century gave a unified shout of rage. Artorius felt his adrenaline levels soar. Instinctively they all stepped off together and passed through the First Century. Artorius did not have to search for a target, there were so many in front of him. Immediately he smashed his shield into a barbarian who was hammering away on the shield of a Soldier from the First Century. The force of his blow knocked the barbarian down. Artorius had to raise his shield immediately to defend himself as another barbarian stabbed at him with his spear. He quickly smashed his assailant twice in the face with the boss of his shield. The barbarian dropped his spear and ran; his face covered in blood from where his nose had exploded. The Germans may have been many, but they could only fight the Romans one at a time. The tightly packed Legionary ranks did not allow the barbarians to use their numbers against individual Soldiers.

Artorius punched away with his shield. As openings presented themselves, he started to stab with his gladius. A barbarian was attacking him high while protecting his face and chest with a wicker shield. Artorius dropped to one knee and in a rare move, slashed with his gladius. The razor sharp blade cleaved through the barbarian's shin, severing his lower leg in half. The man fell to the ground in horrific pain, blood spurting from the amputated limb. Another barbarian quickly took his place, attempting to bring his spear onto the top of his head. Artorius saw him coming. He lunged upward, catching the barbarian under the chin with the top of his shield. He then stabbed the dazed German beneath the ribs. He looked to his left and right and saw nothing but barbarians. He then realized that he was starting to step away from the line. In a near panic he stepped back into line as another German attacked him. This one carried a massive two-handed club, which he swung in an overhand smash. Artorius did not even bother punching with his shield. Instead he rapidly stepped in and stabbed the man in the armpit, penetrating to the heart. It felt as though his gladius had were a conscious entity, able to seek out the most vital of organs on the human body. He stepped back and took several deep breaths. He had been fighting for no more than a minute, and yet he was already breathing hard. The barbarians kept coming at him in force. Every fight took huge amounts of energy and strength.

All up and down the line, Soldiers of the Second Century fought with vengeance against the massive wave of barbarian warriors. The Legionaries relished the thought of everything ending with this action, and they fought as if this were to be their last battle. The barbarians in turn would surge forward, smash and stab with their weapons and then try and break away before the Romans could cut them down. The steady Roman advance, combined with the pressure from the warriors to their rear left many of them with nowhere to go. These could only swing their weapons in desperation, trying in vain to penetrate the wall of Roman shields before they were fatally stricken.

Magnus rammed his gladius into the side of one barbarian's neck. With a vicious jerk, he pulled his weapon free, ripping out the man's esophagus in the process. Blood sprayed all over his face and chest. Valens caught one with a blow to the face from his shield, and with malicious rage, stabbed him in the groin, twisting and turning his gladius about before wrenching it free. His weapon had penetrated the German's bladder, and now reeked of urine as well as fresh blood. Praxus stabbed another German in the thigh. As the barbarian's companions shoved him mercilessly aside, he and Gavius stepped in together and quickly cut down two more with vicious stabs to the vitals.

Carbo seemed to taunt his opponents, quickly moving his shield about, making the barbarians think he was leaving himself open. As one moved in to stab with his spear, the Legionary brought his shield down on the man's foot. He then followed up with a stab underneath the ribs. Sergeant Statorius continued to neither yell nor make any sound at all, as he fought his way through the mob in front of him. His utter silence baffled his assailants, many becoming unnerved by his seemingly tranquil air of contentment. Their confusion only made it easier for him to find openings and slay them.

Artorius watched Decimus reel under the onslaught of one attacker. In order to help his friend, he ducked down, turned sideways while raising his shield over his back to protect himself, and ran his gladius across the barbarian's ankle. The German howled in pain as his Achilles was severed and Decimus subsequently ran him through. While still on his knees, Artorius turned and blocked the blow from another assailant. He brought his gladius up in a rapid stab as he got to his feet, catching the barbarian in the face. The man gave a great cry, turned and ran. It was true; these Germans could not stand to be hurt! As he faced the next attacker, he heard the next order shouted by Centurion Macro.

"Set for passage-of-lines!"

He was relieved at the opportunity to catch his breath as the order to execute the maneuver was given. The next rank crashed into the Germans, who wailed and mourned having to face yet another fresh wave of Legionaries. The Second Century passed back to the rear of the Cohort. Artorius was breathing heavily as he looked around to assess how the rest of the battle was progressing. All four Legions were pretty much online with each other, slowly pushing the barbarian hordes back. In their wake, the advancing Legionaries were having to step over piles of barbarian dead and wounded.

Ingiomerus smashed his sword repeatedly against a Legionary's shield. He stopped once he realized that the Soldier was no longer advancing towards him. He gasped and immediately stepped back. He knew that whenever one line stopped, it meant that a fresh wave would be passing through them. He stepped away just in time as another line surged forward. Others were not so fortunate. Many were knocked down as the Legionaries smashed into them with their shields. Most of these would never rise again. The only way fresh Germanic warriors could be brought forward was when those in front of them were slain. Still they did not lose heart, even as their losses mounted. It was however, disheartening for Ingiomerus to watch as his warriors were cut down one after another. Roman Soldiers were falling as well. However, most of the time their superior armor prevented their wounds from being fatal, and they were quickly pulled from the line before the barbarians could finish them. Ingiomerus figured that maybe one in every five Roman casualties died. Unfortunately, there would be little glory for those who did manage to slay a Legionary, as most of these subsequently paid for their actions with their own lives. Ingiomerus was uncertain as to whether or not he would survive the day. He resolved himself that if he was to die, he was honored to die among such brave men and he renewed his attack on this fresh wave of Legionaries.

As he made his way to the rear of the formation, Artorius looked for his companions. He breathed a sigh of relief as he watched Decimus, Magnus, Gavius, Valens, Carbo, Praxus, and Sergeant Statorius all make their way to the rear of the formation with him. His friends were alright. All were breathing heavily, drenched in sweat, and covered in blood and dirt, yet they were alive and unscathed. Artorius was suddenly thankful and relieved. For the most part, he had been focused on fighting the Germans, staying alive and exacting his revenge. Now he was coming to realize that there was something more to be concerned with. These men were his friends, his brothers, for there was no form of brotherhood in existence like those who were willing to fight and die for each other. These were the finest men he had ever known. They were not simply Roman Soldiers, they *were* Rome! The spirit of Rome was not in some far away city of marble statues and amphitheaters. Neither was it was not on the floor of the Senate. No, *here* was Rome, here on this battlefield!

Artorius watched as the rest of the Century formed up with them behind the First Century. Sergeants started getting accountability of their men, all the while being hounded by Macro and Vitruvius to report if anyone was hurt or lost. The reports were all negative. Though most were battered and drenched in sweat, dirt, and blood, everyone was accounted for. Artorius was shocked that no one from the Second Century had been killed or seriously wounded, in spite of the ferocity of their exchange with the Germans. Other units were not so lucky. He looked back to where litter bearers were carrying away the dead and wounded. Men were falling, however they were much fewer than Artorius had anticipated. For as massive of a battle that he was in the middle of, he thought for sure that their losses would be much heavier.

He looked back to the battle itself. He saw that the Germanic cavalry was in disarray and was starting to break and run, yet the horde of barbarian warriors on the ground continued to press their attack. Artorius saw in the distance that their own cavalry was assaulting the flanks and rear of the enemy, wrecking havoc and destruction.

"Set for passage-of-lines!"

Germanicus led the cavalry around the rear of the German army, stabbing at any target that presented itself. His cavalry chopped away at the barbarians, who surprisingly had not panicked. Many were oblivious to the threat, until they were struck from behind or in the flank. There were still so many on the field that perhaps they still felt that their superior numbers would achieve victory for them. He saw one barbarian with a great sword. He was waiving it over his head, shouting at the other warriors. Obviously, he was some type of leader. Germanicus spurred his horse and rode towards the man. As he closed up, the barbarian turned in surprise just in time for Germanicus to run his sword through his throat. A vicious jerk of the blade nearly severed the barbarian's head. As the corpse lay twitching on the ground, a gushing stream of blood saturated the already blood-soaked earth.

Quickly it seemed that the Third Cohort was executing its passages-of-lines, so that within what seemed like only a few minutes, the Second Century was back to where it started. Artorius watched as Soldiers from the Cohort passed back through the ranks. Like he had been just minutes before, they were all covered in sweat, grime and blood. His own sweat had now dried, his body felt sticky and rank. He licked his lips, thirsty as he was for a drink of water. He had just noticed how the heat of the sun was bearing down on him. He took slow, deep breaths, trying to focus on the task at hand, and not on the heat nor his thirst.

The Sixth Century passed back through their ranks. Artorius saw wounded men being supported by their comrades, biting their lips, refusing to give in to their pain. He turned his head in dismay as he saw two others being carried back, their bodies bloody and lifeless. The men who carried them tried to appear stoic, yet they could not completely mask their sorrow at the loss of their friends.

Artorius stumbled as the line continued to advance. Mobility was being hindered by the sheer volume of barbarian dead that littered the ground they were advancing through. Artorius took a deep breath and wiped his arm across his forehead. In the lull he had started to sweat profusely again and was struggling to keep it out of his eyes.

"Alright lads, let's get ready to do this again," Macro said as they watched the First Century engage.

"You ready to do this?" Magnus asked.

"Absolutely," Artorius replied. He started to rock slightly on the balls of his feet. He shrugged his shoulders, working any kinks out of his joints. His shield arm felt limber, his gladius was balanced, ready to strike once more.

"Decimus, no more getting knocked on your ass either," Artorius muttered, keeping his eyes front. He heard Decimus snort. The battle to their front gave no indications of slowing down. The Germans were suffering fearful losses, yet still they came. Roman losses, while still light, were starting to increase in number.

"A few more goes and they should be committing the reserves," Decimus observed. Artorius blew out a sigh of relief. He had completely forgotten that nearly half the army was behind them in reserve and hadn't even engaged yet. While the battle continued to rage at a standoff, he was certain that once the reserves were committed, the Germans would break.

"Execute passage-of-lines!" The order given, they gave another shout and passed into the fray once more.

Arminius galloped into the woods and soon fell from his horse. He lay on the ground in pain and sorrow. His mind was becoming cloudy and he was dizzy. His armies, his tribesmen, were being utterly pulverized by the Romans. Truly they were getting their revenge for Teutoburger Wald! He now cursed that day. The day that he thought had brought about Cherusci independence and freedom had instead brought about their destruction. He saw other riders coming away from the battle. He was thankful that they were Cherusci and not Roman. One dismounted and helped Arminius to his feet.

"The battle will be lost, my war chief," the man said, hanging his head in shame.

"I know," Arminius replied. "And yet our warriors still fight."

"At least they will die bringing honor to the Cherusci!"

"No, all they bring is death and slaughter. By the gods, have you not seen what is happening out there? Our warriors are not being slain in battle, they are being executed!" He clutched at his side in pain.

"What must we do?" the warrior asked.

"The stronghold," he gasped, as he fought to suppress the bleeding, "We have to get to the stronghold. There we can make another stand. Many of our women and children have fled to there, and we must protect them."

Artorius' lungs burned and his arms ached, the muscles knotted in the agony of extreme exertion. It was the fourth time they had executed a passage-of-lines, and he was completely exhausted. Sweat stung his eyes, and he struggled to keep them open. He found himself fighting with instinct more than anything else. In his peripheral vision he could see the Soldiers on either side of him fighting for their lives. He was certain that everyone in the Cohort was as exhausted as he was. He was then thankful that the Germans had not mounted a full-scale charge to try and break their lines, for at that moment he had doubts as to whether or not they could hold.

He plunged his gladius into an assailant's belly. The German fell to the ground in a heap, twitching uncontrollably in the throes of death. By this time Artorius was covered once more in fresh blood and sweat, as were the rest of the Soldiers in the Century. Thankfully the barbarian attack seemed to be losing momentum. He now had time to step back and assess the situation briefly between engagements. His breathing was coming in heaving gasps as he fought the pain in his lungs and in his muscles. As one barbarian lunged at him, he slammed his shield into the man before he had time to react. The German fell to his side, dazed. A sword thrust to the side of the neck quickly ended it. As Artorius readied himself to face yet another opponent, he heard the Cornicens in the distance sounding the advance. At last, the Legions in reserve were being committed to battle!

Though he dared not to look back behind him, Artorius swore he could actually hear the Legions coming, thousands of men, jogging in step with one another, javelins ready. The Century attacked with renewed vigor. He glanced over to see Vitruvius, in what almost looked like some sort of macabre dance, cut down three barbarians in rapid succession. He had stabbed one in the throat, and then with the exact same motion, stabbed the other two with thrusts to the chest. It was as if they were intentionally running into his blade. Gavius slammed his gladius into one man's groin as Magnus and Carbo smashed their shields into another German before both stabbed him in the chest. Artorius felt a hand grab at his ankle. He saw a stricken barbarian, completely covered in blood and gore, crawling towards him. The man was trying half-heartedly to grab his sandaled feet. His eyes looked hollow and he groaned in pain. In revulsion, Artorius started to slam his shield repeatedly onto the German's head. The metal strip on the bottom, combined with the weight of the shield and the force of his blows soon split the barbarian's head, crushing his skull.

The tide of the battle had definitely turned. One barbarian ran right into Artorius, as if trying to rush past him. He was obviously panicked, and seemed not to know which way to run. Artorius ran him through the heart with his gladius. Another was on his knees, weapons gone, pulling on his hair and howling in despair. Valens kicked the pathetic creature in the head, knocking him down, before slicing his throat open.

"Cohort...stand fast!" Proculus shouted.

Orders were shouted from behind them and soon volleys of javelins were sailing over their heads and down upon the barbarians who still lived and tried to fight. They could not see where this new wave of death was coming from, and it instilled them with panic. Their attack completely ceased for the moment.

Warriors desperately lifted their shields up over their heads as a torrent of javelins rained down on them. Ingiomerus watched as one warrior next to him took two directly through the top of his clavicle. The warrior's eyes were wide, his mouth open in disbelief. The shafts on the javelins bent, and he was pulled to the ground. Another barbarian screamed in pain as he was skewered through the hip. The force knocked him down, the javelin sticking in the ground beneath him. As another wave of javelins struck down even more, uncertainty and panic started to become paramount. The Romans seemed to have ceased in their advance for a moment. As soon as the javelin storm stopped, entire Legions passed through the ranks of those they had been fighting. Warriors in the rear started to step back, uncertain as to what to do. The ones in front, realizing that they had no choice but to fight, charged forward yet again.

Artorius set in place. He knew his fight was over. Immediately, an entire Cohort passed through their ranks, driving hard into the Germans. The Third Cohort, as well as the rest of the Legion quickly and deliberately withdrew to the rear. They would now become the reserve. Again, it seemed remarkable that no one in the Century had sustained serious injury during the engagement. Artorius had witnessed several Soldiers from within the Cohort fall, but none from the Second Century. The barbarian dead, on the other hand, stretched for miles.

Slowly they walked back to where the battle had started. Artorius knew right were it was, because that was where the piles of barbarian corpses ended. He looked to see where doctors were working frantically on the wounded. Again, the numbers were surprisingly few compared to what they had inflicted. He also saw off to the side where the bodies of the dead were laid out in a row and covered with their cloaks. The dead certainly deserved to be mourned and given proper respect. However the sight bore nothing in comparison to the spectacle of death that he had just walked through.

He turned back to the scene of the battle. The Legions to their front were rapidly gaining ground. Within minutes the enemy ranks had completely broken. They were being destroyed from the front, as well as on the flanks and rear by the Roman cavalry. Artorius then looked down at his gladius. It was soaked in blood. "You served me well today," he muttered.

CHAPTER 22

▼

THE ROUTE AND THE AFTERMATH

The barbarians were routed. They were fleeing in every direction. Germanicus spurred his horse and followed.

"Come on!" he shouted to the Cavalry Troopers with him. "This is not over yet!" He rode towards a slow moving German who was limping from a wound. With a shout he thrust his sword into the man's back, violently tearing his weapon loose as he rode by. Cavalrymen continued to slaughter the barbarians as they ran. Most would probably escape, though. The cavalry were too few, and the reserve Legions had already been committed to battle. Those who now occupied the reserve were in no condition to conduct a full blown pursuit in their state of battered exhaustion. Still Germanicus insisted on pressing the issue.

Ingiomerus ran as hard as he could. His mind raced wildly, unable as he was to control it anymore. Memories of the past flooded into his conscious as he fled through the trees. He was suddenly taken back to when he was a young man, and had suffered a similar defeat at the hands of Tiberius. Ingiomerus had watched helpless as one of his brothers was butchered by the very man who was now Emperor of Rome. Tiberius had ridden through the ranks of the vanquished, running Ingiomerus' brother through from behind. Now the Emperor's nephew could be seen riding in similar fashion, slaying all in his wake. Ingiomerus had no doubts as to which one was Germanicus. With his dazzling armor and purple crest on his helm, the young General purposely drew attention to himself. The shine on his armor had dulled as he was awash in blood, *Cherusci* blood!

Ingiomerus also remembered back seven years before to the destruction of the Rhine Army in Teutoburger Wald. That had been a different army altogether. He himself had killed five Romans during that battle, one of whom was a young Tribune. He had taken distinct pleasure in gouging out the man's eyes before beheading him. Never once did he imagine that the Romans would lash out against them like they did!

As he continued to run, the sounds of battle slowly faded into the distance. Still he forced his legs to work beyond the limits of his physical stamina and age. His legs ached, the veins in his head pulsed as sweat ran over his face, and his lungs screamed in agony.

Better this kind of pain than that of a Roman sword! he thought to himself.

Germanicus stopped his horse and surveyed the scene around him. Every German that had not fled the battle lay dead or dying on the field. Only his small contingent of cavalry was with him. All were breathing hard, covered in sweat, grime and blood. Though the Germans had been routed, there were still enough of them to conduct a counterattack against his small force should they press out too far ahead of the main body. Germanicus gave an audible sigh. His men had pushed themselves so hard during the pursuit that they had started to scatter.

"Sound recall," he told the Cornicen that rode next to him. Reluctantly, he turned around rode back to his Legions as the Cornicen sounded the notes on his horn, ordering the rest of the cavalry to do the same.

Germanicus smiled with pride as his army came into sight. All eight Legions, along with their auxiliary counterparts, were arrayed in parade formation. He rode by their ranks, surveying each. All stood solemnly, each man covered in blood and gore from the enemies he had slain. Yet every last one stood more noble and dignified than if they had polished their armor and looked their parade best. To Germanicus they looked magnificent! He rode to where a group of officers stood together at the center of the massive formation. A Centurion walked forward and handed Germanicus the spear of a slain Cherusci.

He gazed at the weapon, reveling in its significance. It was not well-crafted by any means. Really it was little more than a six-foot wooden shaft, with a sharpened stone tip strapped to the end. It was sturdy, though not very well balanced. The lack of blood on the tip told Germanicus that it had not served its owner well that day. He smiled at the thought as he turned the weapon over in his hands. This simple spear, devoid as it was of having killed a single Roman that day, was to Germanicus the ultimate symbol of their enemy's defeat. He held the spear aloft and gazed upon his men.

"My friends, brothers in arms," he began. "Today we have won a great victory. Today we can truly say that the blood spilled by our comrades in Teutoburger Wald has been avenged. This weapon is a symbol of our vanquished enemy. We will take one from each of the tribes we fought and destroyed today. We will erect a trophy in honor of our victory, in the name of the Senate and the people of Rome, and in the name of the Emperor. *Hail Caesar! Hail Tiberius!*"

"*Hail Caesar! Hail Tiberius!*" The Soldiers sounded off in return.

Twelve spears were separately inscribed with the names of the tribes they had fought. They were then stood up and bound together. The trophy was paraded in front of the army, Soldiers cheering loudly as it passed by them. Haraxus watched from cover of the woods at the hated spectacle. The Romans were making a mockery of the bravery of their warriors! He turned and ran back through the woods.

*   *   *   *

Ingiomerus placed a damp cloth over the gash on Arminius' face. Warriors had started to return from where they had scattered. They were occupying the stronghold that marked the border between Cherusci and Angrivarii territory. Many warriors bore injuries from the previous day's fighting. All were somber. There was no drinking, no revelry. So many had died fighting the Romans, and so few could claim the honor of having killed even a single Roman.

"You have nothing to be ashamed of," Ingiomerus said as he tended to his nephew. "Your warriors fought bravely. This just was not their day. Their day of glory will come." Arminius sat in silence. At least his wounds did not hurt as they had the day before. However, the loss of blood had left him dizzy and weak. He felt beaten. Haraxus ran up to where Arminius lay. He was out of breath, having run a great distance. He dropped to one knee before speaking.

"Oh Arminius, war chief of the Cherusci, I bare news from Idistaviso. The accursed Romans have made a spectacle of our dead, and have erected a trophy made from the weapons of our slain." Arminius rose up on one elbow, listening intently.

"A trophy you say?" Ingiomerus asked.

"Yes," Haraxus answered. "It is inscribed with the names of every tribe that fought against them. They were parading it in front of their army when I left."

"This is intolerable!" Ingiomerus shouted.

"Where are they moving to now?" Arminius asked.

"They are coming this way," Haraxus answered. "It would seem that they are goading us into fighting them again."

"Then we shall oblige them," Arminius said quietly. "We will defend the stronghold with our infantry. Cavalry will occupy the woods to the east in order to attack the Romans from behind. The west is a swampy marshland; they will not dare use that. Many of our women and children have come to this stronghold in order to seek protection. We need to offer them that."

Haraxus smiled. "Perhaps this will be the day of our victory. There are still many warriors who survived the battle. From a defensive position, there is hope!"

*   *   *   *

"Are you certain?" Germanicus asked the scout.

"Without a doubt," the man answered. "From what we were able to see, it looks like Arminius has rallied all of the warriors he still has under his control. They are occupying this stronghold here." He pointed to a section of map. "They have many noncombatants in this stronghold as well. It is doubtless they will try and evacuate it while their warriors defend against us."

Germanicus sighed and looked over at Severus. "Do you feel up to another major battle?" he asked. The older General shrugged.

"Giving Arminius another good thrashing can certainly do no harm," Severus answered. "We can bombard the stronghold with artillery and storm it easily enough."

"I'll lead the attack myself," Germanicus stated. "We will send another contingent to route whatever they may have massed against us in the woods here. Shall we go and have a look?"

Later that day they rode forward to where the stronghold was just coming into view. There was a deep, swampy marsh on the left and a thick forest on the right. It only left one avenue of approach available. Germanicus knew that Arminius would keep a large force within the trees, hoping to draw him into a fight there. Artillery was already being set up in a long line, facing towards the stronghold.

"Severus, you will take half the army and assault the wood lines," Germanicus ordered as they surveyed the scene in front of them. "Use your infantry. I want the cavalry kept in reserve. Once you break them, go ahead and use the cavalry to conduct the pursuit."

"Yes Sir," Severus replied calmly. The woods were thick, but this would work to their advantage. The barbarians, with their massive spears and clubs, would have less maneuverability. Their cavalry would also be greatly restricted by the terrain. Severus turned to the Legates of the Legions who would take part in the attack.

"Men, you need to reassure your Legionaries before tomorrow's battle. I know they do not like to fight in restrictive terrain. They feel that it breaks up their formations too much. What they need to do is stay online with each other, and make sure that each of them uses the trees for flank protection, like they would each other. The barbarians will be even less maneuverable with their larger weapons. By utilizing the terrain, the enemy will not be able to mass his numbers against our Soldiers. Make certain they understand this."

While Severus discussed these things with the Legates participating in the wood line attack, Germanicus surveyed the stronghold itself. The rampart was rather long, though it was no more than twenty-five feet high. Thankfully the enemy had absolutely no concept of siege warfare whatsoever. If he did, then the next day's fighting would be desperate and difficult. Enemy archers were few and far between. The Germans could do little more than hurl spears and stones down upon the Legionaries when they scaled the wall. Germanicus looked over to where Tribune Pilate was supervising the setup of artillery. The Scorpions would more than suppress whatever the enemy managed to mass on the walls. Onagers would rain fire down upon the inside of the stronghold. Germanicus could only speculate as to the sheer havoc that would cause. He saw Pilate inspecting one of the Onagers while the weapon's section leader looked on nervously.

"Everything alright, Tribune?" he asked. The section leader snapped a sharp, if rather nervous salute. Pilate, though not intimidated by the presence of his Commander, still looked worried.

"To be honest I'm not sure, Sir," Pilate replied as he continued to pull and inspect the catapult's tension ropes. "The Scorpions all checked out fine, but these Onagers I'm a little nervous about. They have never been the most stable type of siege weapons, and I worry about these tension ropes."

"Will they at least hold through tomorrow?"

Pilate thought hard before making his reply. He did not want to look incompetent in front of the Commanding General. Then again, how bad would it look if one of his weapons failed during the assault the next day?

"They should hold up through tomorrow, Sir," he finally replied. "However I am going to keep an eye on them. First sign of trouble, and I'll have to order a cease fire on the line."

"Be sure that you do," Germanicus said, standing with his arms folded, "because I really don't want to get struck by a stray firebomb tomorrow." With that he gave the Tribune a half smile, turned and left.

"What did he mean by that?" the section leader asked.

"It means that he plans on leading the attack himself. It also means we need to make damn sure these weapons are functioning properly. After all, I don't think either of us wants to explain to the Emperor why the Commanding General, who also happens to be his nephew and adopted son, was killed by his own artillery." As Germanicus walked away, Pilate turned back to his work of inspecting his heavy weapons. It would soon be dark, and he needed to be sure that all weapons were up to standard before the attack commenced in the morning.

"Ever scaled a barbarian fort before?" Statorius asked.

"Never," Artorius answered.

"Well it's not too bad," the Sergeant answered. "Those turf and sod walls are slanted and not that difficult to climb, so I doubt that we'll even bother with ladders, which can be tipped over. You just sling your shield across your back, look for hand and footholds, and up you go. The only tricky part is once you get to the top."

"Why is that?" Artorius asked.

"Because you have to be able to pull yourself over the top, get your weapons out and find your bearings before the barbarians at the top can skewer you." Artorius cringed at the thought.

"Decimus here claims to be the fastest climber in the Century," Statorius continued.

"Is that so?" Magnus asked.

"What's more, I'll prove it when we attack that fort tomorrow," Decimus replied confidently.

"You see, Decimus has been decorated with the *Rampart Crown* twice for being the first over the wall of a siege," Statorius said.

"And I intend to make it three times!" Decimus retorted. Carbo shook his head at that.

"Decimus, some days I swear you have a death wish," he remarked.

Artorius sat back and started to sharpen his gladius. There were a number of nicks on the blade that needed to be worked out. Besides, he always took pride in keeping the blade razor sharp.

"What do you think about attacking this German stronghold?" Magnus asked, taking a seat on the ground beside him.

"If we execute it right, it shouldn't be anything to worry about," Artorius replied, running the sharpening stone across his blade.

"I just hate the thought of not being able to see the enemy at the top, not knowing where they are going to be."

"Would you rather they were where they could see *us*?" Artorius asked. "The last thing I want is to get picked off the wall by one of their spear throwers or archers." He hefted his gladius, admiring the blade. One would scarcely guess the amount of use it had gotten over the past year and a half.

Later that night, Artorius was coming off of sentry duty when he saw torches over by the artillery positions. He walked over to investigate and saw that Pilate was inspecting the tension rope on one of the Onagers. Artorius walked up and saluted.

"Out for a late night stroll?" Pilate asked, returning the salute.

"Just thought I would check and see what the commotion was over here," Artorius answered.

"It's these damned tension ropes on the Onagers," Pilate said, pulling on one as he did so. "I've never placed a lot of faith in the construction of these small catapults."

"They've served us well so far," Artorius replied. "I guess that could have something to do with the officer in charge of them?"

Pilate laughed. "Come on, Artorius. No need to put your lips to my backside just because I happen to be a Tribune." He turned to faced Artorius, leaning back against the wagon as he did so. He looked at his old friend and sighed. So much had changed since both of them had left home. His old school mate was now a Legionary infantryman, while he himself was a Military Tribune. "Has it really been so long since your father tutored us both?"

"Feels like a lifetime ago," Artorius said, looking down. "This is definitely a completely different world than the one we came from."

"Back home we could lay aside the differences in our birth and social upbringings. And yet we now live in this world in order to protect the other," Pilate mused. "You know, most Tribunes only serve on the line for six months. I've been gone for four years and have been home twice during that time."

"Well perhaps you'll get a third chance soon," Artorius observed. "Surely our victory over here will not go unnoticed back home."

"I daresay not," Pilate answered. "However we still have at least one more battle to get through before we can go home and celebrate."

"Have you ever done a siege before?" Artorius asked.

"Only once," Pilate answered. "I had the privilege of laying down an artillery barrage on a Cherusci stronghold when we went to liberate our ally, Segestes. If executed properly, an assault on a fortified position is not something to get overly concerned about. However, the timing has to be perfect. The artillery needs to lift their fire at exactly the right moment as the assaulting element goes over the top. Otherwise the enemy will have time to regroup and possibly throw back the assault. And if the artillery waits too long, well let's just say it could cause a number of our own people to have a very bad day. I take it you are going to be part of the assault tomorrow."

"Yes, in the front rank, in fact" Artorius answered.

"Be careful then. I'll do my best to keep the barbarians off of you long enough for you to get over the wall. After that, I'm afraid you are on your own."

"We'll be alright," Artorius said. "The Second Century hasn't lost anyone yet on this campaign, and we've had fewer combat related injuries than any other Century in the Legion."

"Well I hope you can maintain that," Pilate said as he went back to checking his machines.

As Artorius returned to his tent, he saw Magnus and Praxus talking quietly and eating a small meal over a fire.

"Can't sleep?" he asked his friends as he sat down beside them. Magnus was stuffing his face with bread and bacon. Artorius laughed at the sight. Praxus found it amusing as well.

"Just trying to help our friend Magnus here calm his nerves a bit before the morrow," the older Legionary replied as he handed Magnus another biscuit. Artorius looked puzzled.

"What is it, man?" he asked as Magnus crammed the biscuit into his mouth and took a long pull off of his water bladder. With great effort he managed to swallow it all. He then took a deep breath before answering.

"To tell you the truth Artorius, I'm afraid of heights." Magnus looked downwards, as if ashamed. Artorius was surprised by this, and had to stifle a laugh.

"You mean to tell me that after all we've faced here, you're afraid of climbing over a little rampart?"

"What can I say? I get nervous when I think about falling. And you can't tell me that you aren't the least bit worried about tomorrow! After all, we are to be the first ones over the wall."

"I never said I wasn't concerned," Artorius replied. "I just have a little bit of faith in myself, and in those who will accompany me tomorrow." He gave Magnus a friendly slap on the shoulder.

"Besides," Praxus added, "if you do fall on your head, it will only hurt for a second!" Magnus elbowed him in the ribs, though he was smiling and seemed to have relaxed a bit.

*   *   *   *

"The Roman auxiliaries are covering the rear of the stronghold and the tree lines. They are supported by archers," Ietano reported.

"With the Legions to our front, and the swamp on our flank, the Romans have us surrounded," Haraxus observed. Arminius was laying back with his head on a rock. He seemed to be only half listening. Ingiomerus leaned over and placed his hand on his nephew's shoulder.

"If we leave now, we can organize a breakout," he said. "I can lead the cavalry straight into the auxiliary lines, allowing us to get the women and children away."

"And then what?" Haraxus scoffed. "As dark as it is, our people won't be able to see where they are going. It will be little more than a disorganized route! And even if we do manage to break out, then what? Run away until we are hunted down like dogs? At least here we have a fighting chance, a chance to live!"

"A chance to be incinerated alive, more like," Ietano retorted. "Have you not seen those hated machines the Romans brought with them? They will turn this stronghold into a pit of fire and ash before they even scale the walls!"

"What say you, Arminius?" Haraxus asked. Arminius' eyes looked lost and distant. Clearly, his wounds still affected him. After a minute he finally spoke.

"Whether we run or we fight, we are damned. We will fight long enough for the Romans to commit all their forces to the storming of this stronghold. During that time, we will try to evacuate the women and children. I know that many will refuse to leave, not wanting to abandon their men to die alone. If we are to die, then we will die with Roman swords in our guts, not in our backs."

▼

The Stronghold and Final Justice

The Legion was arrayed in full battle order. The First and the Twentieth Legions had been selected to carry the assault, along with the two Cohorts of the Praetorian Guard that accompanied Germanicus. The General himself was on foot and conspicuously devoid of his helmet. He was pacing back in forth in front of the assaulting Cohorts. He was smiling and bantering with the men of the Praetorians.

"Is he really going to lead this assault?" Valens asked.

"That's what it looks like," Magnus answered.

"I guess he wants to make the Emperor proud," Statorius remarked. Were he still in the field, most veterans had no doubt that Tiberius would have led this attack personally as well, such had been his reputation.

"Quite a reputation to try and live up to when your adoptive father is not only Emperor of the known world, but also one of the most aggressive Soldiers to have ever lived," Vitruvius remarked. The Optio was at the left end of the line, right next to where Statorius' section had fallen in at.

"I think he's lived up to it pretty well," Artorius replied.

"He'll get his chance to add to that reputation soon enough," Praxus added.

"Yes, quite soon," Vitruvius muttered to himself.

Horns sounded, and the Legions tasked with scouring the woods around the stronghold moved out. This was also the signal for Pilate to begin his artillery barrage.

Arminius sat brooding, his back to the rampart. The wounds on his face and abdomen still troubled him. He reached up and felt the gash on his face. It was fresh, and would leave a scar. That was alright, he had plenty of scars. His side was still bandaged up. He had packed the wound with medicinal herbs to speed healing and prevent infection; something he had learned from the Romans.

He looked inside the stronghold. There were scores of huts and buildings inside. Men were ushering their wives and children into what they hoped were the soundest shelters. One woman was carrying a sword and arguing with her husband, while her toddler son tugged on her other hand. Arminius marveled at the sight. Even the women of his tribe were willing to fight to the last. He listened intently, able as he was to hear their debate.

"I can fight!" the woman shouted. "And I will not sit idle while you commit suicide!" Her husband sighed.

"I know you can fight. But what we need now is courage beyond that of fighting the Romans. Somebody has to help our people to rise again. When I am gone, you will raise our sons to be great warriors. You will teach them what it means to be Cherusci!" The woman smiled weakly and averted her eyes downward.

"If you are overrun, what will keep the Romans from slaughtering every last person here?" she asked. "You said so yourself. They do not come for conquest or slaves. They come for extermination! If I am to die today, and if our children are to die, then we will die where we belong; fighting by your side." As she spoke, she placed a hand on the side of her husband's face. Their elder son, perhaps eight or nine placed his hand on his mother's shoulder. He carried a wicker shield and club in his other hand, though both were too big for him to wield effectively. The father lifted his youngest into his arms, and embraced his wife and elder son. Tears were in his eyes.

"I have been so blessed to have such a family," he said. "But you must live. If I die, and we do get overrun, you must make your way into the forests. You must do this for me." His wife clung to him tightly, not saying a word. The warrior then released his family, his face stoic. He nodded, drew his sword, and returned to the rampart.

"Is there no hope for us, Mother? Are we really going to die today?" the eldest son asked, looking up into her face. Her face set and determined, the woman kneeled down and placed both hands on her son's shoulders.

"If we show true courage, and if we face the Romans like Cherusci, then all of us will live forever in the Halls of the Valiant. I do not fear them." She held both her sons close, trying hard to hide her own tears, for she knew their fate. If they tried to flee, they would only be cut down during the Roman pursuit. To die running was unacceptable.

"The Romans are coming!" a young lad shouted from the rampart. Arminius and the warriors rushed forward to see for themselves. Thousands of Roman infantry were formed up on the dry plain in front of them. In the distance, the brightly colored paint and the metal bosses on their shields gleamed in the sun. Their helmets and armor reflected the glare even more so. In true Roman fashion they moved in utter silence. They would only make a sound when the time came to engage. It was unnerving. Arminius looked beyond the mass of infantry. As expected, the Roman artillery was set, crews working frantically on each weapon. Arminius started to breathe heavily. The pending barrage would be devastating.

"Scorpions load!" Pilate shouted. Loaders rapidly cranked back the tension ropes on their weapons. They then placed bolts into the firing grooves as gunners looked down their sites towards the stronghold.

"Scorpions ready, Sir!" Dionysus called back once all crews reported that they were set. Pilate walked up and down the line of Scorpions. Behind them, Onagers were loaded with their fire pots. Beside each a torch bearer stood awaiting orders.

"Monitor your sectors," he told the Scorpion crews. "Only fire at what you can hit. Precision shots, lads!" He looked over at the wall. In his peripheral vision he could see the Legions advancing on the woods. A detachment of Onagers had been designated to cover their advance as well. He saw movement on the wall of the stronghold. There seemed to be excited shouting and pointing coming from the ramparts. It was time to put a stop to it. On the line one of the gunners watched as a figure silhouetted itself fully in his sight. He gave a sinister smile. This was going to be all too easy. He wondered to himself if he could score a head shot.

"Scorpion crews…fire! Onagers ignite!"

The gunner elevated his weapon slightly and squeezed the firing mechanism.

"Got you!" he uttered in a low breath as the bolt flew home.

"The Romans are advancing on the wood lines!" the young lookout shouted. He couldn't have been any older than fourteen, not even old enough to grow a beard.

"Damn, they anticipated our move once again," Arminius muttered. He was still dizzy from the effects of his injuries and was having trouble focusing.

"Tell your son to get off that wall! And get the rest of those men off of there!" Ingiomerus shouted at Haraxus. The other warrior just laughed.

"My son's a brave lad, and he's serving us well as a lookout. *Aren't you lad?*" The boy smiled and turned back to gaze over the ramparts. Suddenly they saw a long bolt fly through the air and smash through his face and head. Blood and bits of bone sprayed everywhere as he fell into a heap on the rampart. A Scorpion bolt protruded from the back of his skull.

"No!" Haraxus screamed as he ran towards his dead son, whose body was twitching and convulsing violently. More Scorpion bolts were seen flying towards the stronghold. Warriors that were standing up conspicuously were picked off by the highly accurate weapons. One lay screaming on the ground as a bolt protruded from his upper arm. Another warrior cried out as he sprouted a bolt from his thigh. His leg started to spasm uncontrollably as he fought to keep his balance. His leg snagged on a section of turf and he pitched head first over the side of the wall. Yet another warrior took a precise hit to the chest and was dead before he hit the ground. Haraxus knelt down on the rampart, cradling the head of his son, tears streaming down his face.

"Haraxus, get down!" Arminius shouted. Haraxus ignored him. All he could do was clutch his son while sobbing uncontrollably. A Scorpion bolt slammed through the grieving father's neck, spraying Arminius in blood. Haraxus bore a look of both pain and relief in his eyes. He still clung to the body of his son, as both tumbled over the rampart, onto the ground below. Arminius turned his head away, trying to drown out the audible screams of his warriors as they were horribly maimed. Then a wave of fireballs came over the rampart in a high arc; flames spewed forth from the bowels of Hell. Their target was the inner structures, where the families of the warriors cringed in fear.

"Look out!" he shouted to the people below. It was too late. The fireballs were already falling inside the compound, exploding wherever they impacted. Huts inside the stronghold burst into flames, their thatched roofs feeding the fire to a raging blaze. Warriors turned back from the ramparts and looked on horrified as their wives and children became the targets of the Roman firestorm. There was nowhere for them to run to. The torrent of fire seemed to find all who sought shelter within. Arminius watched as what looked like a sound shelter burst into flames, the walls quickly crumbling. The screams of horror were almost deafening, those trapped inside slowly suffocating or burning to death. He quickly turned back to the rampart, trying to shut the nightmare from his mind.

"Their infantry are advancing on us!" a warrior shouted, peaking over the rampart. Suddenly the back of his throat exploded as another Scorpion bolt found its mark.

"*Stay down! Nobody goes to the wall!*" Arminius shouted. "We'll face them as they come over. Uncle, you take the right wing." He and Ingiomerus drew their swords and waited. Ingiomerus walked over to the extreme right of the wall. He leaned back against a niche, resting the blade of his sword in his hand. The wait was maddening. He could hear the Romans advancing towards the wall. How long would it take them to get over the top? For the first time since the campaign began he was afraid. Even when he had been wounded during their assault on the Roman fort at Ahenobarbi, he had not felt fear the way he did now. Now they were the ones cornered, and there was nowhere for them to run. If only their plan for defense had been as sound as the Romans' had been!

The First and Twentieth Legions had started to advance. Nobody in the assault elements carried javelins, as they would be nearly impossible to employ. Swords remained sheathed, and each Soldier kept a tight grip on his shield. They stayed in close formation, in case the barbarians managed to engage them with missile weapons. None came. Artorius watched the fireballs from the Onagers and the Scorpion bolts falling almost like rain onto the stronghold. He could see smoke and traces of fire coming from within.

"We have turned that place into Hell itself," he breathed.

It was indeed hell within the stronghold. While turf and stone fortifications were ideally suited for defense during intertribal warfare, they were useless against the technologically advanced Roman war machine. The Germans had no concept whatsoever of artillery, let alone how to defend against it. By having all of their peoples confined in one place, it had made it that much easier for the Romans to employ their siege weapons against them. Warriors howled in pain as they were skewered by Scorpion bolts, women and children screamed in pain and terror as they were smashed and burned. It was as if demons from the underworld were spewing fire and wrath upon them.

"What are they, Mother?" a boy screamed, hiding underneath a shield. Their hut had been burned, and now there was nowhere for them to hide. A fireball exploded nearby, shards and fire spraying them.

"Take courage!" his mother cried, holding him and her toddler close. They watched horrified as one woman took the brunt of a fireball in the back as she tried to run past them. It erupted, covering her in liquid fire. She laid screaming on the ground as she was slowly consumed, the smell of burning flesh and hair overpowering the senses. Many were running towards the rear of the stronghold, hoping to escape through the woods beyond. The woman clung to her children, paralyzed as she was with fear for them. She tried to protect them from the firestorm with her shield as she searched desperately for any sign of her husband. She would not leave without him.

"The gods have abandoned us," she muttered under her breath. She knew the Romans would storm the stronghold with their infantry, but the preceding firestorm had taken all of them by surprise. She did not know that men were capable of such destruction.

Through the haze of smoke, they could see a man walking slowly towards them. His eyes were glazed and distant, his face expressionless. It was only as he got closer that the woman saw that it was her husband, a scorpion bolt protruding from his chest. His breathing was shallow and sounded like a hiss, trickles of blood running from the corners of his mouth.

"No," she moaned as she rose to her feet. Her eyes clouded with tears as her husband fell into her arms. His breathing had almost completely subsided as she gently lowered him to the ground. She gently ran her fingers through his hair as he reached up and touched her face with the last of his strength.

"I go now to be with my forefathers," he whispered. His wife broke into a wailing sob as she buried her face in his lifeless chest, her one arm wrapped around him, the other beating a fist into the ground in sorrow and despair.

The firestorm continued unabated. Onagers continued to rain death over the heads of the advancing Legions. Artorius watched as one fireball wobbled through the air, out of control. It fell short of its mark, impacting on the wall of the stronghold. Liquid fire sprayed everywhere, dousing and burning a section of turf.

"Oh that's not good," he remarked.

"Damn it, who fired that one?" Pilate shouted, obviously enraged. Had that fireball impacted while the infantry were scaling the turf wall, the result would have been disastrous.

"Over here Sir," one section leader called out. "Blasted rope on this thing snapped as we fired!"

"I knew it, I fucking *knew* it!" Pilate shouted to himself. He took a deep breath and looked back to the assault. The infantry were close to the wall. He could not allow another accident like that to happen again. Besides, he could see smoke and the occasional flame coming from inside the stronghold. The Onagers had done their job. He nodded and exhaled audibly.

"Alright," he said. "Onagers cease fire! Scorpion crews, increase your rate of fire. Keep the heads of those bastards down!"

"Sir!" the section leaders sounded of.

"Alright lads, here we go," Centurion Macro said as they reached the base of the wall. The wall itself was part natural, part man made. It was mainly sod and turf that had been built up around a naturally high piece of ground. There seemed to be plenty of hand holds available. Artorius was not too concerned about slipping and falling.

"Make sure that once you are over, you move inside quickly," Macro ordered. "We have to be able to make room for the others. It is critical that we link up as soon as we are inside."

"Let's do this," Vitruvius said as he slung his shield over his back.

Artorius looked over at Magnus. "See you at the top!"

"Yeah," was all Magnus could reply as he took a deep, nervous breath and blew out hard.

"Now to earn my third Rampart Crown!" he heard Decimus announce as he started to climb at an alarmingly fast rate.

Artorius grabbed a section of wall and started to climb. He was encumbered by his weapons and armor; however his enormous strength made the task fairly easy. He reached carefully, but quickly for each new handhold, keeping his body close to the wall and using his legs to propel him upward. At one point a section of turf came off in his hand. He slipped and kept a death grip on the wall with his other hand, hoping that that would not come loose as well.

"Easy there Soldier," Vitruvius said as he grabbed onto him.

"I'm alright," Artorius answered as he continued his climb. He looked over to see that Decimus was already almost to the top. He had purposely ceased climbing and was waiting for the others to catch up before he lunged over the rampart. As Artorius got closer to the top, he could here the sounds of Scorpion bolts whistling overhead. He was almost there.

The fireballs had stopped coming, yet those cursed Scorpions continued to inflict death upon Arminius' warriors. Most of them kept their heads down behind the wall, yet occasionally some would get curious and risk a look. Often these men were felled by the waiting Roman gunners. Then suddenly the bolts stopped coming altogether.

"Here they come!" one warrior shouted as they all started to rise and surge towards the rampart.

"Wait, not yet!" Arminius shouted, but again he was too late.

"Scorpions reload and stand by for one final volley!" Pilate ordered his crews, then emphasizing, *"Wait for my command!"* The idea was something he had conceived after his last siege. He knew that once they stopped firing, the Germans would know that the infantry were almost to the top. At the first sign of Roman Soldiers coming over the rampart they would surge forward. That would be the time to unleash their final volley. Pilate had reviewed his plan with the Cohort Commanders. He hoped that the Legionaries themselves would remember it and wait for the final volley to fire before surging over the wall. It was a calculated risk they were taking. The last thing he wanted was to shoot a friendly in the back. However, he felt there was a much greater risk of the barbarian surge repelling the first wave and inflicting heavy casualties. His plan would give the assaulting elements the seconds they would need in order to get over the wall. He watched as the first group of Soldiers made ready to make the final push. He then saw the heads of numerous Cherusci warriors as they made their way forward.

"Fire!"

Numerous warriors gave a loud cry and surged forward. As they did, one last wave of Scorpion bolts flew in a volley, slamming home into many who had moved to disgorge the Roman intruders. The rest paused, stunned by the shock and surprise of the Romans' final barrage as their companions fell dead or stricken. The delay gave the Legionaries the time they needed.

Ingiomerus watched as one Roman Soldier at the corner of the wall climbed up and over. The Legionary stumbled and slipped onto his stomach as he tried to pull himself over. Ingiomerus gave a loud shout and lunged forward. He swung his sword down in a hard smash. The Roman, anticipating this, rolled to his side, so that the sword deflected off the shield that was still strapped to his back. Before Ingiomerus could strike again, another Roman came over the wall This one kept hold and like a cat sprung to his feet on top of the rampart, drawing his weapon in a flash. Ingiomerus turned to face this new threat as the young Legionary leaped off the wall, shouting in rage. The Soldier plunged his gladius deep into the old warrior's chest. Ingiomerus felt a horrific pain as he was ran through. He fell back into the other rampart, his lungs quickly filling with blood. He gasped, unable to breathe, his eyes wide. He slowly slid down the wall as the young Roman wrenched his gladius from his chest, ribs snapping as he did so.

So this is what it is like to die a warrior's death, Ingiomerus thought to himself as his breath gave out.

On another section of the wall, Arminius ran forward and jabbed his sword into the neck of a Roman who had lost his footing while trying to come over the wall. His warriors took heart and surged to the attack. Several Romans were struck down in similar fashion. One took a spear to the face and was knocked off the wall, his neck snapping as his head hit the rocks below. Another was struck by an axe right on the back of his neck, killing him instantly. But then like a wave, a large number of Legionaries leapt over the top. Arminius turned to face one of these. He swung his sword rapidly, as the Roman tried to deflect with his gladius. Arminius then felt a stabbing pain in the back of his leg. He fell to the ground and lay in a heap against the wall as even more Roman Soldiers poured over the side.

He reached down and felt the fresh wound on his leg. Blood was oozing from it, though it was not gushing. It was a painful gash; however it would not prove to be fatal if he could escape from the stronghold. He turned onto his side and watched as waves of Legionaries stormed into the center of the fort. He then let out a sigh. This would be the last stand of the Cherusci. If any did survive the massacre, they would be scattered to the winds, never to rise again.

Artorius looked down at the warrior he had just slain. The man was old, a lot older than most of the other warriors. Perhaps he was a chief or elder of some sort? He reached over and helped Vitruvius to his feet.

"You alright?" he asked.

"Yeah. Let's go, we have to move off the rampart quickly!" Vitruvius shouted as they unbuckled their shields and looked for the rest of the Century. Macro had been right; they had to move fast. Once the first wave had crested the wall, it was only a matter of seconds before a host of others joined them. The warriors who remained on the rampart were quickly driven off. The lucky ones were slain quickly. The rest had to deal with the horror that awaited them inside the stronghold as they made their way through the devastation.

Many of the structures inside the fort were burning. There was mass hysteria as people tried to flee. Artorius watched as Centurion Macro very calmly descended into the madness below.

"Second Century on me!" The Centurion shouted. Quickly everyone descended the rampart and linked up with their Centurion. Magnus dispatched one warrior with a rapid stab to the back as he did so. Most of the others had fled to go and try to save their families. Artorius watched as their Cohort Commander, Proculus, walked over to Macro.

"No one gets out, no one gets taken alive!" he said.

"Yes Sir," Macro acknowledged. Within seconds the Century was on line. At a slow walk, they moved through the chaos. It was not a battle, it was a slaughter. Artorius saw to his right in the distance Germanicus himself, still without a helmet, slashing and stabbing his way through a crowd of barbarians.

"I guess he went without the helmet to draw attention to himself," Magnus observed.

"Brave, but reckless," Artorius remarked.

"Just like his uncle," Magnus replied as he casually drove his gladius into a barbarian who was trying to run past them. Artorius tried to shut his conscience down as he worked his way through the killing fields. At first he did not really desire to kill noncombatants, but orders were orders. Besides, he reasoned, the entire tribe needed to be punished and purged! His face contorted in the throes of bloodlust as he plunged headlong into his grizzly task.

He came upon a woman who was kneeling over a fallen warrior. She clutched him tightly and was wailing loudly. Her husband's head was held in her one arm, a sword dangled from the other. A Scorpion bolt protruded from the man's chest. A young child kneeled by her side, unable to comprehend what was happening. In what he construed to be an act of mercy, Artorius walked over to the woman, grabbed her by the hair, and ran his gladius through her neck. The woman's eyes opened wide in terror and realization, but then gave a look of almost contented peace as she slumped over the body of her husband. Artorius then heard a scream of horror as a young boy rushed him with an oversized shield and club in his hands. Carbo intercepted the boy, knocking him back against the wall of a hut with his shield. The boy snarled and slashed violently. Carbo gritted his teeth, and with rapid precision pulled back on his shield and thrust his gladius into the boy's heart. The lad's eyes grew wide, though he made not a sound. As Carbo withdrew his gladius, the boy collapsed to the ground in a heap. Artorius looked over to see that Magnus had his sword raised, ready to slay the younger child. He stood frozen, his face wrought in confused torment, unable to ram his gladius home. Artorius briskly walked over, cradled the child's head in his hand and stabbed him beneath the ribs, all the while keeping his eyes on Magnus. A feeling of revulsion welled up inside him and he swallowed hard to keep bile from coming up. Magnus had lowered his arm and was staring at the ground, shaking his head. Artorius grabbed him by the shoulder.

"No one gets out, no one gets taken alive." The words were as much for his own reassurance as his friend's. And yet he could not bring himself to look upon the family they had just slain.

"Artorius, Magnus! What in Hades are you guys doing back there?" Statorius screamed at them. He and the rest of the section were a good thirty meters ahead. Their minds immediately back to the task at hand, the two Legionaries rushed to join their comrades so that they could sooner be done with their nightmarish task.

The firestorm the artillery barrage had wrought only added to the horror of the spectacle. The buildings burned. Those still alive inside cried out in pain, begging for death to come. Artorius sweated profusely as the heat seared him. People ran to and fro, some having caught fire, all in utter panic. He wondered if in fact they were walking through Hell itself.

As they reached the far side of the fort, a line of barbarian warriors stood fast, trying to make a last stand. There were not very many. Many were bare-chested, their bodies bearing numerous cuts and burns. Their faces showed the extreme fear, desperation, and despair of men doomed to die. The Romans moved deliberately and with the utmost sense of order as they moved out of the haze of smoke and fire. The barbarians each carried a pair of spears. Together they threw a volley towards their advancing enemy.

"Get down!" Macro shouted as they dropped down behind their shields. The spears skipped off harmlessly. The warriors then mustered what courage they had left, gave a final battle cry and charged the advancing Romans who had all simultaneously risen to their feet.

Vitruvius smashed a barbarian with his shield. Two rapid thrusts with his gladius and two opponents lay stricken on the ground, both twitching violently, blood gushing from their wounds.

One warrior tried to bring his spear around Artorius' shield and stab him. He kicked the spear aside with his shield and slammed the point of his sword into the barbarian's stomach. Magnus brought his shield down onto one warrior's foot, and followed it up with a stab underneath the ribs. Within a matter of seconds it was over. The Cherusci's final charge had been little more than a mass suicide.

Artorius mounted the far rampart and surveyed the scene below. There were a large number of women, children, and elderly, along with a handful of warriors, who were running for the woods. Roman infantry from Severus' detachment had already sealed off their escape. They were marching back towards the fort, methodically slaying all who stood in their path. Artorius wondered if any had in fact escaped, or were all doomed to die in this place.

Germanicus then mounted the rampart himself and stared in awe at the spectacle of death. Realizing they were trapped, the Germans huddled close to each other in utter terror. The Romans ceased their advance as they came to within a few feet of the mob. Their officers eyed their Commander, awaiting his confirmation.

"Do we take prisoners, Sir?" a nearby Centurion asked. His face emotionless, Germanicus shook his head.

"We have come to destroy these people, not conquer them. Extermination will be their lot." He paused before reemphasizing his point. "Wipe them out...*all* of them." The Centurion signaled to the men below, who then continued in their brutal task, sparing none. Men, women, children, all were viciously slain. The ground became slippery as the earth was saturated in blood and gore.

Artorius turned back towards the scene of fire and death behind him. The smoke was incredibly thick. Fire had consumed nearly all of the structures inside. Bodies were burning as well. The smell was pungent and it made him wretch. His stomach finally overcame his ability to suppress his gagging, and he briefly found himself vomiting uncontrollably. He was at first ashamed, until he saw that he was not the only one. Even those who managed to control their stomachs looked worn and shaken. Germanicus himself was ashen-faced at the sights and smells that assailed them.

Artorius gazed over his shoulder once more, hoping that they would not have to walk back through that nightmare which they had created. He saw the body of the woman he had slain over the body of her husband. Both were burning, along with the corpses of their children. He shook his head, wiped the smoke and sweat from his eyes and looked back at the scene outside the stronghold. Some of the barbarians wailed and sobbed loudly, others just stared blankly into space as the Romans trapped them against the outside wall of the stronghold. Soon not a single one was left alive. Many of the Soldiers hung their heads, taking no pride in that instead of warriors, they had slain mostly women, children, and the crippled elderly. They knew that the repugnant task they had performed had been necessary to exact retribution and end the war, but it brought them little solace.

"Is this what victory looks like?" Artorius asked Magnus, who was surveying the scene with similar feelings.

"I guess it does," he answered. "Though tell me this Artorius, is this what revenge looks like?" Artorius took a deep breath, unable to avert his gaze.

"It does," he said finally. "It is also the symbol of justice, the *final* justice that we have exacted."

*   *   *   *

Arminius fell into the marsh with a loud splash. A mind-numbing pain shot through his injured leg as he lost his footing and fell face first into the mire. Strong hands lifted him to his feet. As he cleared the muck from his eyes, he was pleased to see that it was one of his warriors, escaped as well from the hell that had been their stronghold. Arminius recognized the man's face, though he could not remember his name. He looked around and saw there were a few others who had managed to make their way out. They were mostly warriors, most of the women and children having perished inside.

"Come, we must move quickly before the Romans close this area off," the warrior said. Arminius simply nodded as the man placed an arm under his and helped him make his way through the swamps.

"So much death," he said to himself. He knew that some of the men had taken their families and had tried to escape during the night. Perhaps some of them made it, he hoped. The rest had stayed in the stronghold, believing that Arminius could somehow bring salvation and deliver them from Rome's vengeance. Only a small handful of these had managed to escape into the swamps, mostly young warriors without families. Those who knew that their loved ones could not escape had fought to the bitter end to protect them. Arminius knew that it had all been for naught.

"Such is the price of our vain glory."

*   *   *   *

The sun was setting and the army stood once again in parade formation. The forces that attacked the woods had completely routed their opposition. The dense woods had actually worked to the Romans' advantage, as they were used to close combat and fighting in tight spaces. Though many had managed to flee the stronghold, even more had been slain as they had fought to repel their attackers. Germanicus stood on a makeshift dais, holding aloft an inscribed placard; the final piece of another trophy constructed from the weapons of their fallen enemy. He was an absolute nightmare to look at. Soot, blood and sweat covered him from head to foot, though he had lost none of his persona. He was completely exhausted, and yet filled with elation. He placed the placard on the mound of enemy arms. The inscription read:

The army of Tiberius Caesar, after thoroughly conquering the tribes between the Rhine and the Elbe, has dedicated this monument to Mars, Jupiter, and Augustus. [1]

"Once again we have brought victory to the name of the Emperor, the Senate and the people of Rome!" Germanicus announced to his assembled host. "We have once more wrought vengeance upon our enemies! We can now return across the Rhine, and then to Rome in triumph!" This elicited a chorus of cheers from the ranks.

"My friends, your deeds and your valor will echo throughout all time!" Germanicus raised his blood-soaked gladius in triumph. He could not have been happier or more proud

CHAPTER 24

▼

REDEMPTION

The army marched back to their boats on the Ems River. Though they still maintained proper vanguard and flank security, there was a sense of ease from amongst the ranks. They knew that the Cherusci and their allies were completely broken. So many warriors had died in the battles of the past few days. Roman losses in both battles had been surprisingly light by comparison. The auxiliary infantry had borne the brunt of the losses at Idistaviso. Only a small handful had fallen during the storming of the German stronghold. Sadly the Second Century had lost three men during the assault. Among the fallen was Antoninus, the young recruit who had gone through training with Artorius, Magnus and Gavius. He had slipped on the turf while trying to get over the wall and had taken a sword thrust to the throat.

Soon after the assault, Germanicus had sent Stertinius to make war once more upon the Angrivarii. So abrupt had been their surrender that all knew the Germanic alliance to be truly broken. Keeping his word about showing mercy to those who surrendered willingly, he granted them a full pardon.

Upon reaching the Ems, Germanicus ordered the majority of the army to take the boats home. The Fifth and Twentieth Legions, however, he ordered to take the overland route back to the Rhine. A day after having started their march west, Severus and Gaius Silius, Legate of the Fifth Legion, were holding counsel in Severus' tent, when a Legionary stuck his head in.

"Beg your pardon Sirs, but our reconnaissance patrols have captured a German who claims to be chief of the Marsi."

"Send him in," Severus replied with a wave of his hand. The Soldier nodded and left. Soon a burly, but surprisingly well dressed barbarian was ushered in by a pair of Legionaries. He was wearing custom-made breaches, with a purple cloak draped over his well muscled frame. His hair was pulled back, and his mustache well groomed. One of the Soldiers carried the barbarian's sword, which he handed to Silius. It was a large, two-handed broadsword, sheathed in a highly ornate scabbard.

"His weapon, Sir." Silius took the sword and waived the Soldiers away. Both men saluted and left the German alone with the Legates. Silius drew the sword, admiring its craftsmanship.

"This is good sword," he remarked, hefting the weapon, checking its balance. "Given its condition, one would think it was meant more for ceremony than killing."

"It has seen its share of fighting," the Marsi chief replied in heavily accented Latin.

"Quite," Silius replied, sheathing the weapon and placing it on a nearby table.

"To what do we owe this pleasure?" Severus asked; arms folded across his chest. The German assumed a similar posture before continuing.

"My name is Mallovendus. I am now chief of what remains of the Marsi. Most of our settlements, as well as our people, were annihilated during your campaigns of the last years. Those who survived fear that we will once more face the Roman war machine, being as we are closest to your fortresses on the Rhine."

"Such is the lot of your people," Severus replied with a casual shrug. "But surely you did not come to simply make such an obvious observation."

"No," Mallovendus said, shaking his head. "I have come to offer truce, and to beg for the lives of my people. I personally fear neither pain nor death." He pulled back his cloak to reveal a number of fearful scars upon his torso. "What I do fear is that my people, like a candle, may be blown out of existence completely, like the Cherusci. We have paid for our warmongering. I now ask that those who survived be spared. My sword, please." He pointed over to the table, where his weapon still lay. Severus gave an affirmative nod to Silius, who handed the sword back to Mallovendus. The Marsi chief then dropped to one knee, head bowed, presenting his sword to Severus.

"I ask now that peace may exist between our peoples, that we may draw blades against each other no more." Severus maintained his stance and composure.

"It would indeed benefit your people to enjoy the peace of Rome. However, what are you offering us in return for your salvation; what token can you use to show us your good intentions?" Mallovendus raised his head and looked Severus in the eye.

"I offer you the Eagle of the Nineteenth Legion."

*   *   *   *

The Twentieth Legion was on the march. Artorius was thinking about his lost friend, Antoninus, when he saw riders approaching their column. The scouts were pointing towards where a Marsi settlement existed. He thought he heard the scouts say that it was abandoned. Proculus and Master Centurion Flavius held a brief discussion before Flavius pointed Proculus towards the direction of the settlement. Proculus spurred his horse towards his waiting men.

"Third Cohort skirmish formation, six ranks! At the quick step, march!" The orders were echoed by the Centurions and Optios as the Cohort effortlessly formed up and marched away rapidly.

As they approached the abandoned settlement, torches were passed out, when Centurion Macro gave the order not to ignite them. This puzzled most of the Soldiers, as there were numerous huts and structures. This looked to have been a rather prosperous settlement that had somehow survived the purging of the Marsi lands.

"Take what you will, lads!" Macro ordered. "You have thirty minutes to round up whatever you can carry. The buildings however we will leave intact." The Century cheered as the moved into the village. Even on a mission of plunder, they still moved with order and discipline. Severus may have promised to spare the Marsi villages from burning; however he had made no mention of plunder. Macro had been told the real reason for this. He had decided to keep it quiet, lest their search for the missing Eagle prove futile.

Artorius entered a hut that he supposed belonged to a warrior, given the impressive, albeit archaic décor. There was an animal skin shield in one corner, along with a dagger and belt. He picked these up and examined them. The dagger was quite ornate, though in obvious need of repair and oiling. He found a copper goblet that stank of some foul form of alcohol. He figured it had probably never been properly washed. It would seem that the owner of the house had left in a hurry.

"Who are you?" Artorius asked aloud. "Are you really a rebellious warrior and an enemy of Rome? Or are you simply one of the many caught up in this war who only wants to live free and in peace?" He was surprised to hear such things coming from him. He looked around some more and walked upstairs to an elevated loft. There was a large, crude bed in the center, along with two smaller ones off to the side. Everything was in disarray.

Suddenly he heard excited shouts coming from outside. He quickly exited the hut, taking the goblet and dagger with him. He saw Camillus being carried on the shoulders of other Soldiers from the Century. He carried what Artorius thought was the Century's standard. He then looked over and saw that their standard was planted where Macro stood waiting. Upon closer inspection, Artorius saw that what Camillus carried was a Roman standard, moreover it was an Eagle standard!

"It cannot be," he breathed silently. He rushed forward to see that it was in fact an Eagle that the Signifier bore. The Eagle of the Nineteenth Legion no less!

"I found it in the house of what was probably the war chief for this region!" Camillus said excitedly, once his friends had set him down in front of their Centurion. Macro could not contain his own smile of admiration and elation. The Nineteenth was his former Legion after all. Mallovendus had kept his word. Camillus held the Eagle towards Macro.

"It is only proper that you be the one to deliver this to Germanicus," he said. Macro nodded and took the Eagle. A surge of emotions swept through him. It was as if the lost souls of the Nineteenth were suddenly alive again. They lived through this symbol of their prestige and valor. Macro immediately suppressed his feelings and looked sternly at his men.

"Alright, nobody told you to stop what you were doing! It's been thirty minutes, now form it up at the double!" He smiled to himself as the Century rapidly fell in, every Soldier struggling to carry what he had plundered along with kit. Macro clutched the standard even harder and closed his eyes. Redemption was his at last.

*   *   *   *

Germanicus stood on the command deck of his flagship. Though his men were riding a euphoric high from their victory, he felt uneasy. The wind was cold and was picking up. The waters were rough and choppy.

"We waited too long to return home," he muttered.

"Beg your pardon, Sir?" the Sailing Master asked. Germanicus shook his head. "Nothing. Just talking to myself." The old sailor frowned and nodded.

"Always rough seas, this time of year," he said. His eyes then grew wide with horror as he looked into the distance. He immediately forgot about his Commander and started running about, shouting orders to frantic sailors. Germanicus gazed into the distance and nearly panicked. The clouds were black and racing towards them, as if they had a mind of their own. Lightening could be seen flashing, highlighting waves large enough to swallow the entire fleet.

As Soldiers came up from below deck, Germanicus raced to the front of the ship. Some Soldiers started to panic, unfamiliar as any of them were with an ocean gale. Others rushed about to help the sailors, unaware that their good intentions only inhibited the seamen from doing their job.

"Gods have mercy," Germanicus whispered as he clung to the railing with one hand and wrapped his other in a mooring rope. *"Hold on!"*

CHAPTER 25

▼

THE BITTER-SWEET
AFTERMATH OF WAR

Artorius lay on his bunk back at the fortress. As good as the bathhouse had felt, and as good as it would feel later to go have a spot of whine and perhaps get his hands on a tasty wench, for the moment it felt good just to relax on his own bed. His body ached still, yet he was completely content. Rumor had it that the old warrior he had slain was none other than Arminius' own uncle, Ingiomerus. Unfortunately, the Cherusci war chief himself had somehow escaped. It mattered not. The Germanic tribes were broken. Their warriors lay dead without as much as a grave. Their people had been ravaged and broken. It would be a long time before they even considered contesting the might of Rome again. Artorius was certain that such a thing would not occur again in his lifetime. For the first time in many years he felt at peace. He felt that at last the souls of his brother and mother had been given justice. His quest, his reason for even joining the army was done.

"Just so you know, we've got a full kit inspection tomorrow morning," Praxus said as he walked through the barracks. Artorius sighed. Of course his equipment was immaculate and maintained; it was just a hassle was all. It meant that life was returning to normal around the fortress, whatever that meant. Artorius had never really experienced what one would consider normal life around an army fortress. The day he had joined they had been preparing for war. Now they would be preparing for the return to Rome to celebrate their triumph; that is as soon as the rest of the army had arrived from their seaborne journey. Rumors ran rampant that calamity had struck the fleet, great storms blowing the ships about, scattering all to the four winds.

"Has anyone heard any more concerning Germanicus and the rest of the army?" he asked, sitting upright on his bunk.

"I was walking along, minding my own business, when I saw some dispatch riders heading over to headquarters in a big hurry," Decimus answered. "So I wandered over and heard a bit about how Germanicus was finally on his way back and had just reached the Batavi isles." Artorius shot him a perplexed look.

"Decimus, how is it that you always 'happen to just be around' whenever stuff happens?" he asked. Decimus grinned and shrugged.

"It's a talent, I guess."

Magnus, meanwhile, was working frantically on some popped rivets on his body armor. While the lorica segmentata was ideally suited for close combat and could absorb most arrow and weapon strikes, it was extremely high maintenance.

"Damn it, these brass fittings are a pain in the backside," Magnus muttered as a rivet slipped out of his pliers and fell onto the ground. Artorius laughed.

"If you'd use your shield instead of your body to block enemy blows, you wouldn't have to work on your armor so much," he said sarcastically. Magnus picked up a rivet and threw it at him. Praxus rolled his eyes and walked over to Magnus' bunk.

"Here, let me help me you with that," he said, taking the pliers. Praxus had some of the surest hands when it came to working with small parts, and soon had Magnus' armor put back together. "Just don't think I'm going to make a habit of this," he laughed as he threw the cuirass at Magnus.

*   *   *   *

Germanicus sat trembling as Severus handed him a goblet of wine. The Commanding General looked haggard, was unshaven, and in desperate need of a bath. "No sooner do we reach open sea, but a storm unlike any I've ever seen in my lifetime comes upon us like the wrath of the gods! The entire fleet was scattered. Our men were of little help to the mariners, seeing as how none knew a damn thing about handling of a ship, or of ocean storms. When the seas finally stopped churning and we reached land, my ship was completely alone." He took a long draught of wine before continuing.

"Eventually, the shattered vessels with but few rowers, or clothing spread as sails, some towed by the more powerful, returned. We speedily repaired them, sent them to search the islands. Many more of our men were recovered this way. The Angrivarii had even restored to us several that they had ransomed from the inland tribes, in an effort to show their new found fidelity. Some vessels had been carried to Britain and were sent back by the petty chiefs. Every one, as he returned from some far-distant region, told of wonders, of violent hurricanes, and unknown birds, of monsters of the sea, of forms half-human, half beast-like, things they had really seen or in their terror believed." [1] His eyes were distant as he relayed everything to Severus.

"I received your dispatches concerning this," the older General replied, taking a seat across from Germanicus, "but why the added delays? You made no mention of any pending action against the tribes in the area."

"It wasn't until after I sent the dispatch riders that I decided to strike against the Chatti. They had not been as brutally ravaged as most of the tribes who fought at Idistaviso, so I sought to launch a preemptive strike against them, lest they become overzealous when news of our folly reached them. We attacked them with increased energy, advanced into the country, laying it waste, and utterly ruining a foe who dared not encounter us, or else instantly defeating those who resisted. We learned from prisoners that the barbarians were never more panic-stricken. They declared us to be invincible, rising superior to all calamities; for having thrown away a fleet, having lost our arms, and after strewing the shores with the carcasses of horses and of men, we had rushed to the attack with the same courage, with equal spirit, and, seemingly, with augmented numbers. [2] This was of course nonsense. Our numbers only seemed augmented because in fact the vast majority of our men survived their harrowing ordeals and managed to link back up with the main body once more.

"Our men were overjoyed by the spoils of this fresh mini-campaign, as it lessoned the blows of the calamities we had endured since sailing up the Ems River. The added bounty that I paid them out of my own pockets in recompense to their losses eased their suffering as well." Severus refilled Germanicus' goblet as he sat back and absorbed everything he had heard.

"And now," Germanicus said after a lengthy pause, "we must plan afresh as to how we will finish things for good next year. The barbarians have been sorely whipped and have felt the full wrath of our vengeance. I think that the next campaign will be rather bloodless; rather it will show the barbarians that we can and will strike at them at our leisure. There has been talk of negotiations amongst the surviving war chiefs for a lasting peace with Rome. I think one last campaign will seal that."

"There won't be any last campaign, at least not for us," Severus replied. Germanicus nearly choked on his wine, and he glared at his second.

"What do you mean by *that?*" he asked, his temper rising. Severus very calmly handed a scroll over to Germanicus.

"Only that this letter, and others, came via the Imperial Post while you were away. It bears the Emperor's response to your proposed campaign." Germanicus looked crestfallen as he read the words of his uncle and adoptive father.

From the Emperor, Tiberius Claudius Nero Caesar, etc.

To Germanicus Caesar, Commanding General, Army of the Rhine, etc.

Greetings,

I must first and foremost congratulate you on your triumph over the traitor Arminius, and to send my deepest condolences to your men on the losses they have suffered, both during and after the campaign.

I fully understand your desire to continue in the war against the tribes of Germania, yet it is my opinion that you have had enough of success, enough of disaster. You have fought victorious battles on a great scale; yet you should also remember those losses which the winds and waves have inflicted, and which, though due to no fault of yourself, were still grievous and shocking.

Remember, I had myself been sent nine times by Augustus into Germania, and have done more by policy than by arms. By this means the submission of the Sugambri had been secured, and the Suevi with their king Maroboduus had been forced into peace. The Cherusci too and the other insurgent tribes, since the vengeance of Rome has been satisfied, might be left to their internal feuds. [3]

You are therefore ordered to return to Rome once preparations for a transfer of authority have been made. You will arrive no later than the first of May to celebrate your much-deserved triumph, as well as your second Consulship.

Germanicus set the parchment down and drained his goblet. He sat back, closed his eyes and ran a hand across his forehead.

"Well Severus, my old friend and mentor, it looks like you may at last be getting your long-awaited retirement."

To the family of Quintus Antoninus,

It is with deepest regret and sadness that I send word concerning the death of your son, who died in battle against the Cherusci. He was a brave and honorable Soldier, who fought valiantly to the last. Though his time in the Army was short, he made a huge impact on those who knew him. I know that no words of mine can bring him back; however, I want you to know that all of us who served with him share in your grief, and that he will be missed.

With sincerest respect and condolences,

Platorius Macro, Centurion

Macro set his quill down and leaned back in his chair. This was the last of three letters he had finished writing. Three families of men within his Century would soon be mourning the loss of their sons, brothers, or fathers as the case may be. One of his slain Soldiers had had a 'wife' and three children. Yet since Roman law forbade Soldiers below the rank of Centurion from officially marrying, the man's 'widow' would inherit nothing. He could only hope that the Soldier's other surviving kin would look after the woman he had loved and the children he left behind.

The last letter troubled him. Legionary Antoninus was only eighteen years old and had been a Legionary for just over a year and a half. While the death of a Roman Soldier was always tragic, the loss of one so young sat hard with the Centurion. He always thought hard about how he would word his letters. Would he tell them the brutal truth that Antoninus was dead because he could not get over the enemy rampart fast enough and had been stabbed in the throat as a consequence? No, he would stick with simply telling them that their son died valiantly fighting the hated Cherusci. That at least was not a lie.

"Never an easy task," Proculus said as he walked in. He knew right away what the younger Centurion had been doing. He himself had had to write five such letters over the course of the campaign. "May I sit?" he asked. It was an unnecessary question, but one asked out of courtesy. Macro waived the Cohort Commander to a chair.

"Last year I had to write two of these letters after our battle against the Marsi. I had hoped to delay having to do any more of these for as long as possible,"

Macro said once Proculus had sat down. "Of course once you take command of a Century it becomes an inevitable and never-ending task, doesn't it?"

"I'm afraid so," Proculus replied. "You know Macro; I've held the Centurionate for ten years, three as Pilus Prior. I had to write my first such letter just two months after I took command. And you know what? It has never gotten any easier."

"Your words are encouraging," Macro said with a slight scowl. He glanced at the letters and then set them down. "As much as I try and play the tyrant, these men mean everything to me. Unlike many, I rose through the ranks within the same Century. Most of the time, you're lucky if you get to even stay in the same Cohort once you are promoted past Optio. Many of these men I've known and worked with for nearly seven years. A part of me dies every time one of them does." Proculus sat back, his fingers intertwined.

"I know this doesn't help," he stated, "but consider Calvinus, Commander of the Fifth Cohort."

"Yes, I know him," Macro replied with a wave.

"He had to write over seventy of these letters once. Imagine how much of him died that day," Proculus announced. Macro leaned forward, resting his chin in his hand.

"I know," he replied. "One of my men lost his brother under Calvinus' command. Not that he was at fault. I think it is a credit to Calvinus that he managed to get those whom he did out of that cursed place. My own Centurion did not survive to write his letters." Proculus looked down for a second. He was surprised to see that Macro was not quite so troubled when the subject of Teutoburger Wald surfaced. Before then it was something he had always avoided discussing with his subordinate Centurion.

"Does it still haunt you?" Proculus finally asked.

"Does what still haunt me?" Macro asked in return.

"Don't play dumb with me. You know what I'm talking about," Proculus replied.

"Of course it does," Macro answered. "I swear the spirits of the lost never leave me. But at least now, especially after my men found the Eagle of the Nineteenth, I can at last live in peace with them."

CHAPTER 26

▼

RETURN TO ROME

Camp of the Twentieth Legion, five miles outside of Rome
May, A.D. 17

It would take several weeks to make the journey from the Rhine frontier all the way down into Rome Herself. The army passed quickly out of Germania and through Gaul. Progress was made easy by the quality of the paved roads; roads which Artorius noted had been built on the backs of their predecessors in the Legions. He had also noticed an immediate change once they had reached the southernmost portion of the Alps and passed into Italy. The cold, wetness of the Rhine was replaced by the warm and invigorating climate of the Mediterranean. In spite of being in friendly territory, Severus still insisted upon the troops setting up the standard marching camp, complete with ditch and palisade, every night. Every evening the camp was crowded with locals, mostly curious citizens anxious to set eyes on the famed Legions who had smashed the barbarian giants into oblivion.

One evening Artorius and Magnus were standing outside their tent when they saw Centurion Macro inspecting the covered loads on several carts.

"Macro's certainly anxious about his baggage carts," Artorius observed.

"I noticed," Magnus replied. "What's strange is he packed a lot more than the other Centurions. A bit unusual for him, don't you think?"

"Not only that, but he's so intent on keeping whatever it is hidden from view. I noticed that he never takes anything off of those particular carts, yet he makes certain that they are placed right next to his tent every night. And every morning he checks everything to make sure they haven't been disturbed."

"I think maybe our Centurion's gone a bit mental," Magnus said, shaking his head as he wandered off. Artorius snorted at the remark and went back inside his tent.

As the Army of the Rhine grew closer to the Rome, there was a noticeable increase in traffic. Farmers and merchants from the outlying areas drove great wagonloads of goods with which to feed and provide comfort for the city's inhabitants. Late one afternoon, the men of the Second Century crested a hill and gazed at a breathtaking sight. Though still approximately five miles away, Rome stood out in stark contrast to the surrounding hills. The men could just make out the Temple of Jupiter on Capitoline Hill, the Basilica Julia, the Roman Forum, the Theater of Marcellus next to the River Tiber, and of course the Circus Maximus. The sun at their backs cast an almost divine glow upon the city below, which stretched for miles.

"Well there's something you don't see every day," Gavius said in a low voice.

"Ever been to the Eternal City?" Magnus asked. Gavius could only shake his head. "Neither have I," Magnus replied, himself awestruck.

"There She is, fellas," Camillus pointed, "the one bastion of freedom, order and civilization in the world!"

"Alright, let's keep moving," Macro ordered. "We've still got work to do before dark."

"Are we digging the ditch and palisade tonight?" Vitruvius asked. Macro shook his head.

"No, Severus feels that needlessly tearing up the area so close to Rome would be bad business. Everything else will be set up the same, though."

As the section set about erecting their tent and unpacking their cots, Artorius noticed that Macro and Camillus had both disappeared, along with the Centurion's carts of precious cargo. It wasn't until a while later, as the sun cast its red glow on the horizon that they got their answer to the mystery of Macro's carts.

"*Second Century on your feet!*" Vitruvius barked. The men wasted no time in heeding the call of their Optio. Some had even started strapping on their armor and rounding up their weapons.

"What the hell are you guys doing?" the Optio shouted. He himself was dressed only in his tunic and sword belt. The overzealous Soldiers sheepishly put their gear back before following Vitruvius out of the camp. About a half mile from the Legion's camp, on a ridge with a perfect view of the city, stood the Centurion and Signifier. Camillus had brought the Century's Standard, which he had planted next to the carts. Macro stood with his arms folded across his chest, while Camillus leaned against one of the carts, a wry smile on his face.

"Gather around," Macro said. His voice was extremely calm, though it still projected loud enough to be clearly heard by all. As the Century clustered around their commander, Macro pointed towards the city behind him.

"Down there is a place that many of you had never seen before, yet all have fought for. I want you to look hard upon Rome; gather Her splendor into your very soul, for She is the light in what otherwise would be a dark and twisted world. See and remember, never forgetting what it was that we fought for." He paused briefly, allowing his men to take in what he had said, and what they could see. He had picked the time and place perfectly, knowing full well the effect it would have on his Soldiers, weary and battered as they were after the sheer brutality of their campaigns across the Rhine.

"Over the next several weeks," the Centurion continued, "we will be hearing speeches and accolades given to us by men of the highest offices; Generals, Senators, perhaps even the Emperor himself. This triumph will be a massive affair, one of the most significant events in our time. *This* moment, however, belongs only to the Second Century. Camillus, if you would." He waived to the Signifier, who pulled the tarp off one of the wagons. Underneath the cart was packed tight with vats of wine.

"The best wine, from the best grapes grown in the world," Macro said to his shocked, yet delighted Soldiers, "and it is for the best fighting men the world will ever know. Section Leaders, fill the goblets of your men." Statorius and the other Sergeants grabbed goblets that were on one of the other wagons and started to fill and pass them out to their men. Camillus walked over to Macro with two full goblets, handing one to the Centurion. Vitruvius and Flaccus joined them, their own cups filled to the brim. Once complete, the Second Century waited for their Centurion to finish his speech. As Macro raised his cup, he seemed to glow in the fading light. The image of his Centurion, silhouetted against the backdrop of the greatest of cities was something Artorius knew he would remember till his dying day.

"To Victoria and Bellona, goddesses of victory and war; to our Commander, Germanicus Caesar; to the Emperor Tiberius, guardian of the light that is Rome; to our friends, who did not come home; to the Eternal City and the ideals that our friends died to protect; and most importantly, to you my brothers who give our Legion the right to be called *The Valiant*."

Every Soldier raised his cup in salute and drank. Artorius was shocked by the sweetness and potency of his drink. This was no watered-down tavern wine. This was straight from the vineyards, and indeed was the finest he had ever tasted. *Macro must have paid a fortune for this*, he thought as the strength of the wine seared his throat and stomach. It was a wonderful feeling. The daylight gave out as the sun was eclipsed behind the mountains. The men of the Second Century stood gazing at the city, alive as it was with the nighttime traffic. They stayed on that ridge for some time, drinking their Centurion's wine, talking only in hushed voices. For Artorius, no Triumph, parade, speech or celebration could ever compete with this simple moment.

*   *   *   *

A triumph was a complicated thing to organize, not to mention expensive. There would be banquets, a massive triumphal parade, games and other entertainment, most of which was free to the public. The citizens themselves were exceedingly grateful to the brave Legionaries who had routed Arminius and removed his threat from Rome. Gifts of food, wine, and even the occasional prostitute were heaped upon the Soldiers.

The gladiatorial contests were a huge event, and all of the Soldiers were encouraged to attend. A section of the arena was even reserved for Legionaries wishing to observe the spectacle. Camillus came walking over to where Statorius and the section were lounging, over by their tent. The Signifier was always intrigued by what he described as "exotic entertainment." He was carrying a parchment with the events listed on it.

"Check this out," he said, presenting the scroll to Statorius. "For the next two weeks 'the best gladiators in the whole of the Empire in one place.' What do you think?" The Sergeant said nothing as he read the list of upcoming events.

"I think it'll be a good place to pick up aggressive women," Valens remarked.

"So just how good are these gladiators supposed to actually be?" Magnus asked.

"Supposedly they are the best fighters in the whole of the Empire," Gavius answered.

"Really?" Artorius mused. "This I have got to see."

"You mean you've never been to a gladiatorial match?" Valens asked.

"Never," Artorius replied.

"I haven't either," Magnus said.

"I went once as a boy. My dad thought it would help make me strong," Valens seemed a bit puzzled at the logic behind that. "Anyway, I thought they were quite the spectacle then."

"That was before you learned how to actually fight," Gavius said.

"Who says he has?" Vitruvius laughed as he walked over to the group. He looked at the parchment that the Signifier was carrying. "It says here 'automatic admission and reserved seating to all visiting Legionaries.' Well, let's not disappoint them, shall we?"

As they walked out of the camp, it seemed like quite a few from the Century were going to the games. It was a long walk over to the arena; however, it was made easy by not being encumbered by weapons, armor, and equipment. There was such an air of ease and relaxation that Artorius almost forgot for a second that they were all professional Soldiers. One would almost think that they were simply a large group of friends, going to the games. The red tunics and daggers they wore on their belts revealed their true identities.

Artorius was somewhat surprised to see that even Centurion Macro was out enjoying the day, though he kept a deliberate distance from the men of the ranks. Instead he walked with Proculus and the other Centurions from the Third Cohort. All wore resplendent togas, as opposed to Legionary tunics. Artorius knew that these men, upon retirement, would be enrolled into the equestrian order of society. Because of this, they were granted a lot of the privileges and courtesies normally reserved for those already a part of the patrician class; such was the respect and awe that Romans held for the men who led their Legions into battle.

The road to the city was lined with trees on either side. The air smelled sweet with the scents of the olive and grape vineyards that donned the hillsides. There was little traffic, mostly Soldiers walking to and from their camps outside the city. Most of the city's population would be at the games, or at least trying to get into them.

Soon the city itself came into sight. It had been years since Artorius had last seen Rome Herself. The effect it had had on him then could not compare to what he felt as he saw the immortal city in all her splendor. It was absolutely breathtaking. The Forum, the Circus Maximus, the Temple of Castor and Pollux, the Imperial Palaces, and even the sheer number of houses and apartments occupied by the citizens of the city. These were certainly no mud hovels or rickety wooden buildings so commonly seen on the frontier. Here was civilization! Clean, modern, and above all, organized. The volume of people moving to and fro made the scene seem very chaotic, at least to those who had never seen the true chaos and poverty that existed on the Empire's borders.

At last they reached the Circus Maximus. There was a huge line of people, waiting to get into the arena. They were dancing and shouting, clambering and betting with each other as to which of their favorites would find victory that day. There were wine and food vendors surrounding the arena, as well as gambling tables and ladies of ill repute. Valens eyed them with a glazed-over look on his face.

"I'll see you guys later," he said with a wry grin. He walked over towards a pair of fetching young lasses, his money bag in hand.

"Anybody thirsty?" Artorius asked, turning back to his friends.

"Damn right I am!" Magnus answered, licking his lips.

"Hang on," Artorius replied as he walked over to the nearest wine stand. He turned and looked back to see how many of his friends were still with him. Many had become distracted by offers from merchants, gamblers, and women. Praxus, Decimus, Carbo, Magnus, Gavius, Sergeant Statorius, and Signifier Camillus had accompanied him all the way to the arena. It felt strange to have the Sergeant and Signifier with them. Then he realized that they were still men after all, and perhaps there were in fact times were formalities could be lessoned, if not altogether discarded. Camillus, though senior in rank to Statorius, rarely had a use for formalities as it was. Artorius guessed that Camillus was probably older than Statorius, though his boyish face made him appear to be much younger.

"Eight goblets of your best wine," he said, turning back to the merchant.

"Here you are Sir," the merchant said, after he had poured the last. Artorius reached into his money pouch.

"How much?" he asked. The merchant waived him away.

"Your money is no good here," he said, smiling. "Consider it payment for having saved our city and our Empire."

"Thank you, my friend," Artorius replied as he motioned for his friends to come grab their goblets. They saluted their new found merchant friend with their goblets, and proceeded to quench their collective thirst.

Having been properly refreshed, they made their way into the arena and found the section designated for military guests. The seats for the general public were practically full, the crowd in a frenzy of anticipation. The military seats were a lot less populated than Artorius expected them to be. He looked across the way to where the Imperial box was located. It was filled with Senators and dignitaries. He could see Germanicus and what he guessed to be members of the imperial family, though the box was conspicuously devoid of the Emperor himself. Artorius pointed this out to Camillus, who happened to be seated next to him.

"It seems the Emperor is not a big fan of games or of gladiators in general," Camillus explained. "He thinks they are an expensive waste of time. As frugal as he is with the Treasury, he would probably abolish them altogether, were they not so popular with the masses." At that moment the gates below opened, two gladiators stepped into the arena, and the crowd erupted. "See what I mean?"

Both men wore only sparse amounts of body armor, mainly on their limbs. One man carried a gladius and small, circular shield. The other carried a net in one hand and a trident in the other. They turned to the Imperial box, saluted the Senators on hand and then turned and faced each other. They were very cautious at first, taking only token strikes at each other. Then the one with the gladius made his move and rushed in, his sword high overhead.

"What in Hades is that guy doing?" Decimus asked, annoyed. *"Stab him in the armpit!"* he shouted through cupped hands at the gladiator with the trident. Instead, the man backed away, sweeping with his net as he tried to trip his opponent.

"Oh come on, what's with the stupid net?" Gavius chided. The swordsman chopped away at the net, cutting it. He then continued his attack. The man with the trident stabbed at him, only to have it deflected by his opponent's shield.

"Step in and punch him with your shield!" Artorius shouted. When the gladiator failed to do so, he threw his hands in the air in frustration. Only Camillus seemed to be enjoying himself.

"I don't get it," Artorius stated. "What is so spectacular about this? These guys are complete amateurs!"

"I've seen better fights every time Artorius gets his ass pummeled by Vitruvius!" Magnus stated, causing Artorius to reach over and cuff him across the back of the head.

Finally, the fight ended with the trident gladiator on his back, his adversary standing over him. He looked to the crowd. All were screaming and shouting and waiving their hands. Some pointed to their throats with their thumbs, though most pointed towards the ground.

"What does all that mean?" Artorius asked Camillus.

"If the crowd points to their own throats, it means they want the victor to cut the throat of his opponent and slay him. If they point towards the ground, it literally means 'leave him on Earth.' In other words, let him live. Believe it or not, most fights are not to the death. If the crowd feels a fighter fought well, they usually let him live."

"But he didn't fight well! Both these guys fought like whelps! Magnus was right, I *have* taken bigger beatings from Vitruvius with a practice sword!" Artorius said in frustration. He then sighed audibly. "I guess these people have just never seen real men fight."

The next fight scarcely impressed the Legionaries any more, though the crowd was whipped into an even bigger frenzy. Two men, both carrying long swords and rectangular shields, smaller than those carried by Roman Soldiers, faced each other. Two minutes into the fight and most of the Soldiers had their foreheads resting in their hands in boredom. Decimus had decided to go for a walk and had left as soon as the fight began.

"By the gods, who actually teaches these men how to fight?" Magnus asked loudly. A nobleman, sitting in the next section over, glared at Magnus in irritation. The man looked to be of Gallic ancestry, though he was dressed like a Roman Magistrate. He had a stylus and wax tablet, as well as a number of scrolls and parchments at his feet. He turned back to the fight, making notes onto his tablet as he did so. Artorius saw the man's irritation. He leaned over and elbowed Camillus.

"Who is that man?" he asked.

"That man? That's Julius Sacrovir. His origins are Gallic, though he himself is a Roman citizen, a rather prosperous one at that. He makes most of his money sponsoring these events. In fact, I would say that half the fighters here are from his clan."

"So he's the man whose backside needs to be whipped!" Magnus retorted, purposely loud enough for the man to hear him. "When are we going to get to see a real fight?"

"When one of us steps into the arena!" Statorius muttered. He had been quiet most of the time, yet even he was starting to get irritated and bored. Suddenly the man that Camillus had said was named Sacrovir was standing over them.

"I could not help but overhear your observations in regard to the spectacle we have put on," he said. Though he looked Gallic, he spoke perfect Latin with no trace of an accent.

"All we're saying is that these gladiators are poor fighters who don't know the first thing about real combat," Artorius said as he sat back on his elbows. Sacrovir looked over his shoulder at the fight below. One man was down and the crowd had gone berserk.

"The masses do not seem to think so," he observed.

"That's because the masses have never seen how Legionaries fight," Statorius retorted. Sacrovir smiled at that.

"Really?" he remarked. "Then how about we place a small wager amongst friends?" The wickedness of his smile betrayed that he in no way thought of the Soldiers as friends.

"What do you have in mind?" Statorius asked, sitting up.

"While I admit that many of the preliminary fights here may seem, well shall we say, amateurish, I do in fact have a host of gladiators who would be more than a match for any of you Legionaries." This elicited groans and catcalls from the Soldiers.

"There's no way!" Artorius retorted. "We've got a Soldier who would thrash every last one of your gladiators in a matter of seconds!"

"It's settled then," Sacrovir remarked. "Your best Legionary, against my best gladiator! How much will you be betting?"

✳   ✳   ✳   ✳

"Absolutely not!" Macro shouted. "There is no way I can allow one of my Soldiers, my Optio at that, to fight in a mob induced spectacle, just because some of my men decided to get drunk and volunteer him for it!" He then turned and glared at Camillus.

"We weren't drunk, at least not at that exact moment," the Signifier replied, his speech slightly slurred, and his head hung sheepishly. Macro threw his hands up in the air as Vitruvius sat on a couch laughing.

"You think this is amusing, Optio?" Macro snarled.

"A little bit," Vitruvius replied as he stood up, composing himself. "While I admit, I think our friend Camillus here may have gone a bit far volunteering me to fight in a gladiatorial match without so much as *asking* me, I think it may be time to show the Roman people just how Roman Soldiers fight." Camillus replied with a hiccup and a slight giggle.

"What for?" Flaccus asked, lounging on a couch with a goblet of wine resting precariously on his chest. "I saw the way those gladiators fight. You'll kill the guy in a matter of seconds, I don't care who it is. And the crowd won't want that. They want spectacle, which is something we do not specialize in, at least not in terms of close combat."

"Besides, if I let you go fight in the arena, every drunken Soldier in this city is going to get wind of it and try and prove just how masculine he is by making a complete ass out of himself out there," Macro retorted through clenched teeth. "And the first time one of our Soldiers gets killed or wounded, the Commanding General is going to have my head. That is if Flavius doesn't crucify me first." He shuddered at the thought. Macro had always counted himself fortunate to have never incurred the Master Centurion's wrath.

"Don't get me wrong, Vitruvius," he continued. "I know all about Sacrovir and his scum. And I certainly wouldn't mind watching you thrash one of his so-called best. Just understand the really bad precedent that would set."

Camillus suddenly brightened up. "What if we make it a state sponsored event?" he asked, before hiccupping once more.

"What do you mean?" Macro asked, puzzled.

"Simple, this Sacrovir has lots of money and is willing to foot quite the wager. We simply run it up the chain to Severus. Have *him* sponsor Vitruvius, and we make a fortune! And to avoid precedent, we make it the last fight on the last day of the games."

"Think Severus would go for something like that?" Flaccus asked.

Macro stood rubbing his chin in his hand. "If put to him like that, probably," he finally said. "Most Senators love to gamble, and I think if he were assured to take home a large portion of Sacrovir's fortunes, then yes I would say so."

"Good thing you came to me when you did," Proculus said after Macro had given him the details of his proposal to allow Vitruvius to fight in the arena. In order for him to get the wager approved, he had to run it through his chain-of-command, and that started with Proculus, his Cohort Commander. Next it would have to go to the Master Centurion, and finally to the Legate himself. Macro was surprised to see Master Centurion Flavius in the same room with Proculus.

"What do you mean?" Macro asked in regards to Proculus' remark. The Cohort Commander looked over his shoulder at Flavius, whose arms were crossed, an amused smirk on his face.

"Only that Sacrovir has already posted the fight in every betting house in the city," the Master Centurion answered. "Thankfully Severus has not made his way to any of these yet. If he did before we got to him, he'd have you skinned! Or rather, he'd have *me* skin you." Macro swallowed hard at the statement, knowing full-well that Flavius meant every word of it. Never mind that Camillus and the others had acted on their own. As a Centurion, Macro was ultimately responsible for the actions of his men. After a few seconds, Proculus waived his hand dismissively.

"Anyway, I've got a few Talents I can wager," he said. "Those imbeciles have actually posted five-to-one odds *against* Vitruvius! I figure with a healthy profit at the expense of the money lenders, I can finally build the wife that villa on top of

Esquiline Hill that she's always wanted. She's tired of living in the little hovel we have now." Macro snorted at the remark. Given a Centurion Pilus Prior's salary, he knew full-well that Proculus and his wife lived in anything but a hovel. Just then they heard footsteps echoing in the corridor. Without a word, and with his arms still crossed, Flavius left the room. The two Centurions could just overhear his words as he confronted the Legion's Commanding Legate in the hallway.

"Sir, how would you like to make a spot of money while we're here?"

Severus had readily accepted the offer made by his men. In fact, as word of the proposed bet spread its way up the chain-of-command, every senior officer with a vested interest, and personal knowledge of Optio Vitruvius, added their sums to the ever growing wager. '*The Legionary versus the Gladiator*' became the topic of discussion amongst the social elite. As a mark of professional pride, most military veterans placed their wagers with Vitruvius, while others of a less savory nature placed theirs with the unknown gladiator. Rumor had it that the Emperor himself had even placed a large wager on the Legionary. This was of course preposterous, given Tiberius' loathing of gambling and of gladiators.

On the eve of the fight, Vitruvius stood on a balcony, overlooking the city and the Circus Maximus. He seemed lost in thought.

"Thinking about tomorrow's match?" Macro asked, walking up to him.

"Just thinking about why in Hades I'm even doing this," Vitruvius answered, gazing down at the Tiber River.

"Because you have the reputation for being the best there ever was, Vitruvius," Macro answered. "You've never been defeated in battle; in fact no one has ever even come close to hurting you." Vitruvius turned to face his friend and Centurion.

"'The perfect killer.' That's what the lads call me," he replied.

"Quite the reputation to live up to," Macro observed.

"Yes," Vitruvius said as he turned his gaze back towards the city. "And it would seem that it's all I'll ever be known for." Macro placed a hand on his Optio's shoulder.

"If I bought you a vat of wine and a couple of fetching young courtesans, would you lighten up?" he asked, laughing. Vitruvius found he was unable to control his own laughter.

"Perhaps just a pint and one courtesan," he replied. "Can't risk wearing myself out completely before tomorrow."

Artorius sat at table, a goblet of wine in his hand. He was leaning forward, staring off into space as Soldiers drank and cavorted with the locals of the city. Many of them had never even been to Rome, the heart of the Empire they had all risked their lives to preserve. A gentle breeze blew in from the Tiber. It felt good. It was a far cry from the blood-soaked planes of Idistaviso, or the smoldering hell of the Angrivarii fortress. Artorius took a deep breath, slightly shuddering at the memories. He did not even take notice as Magnus took a seat across from him, a local lady of pleasure sitting on his lap.

"Hey Artorius, you would not believe what these ladies are willing to do, for only a couple of copper coins no less!"

"Anything for my brave boys," the young woman replied, her hands in Magnus' hair, her mouth gently biting on his ear. Magnus was well on his way to becoming drunk and was laughing incessantly. "Come on man, you've got to go and get yourself one before they're all taken! Valens is trying to get a couple of them to go swimming naked with him in the Tiber!"

"Not tonight," Artorius said as he took a drink of wine, continuing to stare off into the direction of the river. Magnus was suddenly aware of his friend's need to talk and immediately sobered up. He slapped his lady friend on the rump and waived her off.

"I'll be waiting for you back in my room," she whispered into his ear. Magnus motioned for her to leave at once, before turning his attention back to his friend.

"So what's on your mind?" he asked. "Thinking about Vitruvius and his fight with the gladiator tomorrow?"

"What?" Artorius looked surprised. "No, I hadn't even thought about it."

"Didn't think so. So what is it?" Magnus persisted. Artorius let out an audible sigh.

"You remember when we first joined the army and I gave you my reasons for joining?"

"Sure," Magnus shrugged. "You joined to avenge your murdered brother. You told me after Idistaviso that you felt like you had done that. So where's the problem?"

"That's just it," Artorius threw his hands up. "I've done what I came here to do. I avenged my brother. I killed gods know how many of those barbarian bastards over the last two years. So now that I've gotten justice and revenge, I'm not sure what else to do now. Don't you understand, avenging my brother was all I ever thought about from the time I was a boy. Now that it's over, I'm not sure what else to do with my life." Magnus leaned forward.

"You see those guys over there?" he asked, pointing to where Decimus and Praxus were becoming friendly with a couple of local ladies while a pair of merchants continued to buy them wine while gambling with Decimus. In the distance they could just make out Valens running towards the riverbank, tearing his clothes off and yelling enthusiastically as he did. A pair of scantily clad women were close behind him. "What do you see when you look at them?"

"I see Praxus negotiating a fare with his lady-in-waiting, and Decimus about to lose his ass to those two merchants who aren't as drunk as they appear," Artorius retorted. What they didn't notice was that Decimus was slipping something into the merchants' drinks. Magnus raised his eyebrows and nodded.

"Well yeah, fair enough," he conceded. "I mean when you *really* look at them what do you see?" Artorius shrugged and shook his head.

"I'll tell you what I see," Magnus continued. "I see *Rome*. Rome is not about politics, the Senate, nor is it even about this city. You said so yourself at Idistaviso." He waived at everything around him in order to emphasize his point. "Rome is an idea, an idea that lives in those men, even when they're drunk. It is an idea that lives in us as well; that the entire world can be brought together in one civilized, advanced, and orderly society. Rome is alive; it lives and breathes through us. As long as we live, Rome will continue to live."

"So our reason to live is so that Rome can continue to live," Artorius observed. Magnus raised his hands in a gesture of acceptance.

"Exactly," he said. Artorius nodded in contemplation.

"Well I suppose there are worse things in life to live for," he said as he took a long gulp of wine. "And it doesn't hurt that they pay us well and let us enjoy some of the finer things in life!" He looked over at where Praxus and Decimus had left with their lady companions, the two merchants passed out with their heads on the table.

"I guess they were as drunk as they looked!" Magnus laughed, rising to his feet and smacking his friend across the shoulder.

"And now I'm going to enjoy some of those finer things, especially since I've already paid for them!" With that he ran back towards the tavern.

Artorius smiled, took another drink of wine and turned his attention back towards the river. *She really is beautiful*, he thought, *especially at this time of year.*

His thoughts turned to the events coming up over the next few days. The games would be over soon, followed by the triumphal parade and then back to the Rhine. Time was running short, and he had yet to hear from his father. The thought disturbed him. He thought that he would at least have gotten a letter or something in reply. Surely his father had to know that he was in Rome! The whole of the Empire knew about their victory over Arminius, so why had his father not made contact with him? The thought vexed him as he finished his wine and contemplated taking a walk along the river. No sooner had he risen, when a voice caught his attention.

"Artorius?" It was a woman's voice, one that he had not heard for some time. He turned to see Camilla standing there, her hands folded in front of her. "I've spent the last three days looking for you."

"The Army of the Rhine is quite large. I'm surprised you were able to find me at all." His face betrayed no emotion. Did she really think that he could still have feelings for her, after she had ran off and married a magistrate's son only so that she could live in luxury? Camilla ran towards him and wrapped her arms around him. Artorius remained motionless.

"Why did you not write to me?" She asked, trying to ignore his coldness.

"You have a husband, and should not be pining after a lowly Legionary," he replied, folding his arms across his chest. Camilla took a step back, leaving her hands on his shoulders.

"Oh don't hate me for getting married," she pouted. She then placed her face next to his ear. "I told you, Marcellus may be my husband, but I still think of you as my lover." She then flicked her tongue against his ear. Artorius shuddered slightly. It *did* feel pretty good, and besides, Camilla had actually blossomed and grown more lovely since he left two years before. He then smiled wickedly. If she wanted him to be her lover, so be it; but it would be on his terms not hers. A series of sinister thoughts came to his mind.

They took a walk over to a block of flats. Camilla opened the door to one and ushered Artorius in. It was plain and unadorned; obviously Camilla and her husband were simply renting the space while they were in Rome. Or could she have gotten it on her own, in anticipation of meeting her proposed lover?

"So where is your husband this night?" Artorius asked as he stepped inside.

"Off at one of the brothels, I do believe," Camilla replied. "You know, under Roman law sex with a married person is not considered adultery if one is paying for the service." She then placed her arms around his neck and kissed him passionately. Artorius felt his body tense up, blood rushing through his veins as he felt the beast inside him come unleashed.

He gave a guttural growl and bit her savagely on the neck. Camilla gave a yelp of surprise and mild pain. Artorius then swatted her hard across the butt before picking her up and throwing her roughly onto the bed. He was immediately on top of her, snarling and tearing her clothes off. Her garments tore in places as they were discarded. Camilla's eyes were wide, her breath coming in near panic gasps. He smiled wickedly at her.

"Be careful what you wish for," Artorius growled into her ear. His lovemaking of Camilla was utterly savage and animalistic; at times it bordered on sheer brutality. His deviant mind conjured up things to do to her that she had never even contemplated. Her screams were at times a mixture of ecstasy and pain, and were loud enough to wake the entire block.

After a number of hours, when he had thoroughly ravaged her to the point where he knew she would not even be able to walk the next day, he finished, took a brief moment to catch his breath, and then started to get dressed. Camilla simply lay there whimpering. He laughed to himself when he saw how her clothes were torn up, not to mention the very visible bite mark on her neck; which would be swollen and purple by morning. As soon as he was dressed, he rummaged through her things and found a purse with some coins in it. As he took one out, Camilla struggled to sit up.

"What are you doing?" she asked, surprised.

"Keeping you from getting into trouble," he said, showing the coin to her. "Like you said, it isn't adultery if the service is paid for. And the way I see it, you owe me one denarius for my services. And now, I will bid you good night." As he started for the door, Camilla started to climb out of the bed, only to find that her legs refused to function properly and she landed in a heap on the floor. Artorius laughed out loud, shook his head, and wandered out into the night.

"Artorius…wait." Camilla found her entire body ached from the ordeal. He was after all perhaps two-and-a-half times her bodyweight, with strength, power, and endurance far beyond her comprehension; not to mention his sheer deviancy and utter savagery. She shook her head and started giggling to herself about the entire affair as she curled up on the floor in a heap.

CHAPTER 27

▼

THE LEGIONARY VERSUS THE GLADIATOR

The last day of the games took place two days before the triumphal parade. That morning members of the Second Century accompanied their Optio to the gladiators' entrance at the arena. Vitruvius was in full Legionary armor. The terms of the wager were that no missile weapons would be allowed, that Vitruvius would use standard military arms, and that his unnamed opponent could use whatever weapons and armor he pleased.

It was dark and dank underneath the arena where the gladiators prepared themselves. It smelled of sweat, flatulence, metal and blood. Vitruvius turned to his friends.

"Go on and take your seats. I'll meet up with you when this is over," he directed. With pats on the back and a few words of encouragement, the Legionaries left their Optio to his meeting with Sacrovir's gladiator. As soon as they had gone, Vitruvius walked around, surveying everything in that dank, dark dungeon. There were racks of weapons, most of which were semi-rusted and in need of work. He looked down at his own gladius, still strapped to his belt. His was a fine weapon, one that had served him for years. It would serve him well again this day. But what was he fighting for?

In another part of the dungeon, on the other side of the arena, a small, sallow-faced man paced back and forth in front of his most prized possession. The gladiator was completely hidden in the shadows, but his deep, nasally breathing could be heard.

"Today will be your finest day," Sacrovir remarked as he continued to pace back and forth, "and I want you to make sure that that insufferable soldier suffers for his outrage towards us. Do that and you shall have whatever you ask for."

"I want my freedom," a deep voice boomed. Sacrovir raised a hand.

"Don't be silly, man. You are my best fighter, my champion. Besides, you can understand that it would be bad business for me to release you upon society. Surely there is something else to satisfy your hunger? A certain girl, even a boy perhaps?"

"You promised me freedom a long time ago! I have done everything you asked of me!" The voice was becoming loud and incensed.

"And so I did," Sacrovir answered, raising his hands in resignation. Though his champion was by far the best gladiator he had ever owned, to say nothing of the wealth his victories had added to Sacrovir's coffers, he was beginning to fear that he was slowly losing control of his most prized fighter. "Very well. Slay this uniformed upstart, and you shall have your freedom. But I want a good show. I want this to be our finest hour, and I want that soldier begging for death before it is over. Am I making myself clear?"

"Yes, Master."

Why are you here, Vitruvius? The Optio asked himself. *Is it for glory, for prestige? No, these things mean nothing to you. What is it then? You are not one to stoop so low as to fight for money. Why then?* He continued to pace back and forth along the corridor leading to the arena. He could hear the sounds of gladiators fighting and the crowd screaming for blood. He then looked down at his arms, his chest, and his body in general. He was thickly set with powerful muscle. By the gods, but his hands had slain many men! He had fought brave and tenacious warriors, yet he had always gotten the best of them, and with little to no effort. Perhaps that was it. In spite of the sheer number of battles he had fought, he had never felt himself to be in any danger. Not once had he even been so much as scratched by an assailant. That was it! He had never been truly challenged before!

The lads all say you are the best close combat fighter to have ever lived. Yet this Sacrovir claims to have a gladiator that's better than you. You simply want to know if in fact there is nobody better than you, don't you? They always say that there is someone better out there. Well perhaps he is here. If so, it is time to meet him.

As he paced back and forth in contemplation, he saw a figure lurking in the shadows. Sacrovir sulked towards him. Vitruvius forced himself to withhold a sneer of disgust. Instead he kept a hard, yet unconcerned expression about him.

"Ready for you meeting with immortality?" Sacrovir asked as he slunk by.

"What do you want?" Vitruvius asked, unconcerned.

"Just making sure that the prey for my champion is ready and fit to meet his fate," Sacrovir replied, shrugging. He then interlocked his fingers, his hands in front of his chest. "I do hope the army has trained you well. The crowd will want a spectacle, and what a shame if you should die too quickly."

"If you've come to try and unnerve me, you're wasting your time," Vitruvius remarked, watching as Sacrovir continued to walk around him, his head hung slightly. By the gods, he really despised this man!

"But you are unnerved," Sacrovir said, his face close to Vitruvius' ear. "Your friends say that you are some sort of god. They say you've killed more men than most of them combined. Yet you are assailed by doubts; doubts as to the true extent of your abilities. And you will never satisfy those until you can find the one who is truly your match! A god? All I see is a man, who when he walks down that corridor will begin his final journey to the land of the dead." With a flash, Vitruvius slammed Sacrovir into a column, pinning him against it with his left arm. In the same instant he drew his gladius and placed the point against the smaller man's throat. Remarkably, Sacrovir maintained his composure.

"You won't even think about killing me. What a pity," he said with much venom in his voice.

"And why not?" Vitruvius replied into his ear. "You said so yourself, I've killed more men than any. What does it matter if I add one more?"

"Because you are not above the law, and to kill me would be murder. Then instead of the privilege of dying at the hands of my champion, you'd have to settle for being strangled, or perhaps thrown to the lions. How boring, how unoriginal." Sacrovir sneered. Vitruvius shoved his weight into Sacrovir, pressing his gladius point hard against the man's neck. Sacrovir gasped in near panic. A trickle of blood started to seep from where the weapon was cutting into him. Vitruvius then withdrew his sword and stepped back. It was true; to kill Sacrovir now would be murder. As the disgusting little man started to breathe easy, Vitruvius lunged forward and slammed his forehead into Sacrovir's. The Gaul yelped and fell back against the column, his hands over his face.

"I'm going to kill your champion," Vitruvius growled. "I'm going to run him through, and deny the crowd and you the pleasure of any spectacle. Today, vermin from Hell, you will see how Soldiers of Rome fight!" He then turned, and with rage in his heart, grabbed his shield and helmet and started his walk down the long corridor leading to the arena.

It was dank and dark in the corridor, yet at the end shown a bright light. He could hear the chants and howls of the crowd. They were filled with lust and fury. Vitruvius slowed to a walk and started to breathe easier. He could not let Sacrovir unnerve him. To cause him to fly into a rage would only give his gladiator an advantage. He then started to calm himself, like he had hundreds of times before. This was nothing to him. He only had to face one man today. The shouts he heard coming from the dungeon only made him smile and relax easily.

"I will have your heart on a spit before I'm done with you, Optio Vitruvius of the Twentieth Legion! I curse you, and all Soldiers of Rome!"

Vitruvius laughed and shook his head. He stopped just short of the entrance into the arena. He donned his helmet, took a deep breath and waited for the orator to announce him.

The arena was packed beyond capacity for the final match of the day. Even the military seats were crowded with Soldiers, anxious to see one of their own take down a famous gladiator in close combat. The orator stood in front of the Imperial box. Artorius was shocked to see that the Emperor was in attendance for this event. Artorius sat towards the edge of their section, and was surprised when he looked over into the next and saw Camilla with a man he could only assume to be her husband. To call him a 'man' was to be generous. He was very thin, with thick, curly hair, a hooked nose, and looked as if he were wearing some form of makeup. He turned his nose up at everything, and talked in a loud voice to his friends who were gathered around him. Most looked equally effeminate. Artorius wondered if he was more interested in little boys than little girls.

He noticed that Camilla was sitting with the side of her head resting on her left hand. Her garments were pulled up around her neck in an obvious attempt to hide her marks from the night before. Her eyes gazed over his way, and she seemed startled to see him. Artorius sat back, smiled knowingly, and winked at her. She gave a half smile back, readjusted to cover her neck up once more, and turned back to the games.

Artorius then noticed the audible silence that had overtaken the arena. He glanced over to see the Emperor standing. Tiberius waived to the orator, who then turned to the crowd.

"Citizens of Rome!" he began. *"On this final day of the triumphal games, commemorating the great victories wrought against the hordes of Germania, the Emperor is pleased to bring you one last match involving two of the most skilled combatants to*

have ever graced the arena! In an historic first, the Emperor has granted his blessings on allowing one of the very Legionaries who won victory for the Empire to compete in this match. Your Emperor presents to you Optio Vitruvius of the Twentieth Legion!" The crowd came to its feet, applauding and shouting accolades as Vitruvius stepped into the arena. He looked very calm as he marched to the center.

"His opponent," the orator continued, *"is not unknown to many of you. In thirty-two matches, he has not been defeated. His name is legendary in the east, as well as in North Africa. The Emperor is pleased to give you, Nubandi!"* On the other side of the arena, a massive African walked through the gates. He looked to be nearly seven feet tall, with muscles the size of tree trunks. He was completely bald, with a slim mustache gracing his upper lip and reaching down to his chin. He wore no armor, only a loin cloth and studded metal belt. In his hands he carried a massive iron round shield, and a broadsword that any other man would have required two hands to use. His eyes were filled with rage as he walked headstrong into the center, just a few feet from where Vitruvius stood eyeing him.

The Optio was surprisingly calm. He scanned his opponent, not in reverence, but rather in the method that a man looks for weaknesses in the one he is about to destroy.

Ok Vitruvius, he's big and he doesn't look too happy, he thought. He did not find that he was afraid of his opponent. Whenever it came time for battle, instinct took over. Perhaps he was in fact the best there ever was. Well if he was, he was going to prove it to all of Rome soon enough. He started to assess his target.

He's too tall to strike in the face, though if I get in close enough I might be able to catch him under the chin. I cannot tell how fast he is, though I must assume that if he's used to putting on spectacles, he's probably well conditioned.

"Good gods, that man is big!" Praxus observed.

"That's no man, that's a fucking beast!" Camillus remarked.

"He makes even Vitruvius look small," Magnus added.

"Since when have you ever been intimidated by the size of those you've fought?" Artorius asked. "Think about all those giants you slew in Germania!"

"Those giants were dwarfs compared to that...thing," Magnus remarked.

"Since when has size been everything?" Carbo asked, offhandedly. Valens gave him a perplexed look.

"Since when has it not?" he retorted.

"Hey, we do need to have a little faith in Vitruvius," Camillus replied, ignoring the off-color remarks of the young Legionaries. "Remember, he doesn't like pain very much, so I doubt that he'll let this guy hurt him."

"Say, where's Decimus?" Praxus asked, looking around.

"I don't know, but the match is about to start without him," Artorius said, leaning forward onto the edge of his seat.

On the arena floor, both men turned and faced the Emperor, weapons raised.

"Hail Caesar!" Both men said together. Vitruvius was then silent as the huge African said the rest of the statement. *"We who are about to die salute you!"*

"Speak for yourself," Vitruvius said in a low voice. Both men turned and faced each other. The African held his shield at arm's length, his sword up at shoulder level, as if preparing to smash his opponent. Vitruvius settled into a comfortable fighting stance, his gladius low and at his side, shield arm cocked back, ready to punch. He quickly started looking for openings. He definitely wanted to end the fight quickly. As the African giant raised his sword up slightly, Vitruvius saw what he figured might be a potential weakness.

"I'm going to spill your guts, Roman!" the African snarled. "You will beg for death before this day is done!"

"Unlikely," Vitruvius replied with a smile.

The African's eyes filled with lust and rage. Spittle sprayed from his mouth, along with a small stream of blood from where he had bit his lip in his anger. He yelled a tribal battle cry and lunged straight at Vitruvius. He raised his sword high and went to smash his smaller opponent. The blow came hard, but slow. Vitruvius easily sidestepped as the gladiator's weapon impacted on the ground. A vicious backhand slash followed, which the Optio deflected off his shield. Both men settled into their fighting stances once more. As the gladiator raised his sword up to smash once again, Vitruvius' eyes brightened in realization.

Got you! He thought to himself. The African was violating one of the most basic principals of close-combat by leaving his flank exposed.

Vitruvius lunged in, raising his shield to protect himself from a potential blow. He stepped inside the African's shield arm and smashed his own shield into his assailant's face. The shield boss impacted just below the chin. Without waiting to see the affects of his blow, using a straight thrust he plunged his gladius into the gladiator's belly, just above the belt. The blade sank all the way up to the hilt, the African giving a jolt of surprise as both arms fell to his sides. Vitruvius then tensed and brought his gladius up in a hard slice directly through the man's stomach to his ribcage. As blood and bodily fluids started to flow from the gash, he angled his gladius up and thrust the point into the gladiator's heart. Just as quickly, he pulled his sword down and out, and stepped away. He turned around, and started to walk away before his opponent fell to the ground.

The crowd stood in a stunned silence. The fight was over, and it had barely begun. This was not the type of match they had expected! Vitruvius was halfway to the gate, when a lone figure started to slowly clap his hands together. The crowd looked around searching for the source. It was the Emperor Tiberius, sporting a rare smile, standing and clapping for one of his finest Soldiers, who had made a mockery of Sacrovir's gladiator. The crowd suddenly broke into frenzied applause and shouts of adulation. Vitruvius turned back towards the Emperor, removed his helmet, and saluted with his weapon held high. The Emperor returned the salute with a wave of his hand as Vitruvius turned and walked out of the arena.

No, I guess the better man wasn't here today, the Optio thought to himself. He couldn't help but allow himself a grim smile. It had felt good to dispatch that pompous fool Sacrovir's prize fighter so easily. *If there is somebody out there that can best me, I won't find him in the arena.*

"No!" Sacrovir screamed. He pulled at his hair frantically. The African giant he had paid so much for, who had won him many victories and great wealth, slain by a lowly Legionary! His hatred only intensified when he saw the Emperor applauding the man. This in turn fueled his loathing. He turned and started to run down the tunnel, out of the arena as the crowd continued to chant the name *Vitruvius* over and over again. Sacrovir placed his hands over his ears. The name had become an abomination for him. In that moment he swore that he would have vengeance upon not only Optio Vitruvius, but on all Legionaries of Rome!

The men of the Second Century were still applauding loudly for their friend and Optio when Decimus suddenly came running up to their seats. He was obviously excited about something.

"You guys have got to come with me!" he panted.

"Hey, where have you been? You missed the match!" Praxus shouted.

"Oh yeah, I saw it. Good on Vitruvius. Don't worry I saved one for him as well," Decimus said, waiving his hand dismissively.

"One what?" Praxus asked. Decimus smiled and winked. He then took off running down the steps.

"Well don't just stand there, come on!" he shouted back at his companions. Shrugging, Artorius, Praxus, Gavius, Magnus, Carbo, and Valens all stood and followed the excited Legionary into the atrium.

In the foyer, behind the seats there was a number of rather striking young women. All wore revealing gowns, and many had laurels in their hair. They smiled and waived at Decimus, who waved back, smiling.

"Who are they?" Artorius asked, mouth gaping. Decimus put his arm around him, eyes never leaving the young ladies.

"Those my friends are courtesans. They are the very best ladies of love that money can buy."

"You mean the ones who only rich, old Senators can afford?" Valens asked.

"The ones they can afford, yet cannot perform properly for, yes," Decimus answered.

"So how do we as lowly Legionaries afford such supple beauty and grace?" Artorius asked.

"We don't. That's the best part! They've already been paid for!" Decimus was giddy with anticipation.

"By who?" Magnus asked.

"Who cares?" Artorius retorted. "Maybe Severus used a share of his winnings from the fight as a way of saying 'thank you.' Or maybe they're just doing their patriotic duty to the State. Either way, does it matter?"

"Indeed!" Decimus laughed as he shoved Artorius towards one of the waiting ladies.

She was a couple of inches shorter than Artorius, with curly hair that reached just past her shoulders. Her green eyes contrasted with the color of her skin. He could tell by the way her gown lay that she was well endowed with a firm, tight figure. Her smile betrayed her lack of innocence. She was definitely something he could understand rich men paying a lot of money for.

"Well hello," he said, trying to sound casual. She slipped an arm underneath his and around his waste. He looked around and saw that all of his friends were similarly engaged. "So, um, anything in particular you would like to, well um," he was embarrassed that he was stuttering. She was a prostitute after all, even if she was a really expensive one that probably hadn't had a real man bed her in years.

"Well, we could go get some wine, find a nice place to dine and pretend that we are courting," she said sweetly, albeit sarcastically. "Or we could just skip the preliminary nonsense and get right down to business." She raised her eyebrows as she said so. Artorius looked away for a second, in mocking contemplation.

"Hmm, alright then," With that, he wrapped his arms around her and kissed her aggressively and passionately. The girl yelped in surprise at first, given his initial awkwardness. She then moaned in pleasure and anticipation as she placed her other arm around him and kissed him back.

CHAPTER 28

▼

THE REWARDS OF
TRIUMPH

Artorius, as well as most of his friends he was sure, was escorted to the courtesan house. It had taken no more than a few minutes to get there, though with his eroticism about to consume him, it had seemed like much longer. He was quick to observe how lavishly decorated the house was from the moment they entered the main foyer. The floor and pillars all gleamed of polished marble. An elaborate fountain with a bronze statue of Pan atop stood in the center. Vases and statues rested on pedestals throughout, exotic mosaics decorated the walls. As they walked down a wide corridor, Artorius saw a familiar face walking towards a room, a beautiful woman in each arm. One was young and fetching, the other was much older, though still beautiful and very striking. He assumed she was the lady of the house. She looked aroused and flattered to have drawn the attention of the strapping Legionary who was probably twenty years younger than she. Artorius laughed to himself when he caught the face of the young Legionary. Valens smiled, winked and shook his fist at him, as if celebrating a conquest. Artorius returned the gesture and continued on his way with his new friend in tow.

The courtesan's room contained a huge bed with comfortable pillows that was doused in exotic scents. Incense burners hung in each corner, and the art and décor was of the finest quality. Yes, it would seem that a number of rich Senators had been busy to have sponsored such a place. Artorius contemplated briefly that just the contents of that room alone cost more than a year of his salary.

He thought briefly about his encounter with Camilla the night before. By Hades, he had been brutal to her! He eyed his companion and wondered if she would be up to a similar challenge. As she dropped her gown and moved confidently towards him, he figured she was. He was then taken in the young woman's arms and kissed deeply. He soon forgot about everything else in the world. For the time he was there, nothing else mattered, or even existed.

His companion, whose name he found out was Lucilla, had been more than a generous host. She seemed genuinely pleased, as well as aroused by the young Legionary. His brute power and extreme physical conditioning seemed to add to her excitement. Artorius prided himself that most rich magistrates did not have his sheer vitality, stamina, or strength. He stroked his ego further by thinking that perhaps *she* should have been paying *him*! Then again, he was quite impressed by her veracity and physicality as well. It became something of an erotic competition to see who could wear the other out first. Each found that they were both worthy opponents in this game of lust and fury. As evening came, they lay relaxing in each other's arms.

"Hmm, think I should get back?" Lucilla asked him.

"Whatever for?" Artorius asked.

"Well, there are a lot of other Soldiers in the city in need of affection," she giggled, caressing his chest with her fingers.

"To hell with them," he retorted. "I'm a Soldier, and you were hired to take care of Soldiers while we are here. I take it your contract did not say how many or for how long? I mean, am I not enough to keep you satisfied…" She placed a finger to his lips, cutting him off.

"Hush, I was only teasing," she said with a smile. She laid her head back onto his chest. "Believe me; you've got more vitality and energy than any man I've met."

"You have no idea," he said, smiling. Without warning he rolled her roughly to her back. She yelped and then laughed as he tried to show her just how much vitality he did have.

It was not until late the next morning that Artorius finally left the courtesan house. He was almost sad as he left. Lucilla stood on a balcony, body aching and scarcely able to walk. Yet still she smiled and waived at him as he walked away. Artorius felt his heart strings getting pulled as he waived back.

"Come off it, man! Don't forget what she does for a living!" he chastised himself harshly. And yet he could not help but feel that he had left something of himself there.

"Well look who finally made it back!" Statorius said, sarcastically. The Sergeant was reclining on the ground, a cup of wine in his hand, lost in his own reminiscing.

"I think I need an ice bath for my groin!" Artorius moaned as he limped over to where his section mates were lounging, the smile never leaving his face. His friends all looked equally serene, though it was obvious that he was the last to return by quite some time. Valens lay flat on his back, eyes closed; his legs spread wide and both hands resting on his crouch. He groaned as if in pain, though he never stopped smiling and chuckling to himself.

"I can never go back to trashy frontier whores ever again," he muttered.

"So what was that last night, the 'mother-daughter' special?" Artorius asked as he slowly eased himself down onto the grass.

"I doubt that a mother and daughter would have done the things to each other that those two did," Valens replied, eyes still closed while continuing to giggle and moan to himself. "You know, I was perfectly happy to just watch. However, they were *so* insistent that I participate as well. I mean, what was I to do?"

Later that afternoon Statorius kicked Artorius' cot, stirring him from his pleasant dreams. "Just so you know, your pass the day after tomorrow has been approved."

"Pass? I didn't ask for a pass," Artorius replied, still half asleep.

"Well I don't think you'll want to miss this," Statorius remarked, handing him a scroll. Artorius heart soared as he read the scroll.

Primus Artorius Maximus does hereby request the presence of his son, Titus Artorius Justus, on the day following the Triumphal Parade in order to oversee the marriage of his father to Juliana Helena. At the gardens of the Temple of Castor and Pollux, three hours after dawn.

At the bottom was written: *Approved, by permission of Platorius Macro, Centurion.*

He had been waiting for weeks to hear from his father, and had hoped that perhaps he had made his way up from Ostia. To know that not only was he going to be able to see his father, but that he had finally done right by Juliana made Artorius beam with pride.

The Triumphal Parade was a spectacle unlike any other. It seemed like every citizen of Rome and all the surrounding areas had turned up to pay tribute to the Legions who had smashed Arminius. On the morning of the parade, the Legions were lined up outside the forum. Each Soldier had taken the time to polish his armor, helmet and weapons, and had draped his cloak over his shoulders. As they milled about, Artorius saw a familiar face that he had not expected to ever see again.

Camilla still walked with a slight limp, and she had at this point given up trying to cover the bite mark on her neck. She waved to Artorius, and he walked over to her, removing his helmet as he did so.

"Looks like you got savaged by a wild animal," he remarked sarcastically. She smiled wryly at that.

"Yes, well it seems I had to learn a hard lesson about trying to get back with a former love after I went and got married behind his back," she replied.

"So what did you tell your husband?" Artorius asked, morbidly curious. Camilla gave a shrug.

"Only that we had both spent the night paying to be serviced by men," she answered. Artorius could not help but laugh at that. "I think he's envious, since his lovers aren't quite so *masculine*." She then gazed downward for a second. "Artorius, I know it was wrong for me to get married the way I did. I did not love Marcellus, and still don't, but I can't take it back."

"Look, if we can at least depart as friends, it will be enough," Artorius replied. Camilla smiled, gave him a lasting embrace, and walked away.

"What did you *do* to that woman?" Magnus asked as they watched Camilla pause and brace herself against a pillar for a second. She let out a stifled groan before she finished hobbling away. Artorius was grinning from ear to ear as he turned and faced his friend.

"I only got even with her for a previous wrong," he replied.

"Yeah, well remind me never to wrong you," Magnus remarked, his eyes wide.

They wandered back over to where the rest of the Century was staged. All wondered why they were there so early, since the parade was not supposed to start for several hours. Then Severus and Germanicus mounted the dais in the center of the formation. They were each wearing their finest military dress; shining breastplates, purple cloaks over their shoulders, ceremonial gladii at their sides, ornamental helmets underneath their arms. They looked so different than when each had been covered in dirt and blood on the fields of battle.

"Soldiers of the Twentieth Legion!" Germanicus called out. "It is my duty and privilege to present to you your Emperor, Tiberius Claudius Nero Caesar!" With that the Soldiers erupted into loud shouts and cheers that shook the Seven Hills of Rome as the Emperor mounted the dais. He was dressed in full military garb, like his Generals. Only thing he lacked was the ceremonial helmet, for instead he wore the laurel crown upon his head that signified him as Emperor. He raised a hand in salute, and the Legion immediately became quiet.

"My friends, fellow Soldiers, *brothers* in arms!" he began. "For each of you that stands before me I acknowledge as my brother. You have avenged the greatest treachery of our time. You have brought justice and honor to your Legion and to Rome. And though we as individuals may be forgotten by history, your deeds and your valor will be remembered forever. Therefore *you*, my friends, will live forever! In honor of your victory, it is my privilege to present each of you with the campaign crest and medal. Wear them with pride, and know that your Emperor is proud of you!" He then raised a medal in his right hand as the Soldiers all started to chant together, *"Hail Caesar! Hail Caesar! Hail Caesar!"*

Once the Emperor had left, Centurions and Optios made the walk down the lines of their Centuries. It was the first time Artorius had seen Macro and Vitruvius in full parade dress with all of their awards displayed. They each wore a harness over their armor, which displayed their medals and decorations. Both had quite a few, though Artorius was surprised to see that Vitruvius actually had more than his Centurion. As they passed in front of each Soldier, Macro took a medal from Vitruvius and pinned it to their cloak. He then clasped each Soldier by the hand.

Artorius gazed at his medal once the Centurion and Optio had presented it to him. For Artorius, as well as many of the younger Legionaries, this was the first decoration he had been presented with. It was slightly smaller than the size of his hand and was made of silver. As was customary, it was emblazed with the image of the Emperor. On the top was inscribed: *For Victory in the Defeat of our Enemy Arminius.* Across the bottom it read: *XX Legion, Valeria, Senatus Populusque Romanus.* Once all medals had been handed out, Macro took his place at the head of the Century formation.

"The campaign crest and medal honors us as a Legion and our deeds during this war," he said. "But there are those who also distinguished themselves individually, and they deserve to be honored and recognized. We have several Soldiers within the Second Century who have been selected to receive awards for valor.

When I call your names, come forward and receive your award." The first award Vitruvius handed to him was a crown of gold leaves.

"Legionary Decimus; you are awarded the Rampart Crown for being the first Legionary over the wall of an enemy stronghold." Decimus removed his helmet as he stood before his Centurion. Macro placed the crown on his head, and then clasped his hand.

"Legionary Decimus is the first Soldier in the history of the Twentieth Legion to be awarded the Rampart Crown three times," Macro stated. Decimus saluted and returned to his place in formation.

"We also have several Soldiers who have been selected to receive the Silver Torque for Valor," Macro continued. "It is awarded for conspicuous acts of valor, above and beyond that normally expected of a Roman Soldier."

The names of several Soldiers were called off, along with the deeds for which they were being recognized. Artorius was pleased to see Praxus was among those selected. As their names were read off, each Soldier came forward and Macro presented him with the Silver Torque. Artorius was shocked when he heard his name called.

"Legionary Artorius; you are awarded the Silver Torque for Valor for conspicuous acts of gallantry during the assault on the Cherusci stronghold, and for personally killing the Cherusci war chief, Ingiomerus." Artorius could not describe his feelings as he walked up to receive the award from his Centurion. Macro clipped the torque to Artorius cloak, just above his campaign medal. He then clasped his hand firmly.

"Well done, Soldier," he said softly. "Your valor is a credit to this Century and to your Legion." Artorius saluted and marched back to his place in formation.

"We have two more awards to hand out, and for these we need to bring back an old friend of the Century," Macro said. He face and his tone betrayed his emotion as he turned his head and called out over his shoulder, *"Optio Valgus, post!"*

There was an audible gasp as the Century watched their former Optio come walking around the dais. He was in full parade dress, and though he now required a walking stick, he had lost none of his presence or aura. With him was a rather striking woman dressed in a resplendent stola. She was very pretty and statuesque in build. Artorius surmised that she must be Vitruvius' sister. In their former Optio's right hand were two simple crowns made of oak leaves. Artorius was impressed when he saw the number of awards Valgus had been awarded over his career, a career that had been cut short by a German spear. Valgus faced the Century as he addressed them.

"The highest award a Soldier of Rome, or any Roman citizen for that matter, can receive is the Civic Crown," he stated. "It is for acts of valor while saving the life of a fellow citizen. For no greater act can one perform in the service of Rome than by protecting its citizens. As brothers-in-arms this has an even deeper and more personal meaning for us. I am here to present two of these awards to the men who saved my life at Ahenobarbi." He then nodded to Centurion Macro, who read off the award citation.

"Optio Vitruvius and Sergeant Statorius; you are both awarded the Civic Crown for distinguished acts of valor in the saving of the life of a fellow citizen and Soldier of Rome. Your valor and selfless devotion to your fellow Soldiers is of the highest caliber, and sets the utmost in standards of conduct representing yourself, the Twentieth Legion and the Army of the Rhine." Each man removed their helmets as Valgus placed the crowns on their respective heads. They then clasped the hand of their old friend before returning to their place in formation. Once all awards had been presented, it was time for them to form up for the actual parade.

The parade itself extended for miles, and the Soldiers were only a small part of it. At the head was Germanicus, in an ornamental chariot. His children accompanied him, and were dressed in their finest splendor. Next were the most prominent Senators and magistrates. Severus rode at the head of these, along with the Legates and Chief Tribunes from each Legion. Enemy prisoners of war, few as there were, were next in the lineup. They were marched together in shackles, heads hung low in shame. Surprisingly, amongst these was Thusnelda, the "liberated" wife of Arminius. With her was her infant son, whom she had named Thumelicus. As she passed the reviewing stands, she glared at her father, who was a guest of honor amongst the Roman dignitaries. Thusnelda had learned only the day before that the price of her and her son being allowed to live was that they be paraded before Rome as prisoners of war during the triumph. She bore the insult with silent dignity, not wishing to do anything that might jeaopardize her son's life. Little did she know that part of the deal struck with Segestes was that his daughter would never be allowed to return to Germania, and that her son would be sent to the gladitorial school in Ravenna, once he came of age.

After the prisoners were all the stockpiles of loot and plunder taken on the campaign. There was not as much as one would expect, but it was still an impressive site. The two trophies that Germanicus had erected were displayed amongst these. The Soldiers themselves came last, though Artorius was certain they received the loudest cheers and accolades.

He looked around at his friends and companions. All were proudly displaying their newly won medals and awards, as well as the awards that some of them had won on previous campaigns. As they passed the reviewing platform where the Emperor stood, they drew their gladii as one and saluted. Tiberius returned their salute, his face rock hard, yet filled with pride. Artorius thought about Magnus' words from the other night. His friend was right, *here* was Rome! Rome did live in these brave men that he had fought along side of. No matter where they went, Rome would be, Her eternal spirit never leaving them.

At the end of the march, Artorius was tired, but elated. As he returned to camp, he knew he would be unable to sleep. All he could think about was seeing his father again, hoping that he would be proud of him. He found himself walking alone along an isolated path, when he saw a lone Legionary gazing off into the hills with his back to him, arms folded across his chest. The sun was coming down, and it gleamed off the Soldier's armor. Artorius removed his helmet and walked up to the man.

"The evenings are beautiful, this time of year," the Soldier said as Artorius approached. His voice somehow seemed familiar, but he could not fathom from where, like something he not heard for a very long time.

"Yes they are," he replied. "Makes one feel good to be alive."

"Quite. You know Artorius, Mother wanted me to tell you that she loves you and that she is very proud of you."

"Excuse me?" Artorius felt his blood starting to boil as he tried to make out the man's face. "Who are you, and how do you know my name? And how *dare* you mention my mother!" The Legionary gave a loud sigh, removed his helmet, and faced him. Artorius gasped, his breath taken from him. He dropped his helmet and fell to his knees, tears welling up in his eyes. He knew that face, its imaged was permanently burned into his mind, though he had not seen it for many years.

"It cannot be," he breathed as he shook his head. He closed his eyes hard, unable to believe what he saw. When he opened them again, the man still stood there. He found himself unable to control the surge of emotions that welled up inside of him and fought to control his speech and his senses. "You're dead. I buried you myself."

"Yes you did," Metellus replied, "and by doing so you brought peace to my tormented soul. For six years I floated between the paradise of the Afterlife, and the agonizing pains of this world. So many of us were unable to find peace after our lives were ended with such savagery. And yet, I took solace and pride in seeing my brother become a man. I have watched you, Artorius. I have watched you grow strong and powerful, in both mind and body. You have the opportunity to accomplish great things in your life. You have learned to control your rage and your hatred. Do not ever let them control you, or your soul will never find peace in the next life."

"How is it that I can see you?" Artorius asked, rising to his feet. "I have not gone mad, have I?" Metellus laughed at that.

"No you haven't. I have been graced with this moment to reassure you that my soul is finally at rest, as is Mother's. My time here is short, and I must leave you."

"Will I ever see you again?" Artorius asked. Metellus contemplated his response to that.

"Not for a very long time," he said at last, "that is all I know. Artorius, I do not know what your future holds, though I know we will not meet again for a very long time. Continue to grow stronger, live justly, and I promise you *will* see me again." With that, Metellus turned and started to walk up a short slope that faced into the setting sun. As he reached the top, he turned and faced Artorius one last time.

"Well done, Little Brother."

CHAPTER 29

▼

SOLDIERS OF ROME

"We may have destroyed his army, but the wolf himself still escaped," Germanicus said. He sat in a chair while the Emperor stood looking out a window, his hands clasped behind his back.

"The wolf of which you speak is now nothing more than an impotent sheep," Tiberius replied. "Did you know we received a deputation from some tribal leaders that survived the campaign? They offered to give me the head of Arminius in exchange for our assurance that we will not invade again."

"And what did you tell them?" Germanicus asked. Tiberius turned and faced his nephew.

"I laughed in their face, that's what I did. I told them that Rome did not need to employ such underhanded tactics in order to win our wars. I told them to pray that we never crossed the Rhine again, and that they never give us reason to. Don't you see? Arminius has fallen. He no longer commands the respect of his fellow war chiefs. They are willing to hand him over to us, when seven years ago they practically revered him as a god. I would be surprised if the Cherusci even survive this as a tribe and nation. They took the brunt of the casualties, and have scattered to the winds. No my son, I have more important work for you." With that, he turned back to the window. Germanicus stood and placed his hands behind his back.

"How may I be of service, Caesar?" he asked.

"I need strong leadership in the east. As you know, the Parthians are always causing trouble. I need somebody who can keep them in check and protect our interests in the Eastern Empire."

"And what of Piso?" Germanicus asked, referring to a Legate in the east whom he mistrusted greatly.

"Piso has done nothing unlawful that I can pinpoint directly on him," Tiberius answered. "He was appointed by the Divine Augustus, and has thus far been steadfastly loyal and a good friend. However I do questions some of his methods and motives. Use your discretion; however do not just go firing Legates and appointed officials simply because they disagree with your policies."

"Yes Caesar."

Later that evening, Germanicus stopped by to see his mother. Antonia was the daughter of Marc Anthony, and widow of Tiberius' brother, Drusus. She was also one of the few people whom Tiberius cherished as a friend. He had never forgotten what she had meant to his brother, and when Drusus died, he promised himself that he would always look after her.

Antonia sat reading by lamp light. She was more handsome than pretty, and age had definitely taken its toll on her. She was a stoic in the deepest sense of the word, though she could never truly hide her emotions from her eldest son. She allowed herself a slight smile as Germanicus walked into the room. He was physically tired and mentally exhausted, however he knew that this may be the only opportunity he had to see his family before he left for the east. Antonia stood and embraced her son.

"I was beginning to think you were going to up and leave without saying goodbye," she said.

"How can I say goodbye when I haven't even had a chance to say hello?" Germanicus laughed. They made their way over to a couple of lounge chairs in the foyer.

"You have done well," Antonia remarked. "I see more and more of your father in you every time I see you. I'm certain he's proud of you, wherever he may be." She gazed upward at her last remark. Germanicus followed her stare into the unknown. There was a long silence before he spoke again.

"I see that you are doing well, Mother. How is Claudius? I stopped by to see him, but he wasn't home." Antonia's face turned into a scowl at the mention of her youngest son. She was embarrassed by him, though it gave her no pleasure admitting it. She was convinced that he was a half-wit and a fool, to be pushed aside and out of the way.

"He is here, out back," she answered, nodding towards the gardens, "avoiding his wife, I don't doubt." Germanicus stared at his mother, eyes ever questioning.

"Why do you hate him so, Mother?" The question took Antonia aback.

"I don't *hate* any of my children! What a monstrous thing to say!"

"I can see it in your eyes, in the way you talk to him. Maybe you don't hate him, but you are embarrassed by him."

"Well who wouldn't be?" Antonia asked with a wave of her hand. "The gods only know what your father would have done with him." She turned and looked away, anxious for the conversation to be over. Germanicus' expression never changed.

"I'm not embarrassed by him," he said earnestly.

"Have you said hello to your sister?" Antonia asked, turning back towards him. When Germanicus looked down, she cracked a half smile. "Oh no, you're not embarrassed by your brother, but ashamed of your sister!"

"It's not that I'm embarrassed by Livilla, I just don't care for her very much." Germanicus' face hardened as his mother raised an eyebrow at the remark. "Well at least I can admit it. She's a wicked, scheming little girl."

"You could still give her the courtesy of a visit," Antonia replied, placing her hand on his. Germanicus nodded.

"Alright," he answered, "I'll try and be nicer to Livilla if you'll stop acting so ashamed towards Claudius. Now, I'm going to go and see him." With that he kissed his mother on the cheek and walked out through the archway leading to the palace gardens.

Night had long since fallen when Germanicus went to find his brother. As he passed by a fountain, he saw a glimmer of light coming from a lamp. He smiled as he saw Claudius sitting on a bench, reading and writing in the dim light.

Germanicus sighed at the sight of his brother. It wasn't fair, really. He had been blessed with a superior physique, a sound constitution and had been fortunate in his military career. His brother, on the other hand, suffered from a bad limp caused by a club foot, his head twitched uncontrollably at times, and he had a tendency to stutter. Because of this, many had thought him to be mentally incompetent. This was of course nonsense. Claudius was an accomplished scholar and historian. He was the author of several books pertaining to Etruscan and early Roman history. Germanicus had read most of them and was an avid fan of his brother's works.

"Am I disturbing you?" Germanicus asked.

"No, not at all," Claudius replied. He continued to write for a few more seconds before setting everything beneath the bench. He motioned for his brother to have a seat with him.

"It's been a long time since we last had a chance to just sit and talk," Germanicus observed.

"T...too long," Claudius stuttered, his head twitching slightly. "Tell me, b...b...brother, how long will you be in Rome?"

"Just a few more days, unfortunately," Germanicus sighed. "I've been reassigned to the east, and there is much to do before I leave. I plan on seeing our old friend, Herod before I leave. That is if I can get Drusus to let him stay sober long enough for me to get some useful first-hand information out of him about the province." Claudius laughed at that. Herod Agrippa was a dear friend of his, though he admitted that his Judean friend, who was the grandson of Herod the Great, did seem to enjoy Rome's excessive vices a little too much. In spite of this, the Emperor was rather fond of him, and he and Drusus were practically inseparable.

"I admit that I am a bit surprised to see you out here," Germanicus said. "I heard about your marriage, and in fact I met your wife when I stopped by to see you." Claudius dropped his head and looked away disappointed.

"My m...marriage is n...nothing but a joke, a cruel and t...twisted joke," he replied sulkily. "It was our grandmother who arranged it. I think she did it out of s...spite." It was well known that Livia had never cared for her handicapped grandson. In fact it was she who spoke most openly about his mental ineptitude. Many, including Germanicus, felt that Claudius exaggerated his afflictions when he was around her and intentionally made himself out to be a bigger fool than he was.

"Well your wife's face is not unpleasant to look at," Germanicus replied, soothingly. "Truth is she's fairly attractive."

"L...like I ever get a chance to see her face!" Claudius retorted. "The woman stands more than a foot t...taller than me. Frankly, I think she was in on the joke as well."

"I think she's a foot taller than *me*," Germanicus said, stifling a laugh. This in turn caused Claudius to laugh, in spite of himself. "Dear brother, it *is* good to see you again." He placed a hand on Claudius' shoulder for emphasis.

Sometimes Claudius felt that Germanicus was all he had in the world. He had been just an infant when his father died. His mother blamed him for many of their family's follies, and his sister...well he preferred not to even think about Livilla. He tolerated her only because she was married to Drusus, their cousin and also one of his best friends. No, Germanicus was the only person Claudius ever really felt comfortable around.

"So tell me about what you saw in Germania," he inquired, his stutter having gone away.

"Teutoburger Wald was a horrific sight. There was very little left of the bodies, though from what we could still gather all had been horribly mutilated. Many had been tortured brutally in some foul ritual that only barbarians could appreciate." Germanicus paused, obviously vexed at the memory. He stared at the ground, drawn into the flood of memories, especially the battles where they destroyed Arminius. "But we avenged them! Oh yes, our vengeance was brutal, and it was twice as savage as anything they had ever witnessed. We spared no one." He then told Claudius of the campaigns of the past two years, the climatic battle at Idistaviso and the subsequent sacking of the Germanic stronghold.

"I wish I could have been there to see it all," Claudius sighed, looking away. The longer he was around Germanicus, the more his stutter seemed to vanish. "There is only so much one can gather from reading books. You have the knowledge that only life experience can give. I admit that I am envious at times."

"Well don't be," Germanicus retorted. "You have a lot to give, dear brother. I don't know how or when, but I know that some day you will be destined for great things. Some day *you* will be the protector of Rome!"

"You place too much on superstitions, brother," Claudius replied. Germanicus had been referring to an incident when they were both children. An auger had witnessed a pair of fighting eagles drop a wolf cub from the sky. Claudius had caught the cub, which the auger was certain signified that one day he would become the savior and protector of Rome. Claudius had never put faith in omens, unlike his brother.

"Yes, I may be superstitious," Germanicus replied. "In fact it is something my men say is a shortcoming. But I believe that some things *are* predestined by the Divine! Do not shy away from your destiny, Claudius. It will come to you some day, when you least expect it." Claudius smiled at the thought. Germanicus' passion almost made him believe it.

The two brothers talked away the rest of the night. In the morning, Claudius escorted Germanicus over to the house of their friend, Herod Agrippa. In a few days Germanicus would leave for the east. Claudius did not realize then that it would be the last time he would ever see his beloved brother.

*   *   *   *

It was over. His lifelong campaign to rid Germania of the Roman scourge was over. Arminius lay underneath the stars and contemplated it all. He had been lucky enough to escape from the stronghold when the Romans stormed it. Most had not. Now his fellow war chiefs, the few who survived, were offering his head to the Romans whom they had sworn to fight until the very last. Ha! Did they not appreciate the accomplishments that he had made? He had driven the Romans west of the Rhine, from which he knew they would never return. Their expeditions of the last two years had been for vengeance, not re-conquest. The Roman invaders would never again occupy the lands east of the Rhine. That had to account for something. Crops could be re-sown, homes could be rebuilt, and the people who survived would once again repopulate the region. He truly had liberated all the peoples of Germania, even if he had been defeated on the battle-field.

He thought about his uncle, Ingiomerus. The old man had been a hothead, and had probably cost him a few battles. However, he had been exceptionally brave and had been part of what had kept the coalition of tribes together. He had also been the one member of his family that had remained loyal to him.

Arminius thought about what he considered to be his greatest personal tragedy. His wife and son were gone. He would never see either of them. He wondered what kind of life his son would have. Would he ever get a chance to know who his father was? Such was a vain hope. Surely Arminius could find himself another bride, and he could have other sons. However, the void now left in his life could never be filled.

*   *   *   *

Artorius roused himself two hours before dawn. He donned his polished armor and cloak, complete with his newly awarded decorations, and started on his way. There was a definite spring to his step as he strolled through the camp. Not a sound could be heard, except for the audible snores coming from the tents, where Soldiers slept off the effects of the previous night's merriment. At the gate, he showed the sentry his pass. It was a cool morning and the city was calm. Remarkably, the streets had been cleaned from the previous day's celebrations and the city now slumbered. After some time he reached the gardens.

There were climbing vines covering the walls on the inside. Roses were still in full bloom, their scent assailed Artorius' senses. As he walked around the garden he came to an elevated alter, where a priest stood with his father and Juliana. They were watching and waiting for him. His father was dressed in his finest tunic, and Juliana wore a white gown with flowers in her hair. They both looked magnificent! His father looked as if he were ten years younger. They smiled at Artorius as he walked over, his helmet held underneath his arm. Juliana immediately ran over and embraced him, kissing him on the cheek. She looked even more beautiful than before.

"My dear Artorius, it is so good to see you," she said, elated.

"Good to see you too," Artorius replied, as he held her close. "I'm glad to see Father has finally done right by you." He then walked over to his father, who extended his hand. Artorius took it, and then pulled his father in and embraced him. Once they separated, Primus gazed in admiration at his son in his military garb.

"My son," he said. "I see you've already been decorated for valor. I received a letter from Pilate, telling me all about your exploits and the deeds you accomplished. He said you stormed the wall of an enemy fort and took it almost single-handed!"

"He exaggerates," Artorius laughed. "I just killed an old man who happened to be Arminius' uncle!"

"You killed Ingiomerus?" Primus looked shocked. He then placed both hands on either side of Artorius' head. "My son that is wonderful news! No wonder they decorated you! Anyway, enough talk of war. We have business to conduct."

"Business?" Juliana asked with a wry smile. "I didn't know that ours was such a formal and impersonal affair." Primus laughed aloud as he placed an arm around Artorius' shoulders and guided him over to his place on the stand. In a short and private ceremony, Primus and Juliana were finally married. It was something that was well overdue in Artorius' mind.

After the ceremony, all three took a walk on one of the hills that surrounded Rome. It was a beautiful day, the most beautiful day Artorius could remember. Juliana walked in between them, her arms laced in between each of theirs. For several hours, they talked about anything but the war that he had just fought. Artorius asked about their health, about home, old friends, and anything else he could think of. Finally, Juliana breached the question about the war to Artorius.

"May I ask, what Germania was like?" she asked.

"Cold and damp in the winter, though the summers can be rather pleasant," Artorius replied. "And it's populated by a race of rather inhospitable people. It is mostly forests and swamps. Teutoburger Wald was an absolutely atrocious place."

"Tell me about when you found your brother," she continued.

"My Love, please," Primus said, placing a hand on her arm.

"No, it's alright," Artorius replied. "I don't suppose you shared my letter with her concerning Metellus."

"I did not," Primus answered.

"The short story is that I met a Cohort Commander, who was Metellus' Centurion. He told me the about how Metellus made his final stand, how he died saving the lives of his friends. We later found a set of remains the corroborated with the Centurion's story, to include the fatal blow that killed Metellus. I told Father he would have been proud of him. And I am honored to not only to have laid his body to rest, but to have done him justice." He contemplated telling them of his seeing Metellus, but thought better of it. After all, he wasn't entirely certain he *had* actually seen his brother, as real as the vision had seemed. Though his heart told him the truth, he knew that no one else would believe his story.

Juliana reached over and placed her hand in his. "Your mother would have been proud of you as well," she said. Towards the end of the day, Primus and his new bride walked Artorius back to the Legion's camp. Each then embraced him in turn.

"Don't you worry about your father, I'll look after him," Juliana said as she took Artorius in her arms.

"I know, Mother," Artorius replied. Juliana smiled at being addressed as such. A tear came to her eye. Artorius then reached over and embraced his father.

"I'm very proud of you," Primus said, beaming.

"And I you," Artorius answered. "It's about time you did right by Juliana." He winked at his new step-mother as he said so. He then turned and walked back to the camp, back to the army, to the Legion and his friends. He felt renewed in body and in spirit. He would miss his father and his new mother. Yet he also looked forward to continuing his life and his chosen career. His vengeful spirit was at last laid to rest. This was a feeling that he had not known since he was a boy. His father would be all right, his brother and his mother's souls could at last rest in peace. He now looked forward to going home, and his home was the Legion. He was, after all a Soldier of Rome.

Bibliography

Note: All quotes cited in this work are taken from the Annals of Tacitus, Book III.

Chapter VI:
1, 2—Quoted from the Annals of Tacitus describing the suppression of the Rhine Mutiny.

Chapter XVIII:
1, 2—Quotes taken from Tacitus regarding the confrontation between Arminius and his brother, Flavus.

Chapter XIX:
1—Quote from Tacitus regarding the Roman response to the Germans' call for surrender prior to Idistaviso.

Chapter XX:
1, 2—Quotes of the speeches given by Arminius and Germanicus prior to the Battle of Idistaviso.

Chapter XXIII:
1—Actual inscription rendered onto the trophy erected after the storming of the Angrivarii fortress.

Chapter XXV:
1, 2—Description of the calamities that befell Germanicus as they sailed home from the Rhine.
3—Tacitus' description of Tiberius' campaigns in Germania.

978-0-595-41737-7
0-595-41737-X

Printed in the United States
104840LV00003B/213/A